Sacred Sex, Heaven's Tears

A Novel

by A.I. Robeshin

Sacred Sex, Heavens Tears
Copyright 2013 A.I. Robeshin

ISBN 10: 0991498003
ISBN-13: 978-0-9914980-0-0

Printed and bound in the USA

Cover design by JH
Formatting by EH

Library of Congress copyright 2013
copyright 2013 A.I Robeshin

For the abused – please, don't give up. Compassionate people and resources exist to help you. Keep praying, asking for His guidance, and open your heart to those He sends your way to assist, protect and heal you.

To the abusers – pay very close attention to the messages from Heaven herein. He hasn't provided them as mere suggestions. He will always forgive a genuinely remorseful heart, but penance and changing your evil ways are part of the package. That has to come from you. You can't hide from Him or His justice, all triggered by your own willful actions in this life.

ACKNOWLEDGMENTS

I am truly grateful to the following people for their help and support with this project:

To my spouse, you mean the world to me. Thank you for your love and friendship during this journey. I am forever thankful for you being in our lives, especially when it seemed to be falling apart and we were thrust into the insane reality of secondary victims without a clear guide. I am grateful for you in my life every day.

To our children and their spouses, thank you for your prayers, and for continuing to energize me with your strength, courage and wisdom. I love you completely.

To Deacon E. A. Greenwell, your guidance, editing, and friendship have been indispensable.

To EH, thanks for guiding me through the publishing jungle. And to JH, thank you for your creative oversight.

To TT2, thank you for your independent reviews and encouragement. Great friends are hard to come by.

To all family and friends who have prayed for this project, thank you for believing in Him, and then in me.

To all who assist with fighting sexual abuse, those who help and not hurt, heal and not destroy, the selfless members of the body of Christ – thank you, thank you, thank you.

To all those who continue to act as though this topic isn't really a big deal, thank you for your ignorance, lack of intelligence and compassion, so much so that it agitated me enough to finally write this book. Inspiration can come in many forms.

And to CKP, whose tenacity and spirit to live robustly inspired me more times than I can count, and who left this world much too soon. Thank you for your help when we were truly in need, and even when we weren't. Rest in peace, my friend.

Chapter 1

It has been said we become what we think about most of the time. In fact, the concept is biblical. When you consider the myriad of professions around the world – law enforcement, artists, bankers, criminals and the like – I believe you would discover they've spent much time perfecting their chosen skillset. Consistently exercising their God-given free will is how they have become good at what they do. And even when their choice has been to do nothing at all, it's still a choice they've made.

Each of us follow this process daily, even on a miniscule scale. Like this journal I am beginning, for posterity – as a gift to you. I will update it as time allows. What I've been through here hasn't been anything like my life back in the Diocese of Brooklyn. It's only been a few months, and my entire world has changed. I've got some unnecessary time to kill right now, it appears, and I'm a bit tired. Excuse the occasional rambling. In the end, I'll print this out for a trusted friend to give to you. Now, back to my world as thoughts race through my mind.

Poor choices by others really do affect us all, no matter how we rationalize them. Sin does that. Oh, maybe not to the extent of an idiot pushing the infamous "big red button" and the world ends; only God decides the fate of our current existence. But make no mistake – truly life-altering decisions abound. That's why I'm about to observe my first execution later today at Central Prison in Raleigh, North Carolina.

The incredibly high number of people who share a "life philosophy" of self-indulgence irks me to no end. You know, the ones who unabashedly live as though the only thing that matters is what *they* want, what makes *them* happy, and how *they* can be all *they* can be. If you're on the receiving end of their unrestrained ways, it's toxic, and they seem to care less. The culmination of their bad decisions has made them who they are, or who they've allowed themselves to become. They call it their right; I call it bullshit.

You may not remember, but I was one of them. That's why I

type with confidence. Oh, not to the same degree as the marked man I will be with later today, but I vaguely recognize his journey. I know at one time his life was driven by sex, an urge I used to be intimately familiar. I can't fathom the twisted violence and hate, but I know the God-given desire.

It's 6:00 a.m. Monday morning. A banana and Emergen-C vitamin pack fill my system. I need energy. It took me 90 minutes to return from Central Prison last night so I was late to bed. The thought of watching an execution didn't help, and I don't sleep well anyway. It's been a problem over the last decade – one my doctor believes can be rectified by a sleep test and a CPAP machine. You know, the things old and overweight people use. I'm avoiding him. My favorite coffee, Peet's Italian Roast, can't even generate a smile. I'm trying desperately not to shut my eyes. I don't want to be any groggier than I already am, and I certainly don't need another anxiety attack. Those little beauties have ailed me since childhood. I'm a worrier, remember? The mind can be a powerful friend or terrible foe. My health concerns me the most. Any disease around, I get. If not, I get sick just thinking I will. It all sucks.

The stress-pit of being a Corporate Chief Financial Officer didn't help either. The upside of that experience? I acquired great skills like project management, meeting deadlines, and managing people – all with limited resources. My previous Bishop said these skills enable me to be an effective administrator in the Church. The downside? When it didn't go the way my perfectionist personality wanted, I would routinely implode on anyone and everyone, and the anxiety attacks multiplied in frequency and intensity. Unfortunately, patience with myself and others is still a challenge.

As I look out the front window of the parish-owned white 1990 Pontiac 6000, the sun is peeking over the ominous prison walls of Hyde Correctional Institution, a 20-year new facility with 756 beds. All filled; all men. There are similar facilities for women around the state. Bad choices brought them to places like this.

Hyde Correctional serves as both a minimum and medium security facility. I have enough faith in the criminal justice system to believe the majority are here because they deserve it. But I also understand some may have ended up here because they had the wrong attorneys, or because the wrong detectives were on their case, or for a myriad of other reasons. No matter the evidence or mistakes that put them here, they appeal, and appeal, and appeal some more. And the taxpayers pick up the tab. But what else are they to do with their time? I mean, wouldn't you work hard to get out of a place that takes all your freedom and traps you with the kind of people you tried to avoid the better part of your free life? Yeah, I think I would too.

So what in the world am I doing right here, right now, on this cloudless, 40 degree North Carolina March morning? After all, the prisoner left Hyde Correctional a year ago when a match of his DNA tied him to three murders, including an especially heinous act in Boise, Idaho. It was that evidence which finally sent him to death row at Central Prison. I'm nervously waiting for my ride with Sheriff Daniel Robert Luder, at his insistence. He's already 15 minutes late. We're going to drive to Raleigh together to watch the execution, Cameron Gambke, a 47-year old Caucasian. I would rather be anywhere else. My prayers this morning have been simple and direct: "God, help me through this, *please.*" Alas, this is God's work, and the life of a Catholic priest.

The parochial vicar who is normally assigned to Central Prison is taking an emergency leave of absence. To help out, my pastor, Fr. Bernard Shoefke, asked me to drive there last night to hear the inmate's last confession. Although visibly displeased with the substitution, Cameron Gambke asked I spend this last day on earth with him. Said it was important. He told me his lawyer was working on an appeal to obtain a more lenient sentence. He said it wouldn't matter. If he isn't executed, he assured me his life will end soon anyway, because of Redek. I pressed him. He said it wasn't necessary for me to know.

An urgent message was waiting at home from Mrs. Susan Bellers, our office administrator, informing me I was to travel with Sheriff Luder today. She said it was imperative I meet him at the Hyde Correctional parking lot at 6:00 a.m. Hyde is another 30 miles in the opposite direction from where I live. However, the execution isn't scheduled until 6:00 p.m. tonight. I'm confused and focus on my controlled breathing, trying not to complain. Once more, I'm failing.

I look out the window once more, envisioning the day last year of the prisoner's transfer from Hyde to Central. I guess it caused quite a media stir. An ingrained vision of Our Lord's Way of the Cross flashes through my mind. The range of emotions reflected in the crowd as He was taken to his own death. Except Jesus was innocent, set up, suffered and killed. Was this man innocent, too?

Oh, I've heard the words "rapist," "murderer," "molester," "thief" and the like thrown around. All the locals seem to be talking about it. Plenty of camera crews were at Central last night. But I'm wary of the media. They can twist anything to their own way if they want, so I never know if what I'm hearing is the truth, their version, or nothing close. Most of the time I don't even bother watching the evening news.

Why all the commotion, you might wonder? Why is this guy finally getting his 15 seconds of fame when so many others sit on death row completely out of the public eye? Well, for one thing, the State of North Carolina isn't the place to be on death row. Apparently it ranks 5th in the nation for exercising this form of punishment, with 322 executions on record; 43 since 1976.

The last two executions were in 2006 by lethal injection since electrocution went away in 1935. The first was for a criminal that murdered a convenience store clerk for $90 in cash and a small change purse containing money and her identification. The second was a man who beat his two-year-old step-daughter so severely the autopsy showed she died from a fatal blow or blows to the abdomen that cut her pancreas in half against her spine and tore her liver. Her attacker felt she was crying just a little bit too much for his liking. His last meal was popcorn shrimp, hush puppies, French fries and a Coke. I can only hope the prison staff shit and urinated on his food before they gave it to him. Sorry, I know. I'm a priest. I'll make sure I go to confession soon. I miss my old job at the Diocese of Brooklyn already.

The sheriff is now 30 minutes late. I'll just keep typing. I have a feeling it will be important when you eventually read this, Father. Let me get to the personal identity stuff that might have slipped from your memory.

My name is Father Jonah Lee Bereo. Mom and Dad named me after her great grandfather Leeson Bereo, someone who was apparently instrumental in her life. I never met him. She also liked to collect whale trinkets – thus, "Jonah." She died last fall at 74 years of age in a rest home in Gardensville, North Carolina, called "Serenity Lane." Dad is still alive. He was living with my older brother Paul and his family in Gardensville. I stress "was." He is the primary reason I have transferred here.

But before I get to that, I grew up in Breezy Point, New York, with Paul, our folks, and a cocker spaniel named "Mopatch." Two years ago, in Mom's memory, I picked up a Siberian Husky, giving her the same name. I spent my days through high school just barely staying out of trouble. Well, at least the kind of trouble that would put me in a place like Hyde Correctional. I couldn't stand middle school. It was my first, but certainly not last, experience with peer pressure, bullying, and humanity's never-ending quest for power. If I could have stayed in elementary school for the rest of my life, I would have.

On to George Mason University where I earned my degree in accounting and soon after, my CPA certification. I was rewarded with five years of big paychecks and healthy bonuses as the CFO for a small financial institution. My workaholic mentality guaranteed success.

It was there I finally realized although everyone around me was technically considered an adult, many hadn't matured beyond their turbulent, self-serving teen years. They were still playing the same infantile mind games, but were much better at it. Sadly, those who were in charge, the ones who were the best at political warfare, also had the unfortunate power to fire people who have families to support. This was domination well beyond name calling or blaspheming a ten-year-old kid. I doubt much has changed in the business world.

I am embarrassed to say I played along, thinking this was the way it was all supposed to be, and I tell ya, I excelled. But none of it felt right. I didn't like myself most days, beginning with the early morning ritual of my conscience screaming at me while I drank my coffee, igniting the engine of my dark grey Porsche Carrera, and mentally plotting my day as I drove down the freeway to my 'dream job' in Manhattan. The backbiting, stealing, positioning and office politics were endless. This was before Enron, Arthur Andersen, WorldCom, and the ensuing financial meltdown. Fortunately, I finally gave in to the call. I continue to thank the Good Lord I wasn't there when it all imploded.

I never married; just never found the right woman. The truth is, even if my heart was in it, and it wasn't, I just went through the motions, the game really, of dating spurred on by all my friends. I knew first-hand that only a minute number of them were faithful – to either their girlfriends or wives – and peer pressure can be very destructive, no matter your age. So I learned to choose my friends wisely. I have learned that Satan wears many masks to try and trip us up, and none of them are ugly. If they were, we would do what our instincts would tell us to do – run.

But marriage was never meant for me, at least not to a woman. Being a Catholic priest is not a profession as many people mistakenly believe. It's a calling. When I finally listened, I realized God had been beckoning me my entire life; He had special plans for me. Like Jonah and the whale, He kept chasing me and I kept running. But with His unending and persistent love I finally pulled my head out and said, "Ah, yes, so that's what I was meant to be." Into seminary at the age of 28, joyfully ordained a priest at 35, and faithfully serving 15 years with the Roman Catholic Diocese of Brooklyn, New York, until now.

Laying my head back on the headrest, I decide to at least doze. My watch says 7:00 a.m. and within seconds, my upper windpipe muscles relax. My snoring wakes me multiple times.

Promptly at 8:00, muscled knuckles rap hard against my driver's side window, causing me to jump, my arm bumping the coffee cup. What remains of my now cold coffee barely misses my laptop but lands squarely on my right thigh.

A voice bellows from the outside, "C'mon, let's go. You're ridin' with me."

Chapter 2

Sheriff Daniel Robert Luder isn't asking, he's ordering. Snapping my laptop shut to force it to power down; I groggily exit the car, instinctively locking my doors. Remember, I'm from Brooklyn, although most people around here aren't concerned with bothersome details like that. I follow the sheriff like a puppy who has been caught chewing something he shouldn't have, but not knowing exactly what he shouldn't have chewed in the first place. Maybe the sheriff is just on edge like everyone else. Thankfully, executions don't happen often in the United States anymore.

As I stride for the front passenger seat, I find the door is locked.

"Nope," he says, reaching for the back right door handle, "Only authorized personnel up front. And you're only here because that convict asked for you." His burly neck, lean head, and securely fastened dark brown cowboy hat nods toward the rear of the car.

"That makes you relegated to the back seat."

Knowing not to argue, I clumsily slide into the black leather seat, moving my legs in quickly, certain he is going to find great pleasure in slamming the car door on my ankle.

"Haven't been in the backseat of one of these in a while," I half-heartedly offer, trying to lighten the mood.

His eyes flash in the rearview mirror, narrowing.

"I, uh, rode along in college with the police for a criminal justice class I was taking." Why do I feel compelled to explain myself to Brigadier General Luder?

No response follows my attempt.

"My message was I was to meet you at 6:00 a.m. this morning."

"Well, you got the wrong message. I told your assistant 0800 hours sharp."

Thank you very much, Mrs. Bellers. Why am I not surprised?

"One year ago when we transferred that craphead, this place

11

was a fuckin' circus. A real clusterfuck. His whole life was about trouble, so I don't know why he wouldn't be a headache to me until the bitter end," he says, firing the engine then ramming the gas pedal hard. My head snaps back into the headrest from the sudden combustible launch. Apparently, my comfort is of no interest to him, nor does my clerical outfit cause him to filter his choice of words.

The sheriff's 2010 white with black and mustard yellow-striped Ford Crown Victoria races forward. I can't help but wonder what went through Cameron Gambke's mind as he looked out the bullet proof windows of the paddy wagon that fateful day – a landscape he knew he would never see again.

A few minutes later, after speeding down Piney Woods Road, the sheriff slows to a crawl as we reach the right turn onto Turnpike Road. On separate, eight foot tall 4" X 4" dilapidated wooden crosses are five animal carcasses. Crucified, if you will. Matted, weather-worn, coats with a slight tint of red. Sheriff Luder smirks. A worn sign underneath, "We will miss you, Gambke!" greets all those who pass by. Obviously a message for Cameron Gambke, but why is it still there? It's been a year. What does it all mean? Why animal carcasses? And what type of animals were they, anyway? Wolves? Coyotes? Foxes? And why five?

"What was all that about?" I ask, as we speed off again, heading towards U.S. 64.

"Just a message." A genuine laugh erupts from the sheriff, clearly pleased with the meaning behind it all, one to which I'm obviously not privy. Miles of silence follow.

Firing up my laptop again, I think about what brought me to this area in the first place. I was in Brooklyn when Superstorm Sandy hit. Breezy Point was practically wiped from this earth, not from the rain or wind, but from the fire that took 100 homes. Dad took the news pretty hard. That was the first home he and mom bought before relocating to Gardensville a few decades ago. Looking back, I think God was preparing me for an eventual geographical change.

A few months ago, Paul accepted a VP position with a global telecommunications company. Along with his wife, Sarah, and their youngest daughter, Emily, they moved to Japan from Gardensville. Their older daughter, Rebecca, didn't make the move, choosing instead to attend the University of Pittsburgh as a freshman.

Dad refused to move with them but even he knew he couldn't live alone in the house anymore. He also wanted nothing to do with the rest home mom had been at. Even now, he keeps talking about how they mistreated her, how she kept saying she was being sexually molested. No one would listen to her, him, Paul or me. The administrators of the facility refused to talk to us in detail about it. Their attorney-coached spiel was that absolutely nothing went wrong, that mom's dementia was the real problem. She passed away within a few weeks after our inquiry, before we had a chance to relocate her. That was last year, a very tough one on all of us.

I tried to get dad to move back with me to Brooklyn, but he insisted he wanted to stay in the town mom is buried, so we collectively arranged for him to live in a wonderful elderly group home. It's located in a residential neighborhood just outside of town and the caregivers reside in the home. An absolute blessing of an arrangement.

To be closer to him, I was able to transfer to Gardensville, where I have been assigned to Our Lady of Perpetual Help Catholic Church. I am supposed to learn the ropes from Fr. Bernard, who will be retiring next year. I'm to take over at that time. Before then, I still have a few pilgrimages to lead with my previous diocese, which I'll document herein as they come up.

Taking a moment to stretch my neck and refocus my fatigued eyes on my surroundings, I can't help but wonder, given the typical occupant of the sheriff's car, how many germs are roaming about on this seat. I don't believe asking the sheriff how often they fumigate the vehicle would generate a helpful response, if he even bothers to offer one at all. I notice the impressive computer technology connected to his front dash, guarded well by a number of firearms. I'm tempted to ask him for his thoughts on gun control. What the heck. Maybe we can find common ground.

"So, what do you think they should do with the kid in

Arvada, Colorado, and any other state where they are holding people who have committed mass shootings?"

His head slowly turns, eyes fixing squarely on mine once more through the rearview mirror.

"I think they should all watch and learn an important lesson from this pro-active State today. We are sending a message to those who choose to take the life of another."

Gotcha. I'll try another angle.

"How many guns do you have in this car?"

"Plenty," he snaps.

"Cool," I nod.

Yes, it is a juvenile response. I really want to ask him if I can shoot any, which is juvenile, too. I just want to tweak him a bit since he doesn't seem to like me much. It's obvious he doesn't realize I've got a pretty thick skin, grown and toughened by my years of experience in Corporate America, as well as my tenure as a Catholic priest wearing clerical garments.

In a surprise twist, he makes an effort at a conversation, and it suddenly becomes clear why I was requested to ride with him to Raleigh.

"What do you think about our celebrity, death row inmate Cameron Gambke?"

Our eyes meet once more in the rearview mirror. I'm not certain what he's after so I hesitate in order to properly formulate my response.

"You saw him for his last confession last night, right?"

He's done his homework.

"Well, he seems personable, respectful, and genuine. Nice."

I know he's not going to like that answer even though, given my time with the inmate last night, it's my honest opinion. It's all I have to go by.

"Death row inmate Gambke has you fooled, just like he deceived everyone else in his life!" he barks, the grip on the steering wheel tightening by the looks of his now bloodless white knuckles. Fortunately, he keeps his eyes on the road ahead. I don't want to end my day in the deep ditch off the side of the road.

I don't reply. It has taken me years to understand the only

way to deal with angry people is to give them time to simmer down before trying to continue with any conversation. It's not that I'm afraid of him losing it. With his Herculean body, readily-accessible weaponry, and special combat skills, he is, no doubt, quite capable of dismembering me.

Actually, I'm more concerned how, with my own work-in-progress ego, I might react to him. My spiritual director is constantly reminding me I need to pray and work on this. I often take comfort in knowing St. Peter was a cantankerous disciple who, with God's grace and much molding by the master potter, became the first pope of the Church. I was once told we are all "cracked pots."

After 15 or 20 minutes of tense silence, he again attempts to rev up the conversation.

"What do you folks think about capital punishment and gun control, anyway?"

Yes, we are actually going to try again to communicate like human beings.

"Us folks? Us 'Catholic' folks? Well, before I answer, let me ask you something. Are you part of any religious organization?"

The sheriff pauses, thinking. "Not anymore." Then he adds, "But I was baptized and confirmed in the Catholic faith if that makes you feel any better."

I pause, wondering why he offered that information up. A door opening? Pride?

"Okay, well, as it relates to capital punishment, the Church believes it may be necessary when there is no, and I emphasize the word 'no,' possible way of effectively defending human lives against the individual in question. But if there are non-lethal means of doing this – like life without the possibility of parole – and the opportunity to harm others does not exist, then the State can and should take that option. The ultimate hope is, given the chance, the prisoner will choose to make restitution and change his or her life and have the time to do so, as would be the case if he were sentenced to life without the possibility of parole."

The sheriff's eyes narrow; his door of communication closing rapidly.

15

"Well, that better not happen to his sentence. He better die today."

A pause before he continues. "So you think these bastards can change?"

"All things are possible with God. But this also requires every person, using their free will, to want to change. Only God knows the answer to that question."

Looking out my side window, I then address the second part of his question.

"And regarding gun ownership, the Church has no issue with it, as long as those possessing firearms abide by the law. Every nation and person has a God-given right to self-defense, even if it means dealing their aggressor a lethal blow. The Church calls it the 'Legitimate Defense' doctrine."

"So what about the people who can't defend themselves? Children, mentally ill people, the elderly – people like that?"

"Well, with all due respect, that's where you come in, Sheriff, and everyone else in the criminal justice system, all of you who have the legal authority and the duty to protect the public at large. It also includes everyone who is charged with protecting children, namely parents, teachers, coaches, counselors, babysitters, and the like. And it also definitely applies to religious and priests, people like me. In reality, every single person on earth is called and expected to protect the children, the poor, and the oppressed – really, all who can't protect themselves. In the Bible, Our Lord tells us repeatedly we are called to love our neighbor and care for those in need. His Church teaches and encourages us to go and do likewise."

We drive in silence, and I absorb the green country around me, welcoming the sun's warmth as it rises from its slumber. I finally feel fully awake.

"So, what did convicted killer Gambke say to you last night?"

"He gave me his last confession. And, as you may recall from your religious education days, I am bound under very severe penalties to hold any sins that have been admitted in the sanctity of the confessional in absolute secrecy. It's called the 'sacramental seal', and there are no exceptions."

"You mean every piece-of-crap convicted killer, rapist, child molesting asshole can just come to you for confession and all is good? They can just waltz right into Heaven?"

"Well, kind of, sort of, maybe. They can all come to me, or any other ordained priest, and confess their sins. We merely act as the servants of God's forgiveness. However, there are requirements every penitent must meet. First, they must really be sorry for their sins. Then they must personally come before an ordained priest, and confess all their sins. If need be, they must make satisfaction to the neighbor they wronged, like returning stolen goods, for example, if it is possible to do so. Then they must do whatever penance the priest imposes on them.

"If I, as the confessor, feel the penitent has satisfied all of these requirements, then I give them absolution which, although taking away the sin, doesn't remedy all the disorders the sin has caused. Before any sinner can enter Heaven, we believe their souls must be as white as fresh linen. That's where Purgatory comes in. But God decides who, and when, a soul gets into Heaven, if at all."

Sheriff Luder waves his hand, apparently not wanting the details.

"What I want to know is, Father, do *you* think that convict sitting in Central Prison up there in Raleigh, who at this moment I truly hope is pissin' all over himself, made a good confession and if he's goin' to Heaven? Or is he going to Hell which he deserves; assuming those places even exist?"

He drives dangerously close to an 18-wheeler in front of us, and I can't help but wonder whether at some point in this journey he's just going to ram into another vehicle in order to make somebody pay for his pent up anger.

"I can't tell you about his confession, as I already said. And if he's going to Heaven, Purgatory or Hell, that decision rests with God alone."

Personally, I believe Cameron Gambke met all the conditions for a sound confession, and I did give him absolution, but that information I am not free to offer.

"Well, whatever he told you, he's lyin'. How do you know if a sinner is lyin' or not? What, can you read minds or somethin'? Is

17

that a special gift you have? Or are you just naïve? Maybe stupid?"

Thirty incredibly long, grueling miles still to go to Raleigh as the road sign agonizingly screams to me.

"I am only standing in the place of God when I hear confession in the Sacrament of Reconciliation. "In persona Christi," in the place of Christ. If a penitent is lying to me, he's actually lying to God. This is between him and God. And God is all knowing, all powerful. It will all be worked out on that person's judgment day."

"Well, today is his judgment day, I tell ya. And I'm certain God is waiting with a big baseball bat."

I look out the window, knowing his heart is closed, and choosing not to add any more fuel to his fire. He's not finished with his interrogation.

"One more thing. Did he give you anything?"

My pause gives away the answer. Yes, he did give me something. A letter for someone who shares his last name and another letter for an address in New Mexico. I promised him I would deliver them both, without telling anyone else and certainly not letting anyone see them.

"That's between me and him."

Sheriff Luder is clearly not pleased with me. Fortunately, I stopped trying to impress people long ago. I have discovered no matter who they are, from budding grade school stars to corporate executives, whenever I assumed they knew what they were doing or where they were going in life, eventually I found myself led down the proverbial rabbit-hole and away from what was best for me, God. What I now know is, at the end of the day, the only thing that matters is what He thinks, no one else, especially one as bad-tempered as my escort.

Mercifully, we arrive at Central Prison. The crowd is enormous, and even more media is present than last night.

"Son of a bitch!" he barks, ramming the car into park and quickly exiting, heading towards what appears to be a command post set up for law enforcement.

I sit, locked into the back seat of his car, and wait.

"Are there any more questions I can answer for you, Sheriff?"

18

I ask, a solid 40 minutes after our arrival. Sheriff Luder has been studiously ignoring me, while hanging out with a handful of fellow officers well within my line of sight. It is obvious from the laughter and glances thrown my way they have been enjoying themselves at my expense.

"Yeah, actually."

A cocky grin overtakes his face as he looks back towards the group of his smirking brothers-in-arms.

"Since you won't tell me what I need to know, it's clear we're not going to be friends. Well, here goes – screwed any little boys lately, Padre?"

He can't hold in his sarcastic laugh, a signal to the others he actually had the gall to ask me this question. They turn from us, either bending over in laughter or holding their hands over their mouths to cover their undeniable grins.

Did I remind you already of my lack of patience, something I really need to work on? I am no Mother Teresa. Stretching my back and standing within a foot of his face, I reply.

"Oh, I guess as many boys as teenage girls you've ordered into the back of this official company vehicle over the years so you could molest them, knowing they couldn't, or wouldn't tell on you because if they did, you could make their life hell. Plus, who would ever believe them, right? How many have you done that to, Mr. Sheriff-Officer-Sir?"

I have only read of an incredibly small number of law enforcement members taking advantage of their authority in this manner, but I am done with his condescending attitude. And this is one topic I am tired of hearing about.

Yes, the Catholic Church failed in the past to appropriately handle the priest pedophile cases. Yes, there were many guilty priests. Yes, great injustices have been done, and these poor victims need love, care, understanding, apologies, and healing. All of it upsets me as much now as it did then. How could it not? But the late Pope John Paul II made great strides within the Church to address this issue. And his successor, Benedict XVI, has picked up the torch and continues to move it forward.

But there is much more to this issue. Every religion, I would venture to guess, has this problem. And it runs through long-trusted institutions like public and private schools, the Boy Scouts, Girl Scouts, Big Brother and Big Sister programs, foster homes, just to name a few. Why? Because evil like this comes from the heart of all persons, and it knows no institutional boundaries. Sexual sin is not reserved only for the religious, nor is it reserved to Catholic priests and religious.

Even though the media loves to crucify the Catholic Church when matters like this come to light, I refuse to hear it from this back-country ogre who is just in a mood to pick a fight. And Our Lord certainly didn't back down from the elders, Pharisees, and Scribes when they were out of bounds. Why should I? I just wish I had Jesus' wit, candor, and eloquence when replying.

His eyes open wide, floored I would actually confront him. I don't get the impression many people ever have.

"Fuck you! I've never done anything like that!" he glowers back.

"Very kind of you, Sheriff, thank you. Now, let's get back to your accusation. You say you haven't done anything like that. Although I have read stories of others in a law enforcement capacity doing so, I have no reason to believe you personally have engaged in such activity. Conversely, I now tell you I have never done anything like what you have insinuated, even though *you* have read stories of other priests being guilty. Understand? Make sure you relay it to your 'boys' over there, will you?"

Walking away, I can feel the physical effects of my sudden angry outburst. I need to calm myself quickly, but against my better judgment, I offer one last sarcastic wave at the fuming sheriff. He knows fully well that any last parting shot he undoubtedly desires to send my way will be overheard by the media who are only steps away.

"I'll get another ride back to town when this is over, but thank you for your hospitality on the way down, Sheriff. It was great getting to know you, and maybe we can grab a beer sometime."

My comment is clearly facetious. His parting eyes bulge with a need for retaliation, especially since his boys are laughing even harder now. Only this time, he's well aware they're not laughing at me.

Chapter 3

It's noon, and I've finally begun to calm down. The impending execution has necessitated a prison lockdown, and I've been standing in the growing heat outside the prison along with everyone else.

I bide my time staring at the prison walls. I wonder how many of these prisoners still haven't grasped why they are behind bars, their minds so full of a lifetime of excuses and justifications. They blame the world around them; their situation is the world's fault as far as they are concerned. The famous line from "The Shawshank Redemption" comes to mind, *"Everybody's innocent in here."*

Glances keep coming my way. Some full of disdain, others respectful. Not far from me, a boisterous group parties, anticipating the end of Cameron Gambke's life. They remind me of college tailgating parties, including the coolers, barbecues, and sodas. The smell reminds me I haven't eaten for hours, but it's obvious none will be offered from this group. I'm apparently on the opposing team. God's team, to be more specific, and He has many enemies on this earth.

Sheriff Luder strides through the crowd, looking elated to see me. I'm immediately cautious. He has the look Paul did growing up, right when he would tell me that Mom and Dad would be home in three minutes and, unless I cleaned his room, he would tell them I had eaten all the chocolate chip cookies he had devoured when they left. Not a big deal, unless you're six years old.

"You can't see the convict until 5:45 tonight – 15 minutes before the scheduled execution. Warden's orders." He grins, pleased he was the one chosen to relay this news to me, his new nemesis.

He turns in the direction of the prison administration building, and I search for a place to get lunch within walking distance. The spit comes at me quickly, catching me in the right eye, then oozing down my cheek. I turn towards the offender.

Silent, angry faces glare back. Giggles break into laughter, and I quickly wipe off what I can. Germs from the offending saliva are hastily working their way into my blood stream, I'm certain. The prison restroom is no option until I am allowed in for the execution.

I quickly walk to a Hardee's restaurant a block away, and am pleased there isn't a long line for the restroom. My heart pounds with anger, and my health worries shift into overdrive. Spit in my eye, are you kidding me? The mouth is the dirtiest part of the human body. My anxiety, combined with the unnecessary early morning start and the lack of sleep, is now causing a full frontal assault on my battered immune system. I pray the Emergen-C I downed this morning helps to protect me. Cleaning my face with soap and water, I wash my hands multiple times, still not believing what just happened. C'mon!

The last and only time I had been spit upon after being ordained a priest was in the airport in Newark, New Jersey. A woman in her mid-30's felt a need to express her views the only way she felt was appropriate. I vividly recall her standing squarely in front of me, nostrils flaring, eyes wide, and a green lump of body waste entering my partially-opened mouth and nose. "Bastard!" was all she screamed. I never knew what her beef was. The Church in general? Abortion? No ordained female priests? Pedophiles? The rising prices of milk and eggs that somehow was the fault of the Catholic Church? My only consolation was Our Lord was also spat upon as He was being beaten, mocked, and scourged.

"Offer it up, offer it up," I said then and say now. My spiritual director reminded me that the Church, and especially His shepherds, will always be targets – either physically like I just was – or spiritually by the evil one. He cautioned we should always be aware of our surroundings, prepared to protect ourselves as needed. Fortunately, the overwhelming interactions with people since I have entered the seminary have been warm and welcoming. Still, I make a mental note to be on special guard.

Instead of buckling and cowering like I would have years ago, I am resolved to stand tall and re-enter the Roman Coliseum, to

22

return to the parking lot where anger towards Christians awaits. Everyone deserves respect, and that includes me.

My cell phone rings.

"This is Fr. Bereo," I snap, throwing away the paper towel I used to open the restroom door. It's the parish office.

Mrs. Bellers, the 53-year old office manager's belligerent yet questioning tone blasts into my ear.

"Where are you?" Apparently she's irate I'm not where she believes I should be. No doubt she expects either a confession of guilt or at least an apology on my part. She'll get neither.

"Excuse me?" I bark, moving outside to the parking lot and blood pressure rising. I have no desire to have a verbal confrontation in front of witnesses, especially as I stand in my clerical outfit. I'm tempted to sarcastically thank her for having me arrive at Hyde Correctional two hours earlier than needed this morning, but know my best move is to calm down.

Mrs. Bellers has been a thorn in my side ever since I arrived in Gardensville. She wasted no time, upon my arrival, in telling me that for the past 15 years, in addition to being the office manager, she handles all business and religious education needs, the scheduling of Lectors and Extraordinary Ministers of Holy Communion, and the use of the hall that is used by various church groups. Apparently she's as important to this parish as the Pope is to the entire Catholic Church.

She, an indispensable gem, firmly believes everyone reports to her which she mistakenly thinks includes me. I find that odd, since there is only one other paid employee, who happens to be a part-time retired parishioner. The remainder are volunteers from the 365 registered families in the parish. Oh, and one other thing – I'm certain she thinks she's smarter than everyone else because we're all idiots.

Remember, I'm from Brooklyn, and if I wasn't so serious about my job and the future of this parish, I would think this game with her might actually be fun, similar to what our parish house cat must feel when stumbling upon a cockroach. Unfortunately, right now I don't have the time to deal with her.

Shortly after my arrival, I made the mistake of interfering in her queenship's domain. Eager to familiarize myself with parish operations, I had the apparent nerve to ask her if I could spend a few days with her. I just wanted to see what she does to gain a better understanding. This, of course, prompted her to cause a major scene. I was kindly asked by Fr. Bernard, who also happens to be her brother-in-law, to perhaps do this sometime late in the fall. I could sense he had no solid reason to request this; he just wanted to quiet her down. It's clearly evident he tries to avoid her as much as he can. She has been able to create the perfect environment for herself – one in which she does what she wants when she wants and everyone leaves her alone.

"Fr. Bernard would like to know where you are."

"Fr. Bernard knows exactly where I am. I called him last night to tell him I would be in Raleigh at the prisoner's request."

Silence. "Well, he must have forgotten because he was just in here asking where you are." Certainly. Fr. Bernard's mind is still sharp enough to remember a conversation he had less than 15 hours ago. "But since you are there, I need you to go over to the Diocesan office and pick up a very important package for me that I need by tomorrow."

I know I have the time to do so. Since hanging around the parking lot with the sharpshooting spitters isn't my idea of a productive afternoon, I'm open to anything to occupy my time. My pride begs me to make up a lie and tell her I can't do it; my vows state I need to say the truth, but first …

"Are you asking me or telling me, Mrs. Bellers?"

She may be mean-spirited and querulous, but she's not stupid. While she is like an aggressive bulldog when she senses weakness, she becomes a sniper, hiding behind feigned humility, when someone stands up to her. If she ever decides to enter Corporate America, I'm certain she'll rise to the top quickly.

"Well, I mean, if you can fit it in, of course."

Uh huh. Fortunately, grace wins out once more, and I choose the higher road.

"Certainly," I reply.

"When will you be back?" she questions, subtly trying to regain control and maintain her power through the end of this wasted conversation.

"When I have completed my duties here, Mrs. Bellers. If Fr. Bernard needs me, he has my number."

I cancel the call before she can reply and store this interaction in my memory bank for later. I'm doing all I can to not make this personal. I find solace knowing that when, not if, her services are no longer required, it will have been because of her own self-inflicted actions.

After picking up the package for Mrs. Bellers from the Diocesan offices, I hop in a taxi and arrive back at the prison at 5:30 p.m. As I suspected, her all-important packet wasn't all that important nor close to urgent. It contains pamphlets for the annual Catholic Services Appeal which raises funds to support many charitable programs for the needy within the Diocese. We have three weeks to mail them out.

Sheriff Luder is waiting for me when I return, visibly disappointed I have done so. I'm ushered into a holding area along with three members of the press. Three elderly couples are present, standing arm-and-arm, with two males and a female off to the side. All nine have red, swollen eyes. I assume they are the parents and possibly siblings of the victims.

Also present is a petite, 20-something female with a stern look on her face. She sports a jet black pixie cut and her features remind me of an Anne Hathaway/Liza Minnelli look-a-like.

On her left is a perfectly attired dirty-blonde haired woman in her mid-40's. She keeps checking her watch as though she has something much more important to do or somewhere else she'd much rather be. Her emotions are visible for anyone to see, alternating between gleeful anticipation, as though she is waiting to board a thrilling ride at a theme park, to the stark reality of waiting to watch a man die.

The image of Irma 'The Beautiful Beast' Grese flashes in my head from a story I read not long ago. She was the Senior SS Supervisor at the Auschwitz/Bergen-Belsen concentration camp, where she treated the female prisoners with extreme cruelty, including whipping and beating some to death. When they arrested her in 1945, they allegedly found in her quarters three lampshades made from the skin of prisoners.

Sixteen witnesses are allowed in this room. It will be a full house.

Within moments, the prison warden, a stout, serious man of around 60 years of age, joins us, introduces himself, and begins to describe how death row inmate Cameron Gambke spent his day. All three reporters check their tape recorders to ensure their "on" buttons are activated.

"As you may know, right now there are 150 inmates on death row within these prison walls. As with the Hyde Correctional Institute, only male prisoners are detained here. All female death row inmates are kept at the North Carolina Correctional Institution for Women also located here in Raleigh.

"I personally offered to be close by his side since this morning, but the prisoner opted to sit quietly in his 11 X 7 foot cell until lunch at 11. As per department policy, lunch was given to him in his cell, but he refused to eat it."

One of the reporter's hands shoots up. "Excuse me, Warden, sir, but what did he have for lunch? And, what is in his cell?" The dirty blonde leans forward, desperate to not miss a word of his reply.

"Pork chops and apple sauce, with a Coke."

My mind goes back to a funny scene in the Brady Bunch series when I hear this, except this isn't TV Land, and this isn't a comical moment.

"As far as the question pertaining to the content of his cell, there is a bed, a toilet, sink, and a wall-mounted writing table."

Turning back towards the group, he continues.

"Before it was determined he would be executed, he would venture out to the community room with the other death row inmates, where he had the opportunity to play chess, watch a small TV, or listen to music, although he never had the chance to spend time with the general prison population. That was for his own safety as well as the safety of the others.

"His attorney has been his only visitor yesterday and today, and all I will say is it appeared to be a heated conversation. The attorney left with a hopeful look on his face, yet the prisoner didn't seem to share in his guarded elation."

I notice the scowls forming on the faces of the victim's parents. Suspicion and concern flash from the eyes of the well-kept drama queen, her tentativeness only matched by the sheriff's. Their eyes lock. Do they know each other outside of these walls? I can't help wondering what their connection is, if any, to Cameron Gambke. Is she Gambke's wife, or possibly another relative? If so, why is she happy at times?

"He did not ask for the prison psychologist, but did ask for his priest. Unfortunately, I had to inform him that after much searching, his priest could not be found."

The warden looks at me disapprovingly, as does the rest of the group. I shoot a glance at the sheriff, who won't meet my stare but I see his shoulders bouncing up and down, a failed attempt to stifle his sick humor.

"Immediately after his last meal we began preparing the inmate for his execution, at which time we secured him with lined ankle and wrist restraints to a gurney in the presence of the trained physician who is required to be present. He also had a cardiac monitor and a stethoscope attached, with two saline intravenous lines started, one in each arm, and, as you will see in a moment, he's now covered up to his neck with a sheet."

Turning his gaze to me, he says: "Once you are all ushered in, he will be given one more chance to speak and pray, if he wishes, with you. He will also be given a chance to record a final statement which will be made public."

I nod to acknowledge my understanding of the role I am to play.

"The syringes have been prepared in advance following very strict, specific Department of Public Safety standards. Each contains only one drug. There are no less than 3,000 milligrams of sodium pentothal, which is a quick acting barbiturate that will put him to sleep. The second syringe contains saline to flush the IV line clean. 40 milligrams of pancuronium bromide, also known as Pavulon, a chemical paralytic agent, will then be injected. Another syringe will contain no less than 160 milli-equivalents of potassium chloride. This will interrupt nerve impulses to his heart, causing it to stop beating. A final injection of saline will flush the

IV lines clean once more. The final step will take place after five minutes of a flat line on the EKG monitor. I, according to Department of Public Safety policy and as warden of this institution, will then pronounce him dead, and the physician will certify that death has indeed occurred. His body will be released to the medical examiner at that time."

The warden informs us he wasn't here during the last execution and this will be his first. He looks like I feel. Ironically, I note that other than the sheriff, the female SS officer, and one of the three reporters – a young up-and-coming male in his red Oxford shirt – everyone else also appears to desire to be anywhere else rather than watching a man be executed. Pixie-haired girl stands still with no trace of emotion. The thoughts of our own mortality are causing our skin to crawl. After a pause, he asks those present. "Are there any questions?"

"What's his state of mind right now?" asks the clear leader of the reporters. Like the others present, he has been trained to ask the five W's – who, what, when, where and why – no matter how idiotic they may sound. Most of the information they have already, but what they write will be read worldwide. They will also be on television within the hour after this event is completed, so obtaining the facts is critical in order to allow the world to live vicariously through them.

A scowl creeps across the warden's face. "We didn't have that particular conversation."

Checking his watch, he nods at one of the prison guards to open the door to the viewing room adjacent to the old gas chamber. Lying on the table, exactly as described by the warden, is Cameron Gambke.

I have witnessed death before, at the bedsides of dying patients in the hospitals, and was by the side of mom when she passed from cancer, but there is nothing that has prepared me for this moment. Here is a healthy man whom I still am not sure is guilty. "God give me strength," I whisper, my head down. If any of the reporters had asked me my thoughts at that moment, I would have told them straight out, "I don't want to be here right now. I am not afraid; it's all just very bleak."

All of the victims' mothers and one father begin crying, and I can see the other two fathers desperately holding back tears of sadness mixed with indescribable rage. The other two young males stand aside, fists and jaws clenching in unison. The young female appears to be in a state of shock.

In contrast, beautiful beast lady cranes her neck to see as much of the room as possible, throwing a wicked smile the inmate's way, leaning forward, not wanting to miss any of this incredible show, and grabbing tight the arm of the 20-something. Her ups and downs make me wonder if she's on meds. I'm thankful this will probably be the only time I have to be in close proximity to this woman, my intuition telling me she represents a personality I want to avoid.

The warden makes his way to the door adjoining our rooms. A guard opens it for him.

"Father, please come with me." My legs are numb. My stomach is in my throat. My mind goes blank.

I leave behind the room of absolute freedom and enter one of stainless steel, wall-to-wall concrete, and abject coldness. No strange smells enter my nostrils, at least any I can identify. I want to escape. I want nothing to touch me or to be touched by anything. A warm shower right at this moment to try and wash all of this away would be ideal.

Our eyes lock and death row inmate Cameron Gambke tries to reach for me.

"How are you doing?"

Yeah, that must be the dumbest thing I have ever said to anyone, ever, and immediately regret what I just said.

His eyes blink, trying to process what he just heard. His face says it all. He's trying to decide whether he heard me correctly, or if I am truly a moron and he's chosen the wrong person to spend these last few moments by his side.

"At least I won't die by the hands of Redek."

There's that name again, but before I can ask, he beckons me to lean forward. "Don't forget the deliveries."

"It's already been done," I whisper. I can feel the eyes of Sheriff Luder burning through the glass, trying desperately to hear every word.

"I dropped them directly in the post office after-hours slot in Gardensville as soon as I got back last night. I didn't want them lying around."

"And no one looked at them?"

"No one. Not me, not any of the prison staff, not a single person. Just as you asked."

I didn't think twice about his request last night, as my focus was more on his confession and my desire to leave the prison walls to get back home. But the intensity on his face now, coupled with Sheriff Luder's insistence that I am a fool for believing anything positive about this man, suddenly makes me nervous.

"What I did for you, it's all, well, legal, isn't it?"

"Is sending a letter against the law, Father?" he hisses.

"No, no it isn't."

His insistence makes me consider his motives. Was he simply saying goodbye or did the letters provide instructions for unlawful activity? I certainly do not wish to be a party to a crime, whether willingly or not. At this point I am pleased that I have absolutely no idea what was in those letters, and no matter how hard the sheriff pushes, I can plead ignorance with conviction.

"Not the sheriff?" glancing his way.

"Not the sheriff. Nobody."

He looks relieved, and the warden takes a step our way, indicating our time is up.

Quickly I ask, "Is there anything else you want to say?"

He looks away towards the room, past the approaching warden, and back to my eyes. "Yeah."

Pulling me even closer so my ear touches his lips, he mouths in a barely audible whisper, "Renae is in that room with you."

It takes a moment for the name to register. Renae. Renae Gambke? Yes, one of the two letters he had asked me to mail was for Renae Gambke! Maybe she's the dirty blonde ponytail tormentor; maybe the 20-something female. Since I had told him I had already mailed the letter, maybe he wishes me to speak with her, get to know her, help her through all of this. I freeze, wondering if the Good Lord is asking me to spend time with epidermis lampshade lady.

Thankfully, his imploring eyes suddenly fill with tears, telling me what I need to know. He wants me to reach out to Renae. God's will needs to be done.

"I will search out Renae for you."

Glancing at the warden, I begin to pray the Our Father, and Cameron Gambke's lips begin to move, his words uniting with mine. I had discovered during his last confession that he, too, had been baptized and confirmed a Catholic, but he had found the "true path" when he got older as he told me twice during our time together, one of true love and life. For who? Himself? Being on death row and scheduled to be executed clearly reflected he was a criminal. And we're all sinners, including him. Yet somehow he had managed to justify his parallel worlds of life and love, and, if true, criminal activities so horrid he was about to have his life taken from him. Or was his belief system just a cover? If that was the case, his theology is grossly out of order, or his self-serving rationalization is deep and disturbed. At least he remembers the Lord's Prayer.

The warden stands by patiently, hesitatingly awaiting his role in the drama that is unfolding before all our eyes.

We squeeze each other's hands and I am escorted back into the viewing room. Sheriff Luder is staring at me, I know, but I ignore him. I stand motionless, wishing I had brought in my hand sanitizer, not knowing what Cameron Gambke has touched since his arrival here.

"Do you have any last words you wish to speak?" the warden asks, looking at him and then our group, panes of glass separating us, but designed in such a way that we can hear everything happening, thanks to the presence of microphones and speakers.

Looking awkwardly from the gurney, he begins from his right, locking eyes with Sheriff Luder, a wretched smile immediately forming on the prisoner, with matching narrow eyes, more venomous than I imagine the sheriff could begin to muster on his angriest days. The sheriff tenses, but Gambke's gaze moves away quickly. Passing over me and the reporters, he locks onto the eyes of dirty blonde ponytail. "I'm sorry," he mouths, and she lurches forward, hitting the glass partition. Sheriff Luder barges past me to grab her and she buries her face in his arms, wailing. Moving towards the 20-something female, a look of true sorrow comes over his face, as he says "Please forgive me," tears forming in his eyes. Guilt? Shame? She remains steadfast, and doesn't seem moved by his remorseful gesture. Finally, he pauses a brief moment on each face of the victim's families, scanning while holding their stares.

"There is nothing I can say that will make your lives better, other than I am truly sorry for any pain you have felt. But your daughter's killer is still out there because I didn't do it. I believe in family and the order and protection it affords, and I would never do anything to tear one apart."

The sheriff can't hold it in any longer, and ignoring the certain reprimand that will come his way as his words are printed and shared with millions around the world, he shouts:

"You're only sorry you got caught, you piece of shit!"

Releasing the blonde from his comforting embrace, he pounds the separating pane of glass. His body oil leaves a perfect imprint of his closed fist, reminding me of the poor dove that attempted to fly through the clean living room window back at the rectory in Brooklyn, instantly breaking its neck as it dropped dead to the ground.

All heads turn towards the sheriff. The victim's families hold each other tight in a group embrace, the sharp outburst startling everyone. Surprisingly, pixie-girl breaks into guttural sobs. For these secondary victims, the raw emotions that they have, over time, suppressed, now reappear in full force.

Without a reply, Cameron Gambke lays his head onto the pillow, his stare focusing on the white ceiling above. I can't tell for certain, but I think I see a slight smile creep onto his lips. The warden nods to the physician who has been standing near the medical equipment.

Suddenly, a shrill buzzer startles everyone present, including the warden.

Motioning one of the guards to open it, another uniformed guard enters, whispering in his ear. The warden composes himself, fixing a determined look our way. Something important has clearly transpired.

"All be advised the Governor has issued a stay of execution

for death row inmate Cameron Gambke. Details will be provided to the family of the victims within the next hour, and to the media during a news conference to commence at a still to be determined time later this evening."

Shouts of revulsion and cries of angst fill the observation room. There are no yelps of joy or pleasure. Cameron Gambke remains motionless. He had told me he was prepared to die, but I sense he is equally afraid to live. We are immediately ushered out of the observation room.

It suddenly dawns on me I now have more time – time to learn more of the story, and, by God's grace, time to determine what He has in mind for me. I need to find Renae Gambke, before this crowd engulfs us.

Chapter 4

Mass confusion has broken out. The talking heads from all the news agencies can be heard shouting phrases such as *"Tampering with the evidence," "Not following the correct judicial process,"* and *"Political maneuvering."* But the rationale for the stay issued by the governor is nowhere near this place.

I have neither the time nor the interest in sorting out the machinations that led to Cameron Gambke's reprieve from death. I just need to find Renae Gambke.

Scanning past the reporters as they sprint by me, I search the sea of heads. The outwardly flawless siren from the Execution Witness Room is only five yards away.

"Excuse me, but are you Renae?" I yell to her, hoping all the while this isn't the person Cameron Gambke wants me to reach out to.

She swings around wildly, her eyes quickly scanning me from head to toe. It is quite clear she has, in an instant, made a calculated judgment and found me wanting, a skill she has undoubtedly mastered over the years. Is it my black outfit? It's all the rage with my fellow Catholic priests. Are my shoes scuffed? A smudge on my white clerical collar, maybe?

"No!" she sneers, "My name is Michele Jerpun. Why do you want to know?"

She had seen me speaking earlier with Cameron Gambke, and probably now connects me with him, maybe even thinking we are long-time friends.

"I, uh, I just need to speak with her."

An awkward pause, then no response. I get the distinct impression she is very good at controlling everything and everyone who happens to come near. Yet, are those tears now forming? At this point, since I've confirmed she isn't Renae, I don't have the time to hear her story.

"She must be the young lady with the jet black hair?" I ask, spotting the back of the Anne Hathaway/Liza Minnelli double who is rapidly moving away from where I'm standing, now at least 30 feet away.

"You don't need to know." Yes, the flood waters are indeed

beginning to flow as she flicks her head towards the prison. "But since he won't take the time to talk with me, you let that motherfucker know he's gonna die sooner rather than later, and we won't rest until he does. Unless you need something else from me, I'm leaving. I need to be at the hospital right now!"

'We' won't rest until he dies? Who's 'we'? A wickedly long, silver fingernail confirms her demand I relay that specific message. Yet, within an instant her face changes, as she seductively rests her right hand on my left shoulder, letting it slide down my black jacket. I pull away immediately. I don't know how her brain is wired, but it's tweaked for sure.

She smiles playfully, turns, and strides away from me, throwing her oversized Coach purse across her left shoulder, leaving her right hand clear to roundhouse blow any of the reporters moving her way in case they say anything flattering about Cameron Gambke.

Turning back to who I hope to be Renae Gambke, I shout a little louder than I mean too, hoping not to cause her to run away.

"Renae Gambke?!"

She stops, turning towards me, and pauses. Not wanting to lose her, I close the distance between us with an awkward jog. I am an avid walker, but running is not my thing. A twinge grabs my thigh from the quick, unexpected start, but I push through it.

As I approach it suddenly strikes me she could easily be the daughter of beast woman. As such, I stop about five feet away from her.

"Hey, uh, sorry to call after you like that."

Sadness and pain etch her face, her eyes red and swollen. Looking at my left hand rubbing my knee, she asks, "Are you all right, Father?"

Her voice is direct, yet not berating nor accusing. An inner strength and calm pulls me toward her. I haven't felt this hint of emotional warmth from another soul all day.

"Oh, yeah, uh, I'll be fine. Haven't run in a long while." I crack a smile.

"Hey, Gambke, did you pull some strings to get your old man off?" yells a slightly overweight grizzled man in his late 60's,

35

sporting a *"Life Is Shit Unless You're the Shitter"* yellow and black baseball cap pulled firmly over his white-haired scalp. She eyes him coolly, hesitates, glances at her watch, and calmly chooses to ignore the heckler. My instinct is to protect her, and I begin to step towards the man. She reaches for my arm with surprising swiftness and strength, holding me in position.

"He's so not worth it, Father."

Her eyes leave mine and pan to the reporters hustling our way, done with their interview with Ms. Jerpun who is comically chasing after them, apparently not feeling she has said all she wanted to say. Renae's eyes lock back on mine, semi-patiently waiting to hear what prompted me to chase her down to begin with.

"May I talk with you? I mailed a letter to you last night on behalf of Cameron Gambke."

Her face turns sour, eyes narrowing, yet not a hint of moisture now arises in them.

"His last request was I make sure you got it, and now I think he wants me to talk with you. I don't know why…can you help me?"

Glancing at the rapidly advancing coterie of reporters and cameramen, she hesitatingly inquires, "Where are you parked?"

"I don't have a car. Can I catch a ride with you?"

"Where are you going?"

"At this point, wherever you are."

Back on U.S. Highway 64, we head east as I settle in the front passenger seat. As providence has it, Renae Gambke lives in Belhaven, just 30 minutes from Gardensville, and graciously agrees to go out of her way to take me home. The inside of her car looks strikingly similar to the sheriff's cruiser. Law enforcement? A relative of the recently spared death row inmate Cameron Gambke is an officer of the law?

I decide to move slowly into this conversation given her cautious demeanor, her trauma from the Execution Witness Room, and her kindness toward me.

"How long have you been living in Belhaven?" I ask.

I find out quickly that Renae Gambke is short, yet not unkind, with her answers, and long on listening. Given I like to talk, this might be the beginning of a great professional friendship. However, Cameron Gambke is still alive, and he wants me to reach out to her, so it will be much more beneficial if she talks and I listen. I don't know what role the Good Lord wants me to play in this, but maybe on this drive home I can get a better idea.

"Three months."

"Do you like it there?"

"Yes. I love it. Great people. Beautiful part of the state."

I feel like I am interviewing for Susan Bellers' replacement. Hey, maybe...?

Returning my focus to our conversation, I begin to ask multiple questions, hoping to speed this process along a little bit.

"What brought you there? Where did you live before? What's your favorite color?" I laugh, trying to ease the situation, hoping we can just talk, like two normal people.

She stares at me, shrugs her shoulders, then finally smiles, thankfully catching my attempt at humor. Before she can reply to this barrage, I try to set her even more at ease.

"Hey, no pressure. We just have some time together on this car ride. I don't know why we are even in this car right now, together – spiritually, I mean – so maybe we can just get to know each other, if you're comfortable with that."

"I understand."

Fifteen-mile markers pass in silence. I can tell she's thinking of exactly what to say, and how to say it. I don't press the issue, giving her time to collect her thoughts. I can't imagine this morning she drove to Raleigh thinking she would be returning with a Catholic priest.

My eye catches the sticker she has placed on the top of her notepad binder she carries with her from Matthew 6:24: *"Therefore do not be anxious about tomorrow, for tomorrow will be anxious for itself. Let the day's own trouble be sufficient for the day."* I'm tempted to make a comment, to reach for a connection, but let it pass.

Eventually her face grows darker, a scowl appearing. She rubs the steering wheel tightly. 65 wordless mile markers have passed since we left Central Prison and I'm wondering if I should fire up my laptop again. I am about to comment on the strange cloud formation when she says, "Look, I'm sorry. There is just, well, so much going on right now, and so much has happened."

"You can tell me everything, or you can tell me nothing. It's really okay."

A deep sigh. It's an opportunity to talk with someone who is unbiased and independent from her life. I hope she still thinks well enough of Catholic priests to open up to me. Get things off her chest.

With limited advance notice, like the fury and speed of a Midwest thunderstorm, the words hastily come out. Emotionless. Direct. Exact.

"Cameron Gambke is my biological father. My biological mother died when I was twelve. My dad told me it was from a car accident, but I still don't know if that's the truth. I moved to Scottsdale, Arizona, with my aunt on my mother's side when I was ten, so I wasn't there when she died. I really wish she were still alive. I really would like to ask her some questions."

It's obvious from her icy tone she didn't have an ideal childhood. If she did have the chance to speak with her mom again, I have the impression it wouldn't be about baby blankets, flower gardens, and beautiful sunsets. Sadly, from my experience as a priest, an incredible number of young children don't have ideal homes anymore, either.

"I have one brother, Matt, who I'm told dropped out of the Community College and left the area about two weeks ago, but I have no idea where he went. I just know he really needed to go, for reasons I have yet to figure out. But I miss him. Well, I miss who he used to be."

I know not to ask any questions at this point. By all indications, more information is yet to come.

"I went to junior and high schools in Scottsdale, and then on to college at Notre Dame."

She turns to me.

"My aunt saved my life."

A new round of quiet envelopes the vehicle. 25 minutes to go.

In the very short time I've known her, she seems well-balanced. She looks healthy, both physically and emotionally, and her breakdown in the prison is pretty understandable given the tension we were all feeling, especially with the intimate, yet public, communication between Cameron Gambke and her.

"What did you study at Notre Dame?" I ask.

"Criminal Justice."

"Ah. That's interesting. All I know is they have some great athletic programs."

I really have no idea how sound their academic programs are. And I have no idea if they still teach appropriate Catholic doctrine, something many "Catholic" schools and universities around this nation no longer choose to do. What I do know is I sure pulled for them to win the last national football championship. Hey, remember that as a young boy, football was one of my favorite things to watch and play. That is, until I found a deep love for the game of soccer. She absently nods her head, as though her thoughts are miles away.

The drone of the rubber tires hitting the imperfections in the road beneath us takes center stage. It's another mile before she continues.

"I'm sure you're wondering what the rest of the story is. I'm not sure how much you know about Cameron Gambke, but he was convicted of raping and then murdering a young 22-year old girl in Boise, Idaho, on one of his business trips. He traveled extensively internationally, as well, so who knows how many more victims there might be. Unfortunately, they could only tie him to two others."

Why would she think he has more than three victims? This certainly doesn't match with the man I spent a few hours with last night while hearing his confession. His demeanor before and after, and the time I spent with him this morning, were quite the opposite. Granted, if he is guilty of these crimes, he could have shared it with another priest before me, but is this the same guy we're talking about?

Disgust is oozing off of her tongue, a granite-like expression now firmly clutching her face. The contents of the letter I placed in the mail for her now begin to pique my interest.

"I'm in town because I got news his appeals were running out and he might be on his last leg. I didn't come for an apology," she seems to be telling herself this more than me, "but when I last talked to the son of a bitch, well, let's just say that even to the end, he couldn't give me the freedom from my nightmares, and I know for damn sure he owes me that."

I now have many more questions than answers with only a few miles to go. Before I can ask, she offers another piece of the puzzle.

"But once I got here, I heard about Gina."

"Gina?"

"Yes. Gina Jerpun. I guess she's technically my step-sister. Her mom was in the room with me today, Cameron's second wife. Ex-wife, I should emphasize. Cameron is not the father of Gina. I guess the biological father left when they learned she was going to be born with Down syndrome and she refused an abortion."

Michele Jerpun. Of course. A mother with a child with Down syndrome. I am amazed once more by how many intricate layers make up the people in God's world. I didn't see that one coming. Yet I can't shake the ease with which Mrs. Jerpun altered between rage and attempted seduction. What I do know is I need to stay clear of her as best as I can.

"What happened to Gina?"

"She was gang raped a few weeks ago. Some bastards gave her a date rape drug which, combined with the medication she was already on, put her into a coma. She's only fourteen years old."

My mind is racing now. Michele had said she had to get to the hospital. Gina is her daughter and she's in a coma. She wanted to be with her, as any good mother would, yet she had to travel to Raleigh to watch the execution of her ex-husband. Maybe that is why she kept checking her watch.

"I've transferred here to work the case. My boss is a real hard ass, with me mainly, because he doesn't like my father. I know that to be true because he tells me about it every chance he gets. Problem for him is, he's overwhelmed with the cases on his plate and he needs my help, even though he won't admit it."

"Who's your boss?"

"Sheriff Daniel Luder."

My eyebrows shoot up, and she catches my reaction. It all makes much more sense now. Both she and the sheriff have identical department-issued vehicles. But what role does she play to warrant an unmarked car?

"Let me guess. He is aggressive, short, and even combative with you?" I ask.

"Only when he's trying to be nice."

We have a common foe and share a collective laugh. She continues.

"He is like that with me all day, every day. And I think pretty much everyone else. Since you're talking with the enemy, Cameron Gambke, and I'm the daughter of the enemy, that puts you and me on his 'make-life-miserable-for' list, I'm sure.

"But you should probably know something else to better clarify what lies below the surface. I knew the sheriff when I lived in this town a long time ago. I was friends with his daughter in elementary school before I was moved by Child Protective Services. He really was a nice man back then. I try to always remember that part of him to get me through my day. Fun, gentle, and, you'll also be surprised to hear this, even going to the Catholic Church, as I recall. I went to a few birthday parties at their house, barbecues, you know, time at the lake. Stuff like that."

She smiles now, recalling the good times that fortunately still exist somewhere in her mind. Maybe this was what Cameron Gambke wanted me to do for his daughter – to get her to talk and get whatever she needs off her chest. But if that is what he wanted, why didn't he let her do that when she visited him in prison?

"I'm sorry for asking," I press, "but if Sheriff Luder knows you had to be rescued by CPS because of a bad situation at home, living with Cameron Gambke, why is he upset with you now? I mean, wouldn't he feel sorry for you and try to help you?"

"I think he's upset with life, really. I just think his way of handling it is to take it out on everyone. He was only a deputy when I knew him, working his way up in the department, but then he ended up running the entire operation. He was a great choice for the job, I think. Really a great, hardworking man. Very professional, knew and followed all the rules. Still does as far as I can see. Then his wife got breast cancer. She battled it and has been in remission ever since, as far as I know. Ever since then he's been a real asshole to everyone."

I interrupt, a bad habit I have when I'm trying to make sure I get all the necessary information.

"What's his wife's name?"

"Mrs. Luder? You know, that's a good question. I haven't seen her in a long time, but as I recall, it's Jean. I just always called her 'Mrs. Luder' when I knew her as a child. I do know she's now a Substance Abuse Counselor.

I nod my head. She continues her trip down memory lane about Sheriff Luder.

"Like I said, I heard that's when he started to change. Maybe it was the stress of the new job and almost losing his wife that got him. I don't know. That combination can really wreak havoc on people. But then another bad thing happened that was the final tipping point. He found out his own daughter had been raped. In their own house, to make matters worse."

"The sheriff's daughter was raped?" I blurt out.

This day is getting even more depressing and I find myself wanting to veg out and watch ESPN. Or, maybe there's a good match from the European League soccer channel that can give me the mental break I'm in need of right now. All this is too much and I really need to clear my head.

"Yes. The sheriff and his wife were at the hospital for final treatments and his daughter had just gotten home from school. A guy had broken in and was waiting for her. Black mask, oversized black outfit to hide his body frame, the works. A well-planned attack. The guy beat, then raped her. One of the deputies told me the other day that when it all happened, he went to the house, and he'd never seen the sheriff like that. Trying to be strong for his wife and daughter, holding them both, holding back tears and a look far beyond rage in his eyes. All he said to the deputy was, 'I should have been here to protect her.'" She pauses. "His daughter tried to commit suicide not long after, but fortunately she didn't succeed. She moved away for a fresh start. Since I had already moved away before all of that I haven't seen her since. So I give him a lot of leeway because he hates sexual predators. And that's what we have in common. He needs me to help him, but probably won't ever admit it."

She grips the steering wheel hard again, turning her focus on me.

"But I'm damn good at what I do, Father, and since Cameron Gambke was a sexual predator, that makes us both despise him. In the end, Sheriff Luder and I are on the same team, and I will try to support him as he works through his painful memories."

For the second time on this brief trip, I feel horrible for my thoughts about a fellow human being and offer meekly, "That's a great deal of pain for him to go through."

She nods her head in agreement, and we both know the emotion of anger is strong and can decimate lives. It's also a hard one to control. Fortunately, I also know that with God, all things are possible. That sounds trite, I know, but I really believe it to be true. With God's grace, I've seen anger dissipate too many times to think otherwise.

I guide her down a few streets to my home as we head down Main Street in Gardensville.

Pulling up to the rectory, I ask, "So what do you do in the department?"

"I'm the new Sex Crimes Detective."

***

As the sun goes down on this emotional rollercoaster of a day after I have my ESPN and soccer "fix," I turn off the TV after briefly listening to CNN postulate about what is really behind the stay of execution for Cameron Gambke in Raleigh, North Carolina. Rolling into bed, I ask the Holy Spirit once more for the fullness of His gifts – Fortitude, Counsel, Fear of the Lord, Piety, Understanding, Knowledge and Wisdom – and absolute guidance to know what He wants me to do, and I pray the same for all those wounded souls I met today.

Chapter 5

A statue of our Blessed Mother stands nestled in a grotto within the garden at the rear of the church property. It is a peaceful oasis where I can be alone with God and our Lady. It is where I begin each day praying the Rosary; where I can, if only for a few moments, dismiss distractions, reflect on the issues of the day, pray and listen to God's voice. I always take a moment to thank Him for all of the gifts I have received.

I am reminded the Rosary was the favorite prayer of the late Blessed Pope John Paul II. This great pope credited Mother Mary with saving his life. Specifically, Mehmet Ali Agca attempted to kill him in St. Peter's Square in Rome, exactly 64 years to the day our Lady began appearing to the three children at Fatima, Portugal. Two years later, Pope John Paul II visited Agca in prison and forgave him.

I begin my prayers this morning by thanking Our Lord for His church's guidance in electing the new Vicar of Christ, Pope Francis, asking he be blessed in all his upcoming duties as the new Pope of the Catholic Church. Although I've yet to meet him, I understand from our Bishop he has great humility, a true concern for the poor, and is committed to building bridges between people of all backgrounds, beliefs, and faiths.

I also pray for the wonderfully blessed Benedict XVI, who retired recently. I often meditate on the latter's quote, *"What does Jesus want from us? He wants us to believe in Him. To let ourselves be led by Him. And so to become more and more like Him, and thus, to live rightly."* I will be forever grateful for his intellectual contributions to His Church, especially as a defender of Catholic doctrines and values.

Turning back to the Rosary, I recall that we honor Mary as the Mother of the Son of God. We don't worship her as though she is God. I have this vision of our Lady as God's chief-of-staff, you know, the person who has His ear. We believe she can't do anything on her own, but she definitely has great influence with her Son and can intercede on our behalf. Do you remember Our

44

Lord turning water into wine at the wedding at Cana? Remember the Gospel reflects He did this at *her* request.

As a self-imposed rule, I bring only my Rosary and breviary with me to this place. But today I felt the need to bring along a few documents I have collected during past pilgrimages. I am hoping their review will help me in preparing for the upcoming video conference meeting with my fellow pilgrims.

We will be journeying to a number of places where our Blessed Mother has appeared. Through her apparitions, Mother Mary has continually asked the Rosary be prayed.

The story of the Rosary is the story of our salvation. Through it we meditate on the saving power of Our Lord's life, death and resurrection. It is a reminder that through His death and resurrection we were given the opportunity to achieve eternal life with Him in Heaven. Countless blessings, graces and miracles have been granted to those who faithfully recite this prayer.

A small folded pamphlet catches my eye. It points out that although we aren't required to believe this as an article of faith, Church tradition holds that Mother Mary gave 15 promises to St. Dominic & Blessed Alan for anyone who faithfully prays the Rosary.

1. Whoever shall faithfully serve me by the recitation of the Rosary, shall receive signal graces.

2. I promise my special protection and the greatest graces to all those who shall recite the Rosary.

3. The Rosary will be a powerful armor against hell. It will destroy vice, decrease sin and defeat heresies.

4. It will cause virtue and good works to flourish; it will obtain for souls the abundant mercy of God; it will withdraw the hearts of men from the love of the world and its vanities, and will lift them to the desire of eternal things. Oh, that souls would sanctify themselves by this means.

5. Those who recommend themselves to me by the recitation of the Rosary shall not perish.

6. Whoever shall recite the Rosary devoutly, applying himself to

the consideration of its sacred Mysteries shall never be conquered by misfortune. God will not chastise him in His justice, he shall not perish by an unprovided death; if he be just, he shall remain in the grace of God, and become worthy of eternal life.

7. Whoever shall have a true devotion for the Rosary shall not die without the sacraments of the Church.

8. Those who are faithful to recite the Rosary shall have during their life and at their death, the light of God and the plentitude of His graces; at the moment of death they shall participate in the merits of the saints in paradise.

9. I shall deliver from purgatory those who have been devoted to the Rosary.

10. The faithful children of the Rosary shall merit a high degree of glory in heaven.

11. You shall obtain all you ask of me by the recitation of the Rosary.

12. All those who propagate the holy Rosary shall be aided by me in their necessities.

13. I have obtained from my Divine Son that all the advocates of the Rosary shall have for intercessors the entire celestial court during their life and at the hour of death.

14. All who recite the Rosary are my sons, and brothers of my only son, Jesus Christ.

15. Devotion to my Rosary is a great sign of predestination.

Another pamphlet in the bundle describes another prayer devoted to Mary. Known as the Devotion to the Seven Sorrows of the Virgin Mary, it was revealed to St. Bridget of Sweden by the Blessed Mother and approved by Pope Pius VII in 1815. The Virgin Mother encouraged those to whom she appeared at Kibeho in Africa to pray these Seven Sorrows, in addition to the Rosary.

As with the Rosary, the Seven Sorrows of the Virgin Mary is a contemplative prayer in which you meditate on seven sorrowful events experienced by the Blessed Mother. The pamphlet lists them:

1. The prophecy of Simeon that a sword will pierce Mary's soul (Luke 2:34-35)
2. The flight into Egypt (Matt 2:13-14)
3. The loss of the child Jesus in the temple (Luke 2:43-45)
4. The meeting of Jesus and Mary on the way of the cross
5. Mary witnesses the Crucifixion and death of Jesus
6. The body of Jesus is taken down and laid in his mother's arms
7. The burial of Jesus (John 19:38-42)

And for those who pray the Devotion of the Seven Sorrows, seven graces are promised:

1. I will grant peace to their families.
2. They will be enlightened about the divine mysteries.
3. I will console them in their pains and I will accompany them in their work.
4. I will give them as much as they ask for as long as it does not oppose the adorable will of my divine Son or the sanctification of their souls.
5. I will defend them in their spiritual battles with the internal enemy and I will protect them at every instant of their lives.
6. I will visibly help them at the moment of their death; they will see the face of their Mother.
7. I have obtained (this grace) from my divine Son, that those who propagate this devotion to my tears and dolors, will be taken directly from this earthly life to eternal happiness since all their sins will be forgiven and my Son and I will be their eternal consolation and joy.

My tranquil morning is shattered with the slamming of the

screen door from the administrative building. Standing on the front step, glaring at me, Mrs. Bellers brusquely interrupts.

"Fr. Bernard was wondering when you are going to come inside. And did you get that packet yesterday from the Diocese?"

It appears she fully intends to plant herself on that step until I pack up my belongings and follow her directive to go inside. I won't, yet calmly reply. "Good morning, Mrs. Bellers. I will be inside in 20 minutes for our scheduled 8:00 a.m. meeting, just like he and I previously discussed and, yes, I have the packet."

Turning my back to her, I return my focus to the statue of Mother Mary. The statue is smiling. I'm not. *"Be gentle,"* she is reminding me. *"Help me to be kind, please,"* I implore back.

A loud huff emerges from the brawny jowls of Mrs. Bellers. I offer a silent prayer. *Please, God, give me patience.*

One by one, I focus on the five sorrowful mysteries:

- Our Lord's agony in the garden
- His scourging at the pillar
- His cruel crowning with thorns
- His carrying of the cross, and
- His dying on the cross.

My fingers move from bead to bead, the Our Fathers and Hail Mary's creating the perfect background mantra as I meditate and reflect on the mysteries. I sense Mrs. Bellers is still standing on the porch, and I use her intended distraction as an opportunity to work on my ability to slow my breathing and offer up this cross with His. In my hands are the Rosary beads I treasure the most. Mom and Dad had traveled to the Holy Land and brought them back to me a few years before she died. I will make sure I get them to you by the time you are reading this.

The screen door slams twice more – once to go back inside and the other to come back out again. Mrs. Bellers makes a point of noisily shuffling to the outside garbage bin, tossing the contents in such a way as to maximize the distraction, then slamming the top shut. *Breathe, just breathe, and focus,* I remind myself. Me and one of my own crosses, Mrs. Susan Bellers. Focus on the cross Our Lord carried. He will never give me more than I can handle, I am reminded, and I can certainly take whatever she tries to throw my way.

The keys to the doors of Heaven are made from the crosses I bear, the daily struggles I experience. They're a gift, not a curse. When I see them through the eyes of God they make me stronger, wiser, and more compassionate to those around me. Yet accepting the crosses I have been given doesn't mean I shouldn't make the effort to improve my situation in life.

Another screen door slam, my body jerking at the loud sound before continuing my meditation. Mrs. Bellers has gone back in, probably recalling she has an entire list of people to harass today. I heard her telling Fr. Bernard just the other day how a volunteer had the gall to change the font on the Parish bulletin. How dare they.

Refocusing, I remind myself that I must never forget that Jesus is the light of the world. So, as a follower of Jesus Christ, I must also strive to be His light in this world. When people see me, they need to see Him. In other words, if I, as a Catholic, am always following the crowd, looking to be accepted by those around me, trying to please everyone, to fit in, then I am not living as He intended. Jesus was not like everyone else in this world. So that is my goal, yet my state in life is not perfect, and that's why I always need Him and His example, His Church and the Sacraments, and my effort.

I know, I know, that's easy for me to say, yet still hard for me to do. A Catholic priest no less. I mean, I *know* what the Church teaches. Heck, I received a great deal of education through the seminary so I should. So why do I still have challenges with people like Susan Bellers, Sheriff Luder, and Michele Jerpun? Well, I suppose it's because I'm human. I know that's not an excuse and it sure sounds like one. What I mean is I struggle just like everyone else. Full of pride and ego, with all the habits, traits, and characteristics I've managed to pick up during my life. And when I was ordained a priest, it wasn't like I was sprinkled with magic dust that suddenly made me a saint. I suffer the same lot of all humanity.

Once my Rosary prayers are completed, I follow it with the

devotion to the Seven Sorrows of the Virgin Mary. The last four of the seven sorrows allow me to meditate even more on Mary's sorrow as a mother during Our Lord's passion. Can you even begin to imagine her pain?

I end it with this prayer: *"Queen of Martyrs, your heart suffered so much. I beg you, by the merits of the tears you shed in these terrible and sorrowful times, to obtain for me and all the sinners of the world the grace of complete sincerity and repentance. Mary, who was conceived without sin and who suffered for us, pray for us."*

"Thank you, God, for this time," I say, reminding myself to at least try to be respectful, kind and courteous to Mrs. Bellers.

Heading in, I place the CSA packet in her special In-Box. Without anticipating a 'Thank You,' I turn towards Fr. Bernard's office. Once more, I'm not disappointed. No 'Thank You' comes my way, not even a glare, as she steadfastly stares at the computer screen, clearly and silently informing me my presence isn't worth a second of her valuable time.

"Fr. Bernard?" I stand in the open doorway, the 80-year-old priest sitting at his desk, reading.

"Yes?"

He looks up, a kind man, who has worked hard at this parish over the past 20 years. A lit cigarette smolders in the ashtray on his desk, casting a cloud over the office. As much as I enjoy spending time with Fr. Bernard, I try to rush through my meetings with him. What I have read about the dangers of second-hand smoke really concerns me.

"Sorry if I'm late." I know I'm not. It's 8:00 a.m. sharp and our agreed-upon meeting time. I need Mrs. Bellers to hear me say it and, more importantly, for her to hear Fr. Bernard's reply. I should be restrained and not play this little mind game with her, but I simply can't resist the temptation.

"Oh, good morning Fr. Jonah! Late? You're the most punctual person I have ever met and, true to form, you're actually right on time!"

His face is joyful. There is rumor that a form of dementia may be setting in, but as far as I can tell, he seems as sharp as a tack. Glancing back over my shoulder at Mrs. Bellers, I can see she is suddenly busying herself with paperwork. We both know she doesn't miss a thing.

"Come on in. Shut the door and join me. Tell me how it went yesterday, please."

I hesitate, wanting the smoke to vent out the open door rather than being trapped in here, but do as he requests. For the next 20 minutes, I relay the events of the previous day.

"So he'll be on death row for a bit longer? Do you plan on visiting him?"

"As a matter of fact, yes. He has fallen away from the faith so maybe God has given me time to continue to share the Good News with him."

"Will these plans take you away from your responsibilities here?" His demeanor is suddenly serious.

I understand what he is asking. He has spoken to me before of his desire to have me slowly relieve him of a number of his current meetings and duties. We also keep hearing through the grapevine we will be expected to begin the process of building a new church, a monumental task. More people are moving to this area, yet we don't have enough priests to go around. Thus the need for a larger worship space. In short, there is much to do.

"No, not at all. I plan on traveling to Raleigh on my days off, maybe every other week, if that helps."

"For now, that would be good. Mondays are your day off, right?"

"Yes."

"Okay. Now, when is your pilgrimage again?"

"April 12 through the 28th. We leave on the Friday after Divine Mercy Sunday. I will be back here in the office on Monday, April 29. And remember that sometime in the spring of next year, I am still obligated to lead one more pilgrimage. It will be to Kibeho, Africa. I don't have the exact dates yet but, once it's finalized, I will let you know. I would like for you to celebrate the masses during my absence, if your retirement plans allow it.

"If not, I'll work it out with the Diocese."

He nods, remembering this promise I've made with my old diocese in Brooklyn.

As he contemplates all I have just shared with him, I hear the

51

voice of Mrs. Bellers rising. I can't hear anyone responding, so she must be on the phone. I feel sorry for whoever is on the other end. I feel a sudden urge to speak with Fr. Bernard again about her, but he beats me to the topic, and not in a way I anticipated.

"Mondays it is. Oh, before you go, Susan said you were pretty rough with her yesterday on the phone. I can understand it, given what you were in the middle of there in Raleigh, and I know she can be pretty demanding, but remember she's a valuable employee and keeps everything in line around here. I would really hate to see her leave once I retire."

I hold my tongue to fight back my initial, emotional response which is to tell him straight up I can't wait until the day she does leave since I already know he won't let me fire her while he's still here.

"We've all just met. I'm sure we just need time to get used to these new personalities that have come together." I offer, knowing no matter what I say, it won't make any difference. In fact, it may ultimately make it worse for me should he decide to tell the Bishop I'm not a good fit for this parish. My dad needs me here, and I'm getting the impression others do too, thinking about all those I've met over the past few days.

Standing to leave his office, he adds: "Only God can change hearts. Remember that."

"I understand."

I'm not sure if he's referring to me, Susan Bellers, Cameron Gambke, the other death row inmates, or all of us, but he's right, I know.

I remind myself Our Lord will never force us to love Him. Like any relationship, we need to make continued attempts for peace and reconciliation. My challenge is I don't believe Mrs. Bellers is making any effort I would define as "charitable," but I know I can't change her. Since I can't control anything about her interior world, I don't need to be naïve either – I will do all I can to protect myself along the way, and that's well within the teachings of the Church and my role as one of His shepherds.

"Thank you, Father."

As I open the door, Mrs. Bellers slams down the phone.

"Damn people. All they need to do is read the bulletin. Everything is posted in there every single week."

She's clearly not talking to me. No one else is in the office.

Our eyes meet. If she's affected by my catching her self-disclosure, she doesn't show it nor even seem to care. Maybe she's really not intimated by me as her future boss, as I previously surmised. Or, if I would press her on the issue, she might just say that's just "who she is," like it or not.

No words pass between us as I close the door to the building, enjoying the warmth of the sun. The morning chill has almost left entirely for the day.

***

Daily Mass is celebrated here at Our Lady of Perpetual Help Monday thru Friday at 12:30 p.m. Fr. Bernard and I alternate days and Tuesdays are mine. Celebrating Mass is the highlight of my day, truly.

Heading to the rectory afterwards, I hear a car door slam behind me.

"Here, you can have this." Sex Crimes Detective Renae Gambke says, handing me the letter I had mailed to her on behalf of Cameron Gambke just 36 hours prior. She must have gone home for her lunch break, checked her mail, read it, and then drove to my place 30 minutes away.

"What do you want me to do with it?" I ask, watching her stomp back to her department vehicle, the driver's door open and the car engine still running.

"It didn't tell me what I was looking for. It's yours now. Do with it whatever you want. Pardon my language, Father, but he's fucked up, and I'm sure it's all another one of his ploys. Conning people until the very end. Even his own flesh and blood."

As quickly as she arrived, she's gone. I look down at the letter and back to the rapidly shrinking rear window, trying to organize my thoughts. Cameron Gambke is still alive. He asked for me to be with him on what, for all intents and purposes, should have been his final day on earth. He wants me to help her. Help her with what, specifically? Will this letter give me any indication? I plan on asking this very question next Monday when I visit him. I don't care for guessing games.

53

Heading back inside the rectory, I place the envelope inside my jacket. I'll read it tonight while meditating at the Adoration of Our Lord in the chapel.

My cell phone rings. It's a number I don't recognize.

"Hello. This is Fr. Bereo speaking."

"Sheriff Luder here. I need to speak with you."

Same tone as yesterday. How did he get my cell phone number? Maybe Detective Renae gave it to him.

"Certainly. I have appointments throughout this afternoon, and a conference call at five, but that should only last an hour."

"I meant tomorrow."

Why didn't he say that to begin with? I continue listening. Be patient. Sympathetic. Caring. Charitable.

"Are you free at four? I need to take you somewhere. There are things you need to know if you are going to be spending more time with death row inmate Cameron Gambke, especially if you keep thinking he's just an innocent saint who merely got a raw deal."

"I never said anything like that about Mr. Gambke, Sheriff. As I said already, Our Lord above is His judge, not me. At any rate, do you need my address?"

"I already know where you live." he says, hanging up.

Of course. My 2:00 p.m. appointment arrives, and I gesture to the young engaged couple, encouraging with my wave that they head inside.

I wonder if the sheriff knows about the letter to Detective Renae I now have in my possession. Most likely not. If not that, what's on his agenda now?

Nothing is clear at this point, other than the badgering face of Mrs. Bellers glaring at me through her office window.

Chapter 6

Earlier tonight I led a videoconference for our upcoming pilgrimage. All 20 participants gathered at the parish offices in Brooklyn while my image was broadcast from a rented facility in Gardensville. Our parish hasn't purchased this technology yet, but if it's in the final budget for the new church, I plan to ask the Bishop's approval.

I always feel nervous before each trip – the different cultures, food, time zones, diseases or any combination thereof – anything that will certainly force me to a hospital bed and cause me to die away from home. Do you know what I hate the most? That I have allowed my health anxieties to control me. It's exhausting.

I reminded the group that we will be traveling by air and bus over the 17-day period. We'll head into Rome first, and ultimately end our journey in Fatima, Portugal. Mother Mary has chosen to appear in some pretty distant places. She's pleased, I'm sure, that we are undergoing this hardship out of faith.

Tonight my primary aim was to remind everyone the Church's stance on the topic of miracles, and to stress they are not intended to satisfy our curiosity or desire for spellbinding enchantment. I relayed that miracles require divine intervention and must be more than remarkable or improbable; a true miracle must be a supernatural phenomenon.

"Also remember that the messages are not considered divine revelation. Catholic doctrine teaches that divine revelation to man by God began with Adam and Eve and ended at the death of Saint John the Apostle. Messages given at approved apparitions are considered private revelations that can provide greater insight into divine revelation but can never provide anything new to our faith. Church authorities are very clear that these private revelations do not belong to the deposit of faith," I had shared.

I said this doesn't mean these messages from Heaven aren't important. All approved apparitions are reminders, and they seem to occur at critical moments in world history and always in troubled times. And the messages are almost always urgent pleas to reopen our hearts, to pay attention, and to turn back to God. I stressed that God can and does speak to us in many ways, and urged that we not let our pride and ego get in the way by trying to stuff Our Lord in our pre-defined box.

Grabbing my Catechism – the document which holds the entire deposit of faith for the Catholic Church – I read the definition of "miracle" to the group.

"'MIRACLE. A sign or wonder, such as a healing or the control of nature, which can only be attributed to divine power. The miracles of Jesus were messianic signs of the presence of God's kingdom.'

I further shared #548 from the Catechism:

"'The signs worked by Jesus attest that the Father has sent him. They invite belief in him. To those who turn to him in faith, he grants what they ask. So miracles strengthen faith in the One who does his Father's works; they bear witness that he is the Son of God. But his miracles can also be occasions for 'offense,' they are not intended to satisfy people's curiosity or desire for magic. Despite his evident miracles some people reject Jesus; he is even accused of acting by the power of demons."

I made a point to relay that miracles still occur today, and which they'll see clear evidence of on the pilgrimage. And then there are smaller, everyday miracles; miracles happen to people of all faiths and from all walks of life.

"The potential for confusion is one of the reasons the Church is incredibly thorough in its investigations of miracles. Miracles are there to remind us God still exists, He is ever present, and He never has nor ever will leave us," I had said.

Doing their own research is critically important for them to form their own opinion, and I stressed this multiple times during the videoconference.

After a quick break, I reminded the group about the extensive investigatory process the Church follows for apparitions and alleged miracles. I always believe it is important to firmly emphasize that the Church has always been cautious in examining and categorizing reported apparitions, and that apparitions are categorized as follows: 'not worthy of belief,' 'not contrary to the faith;' or 'worthy of belief.'

"In evaluating the evidence of each case," I stated, "the local Bishop must follow specific criteria and answer six fundamental questions, at a minimum. First, are the facts in the case free of error? Second, are or were the person(s) receiving the messages psychologically balanced, honest, moral, sincere and respectful of church authority? Third, are there doctrinal errors attributed to God, Our Lady or to a saint? Fourth, are the theological and spiritual doctrines presented free of error? Fifth, is moneymaking a motive involved in the events? And sixth, have healthy religious devotion and spiritual fruits resulted, with no evidence of collective hysteria?

"So, after going through this all-encompassing, methodical process, if a report prepared by the local Bishop for the Vatican is positive, he is specifically saying that the message is not contrary to faith and morals. Specifically, nothing is contrary to all that's included in the Catechism of the Catholic Church. If for a Marian apparition, this report also infers Mary can be venerated in a special way at that particular apparition site."

I relayed that when the Church recognizes a Marian apparition as worthy of belief, it is not saying that after rigorous scrutiny and discernment, we are *obliged* to believe the Virgin Mother Mary appeared here or there. On the contrary. The Church is merely telling us there are good reasons for us to believe, but without any obligation to faith. We are invited to believe because it would be beneficial and fruitful for us, her children.

I urged everyone to always maintain a balanced view concerning any of these apparitions. We shouldn't be naïve, I shared, but neither should we be entirely dismissive. Whenever anyone hears of an apparition by Mother Mary, I stated we all need to let the Church investigate and determine its authenticity, and then make our own decision accordingly.

"After hearing from the local Bishop," I added, "the Church may also decide, based on other information available to it, they want to set up a separate investigative body for further review. Keep in mind it took four years of intense review before a decision was made regarding Lourdes, France, 13 years for Fatima in Portugal, and 20 years for Kibeho in the Republic of Rwanda, Africa.

"One last thing on this topic. Because of the thorough and lengthy process to which an apparition is subjected, the majority of alleged apparitions actually dematerialize before the public even becomes aware of them."

Since this upcoming pilgrimage isn't traveling to these approved sites, I took a moment to speak about the incredible miracles at Guadalupe, Mexico; Siluva, Lithuania; Fillippsdorf, Czech Republic; Gietrzwald, Poland; and Knock, Ireland.

Wrapping up the evening, I shared some of the miracles identified by the Oriental Orthodox Coptic Church because it is worthy of consideration, in my opinion. I stressed that the Catholic Church hasn't ruled on them because they didn't occur in predominant Roman Catholic territory.

"These apparitions occurred just within the last 44 years – the most recent approved was in 2010. The current population of Egypt is approximately 82,000,000, with the vast majority, around 90%, Sunni Muslims, about nine percent Coptic Christians, and the rest a variety of other Christian sects. As it relates to these apparitions, members of the Catholic, Muslim, Jewish and a variety of other faiths, as well as atheists and agnostics, were witnesses to them, which clearly add weight to the argument these are not merely a Catholic phenomenon.

"You should certainly know of the important and pivotal roles Egypt has played throughout biblical history. After the birth of Jesus, Mary and Joseph took refuge in Egypt in order to avoid the massacre of innocents ordered by Herod the Great.

"All right, back to the apparitions in Egypt. Not long ago, from 1968 to 1971, Our Lady reportedly appeared many times above Saint Mark's Coptic Church in Zeitun, Egypt. Tradition has it the Holy Family spent time there during their exile.

"Witnesses state she often appeared at night and doves were seen flying around her. She was seen walking along the top of the church. Witnesses also saw orbs of light which formed a cross.

"She voiced no messages, but Egyptian television filmed and showed startling images of the apparitions. There were nights when up to 250,000 people were watching. It's estimated that over three years, 40 million people saw the images – mostly those of the

Christian and Muslim faiths. What is truly remarkable is witnesses were actually able to take photographs of the apparitions; uncommon at most Marian apparitions. Although many tried to disprove the authenticity of the photographs and televised images, no one has ever been successful in doing so.

"Then, for four months in 1982, the Blessed Virgin Mary reportedly appeared multiple times on St. Mary's Coptic Church in Edfu, Egypt. As at Zeitun, Our Lady was silent. And again, both Christians and Muslims saw the images.

"From 1986 to 1991, so roughly over a five-year period, the Virgin Mary is reported to have appeared near the two towers of the church of the martyr Saint Demiana in the Shoubra quarter in Cairo, Egypt. The witnesses claim they saw her full body in a halo of light. Apparently, the apparition was originally noticed when the light surrounding her shone into the houses adjacent to the church. The apparition was seen on multiple occasions by members of different religions, including Coptic Church authorities. During one appearance, a young girl's eyesight was allegedly restored; this has been attested to by a medical physician. As with Zeitun, photographs were taken for all to see.

"From 2000 to 2001, at St. Mark's Church in Assuit which is in the southern region of Egypt, the Blessed Virgin Mary is reported to have again appeared in full figure. Witnesses reported seeing glorious lights and big, bright white doves. Supernatural lights and blue-green flashes of lights were also seen above the church. Witnesses stated they could smell incense during these apparitions. Once again, Our Lady was silent.

"And, finally, from 2009 to 2010, just a few years ago, on multiple occasions, witnesses report the Virgin Mary appeared on the domes of the Virgin Mary and Archangel Michael Coptic Orthodox Church in Warraq el-Hadar, Egypt, which is in the Greater Cairo area. Those present recalled she appeared in a pure white dress with a royal blue belt and a crown on her head. Over 200,000 Christians and Muslims witnessed the initial appearance. She was seen surrounded by pure white birds. Behind her a star would suddenly appear and then travel across the sky before disappearing. Like the other apparitions I just shared with you, there were no messages from Mother Mary. However, with the beauty of technology, videos were made on mobile phones by a number of witnesses and shown on YouTube. Plus, the events garnered a great deal of media coverage in Egyptian newspapers and on Arabic TV channels.

"So why was Mother Mary allegedly appearing in Egypt to a predominantly Muslim group? I will leave that for the scholars and theologians of the Church and other faiths to contemplate."

After concluding the teleconference, I gathered my papers, reminding myself about the letter in my jacket pocket from Cameron Gambke to Detective Renae.

Chapter 7

It's quiet and serene in the chapel. There are only two people other than myself here at the moment, gazing at Our Lord exposed in the silver and gold monstrance. His radiant presence brings me peace and often, answers. I come here whenever my schedule allows.

The others sit in quiet solicitude around me, only our breathing a gentler reminder of each other's presence. Although we are not alone, we are alone with Him, each in our own private audience with Our Lord. He loves us that much.

It saddens me so few take the time to spend any time at all with Him. The peace and serenity that pervades this chapel, especially during Adoration, should be desired by everyone. Sadly, far too many no longer believe in the real presence of Our Lord. If they did, this Church would be packed. I mean, if it was the President of the United States standing here or certainly a celebrity exalted and glorified by the media, a mere human being created by God, it undoubtedly would be.

"Please, Lord, let me see and understand what you wish during this time with you, and especially as I read the contents of this letter."

Unfolding the three pages, I begin.

"Ro-Ro, I haven't called you that since you were a little girl, have I? If you were here in front of me now, I would do so, but I don't think you would be open to it like you were way back then. I don't blame you, but maybe this final letter will help ease that pain. If you knew all the truth, you still might not understand, but know sometimes life happens quickly, and we all adjust as best we can.

By the time you will have read this, the State will have murdered me, an innocent man. Given your new job (an interesting career option, I might add, no doubt an influence of your aunt), I'm certain you know the details from the case file, at least what Sheriff Danny Boy has chosen to actually record there. He hasn't liked me for years, and I believe he has set this all up against me. I tried everything I could to prove it, but they've all stopped listening to me. DNA can lie. And DNA is only as good as the investigator interpreting it. And you know why I know that to be true? Because I wasn't there. I've been told it doesn't matter anymore now; deaf ears are all around me.

The last time you and I met, you had many questions for me, but since there are too many ears in here, all with friends out there, I couldn't tell you everything then. Even now, I wonder who will read this letter, and all that I've set up for you and your brother may disappear if what now has to happen doesn't go as planned.

So I will paint this picture of your dad's life in a roundabout way. I write this letter to you, not your brother, because although he received the might of brute force, he has yet learned to control his impulses. You, on the other hand, received a keen intellect, a gift from your mother. I miss that time in my life with her completely, before, well...Back to the point. In your hands this information will come to light, and all I've left for you and him can come to fruition if only you are willing to search for the truth of the wonderful world I created for myself and my loved ones – my family.

Let me attempt to tell you my story via the saga of the wolves, one which we are both familiar with, irrevocably linked from long ago. I don't know who will read this in the future, but I know you're smart enough to put together the puzzle I am laying out for you. The wolf. But for my purposes here, the Canis Rufus, specifically – the red wolf. They're a special breed of angels, babies from junior gods, some full of light and others full of darkness according to the brilliant master of the greatest book ever written. Before being transferred here from Hyde, I had two years to study them with my own eyes, and offer you, my precious Ro-Ro, this information. They greeted me on my daily walks in those screened, razor-barbed fences; they spoke to me as they howled at night. An entire pack lived just over the road, and they were marvelous creatures indeed. I think they were there for a reason, just for me. We seemed to have a connection that went far back. I understood them, and I believe they understood me.

Thousands of years ago, about two million of their ancestors roamed freely across the United States of America where I made my own home long ago before starting my family. One-hundred thousand of those were red wolves. They had families, and friends, too, if you will, a wonderful social structure, and they fit perfectly into the evolutionary map *haphazardly laid out by the big bang a millennium ago.*

The Native Americans knew how to live peacefully with them, but not the European settlers who decided to explore, travel west, and kill as many as they could. Fear drove them. Fear for their livestock, their animals, themselves. Fear can be a wonderful source of knowledge, or it can shut down a brain and instead of thinking with that gray mass between their ears, some people just react, panic. And they did. They still do today. But I digress. By 1960, only seventeen pure red wolves remained in this country. What these people didn't know is these poor animals were more afraid of them than they were of the wolves.

Fortunately, the biologists and scientists got involved, and the controlled breeding began. Almost thirty years ago, the Alligator River National Wildlife Refuge in North Carolina was chosen as one of the release sites. It's about an hour and a half from Hyde. Not a lot of people lived there then or now and there's plenty of land and natural prey for the wolves to live on. And freedom, yes, they had freedom, even though they had radio collars strapped around their necks for tracking purposes. Today there are about one-hundred and thirty that are alive, roaming in and out of that refuge area, and five seemed to have relocated right across the way from that prison hellhole. When the enforcers of the law brought me there, they thought I would be saddened. In retrospect, the Aeons surely brought me there to begin with. It was a blessing in disguise.

"But when they transferred me here I saw they had killed the whole family and made sure I saw them dead. The alpha male, I just called him 'Mac,' and the alpha female, I called her 'Ehslly,' because she reminded me of an old friend on the outside I once knew. They mate for life, but sometimes it doesn't happen as planned. She wasn't the first alpha female either – I think one was killed by a hunter around here and her name was Ilsa. And Mac wasn't always the alpha male, either – the first one, I called him Redek, must have been captured because one day he didn't show up and the entire family left the area; I think they are keeping him at another man-made lockup somewhere, or so I hope. A couple of weeks later they showed up again, and this lone wolf, Mac, was already there.

Lone wolves are the saddest to even think about. They leave the pack for a variety of reasons, but really as a result of physical and mental harassment, intimidation, maybe even hunger because the pack can't kill enough to feed all of them, or maybe they just want to mate themselves.

They are tough, because they travel a long ways after they are cast out to find food, a home, somewhere to belong, maybe a family of their own.

So here was 'Mac' courting Ilsa and the other members of the pack showed up. He must have sensed there was no alpha male around, and only she was in charge. They howled at one another, and for three hours they played this 'cat and mouse' game. He was being tested, and if he didn't play well, she and the other members would kill him for sure. But after all this, she accepted him, maybe because she used to be a beta female herself. I literally saw him put his paw around her, then there seemed to be rejoicing as Ilsa introduced him to the other family members. He was happy. They all were. He belonged to one of his kind once more.

Sometimes during the day they hunted, but mostly at night. Oh, I wish I could've seen them but I couldn't from within those prison walls. The hunt. Man, I miss the hunt. Adrenaline pumping, all senses fully alert, an unmatched feeling of invincibility. I found out they sifted and sorted incredibly efficiently. They run alongside their prey and work as a team. It may take a while, but once they lock in, she's a goner. It's a numbers game, and the more wolves on the hunt, the greater their chance of victory. They have a total of forty-two teeth, ten more than humans, and their jaws are extremely powerful. They smell a hundred times more acutely than humans, too. Very effective. Once they get their kill, they may eat twenty pounds of food at a sitting! But they are only successful one out of four times, so they need to always hunt. It's what they do. It's in their blood. They need it to survive. And when they aren't hunting or planning a hunt, they are sleeping or playing. They know how to live the good life! I don't know who taught Mac how to hunt like that, but I'm certain a sage wolf of the Magbke family had a lot to do with it.

But I do feel sorry for the omega wolf – the lowest member of the pack on their taxonomy organization chart – he's harassed all the time. No one really understands him. Sure, he's gotten himself into trouble a lot, but I think it's because they won't leave him alone so he has to react to all they're doing to him to begin with. And since none of the pack members will reach out and help him, how else is he going to turn out? I call him 'Tamhew.' He had to leave the pack quickly not long ago, but he'll figure it out, I'm sure. He's a fighter.

And there used to be a beta female that the first alpha female just beat up all the time, I mean, really mistreated her. Completely unfair, I thought. But that original alpha female, Ilsa, who was very loved, had to pay for how she treated her. I call her 'Nerae.' She left for a long time, but she's back now. I saw her with my own eyes. She's really grown into a beautiful young red wolf princess. If she can figure it out, like Tamhew, she'll realize they're all waiting for her, a spot of power is open on this clan's totem pole, and it's all ready for her to run someday, run it all, if she chooses.

In closing, if Sheriff Danny Boy has gotten his hands on this and is reading it now, I now address this to him. YOU WILL NEVER BE SMART ENOUGH TO PUT ALL OF THIS TOGETHER. YOU'RE JUST NOT THAT INTELLIGENT AS YOU'VE PROVEN TIME AND AGAIN. NEVER HAVE BEEN NOR WILL YOU EVER BE. IF YOU WERE, YOU WOULD HAVE ALREADY FIGURED OUT YOUR OWN TWISTED PAST, BUT THAT EASILY ESCAPES YOU, TOO.

Ro-Ro, this is very important – know that joke of a law enforcement officer will burn you the first chance he gets. It's what self-serving people do. And when, not if, that happens, after all of your hard work to get where you're at in your career, know there is another way to get what you want in life and achieve your dreams. You deserve happiness and happiness is what awaits you. It's all in place. Think about you, what you want, what makes you happy, what makes you dance. Follow your heart, always, because the many voices in your head can only confuse and paralyze you while the world races by. What's right? What's wrong? Don't let your misguided conscience decide. YOU decide. You are a part of me; you have my genes. Live large. Read "Paideia" by Thomas Victor – it completely altered my world for the better. Find "monstrabilis" and accept my gift. Become the Aeon, the alpha female lobos."

Know that death doesn't frighten me, for I will come back again, in what form only karma will decide.

Cameron Gambke, BHR"

BHR? What's that stand for? And there's that name again, "Redek."

The word "monstrabilis" also sticks out. I just saw that word recently, but where?

Sitting back I look once more at the monstrance, clearing my mind and closing my eyes.

A flash of insight – of course, it's the name of the street that

was on the first letter Cameron had me mail out! #3 Monstrabilis
Court! Albuquerque, New Mexico!

So...what in the heck am I supposed to do with this
information?

Chapter 8

I've read the letter at least six times now, sleeping only sparingly throughout the night. I left a voicemail for Detective Renae. Maybe she can help me make sense of it, if she's willing. Maybe I should let the whole thing go. *Lord, what do you want me to do?*

It's Wednesday morning, and I'm sitting once more in the garden grotto, meditating on the Glorious Mysteries. These mysteries ask us to reflect on the glorious events which occurred in the lives of Jesus and Mary.

- Our Lord's Resurrection which constitutes the confirmation of all Christ's work and teachings.
- His Ascension where He has a mission to begin a new creation, to prepare a place for us, new heavens and a new earth.
- The descent of the Holy Spirit at Pentecost, reminding me of when the Catholic Church officially was "born."
- The Assumption of Mother Mary into Heaven, where she already shares in the glory of her Son's Resurrection, anticipating the resurrection of all members of His body, and
- The crowning of Our Lady as Queen of Heaven and all things.

"Lord, I offer all my continuing intentions I ask for each day as I pray the Rosary. I also now ask you help me to see what it is you wish me to do with this letter, this situation, these scarred souls around me, this phase of my life as one of your shepherds. Please, show me the way," I whisper.

I thank Our Lord for this time to spend with Him, and Our Mother for her intercession and constant help.

My cell phone rings. The now preprogrammed name of Detective Renae displays on my phone.

"Hello, Detective."

"Good morning, Father. I'm returning your call." Direct, to the point, all business.

"Thanks for calling me back. Look, I know you're at work, so I don't want to take much of your time. But, I read the letter over a number of times and, well, if it's all right with you, I would like to talk about it sometime soon."

Silence.

"I'm not trying to cause any trouble, nor bring back more bad memories for you. Let's just say I'm intrigued. I'm hoping you can help me connect the dots."

My spiritual advisor, Fr. Jack, had encouraged me long ago to ask for God's grace to connect the dots, to be better able to see the handiwork of God in the world around me. Right now, I'm just trying to see where I fit pastorally in God's great plan if, and how, He wants me to help Detective Renae.

"Sure. Yeah, that would be fine. I'm tied up today," she says, "But am free tomorrow."

We agree to meet at two p.m. at Swan Quarter after I celebrate daily Mass.

I don't tell her I'm meeting with her boss today. I don't want to give her any reason not to trust me. Neither do I want her to think I am going to share her letter with him, which I have no intention of doing. I know she said I could do whatever I wanted with the letter, but I see no need to pass its contents on to anyone else, especially the sheriff. If I find a need to do so later, I'll speak with her first out of common courtesy.

***

At precisely 4:00 p.m., Sheriff Luder pulls into the parking lot. I appreciate his punctuality. I have always believed it is a sign of respect to others, so I try to do the same. An outgrowth of my days in Corporate America, I guess.

I've already notified Fr. Bernard I will be spending the rest of the afternoon and evening with the sheriff. A small life pleasure emerges as Mrs. Bellers cranes her neck to look through the window. I take the front seat with no hesitation by the sheriff – this must now be "official business" – and hear the window plant crashing to the ground. She'll probably be up all night wondering what this is all about, beating her brain cells to exhaustion, trying to figure out what it could all mean.

"I need to open your eyes to the world around you, Father. There's something I want you to see, something I want you to hear, and then there's something I want you to do. If you want to really help people, and I believe you do, you need to let the scales drop from your eyes."

His tone is less aggressive today, yet his piercing gaze notifies me his boiling anger might only be on hold for a short while. I decide to merely nod in acknowledgement as he puts his "law enforcement issued" glasses on.

A reference to the scales dropping from my eyes? Apparently, he does remember some of his Catholic teachings.

I'm certain he's referring to St. Paul who, on the way to Damascus to persecute the Christians, is met by God, falls off his horse, is blinded, regains his sight, and then becomes one of the greatest saints in Church history. Is he suggesting I'm persecuting people like St. Paul? If so, who does he think I'm after?

He really knows nothing about me no matter how much he researches. Or, is he suggesting he's St. Paul, trying to help people turn their lives around? If that's the case, maybe his approach is to beat them into submission. Certainly something God would never do; He loves us too much.

"Where are we going?" I ask as we pull onto the freeway heading north towards Plymouth.

"A community college. I know the President, and he's agreed to let us sit in tonight."

He abruptly hands me a file folder that was wedged between his seat and the center console. It's thick. He struggles to remove it with his free hand without spilling all of its contents. I see it's marked **"Gambke, Cameron. Case #VJ2-2010. CONFIDENTIAL. Tier III Sex Offender."** He motions for me not to open it just yet. I imagine he's been carefully planning what to say to me and wants my undivided attention.

"Do you have any idea how bad it's gotten?"

I wait. It's a rhetorical question. He's not expecting me to answer. If I knew how bad "it" has gotten, I don't think I would have been asked to go along with him on this field trip.

"The amount of violence, and the degrading nature of it all,

I..." he's becoming exasperated, struggling to keep his thoughts organized. "I can't even put into words how bad things are from when I began my career in law enforcement 25 years ago."

I need him to know I'm not completely naïve to the world.

"As a priest, I've heard many, many things over the years which have truly bothered me. So, yes, I agree, it's gotten dark. And the history of the world is chock full of very bleak periods interspersed with moments where it appears to be more in balance. But we must always remember that although battles will be lost, God will win the war. He's promised it."

Staring at me, he shakes his head.

"With all due respect, I really don't want to get into a religious conversation with you right now, or probably ever. I'm talking about the here and now. This problem. This issue. This moment."

Religion is the here and now, but I don't say it and respect his request to not head down that road, at least for the moment.

"I'm talking about what one person is capable of doing to another. Look..." his index finger stabbing at the file folder I now hold on my lap.

"That guy, and all that shit in there, typifies what I see around me all day long. And it's not just here. I have contacts all over this country and around the world, too. It's everywhere. Everywhere!"

His shout startles me. I'm wondering if the sheriff from the other day has returned. Remaining silent, I focus on my breathing, trying to remain calm. I sense he is attempting to do the same.

From merely being a member of today's society, I have no doubt what he is saying is probably on the mark. It's obvious he is genuinely trying to communicate his concerns to me, and I'm grateful he's not pulling the dominant "tough guy" move from before.

"Do me a favor. Look in that file. Then, when you're done, you and I are going to sit in a college-level class so you can hear the crap that's being fed to our youth. And when all of that is done, on the way home, I am going to challenge you to take an eye opening journey."

"Why?" I ask.

70

"Why what?" His head snaps towards me.

"Why are you asking me to do all of this?" I have every reason not to trust him at this point.

"Because like I said on the phone, you think Cameron Gambke is a saint. Because you probably have people coming to you all day long wanting clear help and guidance, and all you probably give is some pithy advice like 'Oh, just give it up to God,' or 'Just accept whatever pain God is giving you and offer it up for penance.' Bullshit like that. You need to do your homework so you can really *help* people! Now, take a look in there, and see what I see!"

His theology is off; his line of reasoning skewed. Our Lord said there would be darkness, pain, evil and sin in this world due to original sin combined with man's free will. However, He also said we need to look towards the light and that the light is Him – the Good News. He gave us His Church to help and guide us along the way. He offers us the hope of everlasting life if we run the good race to the end. Whenever I come upon such pain, I am reminded of the agony experienced by Our Lord, and I take comfort in knowing that through his suffering and death on the cross, we now have an opportunity to spend eternity with him.

I'll go down this road with him today and see where it leads. If it's the wrong road, God, via the well-formed conscience He formed in me guided by the Holy Spirit, will alert me.

Opening the file, a mug shot of Cameron Gambke stares back. A slight smile for the camera, and a gentle, innocent expression on his face, the same image I have of him from our first meeting. Either they have the wrong guy, or he's one of the best actors I have ever met. I find it hard to believe this overstuffed file folder contains evidence of the horrendous evil that this outwardly nice man supposedly has done. Yet the sheriff is emphatic about the horrid character of Cameron Gambke. He may be right. Maybe I am naïve.

I peer more closely at the file, the smaller font tasking my aging eyes.

Full legal name. Date of birth. Past history of residences. Names of relatives. Past places of employment. All the necessary details are present which allow anyone interested in knowing the standard pieces of identification relative to a given individual.

I read and reread the notations for the tattoos located on his body. *"Grey skull and cross bones, with the letters 'B.H.R.' immediately underneath said crossbones, on top of light gray, ornate design in the shape of a military medal. All superimposed onto a black, gray and white ribbon. Tattoo located on subjects back, spanning from the inside right of the left shoulder blade to the inside left of the right shoulder blade. No other tattoos on subject's body. No piercings."* A picture accompanies the tattoo.

It's the second time I've seen the initials "B.H.R." as they relate to Cameron Gambke in just a matter of days. There's no explanation of these letters. I'm tempted to ask the sheriff, but my eyes immediately catch the label for section two of the folder.

"Tier III Sex Offender – Definition
- *Aggravated sexual abuse under 18 U.S.C. § 2241 or sexual abuse under 18 U.S.C. § 2242; ["Sexual abuse" crimes generally require, among other things, the commission of a "sexual act," defined in 18 U.S.C. § 2246 as contact between the penis and the vulva, the penis and the anus, the mouth and the penis, the mouth and the vulva, or the mouth and the anus; penetration of the anal or genital opening of another by a hand, finger, or any object; or direct touching, not through the clothing, of the genitalia of a person under 16.]*
- *Abusive sexual contact under 18 U.S.C. § 2244 [described above in the tier II offense definition] when committed against a minor under 13 years old;*
OR
- *Involve kidnapping of a minor (unless committed by a parent or guardian);*

Cameron Gambke had been convicted of raping and sodomizing an 11-year old female over a two-year period. On two occasions he took her on a 'vacation,' just he and her, and raped and sodomized her in his hotel room multiple times. Evidence was also found in which he secretly videotaped the female victim dressing and undressing, showering, and masturbating. According to a notation in the file, a plethora of digital images exist that he kept for later use. Thankfully, the bulk of these images are retained in a separate folder.

Turning back to the mug shot, I stare more closely at his eyes, trying to picture this man partaking in these heinous activities. I find it difficult to do. He looks just like the people I see all around me every single day. I chastise myself. What am I to think, that all criminals have a label tattooed on their head telling me what type of person they really are? Shit, I am naïve.

The sheriff periodically glances my way. He knows where I'm at in the file folder and is waiting patiently for my reaction. I refocus on the contents sitting in my lap as he fixes his gaze once more on the road.

Evidence was also found in which he secretly videotaped another female performing the same actions – her mother – with whom he had been married at the time.

Cameron Gambke admitted to this activity, but justified it by claiming he was only doing so in order to "properly educate the young female before she began a sexually active life." He denied having anything to do with the videotapes, however, although this evidence was found on his laptop. When presented with this evidence, he said that since she's his wife and it's his house, he can do whatever he wants.

Some of the pictures, as entered into evidence for the trial to describe his character, are still in this folder. I recognize the individual in one of them.

"Cameron Gambke secretly filmed his wife, Michele Jerpun?" I ask.

"Yep." He's clearly tense.

"This girl in this other picture looks like she has Down syndrome. Please don't tell me Cameron Gambke was having sex with that young girl." I shake my head, a frown quickly forming on my face.

"Welcome to my world, Father Jonah. These are the turds of humanity I deal with all day long. But soon that twisted prick is going to die," he says, jabbing the folder with such impact I'm forced to hang on tight lest the contents spill on the floorboard.

I close the file and lean my head back on the headrest, not certain how much more I want to see.

"There's more. Keep going," he orders.

Dutifully, I read that twelve months ago, a tip came through that prompted a search of the Idaho State Police DNA database. The authorities got a match which tied Cameron Gambke to the death of a young 22-year-old female in Boise, the daughter of an Idaho State Police Officer. Like Gina Jerpun, she was raped and sodomized. But unlike Gina, this poor girl's throat had been slit and her body dumped in a ravine. Pictures of the victim and the crime scene make up the remainder of this section of the file, and two other sections exist with information supporting the other two murders. I have no interest in reading through them.

I've seen enough. Closing the file folder for good, I look out the window, away from the sneer I am certain is on the face of Sheriff Luder. He turns on the radio, an unknown hip hop country song blaring away, tapping his fingers to the beat. The first part of his mission for me has been accomplished – I've seen what he wanted me to see.

My head is about to explode as I try to make sense out of all this new information. Combined with what I already know from Cameron Gambke's letter, once more I have more questions than answers.

We pass a sign for the Alligator River National Wildlife Refuge. He referenced this area as it related to the red wolves. B.H.R. after his signature on the letter and the same three letters tattooed on his body. The disgusting things Sheriff Luder must have to deal with on a routine basis. How does he do it? Michele Jerpun's understandable rage at what Cameron Gambke did to her as well as to her daughter who is now in a coma from, who? Cameron? But he's been locked in prison for some time so it couldn't have been him. Then who? And why her? This innocent young lady, who has an even harder time in life living with Down syndrome, had to be subjected to this? I'm saddened and disgusted by the whole thing, and rest with this thought for a few moments before the sheriff continues.

"So, if I may borrow one of your little biblical terms, now that you've seen the file and have a better understanding of the real murderous wolf in sheep's clothing, you want to tell me what Gambke told you right before his life was spared? I know he said something – hell, I saw his lips move – and he was trying awfully hard to keep me from hearing it. Damn straight."

"Do you honestly think I'm going to tell you that, Sheriff, though I've seen what's in this folder? Were you not listening the first time? I can't, and I won't. Ever."

He turns up the radio, chuckling loud enough for me to hear.

The sun is beginning to set and clouds are forming over the ocean, remnants of Hurricanes Isabel and Super Storm Sandy try to catch my attention. I sense that what I have seen thus far, in this challenge of Sheriff Luder, is only the beginning; that things are indeed about to get worse. To what extent only the Good Lord knows.

Chapter 9

The remainder of the trip is made in silence. We enter the campus of the Robert D. Charles Community College. Spring break has just ended.

"I could have used you when I was going to college," I quip, as we park in front of the building, in a space designated for 'official use' only. My mind is still in a fog, and I welcome the fresh air to wash away the garbage that has covered the grey matter between my ears on our trip over.

"It comes in handy when I need it," Sheriff Luder replies tersely.

He seems quite intent on making this a serious, shaky night for me. I learned long ago if I rely on someone else for my own happiness, I will almost always be disappointed. As such, as he turns off the ignition, I allow the fart I've been holding in during the drive to come ripping out. Yes, Catholic priests fart, just like every other human being. Maybe this will allow us to bond – it certainly worked in Little League baseball. He's not amused. I'm cracking myself up.

"This is a three-hour class, but we can leave at the halfway break if you would like," he says. "Maybe you should sit alone if you feel you can't control yourself."

I shrug my shoulders.

"You're in charge tonight, Sheriff."

Like the last plane out of Vietnam during the war, every seat will be filled. We are in the back row. I offer mine to a young woman, which she gratefully accepts. The sheriff ignores my gallantry, barely acknowledging her presence. I lean slightly against the wall. Another student, a male who appears to be in his early forties, is doing the same a few feet away.

Excited voices echo through the crowd.

"Is there a guest lecturer tonight? I'm just here for the evening." I lean towards the fellow next to me, feeling compelled once more to explain myself.

"I don't think so. At least our syllabus doesn't reflect that. It should just be a regular class with our normal instructor, Dr. Chaffgrind."

Thanking him, I lean back against the wall. After a moment, he turns his head back towards me and relays the professor used to teach at a university somewhere he can't remember, but he seems to think he transferred here a few years ago.

I am about to ask why he transferred from a university to a community college, and what his background and qualifications are, when Dr. Chaffgrind himself enters from a side door. Striding quickly to the front of the class, he drops his backpack on the eight-foot table in front of him, moving abruptly behind the lectern. Silence from 127 expectant faces fills the room, anticipating every word this apparently well-respected 50-something pedagogue is about to utter.

He must have traveled somewhere for his spring break. Either that or he's visited a tanning salon recently. His head is completely shaved, in all probability an attempt to hide a receding hairline or early onset baldness and a bruised ego. His copper eyes are topped by pruned eyebrows and he wears a neatly trimmed black mustache and goatee. His body has that athletic look which comes from an hour a day on the elliptical trainer and weights six times a week. It appears he is going for the tough, sinister look. It's working. All and all, he is an imposing presence. I am immediately repelled. He acts as though another's opinion of him doesn't matter, but his pride and ego clearly drive him.

What draws these students, I wonder? I subtly glance down at the book and paper sitting neatly on the desk of the young lady to whom I gave my seat.

"Studies in Human Sexuality and Erotica."

Ah, got it. It's the topic that draws the crowd and this pompous, self-proclaimed, hedonistic guru probably thinks most come for the privilege of seeing and hearing him. And since he's a full professor, a doctor no less, anything he says must be true, right? If it's anything like my college years, he can also alter their grades in a negative way if anyone dare speaks out against him. He begins.

"I trust you enjoyed your break. You may find this

interesting. Earlier today, the administration informed me the technology will be available this fall which will allow this class to be broadcast to any community college in the state that might wish to do so."

He's far more pleased with himself than Sheriff Luder was when I finished reviewing the file on Cameron Gambke. Generous hoots and roaring claps follow from the crowd.

"I understand we turn away as many as 250 students each semester. You…" he pauses, panning the stimulated faces in front of him, "are the fortunate ones for now."

He smiles, a mischievous look overtaking his angular, well-toned face, framed by stylish, thin black glasses.

Looking in our direction, while waving his hand reminiscent of Caesar Augustus in Rome before the Christians were fed to the lions, he chooses to announce our presence.

"We have guests this evening. An esteemed sheriff and…" he pauses to build the tension. "A Roman Catholic priest."

All heads turn to follow the direction of his mocked greeting. Scattered laughter is muffled. The student standing next to me shuffles a few feet further away, not so much as to offend, but far enough to notice.

Although the sheriff is dressed in his departmentally assigned attire, I am not dressed in my clerics. I am wearing khaki jeans and a green pullover shirt, my normal attire when out on the town.

"No, none of you are in trouble with the law, at least as far as I know. And, well, I'm sure we're all going to Hell anyway, all of us *bad* people, but maybe the good padre can save all of our souls before the night is out."

Many of the students laugh hard out loud, and Dr. Chaffgrind holds up his hand for quiet.

"I warn you in advance," he says, locking his eyes on mine, "I am not going to change any of my presentation due to your presence. I am ashamed of nothing, and stand firmly behind what I will present this evening."

Is everyone waiting for me to reply? If so, I won't give the instructor, nor the students, the pleasure.

"So for the benefit of our distinguished guests, let me

78

welcome you back to my Human Sexuality and Erotica class. It's under the 'Health and Happiness' field of study and primarily covers the topic of sex. It also covers the topic of life around the world and how sex permeates every fabric of it. It analyzes how the world has evolved with, in, and around our insatiable desire for one another. Plain and simple.

"And what's my philosophy as it relates to this marvelous topic? I firmly believe if partaken in often and done well, sex can truly make you healthy and happy – especially unadulterated, anytime, anywhere, anything goes sex; sex with no consequences to worry about. I mean, I truly love this age we are living in – do you have any idea how lucky we are? No real consequences. There's birth control. If you screw up by either not using condoms or using them incorrectly and your partner gets pregnant because she forgot to take the pill or use another form of birth control, she can simply get an abortion. If you get a disease, get medication for it! Finally, in this day and age, most people are getting over their hang ups about sexuality, so it's all good!"

What? Is he serious? Is he always this way? Or is it to mock me and the values I hold dear?

His proud oration brings a "Woo hoo" from a female somewhere in the room, the majority of the students are cheering with even a few standing and applauding as they glance back my way for added emphasis.

Thankfully, I begin to notice more students who choose not to join in this inane, ludicrous frivolity. Maybe they recognize what is happening and are embarrassed to be part of it by association. Yet they remain. Peer pressure is a powerful force. Just talk to those who have ever given into pressure from someone or some group, only to regret it, even decades later. I must admit I have given into the pressure on occasion and understand their reluctance.

"Since our world is driven by supply and demand," gesturing with open hands over the auditorium, "I have hit the mark, as you can plainly see. If you have any questions, Father, feel free to ask me after class." His eyes fix once more on mine, and I hold the stare.

An image from his laptop suddenly is projected onto the overhead screen.

Glancing at the sheriff, I have to wonder if he has arranged this in advance, but his expression is stormier than mine, his anger barely held in check, just ready to erupt. I realize we may finally agree on something.

What the sheriff doesn't know is that before I entered the priesthood, I was of this world. And now as a priest, I see and hear things all the time that I believe have prepared me for his challenge. Or have I?

Maybe I am being shown the way Our Lord wishes me to go as I stand here now, looking at the overhead screen. I asked Him for this, and He is letting me have it.

"As I mentioned on my first day of class, and I know you've heard this outside of this venue, if there is anything I have confirmed in my life, is the old adage that 'Men use love to get sex and women use sex and their bodies to get love, or whatever else they find they want in life.' It is patently true. Hands down. No questions asked."

He pauses, staring down a striking young brunette who has made the mistake of coming into class late.

"Most women today know exactly what they want and how to use their bodies to get it. It has always worked in every single culture back to the beginning of time. So given this is an undeniable fact of life, I will take this opportunity to remind you that being on time for my class is a requirement, not a request, no matter how you look, or who you think you are. Let there be no mistake, while you may believe you can manipulate me as you've probably done many others in your life, you are sorely mistaken. Understand?"

She nods her head meekly, turning her attention to the binder she placed on the desk in front of her.

He quickly regains the momentum temporarily lost with the interruption.

"I also know about Title IX being pushed by all the feminists in the world of academia. Women are getting their way in all the arenas now and men are being forced to take a back seat."

This random declamation, having no purpose whatsoever, hovers in the air. And this is a community college without a football team. Does he do this all the time?

As quickly as he pounced on the latecomer, he switches back to the screen, proudly reading the name showing in black and white behind him.

"GUEST SPEAKER – Alex Chaffgrind."

"As I mentioned a few weeks before the break, we have a very special guest speaker coming in a few weeks. If there is anything good that came from my one and only horrendous previous marriage, it's my incredible son. He travels around the world as a very successful adult entertainment producer, and he's coming to share his experiences with us."

His son produces porn movies? No real surprise there.

"Let me remind you that this will continue to be an interactive class, as long as everyone makes this *productive.* 20% of your grade is relying on it."

He stares at a female in her late twenties sitting directly in front of him, a dainty silver cross hanging around her neck. His tone tells me her involvement before the break wasn't as "productive" as he would like.

"As before, let me be perfectly clear. When I say productive, I mean open-minded. I could care less about your religious views on anything that is said here. College is meant to be a time when your minds are opened to new ways of thinking, when your parents aren't here to play their mind control games on you anymore, where you can explore your sexuality and know it's all okay – everything and anything. Got it?"

No responses. The young lady in the front row holds his gaze with hers. From my vantage point, I don't get the impression she's one bit intimidated, but she may have learned to bite her tongue for the good of her grade and GPA. I recall hearing once that in many higher level educational institutions, at the end of each semester, students are allowed to evaluate their professors anonymously. But as with corporate politics, is anything productive done with them even if these poor students have the courage to honestly fill one out?

"Remember, I was born in the 1950's and grew up in the 60's, 70's and 80's. That was a fantastic time, let me tell ya. Sure, AIDS came along and really scared people, but you had to learn to be smart about sex. Then Magic Johnson got AIDS and the media went crazy, freakin' people out everywhere. But you can see him now as an NBA TV analyst and he looks great! Modern medicine has proven yet again how it can handle something as serious as HIV, so what's the big deal?"

He's ecstatic, beaming.

"The Sexual Revolution was a culmination of years of repression – mostly by the Catholic Church and other religious institutions – and the people were tired of being told what to do.

"Good for them. God, if there even was a God, had shown He could care less and gave us these bodies to enjoy and the world was finally realizing the beauty of that fact.

"I'm 56 years old now and I've yet to find any reason not to continue to firmly believe everything I just shared with you. So I continue to remind you to enjoy! The Sexual Revolution most certainly hasn't gone away, it's only gotten better! With the Internet and more ways for people to get together, and the laws to support it all, there's a freedom now I wish I had back then. I am a big proponent of it being your life and your body. Don't let anyone tell you otherwise. And if anyone tries to tell you God disagrees, just ask them 'What God?'"

I notice a few reddened faces in the class that certainly are not happy with what he is saying, with some turning to see my reaction. But Chaffgrind bullies ever forward, compelled to share his deep-seated views and put me, a Catholic priest, in my spot in this public forum

"As an aside, I'm not sure if any of you have seen this, but a recent study by the top psychologists in Germany concluded that anyone who believes in organized religion is relying upon some outside force to help them in life. They are so weak inside they either become easy victims of sexual abuse or they themselves become the abuser. Why? Because they believe their God gave them the green light to crap all over the rest of us lesser beings."

I have never heard of this study and am absolutely certain this is a bald-faced lie. Maybe he just makes these things up as he goes along. Besides, who's going to check to validate his claims?

And, more importantly, who's going to stand up and say he's lying? I bite my tongue. I need to hear the rest of his propaganda before I decide what to do.

Looking back at the female latecomer, he continues.

"The same study showed prima donna women routinely end up as victims of all around abuse because no one likes them. Do you know who their primary attackers are? Their prima donna best friends."

Her jaw and eyes both drop – it is probably rare a female with her superior physical attributes is put down in such a public way. I get the impression Dr. Chaffgrind was burned once or twice and is taking full advantage of this opportunity to return the favor. A number of males chuckle along with a few females.

Standing arms akimbo with his hands on his hips, elbows out, and legs slightly spread apart, Chaffgrind is clearly in charge and no one is going to dare challenge him.

Glancing at his watch, he says, "But let me move on."

Finally.

"I am now going to prove the oft repeated theory, so all of the males here can see just how true it is, that women are more aroused verbally than physically. And for you ladies, I am then going to prove that men are more aroused physically than verbally, should any of you be questioning this naked truth."

Reaching into his backpack, Chaffgrind pulls out a copy of Fifty Shades of Grey, an erotic romance novel written by British author E. L. James. Showing the book to the class he continues.

"I'm sure this book has been read by most of you females in this class and maybe some of you men. If not, I highly recommend you do so. It has topped best-seller lists around the world. This, and the other books in the trilogy," he pauses as he flips to the end of the book, "Fifty Shades Darker and Fifty Shades Freed are about a twisted and all-encompassing sensual love affair between a guy and a gal involving bondage and discipline, dominance and submission, sadism and masochism. Very erotic and absolutely delicious, wouldn't you ladies agree?"

"Oh yeah," replies a 20-something coed, her perfectly fashioned hair bobbing up and down, holding up a copy in the series for all to see, as she snickers and high-fives two female friends sitting next to her.

"Of note," he continues, his bald head now perspiring from, I imagine, the bright lights illuminating his majesty on stage, "this series has sold 40 million copies worldwide, with book rights being retained in about 37 countries, and they are currently making a movie based on the first book of the trilogy. It's so popular it set the record as the fastest-selling paperback of all time, surpassing the Harry Potter series, for all of you Hogwarts fans. And I'm personally pleased to tell you not only have they made a board game based on this book, but an intelligent small hotel businessman in England tossed every Gideon bible in his hotel rooms and exchanged them for copies of Fifty Shades. He rightfully realized most people don't read or believe in the bible anymore, and, if nothing else, the bible has no place in the bedroom. That's one intelligent business owner!"

Looking at me, he quips: "Sorry, Father, but it's true."

"So close your eyes if you want, but sit back, listen and enjoy as I read to you what the more enlightened part of the world has either already read, is reading right now, or will be in the near future according to the sales figures."

Chaffgrind spends the next hour verbally performing, with the proper accompanying groans and orgasmic reactions, selected sex scenes to demonstrate how the spoken word, accompanied by a healthy imagination, can titillate anyone who cares to do so.

After a 20-minute break, the class rejoins, and most of the students seemed noticeably excited about the path this particular class is taking. Sheriff Luder decides he wants to stay, and encourages me to do so.

"We're already here, and I think you need to see this through to the end," he says, reclaiming his seat. Only three seats in the back are now open. I sit down, stretching my legs.

"Now for the guys. Remember, throughout the world, no matter the culture, men appear to be predominantly visual. You can fight it all you want, but men *need* sex. And, yes, we are turned on by seeing other women, especially when they are naked. It really doesn't matter how they look undressed either. Deal with it.

In my travels around the world let's just say I have had the privilege of either participating in or being exposed to differing sexual practices. Like Epcot Center at Disneyland, over the remainder of this semester I am going to introduce you, visually, to practices from around the world."

As he clicks through different icons on his laptop searching for his first video, Chaffgrind says, "And to show you I do keep up with current studies, I recently read that more and more women are becoming like us guys, more visual. The programming they are receiving from the same technology available to us guys seems to be altering their sexual views, as well."

I wonder if that means more women are acting like some men when it comes to sex. Demanding. Degrading. Aggressive and demeaning to their partner. Garbage in, garbage out.

He finds what he is searching for, and turns back to the class.

"In Japan, around the 1980's, the porn industry introduced something called Bukkake. In short, this is a sex act in which several men have an orgasm as they splash their semen on a woman. Apparently this has found its way around the world and many gay films are introducing it man on man. As with anything, there are critics. They feel it's not fair that multiple men are ejaculating on the woman while she's not allowed to be brought to orgasm herself. But what are they complaining about? She's being paid and porn's a business. A *big* business, I assure you. I'm sure the critics would love to be part of the sex scenes themselves."

Finding his way to a chair set aside for him next to the stage, his gaze looks for and then finds me once more.

"You've been warned, Father. If you're at all bothered by this, you better leave now."

Another profane, arrogant smile wafts my way. Here we go.

For the next 45 minutes, five different videos are shown. Each contains one Japanese female actor – appearing to be in their early 20's – naked with their hair done up and makeup perfectly applied. All five look sweet and innocent. For the first three DVDs, the men stand off camera, and one by one, with the only view of them being from their waist down to their knees, they approach the kneeling woman, their hands on their hardened penises, while taking turns ejaculating on her face. At least 25 men proceed in this manner while the female opens and closes her mouth, swallowing some and rubbing the rest on her face and breasts. In the other two, a plastic device is placed around the female's neck so the ejaculated semen can accumulate. Once each man relieves himself on the female's face and the semen has collected in the container, she drinks it. Most everyone present gasps and gags, including me. At a minimum, I can't even imagine the number of diseases she's just willingly sent into her body. At the most, I shudder for their souls.

As the DVDs play, I glance around the room at the students. Many of the men are smiling along with a few of the women. However, a genuine look of shock is evident on the faces of the majority of the females and, surprisingly, a few of the males. After a 30-minute discussion – the class mercifully ends.

Most of the students file out as Chaffgrind gathers up his belongings. I see him eyeing a spattering of female students waiting to ask questions, wondering which one will ask him to have sex at the end of the semester to ensure a good grade. His nostrils flare again, his breathing intensifying, as the stunning brunette approaches the front of the class, standing alone on the side. No matter how he dressed her down in front of the class earlier, now all he clearly wants to do is undress her. She, unfortunately, appears willing.

I can't leave the class without saying something, as respectfully yet firmly as I can.

"Thank you for allowing me to stay," I say, reaching out my hand for a shake, "but, do you have any idea what you are doing to these students and how misguided your teachings are?"

Recognizing the audience that remains in front of him and ignoring my outstretched hand, Chaffgrind is prepared for this encounter.

"Look, Padre, you really are out of touch with reality, aren't you? I would venture to guess what these people just heard and saw wasn't a great surprise to many of them. For the most part, they could probably stand up and teach this class on their own just from their own personal real world sexual escapades, so the sooner the Catholic Church accepts this the better we'll all be. I'm tired of you guys making us all feel so damn bad about ourselves, about sex, about our desires. If there is a God, which I highly doubt there is, thanks to science, why did He give us these feelings if we can't just enjoy them?"

Somehow, I maintain my composure and stand my ground. "You really have no idea the road you are traveling. And, for the record, *you* are the one completely misinformed – the Catholic Church has no problem with sex if enjoyed in the manner and for the purpose God intended. But you teach filth and the gravely disordered side of sex." I stand firm, continuing.

"However, I do agree with you on one thing. Yes, unfortunately, most of these kids probably are much more experienced at their age than when we were their age. But if they did choose to stand up here and teach the same topic, I'll bet most would do it with far more class. Sex is a holy and sacred act. You really don't know what you are dealing with, or if you do and simply don't care, I give *you* fair warning, Dr. Chaffgrind. You need to reconsider."

"Or what, I'll go to Hell?!"

His hysterical, yet forced laughter follows me as I head towards the exit. I notice the sheriff was close enough to have heard the exchange. The group of students who apparently hung around to watch this unfold part slightly as I walk past them. It's obvious from their dismissive looks they are firmly under the spell of the good doctor. One of the young men has the audacity to bump my shoulder slightly as I pass.

"Excuse me," I offer, hoping beyond hope it wasn't intentional. I'm disappointed as muffled laughter reach my ears.

"You're pretty intuitive, Mr. Greater-Than-Everyone-Else. I truly *don't* care. I don't care to control everyone's life like you do!" bellows Chaffgrind, my back growing smaller as I head towards the exit.

Father, forgive them, for they know not what they do, I pray silently, as did Our Lord as He hung on the cross.

Chapter 10

Reaching the sheriff, I ask, "Why, exactly, did you bring me here?"

He had made no move to join me in the conversation with Chaffgrind, but his interest in the exchange was obvious. Was he hoping I would be embarrassed or put in my place, whatever place that might be?

"I needed you to know what is being taught to our children at this level, to see just how depraved and twisted sex education has become." His indifference to my exchange with Chaffgrind irritates me.

"So you disagree with it?" I inquire.

"You bet I do!" he hisses. He's not getting my point. I'll be more direct.

"Then why didn't you join me in expressing your views to that pretentious degenerate?" I challenge.

We stop in the hallway and he turns toward me. "Because that's your job as a Catholic priest."

"Let me correct you, Sheriff Luder, because once again you fail to understand *our* faith. Since you were baptized and confirmed as a member of the Catholic community, *you* are a member of the same Body of Christ as I am. That means it's also *your* job to stand up against evil. I didn't take you for a coward, but now I'm beginning to wonder."

Leaning towards me, he clenches his fists, but says nothing. I follow him out to the parking lot. I'm glad I challenged him. He's very good at telling others just how wrong they are, but can't stand hearing about his own failures.

Not a word is spoke for 45 minutes and the dark sky outside the car adds to the bleakness of the night.

"Sheriff, I read the file on Cameron Gambke and I listened to the presentation you wanted me to hear from demented Dr. Chaffgrind."

"Yep. I needed to make sure you understood what put him in prison. And, as I said, I also needed you to know what is being taught to our children."

"How did you know about the class?" I ask.

"All the local college kids, and many of the adults, have been clamoring to get into it since it started. It's hard not to know about it. Heck, even Detective Gambke's brother is in it. I don't know why he wasn't there tonight, though."

"Detective Renae's brother is taking this specific class?"

I wonder if she knows this, given her focus on criminal sexual behavior. I don't tell the sheriff he's left town. I know he'd question me on how I know that particular fact and I have no desire, just yet, to tell him Detective Renae and I have communicated with one another.

"Yep. I also know many people around the country and, believe me, this isn't just a North Carolina higher education phenomenon. Not this specific class is being offered elsewhere, of course, but this open sexual mentality is rampant, probably even in Catholic colleges for all I know. You should see some of their co-ed newspaper sex columns they allow to be published. There are probably an enormous number of budding E.L. James' right now in our esteemed universities. Are your eyes opening yet?"

"Yes, yes they are. You also said you wanted me to do something, and I've been thinking about this all evening. Before you tell me what the last thing is you want from me, I want you to promise me you will do something for me in the near future, because I can tell that your eyes need to be opened to my world as well."

Taking a drink of his large iced tea he picked up at a local Food Mart after class, I can tell he's buying time to contemplate my challenge before replying.

"Sure. Whatever it is, it's worth what you've now seen, and especially what you're about to see. I know the next time you speak with Cameron Gambke you'll be much the wiser. When is that, by the way?"

"When I have a chance to," I say. I certainly don't report to Ms. Bellers, so why would I keep him posted on my activities? "Now what's the last thing on your list?"

Turning his head my way, aided by the headlights of oncoming cars racing by, his eyes flash.

"Before you meet with him, I want you to visit each one of these websites." He hands me a sheet of paper then proceeds to click on the overhead light.

"What are these?" I ask, a feeling of uneasiness creeping in.

"The top five porn sites Gambke visited prior to his incarceration. We discovered them during our search of his home computer, laptop, and I-Phone. We could tell he had attempted to erase them, but the lab experts out of Raleigh were able to recover what hadn't been written over with new data. If you don't understand how twisted he is after going through these, then you never will."

"I'll have it done by the end of tonight," I state firmly.

"Tonight?" I can see him raise his eyebrows.

"Yep. I have a great many other things going on right now so I need to get your list for me I agreed to off my plate." His look of surprise lingers, and I continue.

"Are you able to take vacation time in the next month or so?" There's no way he's getting the upper hand on this exchange. I'm going to make sure this "deal" goes both ways, not just his.

"I'm the boss and have plenty of time saved up," he proudly says, then regroups quickly. "Why do you ask?"

"You'll see. Do you have a passport?" His smirk quickly disappears. Mine emerges swiftly.

"Passport?" His mind is beginning to race now, and I imagine he's wondering what he might have made the mistake of agreeing to.

"I trust you're good at keeping your promises," I challenge, sensing his growing reluctance.

His sour look returns. "You bet I am. And I can't wait to drop you off and take a ride on my bike. Clear my head."

"A ride on your bike? A ten speed? And this late at night?" Once again, he throws me.

"My motorcycle. And, yes, it's the best time to clear my head. I do it all the time."

Chapter 11

It's been a tough evening. I need a few minutes with Our Lord before I reluctantly tackle the sheriff's last challenge. Entering the semi-dark church, I kneel before the altar, gazing up at His presence waiting patiently in the tabernacle. I recall my dark dreams. My morbid memories. And Him pulling me out. Procrastination eases my hesitation.

"Lord, you know me through and through because you created me. Not only are you my God and Savior, but you're my best friend. I truly believe this to be true. I beg for your protection and guidance once more as I head back into this lewd, vulgar, lustful world I left long ago. I know I was trapped in this while in college, when Playboy and Hustler were all the rage, when the Internet was only accessible to the world of academia and the military. Not to regular guys like me. Before the seminary. Before my life changed completely for the better. I thank you for your protection then and now, because although I hate to admit this, Sheriff Luder and Dr. Chaffgrind are probably right in one regard - I don't have any idea how bad it has become.

"I remember when you opened my eyes to your truth. I came to understand why you forbade our first parents from eating the fruit from the 'tree of the knowledge of good and evil.' You knew if they did, at that moment, evil would come into their hearts and, thus, the world. That your beautiful, sinless creation would be forever stained with an inclination to sin. You were then and still are now a good parent, forever trying to show us the true way to happiness. Their disobedience made us all pay, as rebellion will always do.

"Like them, no one was about to tell me 'no,' nor was anyone about to tell me I couldn't do what I wanted to do. Not even you. Once attained, carnal pleasures only left me wanting more. It was addictive, and like any addiction, attaining the next pleasure became increasingly more difficult. Satan had no answers then and still doesn't to this day – only empty promises – ones that never satisfy, promises that always left me begging for more. All I found was pain, loneliness, depression, shame, emptiness, sadness, and despair. In the end, Satan was the only one laughing.

"You didn't want to control me, I know. Your love merely wanted the best for me. The filth of porn was *not* the answer. You were trying to show me this truth time and again. But I closed my eyes and heart to you. It's amazing to think I had fooled myself into believing I was using the porn to become a Don Juan, a great lover for a wife someday, or because I was working so hard I deserved this "gift" to myself – oh, the head games I played when I tried to justify my actions. Thankfully, you opened my eyes to see that all I had become was another sex-starved, self-serving, manipulating pervert.

"And then, just when I was about to start acting out, when the porn no longer fed my unhealthy lustful appetite, my best friend died of AIDS. It took *that* to convince me the road I was traveling was the wrong one. Thank you, God, for not giving up on me, because Satan kept trying to keep me down. I could hear his voice telling me I was bad, worthless, small, and insignificant. Yet, even when Satan's hold on me was strong, you were there beside me, holding me and encouraging me to turn away from sin. By your grace and my free will I got back up, headed back to confession, back to the Sacraments, and back into the human race. Only this time it wasn't as a taker, but as a giver.

"Here I go, Lord. Please hold my hand, and guard my heart once more. Thank you!"

Locking up the Church, I head to my office in the Administrative Building. It's 10:30 at night and quiet. The light is off in Fr. Bernard's room in the rectory, probably turning in an hour ago. Mrs. Bellers won't be here until 8 a.m. tomorrow morning.

Plugging in my laptop, I hit the "on" button, sitting back in my chair waiting for it to power up. I think about how powerful the minds God has given us really are. I've seen it time and again – we really do become what we think about most of the time, and that's exactly what happened to me back then with porn.

The human brain has always fascinated me. I've learned God designed me in such a way I have about 100 billion brain cells, and

I can use or lose them in my life in any way I wish, for good or evil. I've learned if something involves strong emotions, I usually remember it very well. That enjoyment and fun are important ingredients in my learning, because they are positive emotions. That the more connections I make in my brain, the more I stimulate it, the more intelligent I become. I also know my brain thrives on originality. It only goes downhill if I don't continue to stimulate it or if I damage it in some way, such as with harmful substances. Thankfully, I've never traveled that road. But even if I did, it could still recover, to some extent, if I stopped using whatever was causing it harm.

I know if I'm stressed I don't learn as well; conversely, if I'm calm I tend to retain information much longer. And I learned if I use all my senses in learning – if I see it, hear it, say it and do it – then I will retain an incredible 90%! God has indeed given me a wonderful gift with my brain. This built-in tool helped in wonderful ways during seminary. But before then, they became lethal when porn became the subject I set my mind on devouring.

My laptop continues to go through its startup machinations, and I shake my head while continuing my train of thought. I think of all the people in the history of the world who used their brains for good. All the scientists, explorers, inventors, physicians, religious, teachers, business leaders, and humanitarians who used their brains and talents to help God's people. From the useful side of the personal computer and the World Wide Web, global positioning systems, cell phones, and cloud computing.

Or the plethora of medical advances in areas like human organ transplants, anesthesia, and all the vaccines now. From the discovery of electricity and superconductivity to the modes of travel like the airplane and high-speed trains, to gas, hybrid and even electric cars. And the Hubble Telescope and space travel where maybe one day, if God wishes it to be, the human race might discover life on other planets.

Finally, my laptop is ready. I make the sign of the cross. It's time to begin. No more stalling. "Okay, Cameron Gambke, let's see where you allowed your mind to travel, to turn your world into one of filth, violence, pain and destruction."

The list Sheriff Luder provided me contains five sites. It seems death row inmate Cameron Gambke periodically browsed through plenty of different sites, including chat rooms and usenet groups where he shared pictures of his ex-wife, Michele, per a note on the list made by either the sheriff or the case investigator. But those aren't the ones he visited most often.

So I don't have to pay for any of this searching, the sheriff suggested I use any search engine of my choice and type in the word associated with each of the five sites, and then type "free" and "pics" or "videos" before and after. I'm alarmed to see just how easy it is for anyone to access this smut.

I decide to start with the last site on the list, typing "free klismaphilia pics" into Google. Hundreds of sites beg for my attention, and randomly click on one.

I find out immediately "klismaphilia" refers to enemas, a standard medical procedure when used properly, where liquid is introduced into the rectum and colon via the anus. It is intended to work like a laxative, except the images I now see are gay, lesbian and straight people using them for sexual pleasure. One of my first impressions is all of these faces in front of me look just like people I might see around me every day in town, on the streets, on television, in the stores, or in my congregation.

I am given opportunities to purchase all the enema equipment I would like, much of it with free shipping and handling, the owners of the site being as customer-service friendly as they can be. Immediately, pop-up windows reflecting invitations for videos on spanking, bondage, public sex videos, extreme porn videos, graphic videos, and sexual abuse videos fill my screen. A web cam offer comes up, too. A young female wanting to satisfy my every sexual request online should I wish to do so, for a fee, of course, pops into my view. I shake my head. Only four more sites to go.

Next on the list, and the fourth most visited by Cameron. I type in the words "free bestiality pics." As with the previous choice, hundreds of sites have apparently been created for those with this particular interest. The decay of humanity continues as evidenced by the images displayed before my eyes. I see mostly women, but some men, performing anal, vaginal, and oral sex with and from horses, dogs, cows, cats, pigs, and I'm certain other animals if I choose to search further. I don't.

I'm feeling a bit nauseated; something I haven't felt since, well, since I don't know when. I get it, Sheriff Luder, I get it. This is indescribably sick. I have to wallow through this, though. I don't want to give him any reason to back out of our agreement. Sure, he'll never know whether I did or didn't finish this challenge, but I'll know. I also firmly believe I need to see this through if I'm going to understand what's happening around me and what polluted the mind of Cameron Gambke.

"Free rape pics" is third on Cameron Gambke's "Top Five" list. I randomly choose one out of the hundred site options that beg for my attention. Images are now beginning to haunt me. Are these staged videos or still pics? Paid actors? Amateurs? Cameras are owned by everyone now – especially high quality ones installed on their cell phones – and their sick use provides the viewers a multitude of options. How much of this is true rape video, I'm wondering? If so, do they know rape is against the law? Do they even care? Are they so brazen and have been doing this for so long they don't believe they will get caught? I mean, I've read stories of abusers being so shameless they complete their rape and then post it online, but is that really what I'm seeing in front of me? If there was ever a reflection on our society of just how confident these bastards feel they won't get caught or prosecuted, it's this, in my opinion.

I can't tell by the looks that so many of the females portray whether or not they're acting. So many seem horrified, shocked, in fear, and trapped. The men seem to relish in what they are doing. Each scene is a group rape, every single one. Sometimes two men, many times four, five or more. I'm angry now. Pissed, really. The pictures go on. They are endless. To say I'm shocked for everyone involved doesn't fully express what I'm feeling. What word can I use to express how mortified I am? Stunned? Traumatized? Outraged? How many people out there are being programmed by these videos? Guys dressed up in black masks and outfits, stalking their prey, and raping them? Not only do I need to wake up, but so does everyone else in the general public. This is the new global classroom, available to more than seven billion viewers as soon as they all purchase the technology, and every sick bastard has the opportunity to be both a student and a teacher. To be a SOMEBODY if only in their sick little minds.

"Be very careful who you follow in life, for you are assuming that person actually knows where they are going," I say out loud. The story of the Pied Piper forces its way into my consciousness. As legend has it, he was a man who lived in Germany during the Middle Ages. He dressed in multicolored clothing and led all the children away from the town never to return.

Cameron Gambke seemed to enjoy this, learned from this, and planned his attacks from this. All of it percolating in his mind and then, thanks to his sick frame of mind, he gave it his own personal twist. All he needed was a victim or victims, as suggested by his daughter, Detective Renae. How far into this was he, I wonder?

I take a break; it's too much.

It's 11:00 p.m. and I need to finish what I started. Can it get worse? I make another sign of the cross and sign back on.

"Free coprophilia pics." The death row inmate was sexually aroused by human urine and feces. I blow through a few pictures before I reach the point of losing the contents of my stomach, the repulsive vortex sucking at my humanity. Men and women defecating and peeing on one another, wiping it on themselves or each other. Licking it. Eating it. Again, it appears to be both amateurs and professionals in the pictures. My head is shaking back and forth, instinctively repulsed. The images of Hell from the apparitions I've studied flash into my consciousness.

"Are you kidding me?" I say out loud. I have never been more concerned for the souls of my fellow man than I am at this moment. This makes Chaffgrind's class look like pre-school.

One more to go. "Erotic Asphyxiation." I soon discover this is the intentional restriction of oxygen to the brain for the purpose of sexual arousal. Sometimes partners do it to each other. Many times an individual tries this out on their own. Alarmingly, I find from a side article that apparently there is a high mortality rate tied into this paraphilia. Most are men. Questions explode rapidly in my increasingly terrified brain. What are these people thinking? Why would anyone even venture down this road? What was Cameron Gambke doing with this information?

The questions continue to fire through my mind as I turn off the laptop, sit back, and run my fingers through my hair, completely exhausted and thoroughly disgusted. The full gravity of what I've seen hits me like a sledgehammer and, by all indications, I know this is only a sampling of what is out there. I've only been given a glimpse of what Cameron Gambke gets off on, but the Internet is massive…

I will now forever pray for and worry about each and every soul I've seen in these pictures and videos. They either don't know the beauty God intended for sexual pleasure, or they actually do understand but simply don't care.

The familiar sound of my computer shutting down echoes in the quiet of my office. I catch a glimpse of a newspaper Fr. Bernard has graciously left on my desk. The word "rape" catches my eye from the fleeting light of the computer screen.

Turning on my desk lamp, I scan the headline: "Rape and Society: How Bad Is It?" Underneath, I scan the article. Two high school football players accused of raping a young teenage girl in Steubenville, Ohio, a similar scenario in Torrington, Connecticut, and a group rape in India of a Swiss tourist and the beating of her husband by five men who confessed to doing it. Many people interviewed seem very surprised this type of activity is happening around the world, but especially here in the United States. Yet the experts interviewed say non-consensual sex occurs more frequently than most people will ever know. One reason quoted is because most women don't report it. Another expert notes that rape is the only crime in which, when it is reported, many in law enforcement and certainly their friends, family or co-workers make comments that clearly place the blame on the victim. *"Maybe it was the way you were dressed." "You shouldn't have been at the party." "You shouldn't have slept with your window partially cracked."*

"Can you imagine if a man who just bought a nice new car went driving around town, had a nice meal, drove it home, parked it, and then had it stolen? When the police come to investigate, the responding officer asks, 'Well, what did you do to allow your nice car to be stolen?' The victim would be rightfully incensed, because *he's* been violated, *he's* the victim. He would become upset and angry as the responding officer continued to make him feel like *he* did something wrong to cause this crime to occur to *him*. He would probably scream at the officer that *he is the victim* and they should be spending their time catching the person who stole his car. He might even be told that even if they find who stole it, the accused thief might just argue the man let him borrow it. I mean, it would just be one person's word against another's," a rape expert advocate is quoted. "Well, welcome to the very real world of rape victims."

I feel the sorrow of Our Lord as he knelt in the Garden of Gethsemane, knowing what He was about to do for all of humanity, knowing many people wouldn't even care, then or now. I feel the anguish of Mother Mary as she held Our Lord in her arms after He was taken down from the cross, as depicted in Michelangelo's Pieta.

My grief is growing, the depression I escaped long ago before becoming a priest is beginning to settle in again, its tentacles attempting to drain every last vestige of my energy.

Thoughts and images pepper my brain. My eyes are spent. My head hurts. I long for sleep. The smell of cigarette smoke permeates every room in this building, a persistent remnant from years of Fr. Bernard's chain smoking habit. It suddenly occurs to me that pornography on the Internet is now the second hand smoke of this day and age – it affects everyone in a negative way, whether or not they are using it or being abused by those who do. And so many are breathing it in, many knowing full well its dangers, and caring less about what it's doing to them and their fellow humans on this earth – to every single soul that comes in contact with the sludge and muck.

I look at the crucifix hanging above my office door, and pray. "What do you want me to do, Lord?"

Some will listen, some won't. Our Lord even said that. My role is to not wonder who, but to give it my all and to make sure I continue to pray for God's grace and guidance.

Chapter 12

It's early Thursday morning as I write this, and I'm back in the grotto after finishing praying the Luminous Mysteries of the Rosary. I asked Our Lady to intercede with Our Lord for all those in the throes of sexual sin, for Dr. Chaffgrind, his past, present, and future students, as well as his son. I also asked her for help in the conversion of their hearts and for protection from the seductive evil that continuously tempts us all.

The Luminous Mysteries remind the faithful of important moments in the life of Our Lord:

- Jesus' baptism in the River Jordan which officially began His public ministry
- Jesus attending the wedding at Cana in Galilee which the Church teaches is a very significant moment signifying Our Lord supporting, and sanctifying, one of the most beautiful sacraments, the Sacrament of Marriage – recalling how this was the first public miracle of Our Lord (turning water into wine), at the request of his mother
- Jesus on His mission of proclaiming the "Good News" of the Kingdom as He went through towns and cities helping the spiritually poor, in addition to performing countless other miracles, to clearly show that He truly was who He said He was
- The Transfiguration where the Trinity first appeared, and
- The institution of the Eucharist at the last supper, the source and summit of the Catholic faith.

As a courtesy to Fr. Bernard, I will make certain I inform him about my Internet searches last night and the purpose for it.

My cell phone rings. It's Detective Renae Gambke. Standing, I stretch my back and legs, thankful I still have the entire grotto to myself. It's a bit chilly, but my jacket keeps me warm enough.

"Good morning, Father."

"Well good morning! Are we still on for today?" I'm looking forward to our time together.

"Yes, 2:00. Did you hear about Sheriff Luder?" Her tone turns serious.

"No. What happened?!" I immediately brace myself for bad news.

"He was hit on his motorcycle last night." Business-like, yet concerned.

"What?! Is he all right?! Is he going to be okay?!" My heart jumps. It's the rare individual who can take bad news about someone they know personally in stride, and I'm not one of them.

"Yes, yes. He's fine. They think he may have a concussion, though. He started talking when he came out of it at the hospital, but he wasn't making any sense."

"What happened? Do you know any of the details?" She's law enforcement. Of course she knows the details! I immediately recall the sheriff telling me he was going to take his motorcycle out for a ride late last night after dropping me off.

"I've seen him on it once or twice," she says. "It isn't a Harley, either, it's a crotch-rocket."

"A what?" The images that enter my mind with that label don't match up; well, that is, with anything in my mental database.

"A Yamaha R-1 sport bike. They're very quick. I guess he always just wanted that kind of bike. Anyway, the thing is, he didn't get hurt while he was riding it. It happened when he was pulled over. At 2300 hours last night he was parked at a strip mall talking on his cell phone when a 42-year-old Caucasian female driving a Subaru Wrx Sti owned by her 28-year-old Caucasian boyfriend apparently hit him from his rear right side, allegedly as she was attempting to finish a text. She told the responding officers she had just gotten off work and was trying to get to a convenience store before it closed to purchase a gallon of milk for the next morning. The officers on the scene said she hit the bike at 30 miles per hour, throwing the sheriff about 15 feet from where he was originally located. Since he was on the cell phone at the time, he didn't have his helmet on. Fortunately, he landed in some bushes but it still knocked him unconscious."

It seemed odd, hearing an officer of the law tell me a story like that, a briefing on the specifics of a reportable event, to the point, with just the pertinent facts. Usually, I hear things like this, accompanied by lots of emotion, crying, yelling, or sobbing from a parishioner begging me to go to the hospital to offer prayer and support. I thank God the sheriff wasn't seriously hurt.

"What hospital is he at?" I inquire. I want to make sure I see him soon.

"Vidant Beaufort Hospital in Washington. That's about 30 minutes for you if you get over to the 64, and it's an hour west of here when you're done. And, Father?"

"Yes?"

"He said he really needs to talk to you. The deputies said it really shook him up. So, and I hope you don't mind me suggesting, how about if we just cancel and reschedule our 2:00 today?" She sounds a little disappointed that we might not meet. I'm encouraged.

"If it's still all right with you, I really would like to meet with you today. How about dinner to give me extra time to see him and then drive your way? That way I can tell you how he's doing. Will that work?" As a priest, I've learned to juggle many meetings.

"Sure. Let's say around six? Swan Quarter Grill right off of Main Street?" she suggests.

"Perfect."

***

Hoping to use this time efficiently, I hit the speed dial button for Fr. Jack Thomis, my spiritual advisor in Brooklyn, glancing at my auto clock. Its noon my time and Fr. Jack will have already eaten his lunch. He's in his 80's now; set in a daily routine, yet his mind and wit are still sharp.

"Hello?" a raspy voice rings out.

"Fr. Jack! This is Jonah Lee Bereo. Did I interrupt you?" I speak loudly, attempting to throw my voice through my cell phone.

"Jonah! Yes, I can hear you just fine. How are you? Haven't heard from you in a while. How's everything going? Are you

101

okay? Boy, glad to hear your voice, my friend!"

Fr. Jack always peppers me with questions. His mind is always well ahead of his tongue. He still manages to make me feel like I'm the most important person to him at that moment, and I have tried to emulate this gift of his whenever I spend time with others. I warm to the memories of our friendship.

I really hope you remember him, too, because he probably won't still be alive by the time you read this journal, unless God has other plans for him, and me.

"Great. Fine, fine, everything is fine. Do you have a few moments to talk? I'm heading to the hospital to see someone who has been in an accident and was hoping I could run a few things your way."

"I hope he's okay, whoever you are going to see. I'll include him in my prayers. What's his name?" I can picture him trying in earnest to listen attentively, just as before.

"Sheriff Daniel Luder."

"You got it. What's on your mind?" Right to the point. He and Detective Gambke would get along well.

For the next 30 minutes, I bring Fr. Jack up to speed on all that's happened to me since I arrived here.

"Still there?" I ask, once I can't hear breathing on his end.

"Yes, yes, of course. Just processing all you said. You've certainly got a lot going on, Jonah. Are you holding up okay? You sound stressed. I would understand why, but I want to make sure you are okay."

Yes, Fr. Jack knows all the important things there are to know about me.

"You haven't forgotten that God has a glorious, wonderful, mysterious plan for humankind and each one of us has our individual roles to play in it, have you? He has the broadest shoulders ever. You can't feel like every single thing in your parish nor in the outside world is your responsibility to fix," he gently reminds me.

"No, I haven't forgotten," I reply, a twinge of defensiveness in my voice. I catch myself, and am immediately disappointed with my sudden, ingrained reaction.

If he caught my defensiveness, he chooses to ignore it and continues.

"Remember you always need to take care of yourself. You're no good to your parishioners if you worry yourself sick. You need to make sure your life is in balance. You must continue to take the time to do deep relaxation breathing, get good aerobic exercise like on those walks you used to love to take, listen to any of your favorite music and call me at any time day or night – talking to someone you trust is one of the best ways to relieve anxiety. And never forget what Our Lord did when he was stressed. He found time to be alone in prayer. If *He* needed time alone for rejuvenation and restoration, there should be no doubt we need to do so as well. Where are you at right now?"

"Huh?" I'm absorbing all Fr. Jack is telling me, and even though the pavement is clipping along under my car, my mind has drifted back to his library at the Diocese of Brooklyn, and I can smell the comfort of the book pages once more.

"Um, about 15 minutes away from the hospital."

"What do you see? I know you're on a freeway, but what do you see?"

I've known him well enough to know where he's going with this, and lock my focus to the things around me.

"Other cars. A billboard for a news station. Rosary beads swinging from my rearview mirror."

"Good. When things get tough in the future, remember to get yourself back to the moment, to the beauty of God's world that surrounds you. And when you take the time to look, wow, you really can see the beauty of it all. It's always there for any person to notice, if we but take the time to look for it."

He pauses. I don't want to hang up the phone.

"The past is the past, and today is a gift from God, that's why they call it the present, Jonah."

We both laugh, as Fr. Jack is playfully reminding me of this well-worn, yet appropriate, saying. I miss his laughter, and I am saddened thinking how much I will miss him when he passes.

"Everything you're telling me will get done with your efforts and God's providence. Always remember it was man who made time, not God. Everything in *His* time, Jonah. Just get up every day and do your best. Rejuvenate yourself with little breaks along the way. Go to bed knowing you did your best and asking God to show you where you might do better, then ask God to give you the grace to do so in the future. Sleep well, then get up the next day and offer it and your energies to God once more. He'll direct your paths. Never forget if God brings you to something, He will bring you through it."

Another popular saying at another appropriate moment.

"As always, you're right. And, as always, I am glad to be blessed with being able to talk with you, my friend." Yes, I will miss him when God finally calls him home.

"Know I am incredibly proud of you, Jonah. It is I who am blessed whenever you have the opportunity to call. I was just getting ready to go for an afternoon walk. It's cold outside today, but that's why we have jackets and sweaters, eh? But before I go, I know you know this to be true, but never forget we all have a part in God's plan. You're a parish priest now. One of your most important roles is to serve the priesthood of your parishioners by building up and guiding the Church in the name of Christ, who is the Head of this Body, the Church. You exist to help them get there, to understand, to comprehend and to bring God to them in the Sacraments and His Word."

He coughs now, taking a moment to clear his throat before continuing.

"I know you know this, but never forget *all* the faithful have a role to play, too, initiated by their Baptism and instilled by their Confirmation. They've been given charisms – we all have – gifts of the Holy Spirit which helps them to live out their Christian lives and to help build up His Church. Any chance you get, remind them of that, with love, compassion and gentleness. If you are the one doing everything, if you are the one always serving them but they aren't helping you and serving each other, then you should find a way to fit that fact into some of your homilies. Don't let them forget Christ showed us how to live by serving others, and not by being a so-called King and demanding everyone serve them hand and foot. He wasn't born in a stable without a purpose.

Remind them of the example Our Lord gave with the washing of the feet. He meant it.

"And for the sheriff and the other folks who seem to really need assistance and guidance, never stop praying God will show you what He wants you to do. Also pray for the grace to know when to walk away. You can only do so much, Jonah, and God never expects you to solve all the problems of the world, just your small part. Take care, my friend."

"God Bless, Fr. Jack, and thanks again. Enjoy the walk."

Chapter 13

Vidant Beaufort Hospital is nicely landscaped, a light red brick façade welcoming all patients and visitors. I don't like hospitals and check my pockets multiple times to ensure my hand sanitizer is present and ready. If I could wear a mask right now and not look too ridiculous as a Catholic priest, I would.

Checking with the receptionist at the front desk, I am told Sheriff Luder is in room 316. The friendly receptionist tells me he was moved out of ICU at noon. At the elevator I punch the button for the third floor, wishing I was on my way out and not in. I hear the chime and, as the door opens, I'm surprised to see Michele Jerpun standing inside.

At first looking directly at me, she redirects her gaze quickly to the lobby behind me. No acknowledgment. She's been crying. Gina Jerpun must be here as well. I make a mental note to catch up with Mrs. Jerpun at some point and offer my assistance if she's open to it. We had a rough beginning, but I'll give it a shot.

Entering his room, the sheriff is sitting up in his partially raised hospital bed, head wrapped, eyes closed, the machines that surround his bed measuring every important bodily function.

A nurse is in his room, removing his food tray. She looks at me and noticing my clerics says, "You must be Fr. Jonah."

"Yes. Nice to meet you, Amanda," I reply, catching the name printed on her employee badge.

"Same to you. I'm glad you're here. He's been asking for you ever since he woke this morning. They placed him in a medically-induced coma overnight to allow the swelling inside his skull to go down. We've only let one visitor in today, and she left not long ago. We've kept everyone else out. The entire Sheriff's Office from Hyde County and many from the surrounding counties have come by, trying to speak with him, but no one else has been allowed in, other than you and her."

I'm glad to hear Mrs. Luder came to visit him. Maybe she had to get back to work which is why she isn't still here.

"He needs his rest. Do me a favor and make your visit as brief as possible. Maybe then he'll allow himself to sleep, okay? He keeps trying to stay awake to see you, I think, so I'm glad you're finally here."

He opens his eyes and I smile. He doesn't. There's a look in his eyes I've never seen before. It's not pain; no, I've seen that many times. Certainly not anger, either. He's perplexed, and it looks like he's been crying. All understandable. He's probably very sore and still in pain, even though he's on medication. Maybe his confusion is from the trauma of the hit.

A handful of bouquets are in the room, brightening the grey and white décor.

"I heard what happened. I'm glad you're all right." I smile again; he doesn't meet my glance. He's looking up towards the ceiling, his focus on something, or somewhere, else.

After an awkward few minutes, I ask if I can get him anything. He shakes his head.

"Father, make sure the door is completely shut, will you?"

His voice is soft and low, yet still firm enough for me to hear him plainly. It's the nicest he's spoke to me since we've met. I suppress a laugh, thinking I might talk Nurse Amanda out of a prescription of whatever he's on for the next time I have to spend any time with him. I plan on staying no more than ten minutes before I bail. There are far too many sick people in here.

"I need to share something with you in confidence, okay? If this ever gets out, it will certainly get me put on a leave of absence and may cost me my job, all right? Please?"

"Of course. What is it?" I focus completely on the sheriff; his intensity compels me.

"When I was hit last night, I went somewhere. I mean, my mind. Or maybe my body, too. It felt like all of me. I know this will really sound strange, but I've never felt so alive, so convinced that what I believe happened, truly happened."

He's fragile now, his manliness stripped away. He seems, well, humble.

"When they revived me, I guess I asked for my tape recorder." He sees the look of surprise on my face, accurately reading my reaction.

107

"I always have my small tape recorder with me. Whenever I'm working on a case or just driving around during the day, I like to make verbal notes. I just naturally carry it with me, whether I'm at work or not, because I never know when something about a case may pop into my mind, or whatever. I use it all the time."

Speaking slowly, he gestures slightly with his hands.

"They apparently found my tape recorder for me in the backpack I had with me on my ride, and I guess I automatically hit the 'Record' button and started talking."

Handing me the tape recorder, I notice his eyes look behind me to make sure the door is still firmly closed, and winces when he leans over to show me where the "Play" button is. Lying back, we both listen to what he recorded less than 24 hours before.

"I was whooshed upwards in a dark tunnel, and I knew I was traveling at a great speed as there were light beings heading up around me, while others were heading back down. I couldn't make out any features, only outlines of what appeared to be in the general form of human bodies. I was heading towards a bright light, but felt no wind resistance. The peace I felt was deep and indescribable.

"Then I sensed a presence on my right side, and seemed to know immediately this was my guardian angel. I don't know why I knew, I just did. Everything felt completely right.

"Then I hear, 'Oh, God! Shit! Shit! Oh, God!!! Help me! Help! Shit!!!!!!!!!!' I think it was the poor lady that hit me. I'm lying there, and I open my eyes. A few people are standing around, and someone says the ambulance is on its way. I try to move but can't. A red-headed kid is holding her and bending down towards me, telling me to not move. I'm trying to tell him my head is killing me, and I just wanted to get back to that feeling of peace.

"Then I'm whooshed back into this tunnel. I'm drawing nearer to the light, and the peaceful feeling was back. Closer, closer. I definitely liked being there.

"Then I'm awake again, and opening my eyes. I'm on an operating table and they are shocking my heart. Pain shoots back into my system. 'He's back!' shouted someone. 'Hang in there, hang in there' one of the hospital guys say. There's organized

108

commotion everywhere. Hospital personnel running around. They're all just barely missing each other as they move around the room.

"And I know they're barely missing each other because I'm floating up above them.

"Peace. Floating now, I looked down and saw my body below. There were four medical personnel in the room. Clean. Aluminum. Medical utensils. Tubes. Attempts to resuscitate me.

"Flatline!" barks someone, and I watch from above, detached. Calm. Peace. Surreal. Observing, like someone watching a fish aquarium because there is nothing better to look at, but losing interest quickly at what I'm seeing.

"Then, to my surprise, I realized I could move with just a thought. I thought about the wife, and immediately I was in our room at home. She wasn't there, but I know it was our room. I searched around the house and couldn't find her. All the lights were off. I am able to see through the walls a flashlight. A teenage boy dressed in dark clothes in my garage attic. He's looking through a rare gun collection I keep in a safe up there. I get closer to his face and see the reflection – he's the kid that has been mowing our lawn for years and lives just a few houses down.

"Our daughter used to babysit him when he was little. My daughter. I think about her and suddenly there I was, in her room at her apartment, sleeping. I touch her on her head. She doesn't move. She can't feel me. I love my baby girl so much."

There's a pause in the recording, and then it picks up again.

"And then I'm in Cameron Gambke's cell on death row. At first I think he's sleeping, but then it looks more and more like he's dead. His blood-stained pants and underwear are around his ankles. A rounded, wood stick is protruding from his rear end. His eyes are bulging; it looks like he's been strangled.

"But it's weird. Other than seeing my daughter safely asleep in her room, I have no emotion over any of these other experiences. Just floating, observing.

"Then pain again. 'Ahhhhh!' I'm screaming, another shock bringing me back to life once more in the ER. My head was pounding, as though in the middle of a vice. The doctor is looking into my eyes again, yelling once more to "hang on." A male nurse is shooting chemicals into my body with a needle, hoping they can keep me revived permanently.

"Flatline!' I hear again. Why won't they just leave me alone? Just let me be, I want to say. I want to stay with the peace.

"Now back in the tunnel. The light. Growing brighter and brighter, enveloping me in a wonderful feeling of love and peace. A luscious green landscape now, all hues of greens, yellows and blues. The perfect temperature. On a rolling hillside now, I glided slowly to the top. Looking back, I saw the features of another being, somehow recognizing intuitively, again without thought, that this was my guardian angel. I knew this being, this angel, without question from sometime before, but I can't place it. The angel motions me forward to the light which was brighter than anything I had ever seen before, yet I felt no strain on my eyes.

"And then I saw Him. Jesus. I immediately knew who He was. I didn't question it at all. My heart told me all I needed to know. He's smiling. His arms outstretched to me. I felt a magnificent, powerful, unconditional love from Him and then for Him."

I look toward him on the bed as I hear this, and he is looking at me with piercing, imploring eyes. I turn my attention back to the audio recording as it continues.

"A three-dimensional film began in front of me, a review of my life. My early childhood up until the accident last night. In living color. Fifty-one years were covered, in what felt like an instant. I felt the emotions of each life event, and Jesus was pointing out, not in any words but in thought that traveled effortlessly between us, the good I had done, and the wrong choices I had made. I was shown the times how what I had done positively or negatively affected other people. All my thoughts and actions were covered. Jesus was showing me the times I could have loved and didn't, the times I was given the opportunity to learn something important that would help me and others but was too lazy to do so and disregarded it. I felt happiness in many instances, mostly when I was young, with another young boy by my side, who I just vaguely remembered, and a great deal of shame and embarrassment as the review of my life progressed. I was made to understand my life thus far was based on the choices I had made, by my own free will, each and every time, yet I knew Jesus loved me through it all. He was smiling at my good moments, and looked incredibly sad when I made wrong choices, especially the serious ones. Not mad, just sad.

"What surprised me the most was that Jesus was not judgmental, like the cold, hard, eye-for-an-eye and tooth-for-a-tooth dominator of the universe I had always figured Him to be. But a theme had become very evident – I was responsible for every thought, word, and deed of my life and I knew in my innermost being I would be judged in light of the choices *I* made, based on a timeless, universal, unyielding ethic of love and justice; that it wasn't a choice as much that Jesus made for me when my life ends, but a result of the cumulative choices I had made.

"As my life's review ended, I stood before Jesus once more, and the love pulsed like ocean waves through Him into me. I was told in thought once more that the purpose of life is to love other human beings, and the life lived and died by Jesus on earth was the model He wants us to follow. That He died to save us from Satan and to give us a chance to live in eternal happiness with Him someday, but this wasn't guaranteed. He made me to understand He has given everyone all we need to live this life, if only we're humble, listen, repent, and walk the path He laid out for us.

"Jesus smiled again, and I couldn't believe all I had been shown, all I now understood, and all I had ignored and mocked. That's when he showed me Fr. Jonah Lee Bereo."

My eyes turn towards him again. His eyes are locked intently on me, tears forming.

"I was made to understand how important he and all His shepherds are. They are His chosen ones who are here on earth to bring Him to us, and to help us on our journey back to Him. He told me many of His shepherds continue to go astray. Satan attacks them the most in life because they have been given a special gift, a gift they are to give to all of God's people. He asked me to pray for them always – all of His shepherds.

"Jesus then looked behind me, and I turned to follow His gaze.

"An aunt of my dad's stood before me, smiling. She's a lady that meant a great deal to him and mom, they said, but I never met her. I know her from a picture I keep locked in a box in my bedroom closet with other things from my childhood. It all felt natural, very real, and incredibly lucid. She said something to me.

"You have to go back now, my little Danny. But remember, both of you – trust God, live as He wills, help your father, and the others. God loves you, my little Danny.

"I don't want to go. Please. No. I want to stay,' I pleaded.

"Then more pain. Another shock. I am back in reality. The resuscitation worked, the drugs kicked in and finally held. I'm looking up at the doctor, and he tells me I was medically dead for three minutes, and I wonder why it felt like what I had experienced was hours long."

The recording ends. We both sit in silence.

"Do you remember any of this?" I ask.

"Yes and no. Everything just seems like a blur. When I woke for the last time, which must have been after I had recorded all of this, I had been dreaming about giraffes with kitten heads driving Ferraris. *That* felt like a dream, but not what I went through before. But now I have no idea what to believe. Do you think any of it was real?"

I shrug. I've heard of near death experiences before but am certainly not qualified to tell him if this was real or not.

"Has anyone from your office spoken with you today?"

"The nurse told me every employee that was off duty has come by, and some on-shift, too, but none were allowed to come in here. So, no."

He doesn't tell me Mrs. Luder came in, and I don't push it, but I'm wondering if she told him what she had heard from the hospital staff and relayed it to him and that's why he remembers it. But how could it have been on the tape recorder if she didn't get here until after he was in this room, after he was out of the coma? That had to have been recorded before she had a chance to see him because he was still in the emergency room.

"Then I'm told I passed out again, but only this time by a medically-induced coma. I had an epidural hemorrhage, brain contusion and skull fracture, with significant bruises on my back and left arm where I hit the ground. Other than the head injuries, I have no broken bones. The trauma stopped my heart a few times, but the doctors expect a full recovery. I should be out of here in a few days."

I let the information settle in. The experience has clearly altered the sheriff's outlook on life. Again, however, I know the experience could be real, or it could be from the head injuries. Quite frankly, it could simply be the effects of the medication.

"Do you want to know what's so weird about this? I don't have any idea who that other little boy was next to me because I never had a brother. Maybe he was a cousin from way back when that I don't remember. Why did my aunt come to me and not my parents or someone I actually had met before? I don't get it. Maybe this is just a bad, weird dream. And what was that about with Cameron Gambke, my daughter, the wife, and the damn kid in my attic? And why in the world did it all feel so real?"

Nurse Amanda enters the room, completely ignoring the closed door and the "Keep Out" message it portrays. Forcing her mouth into a smile, her eyes remain all business. She heads towards the sheriff while simultaneously reading the digital information from the plethora of medical equipment attached to his body.

"How are you feeling?" she asks, readjusting who knows what on the machine.

"My head hurts. Tired."

"He really needs his rest now," she says, looking at me.

"Three minutes, please," the sheriff says, barely audible now.

He motions me closer, pain etched across his face as the nurse exits the room, leaving it partially open.

"Was it real, Father?"

"I don't know. But look, when you're better we can talk about this in more detail."

"Yeah, okay. You're right." I begin to move way, but he grabs my coat jacket. "Hey, look, Father, I'm really sorry about the crack I made about you and little boys back at the prison that first day."

"It's okay, Sheriff, and I apologize for my comment about you and girls in the back of your car. We can all say things out of spite that we fully regret later. It doesn't make it right, but I slip just like you did."

I pat him lightly on his shoulder.

"You need to rest and get better. But before I leave, know I did do the homework you assigned to me."

"And?"

"You have my complete attention now. And, before you ask, although I had an inkling, you were right. I really didn't have any idea how bad it had all gotten. Let's see what the doctors say, but if you can physically, you need to uphold your end of the challenge. We're going to Europe for a couple of weeks and we leave in less than a month. I wish I could postpone this but I've been locked into this pilgrimage for a year, and I believe it's imperative you go with me. You look like you need a vacation anyway."

I smile, and he finally returns it in kind. I like this kinder, gentler Sheriff Daniel Luder.

"Department policy will have me out until the doctor officially releases me to return to work, and I have plenty of weeks saved up for PTO time. If the place can't run without me, then I haven't done a good job of managing it, right?"

He's falling asleep as he says this, and I noiselessly leave the room, happy I didn't touch anything, not even the elevator buttons since I used my shirt to cover my fingers when I pushed them. I don't want to end up back here as a patient with a strange virus. Hospitals can be extremely dirty places.

Chapter 14

As I make my way through the Swan Quarter Grill to the booth Detective Gambke now occupies, I wonder if she ever suffered from an eating disorder. She doesn't have that appearance, but it seems to be fairly common these days. The pressure to look like the fabricated and air-brushed models that define fashion and style is enormous, especially for women. Past exposure to the epidemic of eating disorders has led me to look for and more readily recognize the signs among members of the parish, primarily the young women, but even with some of the young men now. My first experience came during a summer church picnic. I happened to notice a young girl furiously consuming a variety of potato chips, hamburgers, hot dogs and ice cream. A short time later, as I was searching for an errant Frisbee I came upon her, behind a bush on the outskirts of the park, purging what she had just recently consumed.

I later learned this young girl suffered from bulimia nervosa. She ended up in the hospital and after she began her treatment, she shared with me some of what she experienced and also what she had learned. She told me she was glad she got the help when she did, as the doctors were concerned about the damage to her heart and other major organ systems if she hadn't. Death would have soon followed. She told me about the hope she gained during her recovery process, and that she was able to overcome her eating challenges. And I'll never forget what she told me was one of the most harmful comments made to her by ignorant friends and family members as she struggled. "Oh, just eat. It's all in your head. Are you just trying to get attention or something?" I pray I never do the same to any person suffering from this disorder.

Detective Gambke looks my way as I close the distance from the front door. If she did suffer from this in the past — whether from her family environment, peer or media pressure – I can see no evidence of it. Her intelligence and inner strength I discovered the day I met her at Central prison stays with me. Coupled with a great deal of study, a lifetime of hard experience, and a solid work ethic, she is undoubtedly someone I admire.

"And how are you this fine, sunny day?" I ask, pulling out my chair. She looks distracted, bothered. A half piece of dry wheat toast and an unopened water bottle she must have brought along sit on the table in front of her.

"I'm fine, Father. And you?"

"Fantastic. Sorry I'm late. No GPS in my old car." I smile. She struggles to do the same, something clearly on her mind.

The waitress is on my heels, asking if I'm ready to order. Glancing towards Detective Renae, I had hoped to have a little time to look over the menu.

"Oh, I've already ordered and eaten. Sorry, Father. I got here early and was starving."

It's Friday during Lent.

"Um, an egg salad sandwich is fine. And water is perfect for me as well."

The waitress leaves, and our eyes meet momentarily. Her normally calm demeanor appears to be among the missing, but not her straightforward business style.

"How is the sheriff doing?"

I know I won't say anything about his possible near death experience, and reply with the usual. "He'll be fine. Quite the accident, huh?" deflecting.

She nods her head.

"How's the investigation going?" I ask, hoping to encourage her to open up more about her life.

"It's all I'm spending my time on now. The media is still all over it. A young girl with Down syndrome in a coma after what appears to be a rape – maybe a gang rape – makes a lot of people understandably upset. People are rightfully incensed and they want this person, or persons, caught and put away. It's very upsetting to the community, as you can imagine."

I nod.

"Cameron Gambke is dead," she states simply. She reaches for a lone slice of toast remaining on her plate and plays with it but doesn't take a bite.

"What? When?" My pleasant state of mind on the drive down is blasted away as I think about the sheriff's vision of Gambke's death.

She proceeds to describe how they found him in his cell. The details match *exactly* what the sheriff claimed to see during his out-of-body experience.

"Blood was all over. Whoever did this either ensured no lubrication was used, or he didn't have access to it before he sodomized him. Or maybe he just didn't give a rat's ass."

Chills fill my body. We sit quietly for a few moments.

"Are you okay?"

"He had it coming. I only wish..." she cuts herself off.

The sudden stab of fury reflected in her eyes quickly dies into a distant stare, showing nothing of her thoughts or feelings. She's mastered this control over the years, and now it retreats to the dormant spot inside her.

"I read the letter he gave to you a number of times," I offer.

"It's garbage. It doesn't make any sense. He doesn't, didn't ever, make any sense. It's only his word games, playing everyone around him to the very end."

"So you don't think he is, uh, was, trying to tell you something which might help you?"

"Help me with what, Father? When I met him in prison and tried to say what I wanted to say, what I needed to say, he kept changing the subject, blaming everyone else for his state in life, accepting no responsibility for anything. He's no different than any of the other pieces of shit I've run into every single day of my working life."

She doesn't look away this time, her eyes piercing through my retinas, yet her words remain controlled. This is a new Detective Renae. It's clear this topic carries with it an enormous amount of underlying pain of which Cameron Gambke played a pivotal part.

We stare out the window at the scattering of gulls fighting over discarded lunches from tourists, watching the clouds roll in and the afternoon breeze pick up.

"So, tell me about your world," I gently prod, sensing she

doesn't wish to speak specifically about Cameron Gambke, at least not for the moment.

"My world?" Her analytical mind is turned back on. She's not into guessing games.

"Yeah, I mean, what's your life like? Is there someone significant in your life?"

She's calmer now, realizing I'm not one of the many threats she faces each day.

"No, well, kind of. I don't have time for relationships and, I really can't find the right man. Maybe my job has tainted me; or maybe I'm right on target and they're all assholes."

I laugh, which brings a smile to her face. "Sometimes it's hard to tell, isn't it? Your aunt, the one you told me about, do you still see her?"

"Not as much as I would like. She was my mom's big sister," she adds, just in case I think her aunt was related to Cameron Gambke. "She couldn't stand him and came to get me when CPS contacted her. She's a therapist, and I will never be able to thank her enough for how she's helped me."

"Did she help your brother, too?"

"No. He's about five years younger than me. Maybe Cameron and my mom had figured how to keep CPS away by that time. But I can't believe they got any better as parents before my mom died. He knew how to fool people and control my mom so keeping CPS at bay was child's play. All I know is my own parents never asked me to come back home. But even if they had, there's no way I would have gone back."

I can't imagine the pain she must have felt, feeling this lack of love from her own parents. And, her own father refusing to explain or apologize years later. Everyone likes to feel as though they matter.

"You said your aunt was instrumental in your life. How so?"

She turns again to gaze out the window.

"My aunt took classes in EMDR because she was seeing so much trauma in her practice. The sessions she put me through meant everything to me, allowed me to refocus on life, get my degree, and get this job, this career, this hope."

"EMDR?" I ask.

"Yes. It stands for Eye Movement Desensitization and Reprocessing." She takes a drink from her water bottle, and fiddles with the plastic cap.

"What's it about? You know, high-level," I prompt, very curious about this tool. I see an enormous amount of trauma in my line of work, too.

"Well, basically, although there are different variations of it, my aunt made sure I always felt safe before and at the end of each session so I could trust the process. She would then stimulate my past trauma neural network, and then she would add alternating bilateral stimulation like audio, eye movements, stuff like that. It's been in the news a lot lately with a lot of success stories, especially with our returning soldiers who have experienced a lot of trauma."

"Wow. Very much a blessing then, your aunt."

"Yes." My food arrives and my water glass refilled.

"How about your job? Do you like what you do? I mean, if you were to describe it to someone, what would you tell them?"

I relay to her what the sheriff challenged me to do and how horrified I was by what I saw and what he has to deal with every day, but don't include what I read about her father in the file.

Although her eyes are locked on mine, I sense she's gone to a different place. Not like the sheriff as he traveled outside his physical body, but rather into her past, full of experiences that have caused her deep pain.

"Do you really want to head down my professional road, Father?"

I grab my sandwich, take a bite, and nod.

"If you say so," she says.

119

Chapter 15

Detective Renae sits back, staring at me intently, and begins. Her rant is far from an organized presentation – it's a brain dump. Nonetheless, her passion for this topic is immediately apparent and I'm pleased she's finally opening up.

"I've never been more sickened in my life, nor driven more to make a difference in going after the abusers and helping the victims, than I am as I sit here with you today. Sex seems to be on a lot of people's minds all the time, but in a lustful, not loving way. I don't have a problem with sex, and have no problem telling you, even if you are a priest. But I see the violent side, the predators. And even if the predators haven't physically harmed their victims, they've taken something very important from them – maybe it's their soul, their sanity, their sense of self-worth, their ability to feel safe in this world. No one has the right to take sex from anyone. No one. And that's why I got into this business. I want to put all the bastards away, every last one! But to your question about what I do for a living, I'll answer it by telling you the people I have to deal with. First, let me ask you one to put this all into a crystal clear perspective."

She's leaning forward, speaking slowly and methodically to make sure I don't miss this very important point.

"Did you ever lie to anyone, Father? I mean, seriously. Did you ever lie, even with little stuff like eating the last cookie?"

I nod. Of course I lied. Growing up. In college. In Corporate America.

"Well, try this on for size. You've committed a sex crime and you know you did it. You know for damn sure, deep down inside, you did something wrong. You have your back up against the wall because if anyone who means the world to you like your parents, girlfriend, wife or children find out, your entire world will explode. I mean, KABOOM! At that critical moment in time, if confronted, would you lie with as much skill whereby any self-serving corrupt politician would come to you for coaching?"

She's made her point well. These people are expert liars, and we fools are taken in all the time.

"Welcome to the world of the sexual predator. Most people don't know and haven't taken the time to find out how they do what they do. They would much rather think the victims are making this shit up than face the truth. And it's their own ignorance, or incessant bad habit to deny what isn't coming close to passing the bad smell test, that allows the predators to do what they do, unscathed. And with each successful attack, the bastards become less afraid they'll suffer any consequences. I can picture them doing cartwheels now, laughing as they say, 'You mean I could get away with *that* and *nothing at all* happens to me?'

"You see, many people just don't want to know. They look the other way. They don't want to know they're our sons, grandsons, brothers, fathers, grandfathers, cousins, husbands – and more and more their female counterparts – are capable of doing this to other people. They close their eyes and bury their heads.

"So the numbers of victims continue to climb. Unfortunately, 20 years ago they were successful one out of six times; ten years ago one out of five. I believe it's approaching one in four women in their lifetime who can expect to get raped unless something changes. And, yes, I know it's changing for the better, but it's too damn slow. Why? Because one victory for them is still one heartbreaking, unnecessary loss for the victim, especially if you're the victim."

I want to apologize for taking her down this road, but she moves forward quickly, the madness of it all exercising complete control over her tongue.

"And, for the most part, they're intelligent, patient people with exceptionally calculating, premeditative minds. While on the other hand, some can't even have a conversation with a woman; they just want to have sex. Others just can't stand women, especially the confident women of today that they only want to control. And think about this very important point – a large number of them already have wives or girlfriends, or both, so they most definitely already have a sexual outlet, but that's not enough for them. Sex with that partner is getting old, boring, and routine. They want more, always more.

121

"These predators know exactly what they are doing in life, always. They know when to lie, and they know how to weave credible-sounding stories exceptionally well, on the spot, without flinching. So much so that you think you might actually be wrong despite all the evidence against them. So whenever you read a story about some bullshit pervert claiming he couldn't help himself, or he was drunk when he did it and can't remember any of it, or any other lame excuse, know in your heart, Father, that it's all crap. Hell, they knew enough to dress themselves, shave, eat, go to the bathroom, and do anything else it took to get ready the morning they committed their sexual crime. And they certainly know that what they're doing is wrong. If they didn't, why do they insist on lying about it? I mean, if they don't know it's wrong, why bother to lie at all? Please.

"The truth is they've been liars all their lives. It's the incredibly rare rapist who confesses to the crime they've committed when they are caught, and even then, most of the time, they will still try to dish out excuses to make the crime seem less severe. Like, it's *her* fault because *she* chose to go out on the date with him. Or maybe it's because *she* wore those shorts, so *she* caused him to react the way he did. Maybe she just hugged him too long, or danced with him in a provocative way. Or, here's a good one that is far from unique – she's crazy and making it all up, a point he always seems to say to his family and friends so they think she's the one who's whacko, not the perfect gentleman standing in front of them."

She's pissed, and now so am I. Righteous anger for the victims has my heart pumping hard.

"And, no, they're not psychotic, don't give them that out. And they don't have split personalities either. They're merely calculating, very detail-oriented sexual predators, and silently proud of it. I've seen it where even when they killed for that high – the stalking and rape began to bore them – they claimed they did so out of an uncontrolled anger. But what they don't realize is everything about the crime scene showed us they were *very much* in control – a controlled anger – not the blithering idiot they try to convince us they were.

122

"And another thing we find? A whole shitload of them are narcissists, big time. Not all of them; some are just inadequate blips on the history of humanity; immature even though they are well into their late teens, 20's, 30's, 40's, 50's and now older. But many of them really do believe the whole world revolves around them and, if it doesn't, it better. These types are described by their victims as truly manipulative; incredibly dangerous; effortlessly charming; intimidating. They really think they are special, and they crave admiration from people.

"What's concerning to me is in today's 'Me-Me-Me' society, I'm seeing many more of these narcissistic types. Shit, I've dated enough of them to know. But these egotistical sexual predators really believe they *deserve* sex with whom they want *whenever they want it*. And if they can't get it for free, they'll just take it."

She stops to catch her breath as the waitress hesitatingly passes by to see if I want a refill. Her tone has been higher the last few minutes, and heads have turned.

"By the way, I just described to you my father – he fit the narcissistic mold perfectly."

The break from her professional life to a personal tidbit catches me off guard. Not hesitating for me to reply, she continues.

"One of these perverts did at least tell me, and this I've found to be true with the sexual predators across the board, is more than anything else, they are looking for easy victims. Naïve people. People who show fear or apprehension. These guys smell this stuff, like a wolf smells wounded prey. And, unfortunately, there are so many gullible people out there. But, if someone stands up to them early on, they quickly understand that person won't give in easily. Now, some of them may still go forward and commit the rape anyway, but many move on because they're cowards. They want free, easy sex. And if they can get someone to help them like with a gang rape, they will. Heck, if they can push date rape drugs, they will. But many operate solo.

"But think about why their ploy works. If the meanest bastard or bitch who looked homeless, or evil, or out of control approached any of these women or men, most would turn and get away because their instincts would tell them to do so. These perps know that. So they won't approach their potential victims in that manner. Remember, they're predators, and like all predators, there's a strategy, a game they play. They'll be nice, accommodating, maybe acting like they need help or are really humble, gentle souls in dire need. But it's all a game aimed at getting potential victims to let their guard down."

She's bouncing all over now, spewing a career full of information my way.

"Fantasy and ritual is a big thing for them, too. They've practiced it over and over in their minds and they want it to play out just like that in real life. But it never does and why would it? When they're watching porn, everything is right – it's all under their control. There aren't any bad smells from parts of the victim's body coming through the Internet, and their makeup or body type is just right, and their fantasy victim doesn't talk back or say the wrong thing; in fact, many times they are telling them how much of a sexual master they are. But that doesn't happen in real life so their sought-after fantasy isn't met. That's why they need to keep trying until they get it right. That should be very alarming for potential victims out there.

"Since it's clear these predators are on the hunt, we have to understand *we* are the prey. That means everyone has to have their head on a swivel, always knowing what and who is around them. People can't walk around everywhere with their ears plugged and their iPods blaring, completely oblivious to what is going on around them or who could be tracking them. In our car we need to know who is in front of us, on the side of us, behind us. We don't have to stare them down, but we can't be oblivious. Pay attention."

"How do they get like this?" I ask. Like my desire to learn more about the symptoms of an eating disorder so I can help where I can, I also want to know more about who these perpetrators are.

"You mean, the Cameron Gambkes of the world?"

I actually don't mean him specifically, but she's perceptive.

"Well, let me start with this. Many states have a slightly different definition, but the essence is the same – if a woman or man is not consenting, if they're forced to have sexual intercourse, its rape, even if they are a married couple. If they can't consent, it's also rape, like if they're on a date rape drug or too inebriated, situations like that. Sexual intercourse must be consensual among adults.

"Sexual criminals are so varied there's no one phrase that labels them all adequately. What excited Cameron Gambke might not excite another. But what we look for are *patterns*. That's really the key. It's not like this is such a big mystery we haven't figured out. The problem is there are just so many of the bastards."

She's on an educational roll, so I sit back in my chair and continue to listen intently.

"But here's where it really gets concerning. For many, the porn that used to get them off just doesn't do it anymore, so they search for more of it, and more violent porn, too. Then they start to act out on others and that's where I get involved. All the while they tie what they're seeing with the pleasurable feelings of masturbation, for instance, and they're hooked. Many like the power. Many like the possession. Most of all, I think many of them just like the sex, plain and simple. I'm sure a ton of them are just plain addicted to it, the pricks."

I can't help concentrating on an overriding thought, *"We become what we think about most of the time."* She continues.

"Back to the patterns. What the experts have seen, and what I myself have seen repeatedly, is there is a blueprint that becomes evident early in their lives. Heck, I've seen seven year olds addicted to sex. See, people used to think the things these guys did, and this also applies to girls and adult women more and more, was just them innocently experiencing their own sexuality, sowing their oats, if you will. But it has become evident there's a clear tie to early sexual activities. And the type of activities we've seen run the gamut from making indecent phone calls or sending indecent texts, to peeping in windows, exposing themselves to men or women in public, video voyeurism where they hook tiny cameras to their shoes so they can look up the skirts of girls, or placing hidden cameras in rooms so they can watch people dress or have sex.

"This early activity is a clear indication of potential future trouble. Some stick with their fantasy, the object of their desire – like black hair, brown eyes, young, etc. – which is part of the pattern we need to watch for. The possibilities are endless, really; it's only limited by the technology and their disordered imagination.

"There are additional factors that help to round out the profile, such as alcohol abuse in their youth, routine shoplifting, burglary or petty theft, and aggression towards adults. In short, many, but certainly not all, had a tendency to say 'screw you' to authority around them early on. Unless they had something stop them as they got older, they just got better at their 'trade' and more aggressive until they were caught, convicted and finally put behind bars.

"Another certainty is many of these people are taught to see their world by the people closest to them. You know those with the greatest influence on them. Like their parents, grandparents, coaches, youth group leaders, friends, or fraternity brothers and sisters. Plenty were even influenced by the famous, you know, musicians, sports figures and movie stars, all those the media glorify. These people help these predators to believe that, in many respects, what they are doing is *just fine, normal behavior.* The underlying, unspoken 'wink-wink' message is just don't be stupid enough to get caught. All of this just reinforces their pathetic behavior."

She stops only for a moment, long enough to take another drink of her water bottle.

"Those who regularly view porn often end up acting out what they see on film and over time they need for it to be harder, rougher, and longer, in order to just get off. They will begin to demand more violent activities such as sexual bondage, constantly demanding anal sex, or other forms of rough sex. Their partners should be very cautious. It's not gentle and sensual love they are making with their partner, it's screwing, pure and simple, all the time. Many times these are some of the same guys on the other end of murder charges. Not always, of course, but their mentality and need for this type of rough sex makes me wary of them and their partners should be aware of the possible outcome.

126

"Now, we're very leery of the sexual predators who are willing to kidnap, either forcefully or by intimidation, and then transport their victims to another location. These predators always have a master plan. They work out to the last detail how to snatch their victims and then transport them to a place where no one can hear or see them. They plan out exactly what they want to do because they do not want to be rushed. It's all premeditated. Ultimately, this may, and often does, end with the victim's death! If I could castrate them and not get in trouble for it, I would. Believe me."

Her fists clenching now, she picks up the pace.

"A big challenge we are facing right now is when current or old boyfriends or girlfriends install a program onto a victim's laptop computers which allow them to see, from their own computer, what's going on in the victim's life whenever they have it powered on. One lethal version works when an unsuspecting victim opens an 'electronic greeting card' which immediately installs malicious software to capture emails and instant messages, in addition to activating their webcam. Computer shops can install these, too, when the customers bring them in for repair. That's why I have a piece of black tape covering my camera."

She turns her laptop to me so I can see what she's done.

"Why doesn't the public know about all of this?" I ask.

Her eyebrows raise, a flash streaking through her eyes.

"With all due respect, Father, we are doing the best we can. Well, most of us. Do you actually think these perps have a web site called www.badguystrategies.com so anyone can just go there to find exactly what the maggots are up to? Their whole lives are about *not getting caught*, staying under the radar, trying to fit in with everyone else so their bullshit cover isn't blown. And they're damn good at it. But we do catch some of them, make no mistake about it. If we can all team up – law enforcement and the public – we'll change the odds, I know that to be true."

"You're right. I get it." I look down at my plate, embarrassed.

She takes a breath to slow her breathing and apologizes, although I am in no need of one.

"Look, I'm sorry for my reaction. This is just a constant cat and rat game, but there aren't enough cats to grab the explosion of rats. I do agree with your thought process, though. Self-education is key, and combining forces helps create the all-imperative hammer society needs to force an end to the sex perps' activity."

I nod my head and she continues.

"And these same people, as they're exposed to more of this media, coupled with their incessant masturbating practices, truly jerk-silly perverts, become increasingly aroused. I mean, even if they have been told to practice self-control, they ignore it. Why? Because they don't believe they have a problem, or they don't think it will lead to more problems down the road, if left unchecked."

My mind goes back to my high school and college days, recalling how the more I masturbated the hornier I got, not the reverse. And I angrily remember the Catholic counselor who encouraged me to masturbate whenever I felt the urge to do so, because he said it was a natural human desire. That was exactly what I wanted to hear at the time. Heck, he was "Catholic" after all and someone in authority, so I didn't question a thing. I often wondered later in life how that logic would have worked if every time I was thirsty for a beer I drank one, or any time I felt a twinge of hunger I ate more food. Whatever happened to good old-fashioned temperance?

"One guy I busted admitted to masturbating only two or three times a day. When his case came to court and the psychologist testified, we found out he had admitted to that same psychologist he masturbated up to *ten times a day*. She also reported he wasn't a mentally challenged person who had no way of controlling this urge. His excuse for masturbating so much? That it was part of him, you know, his sexual drive, and there was nothing he could do to change it. He also said women existed in life to give him sex. It was *their* reason for even existing here on earth. Not once did he take responsibility for any of his actions. Not once did he talk about self-control. He truly didn't believe he needed to practice it because he didn't think it was necessary. Do you know the only thing he was upset about?"

"No."

"That he got caught. That was it. He made the mistake of admitting to his psychologist he would make absolute certain he was more organized the next time, to ensure he didn't get caught. The perfect sexual crime was his goal. My experience tells me he is far from the exception in his screwed-up thought process."

Sitting back, I cross my arms as I try to absorb all this information. I look past her, out the window, and my darkened mood matches the changing sky.

"I'm not saying everyone that looks at porn becomes a rapist. Of course not. We haven't seen that to be true at all."

Good, because I was about to make a rebutting comment. I did look at porn when I was younger and I didn't become a rapist, but I understand what she's saying.

"Many of the bastards are proud of it; they are actually pleased with what they have accomplished, and that's really twisted, isn't it? As I said before, if they're not caught, or if something doesn't happen in their lives to make them stop, they get bolder, and cockier. We can only hope we'll catch them when they slip up.

"Some of the guys we've caught, they've confessed to 40 or 50 rapes that we've been able to verify. So it's not just them bragging. For some of them, we have every reason to believe they've been involved with a hundred or more rapes. It's like they get going and are unwilling to stop themselves, a kind of mentality where they believe they're already in big trouble anyway, so why not just keep going and enjoy it while it lasts?

"The good news, at least minimally, is some actually don't act out because of their belief in Hell, or maybe their high profile career they can't risk, or it's their fear of being incarcerated. But all too many times that doesn't even stop them.

"But think about this. They spend an enormous amount of time and energy every single day trying not to get caught, covering their bases, replaying their alibi over and over and over again in their minds. Did they cover the crime scene? Did they throw away all the evidence; their clothes, gloves, or anything else which might have DNA evidence on it? Were they seen going to and from the scene? Were any cameras around to catch them?

They are probably more obsessed with this part of their life than their desire to rape, and it can drive them crazy which I think is fantastic. But even that doesn't stop some of them.

"I can't tell you how many people we've arrested where their wives, girlfriends, family, or neighbors always said the same thing – they had no idea. You know why? *Because not getting caught was their overarching, primary goal. It consumed them, and they became incredibly good at it until their world rightfully came crashing down on their pathetic heads.* Remember, all sex perps know that what they're doing is wrong and they know they're in deep shit with everyone around them if they get caught. Because if they do, the double-life they've been leading, the world they've created, goes up in smoke. And if they are put away into prison, they've now entered the one place on earth where men have an incredibly high likelihood of being raped themselves. That's why they work so hard at their M.O. They learn something from each attempted or successful rape in order to get better and reduce their chances of getting caught the next time. And there's always a 'next time.' Like going from wearing normal clothes to dressing up in oversized black clothes, gloves, shoes, cloth masks – the works – so they don't leave a trace."

"Really, they dress up like that? Like in the movies?"

My intent isn't to question what she is saying, rather, it just sounds like more of a fictional book or movie than real life. Suddenly remembering the rape site I saw on the Internet and how I wondered then how much of this was fake and how much was real, I wish I could take back my question. Still I wonder: Do people actually post their "victory videos" for the world to see?

Rather than verbally reacting, she redirects.

"Did you see this in the paper this morning?"

"No. I haven't had a chance to read the news today." More bad news, I'm sure.

"In California. A fifteen-year-old girl committed suicide. Three 16 year olds have been arrested on sexual battery. She was allegedly sexually battered while passed out at a party. Then the pictures taken by the little bastards were posted online so they could broadcast their victory over this helpless young girl. They're

130

either stupid or so cocky they believed they could get away with it. I'll bet you anything they slipped her a date rape drug. Her parents are pissed and want justice. Good for them, because they, she, hell, all the victims and their families, deserve justice."

So it is true. Some of these worthless bastards post their "victory" rapes. Is any agency searching through this "evidence" for cases? I keep this to myself. I don't want to set her off again. She genuinely cares about doing her job well, and I have confidence that whatever will help her cases, she'll use – including this ready tool that is waiting in cyberspace for discovery.

"Then there's a related story up in Canada. The authorities are looking further into the case of a teenage girl who hanged herself after an alleged rape and months of bullying. A photo said to be of the assault on the 17 year old was also shared online.

"I'll bet you anything that someone has already said these girls were whores or sluts. That they shouldn't have been there, implying the victims somehow deserved what happened to them. Or they were lying, making it all up for the attention. The bad boys will probably say the girls asked for it, were part of it – even enjoyed it."

I've lost my appetite. She's not done.

"There' so much more, Father, so much more. Do you want to hear some quick stats?"

My anxiety is already on high. Why not.

"Except for child porn, pornography use is legal in almost every part of North and South America, although there are pockets of restrictions here and there. It's also either completely illegal or legal with restrictions in the rest of the world. But even in those places where it's restricted or flat-out illegal, it's difficult to adequately control. You know, like the laws that ban the use of hand-held cell phones while driving are difficult to enforce because the vast majority of people just completely ignore them.

"Why? What agency really has the resources to really do anything long-term about it? I mean, in the United States, we have to battle everyone from the court system to the ACLU and its allies. The legal system is all about letting the door remain open for personal freedoms, no matter the filth that is produced.

"They think they make a strong argument when they claim that regulating morality shouldn't be the privilege of any one consenting adult over another. The flip side is even if that's the case, the innocent continue to suffer because not enough people are standing up to say this is bullshit, and it's incredibly damaging. It does affect everyone in so many ways and is certainly not a victimless crime. I've seen firsthand what it can do to people, families, homes, and children."

She's clicking through the tabs and has my full attention.

"As a big part of the adult entertainment industry, Internet porn pulls in around $4.9 billion a year. Every second you and I are sitting here, there are 28,000 Internet users viewing porn. There are 2.5 billion emails per day that are pornographic flowing around the net. One of the biggest revenue producers for hotels are the in-room adult entertainment options. And listen to this, Father. The least popular day of the year for Internet porn is Thanksgiving. Football, parades, and too many people in the house probably keep people away from looking at it freely. The most popular day? Sunday. Looks like people have too much time on their hands on the Lord's Day, huh?"

Neither of us are smiling.

"The adult video industry rakes in about $1.8 billion a year. And there are an estimated 211 new porn films every week in the United States. However, Los Angeles County started requiring condoms for the porn shoots there to try and stop the spread of infectious diseases like AIDS. The permit fees dropped through the floor, so now many of those companies just moved on to other towns and cities who won't make it so hard on them."

I think about Dr. Chaffgrind's son, Alex, and how proud he is of his success in this field.

"One very disturbing fact, if that isn't enough, is there are about 116,000 searches every day for child porn. *116,000* searches for child porn! Can you believe it? I'm amazed our government continues to protect everyone's freedom of expression, which I certainly do believe is a good thing within appropriate parameters, but doesn't do much to protect the children or give the parents any true help on the matter.

"Incest, bestiality, transman, tranny, transgender, hermaphrodite, Futunari, Human corpse stuff, cartoon porn Hentai or anything digital, and that's just off the top of my head. The genres are endless and evolving daily, and I've seen this stuff firsthand.

"And who knows what Cameron Gambke was into by the time he was caught? One thing's for sure, when I was living with him, he was definitely into swinging."

"Swinging, like, well, I'm sorry to say this, uh, dancing?" I've heard the term but am trying to make the tie to what Detective Renae is attempting to describe to me.

"No. Not at all. Swapping sex partners. It's how he and mom met, I know at least that much. And it's a big thing now in the world."

"By the way, you have met someone recently that's still very active in this lifestyle."

I don't have a clue. I have met many people since I've been here, so it could be one of any of them. Whoever it is, at this point, I don't know if I will be surprised, if and when I find out.

"I'll let you discover that out on your own, if she ever volunteers to tell you. Excuse me for a moment – I need to head to the restroom."

I ponder an overriding thought as she leaves: *Eating from the tree of the knowledge of good and evil.* They think its freedom they are exercising – 'no one is going to tell me what to do' kind of thing – yet it only leads them into the slavery of sin. And many times, it just doesn't affect them, it affects us all.

Chapter 16

I picked up the tab for lunch, and Detective Renae has just returned from the restroom. Sitting down while we wait for the change, I try to make the most use of our remaining time.

"What about gang rapes? Didn't Gina experience something like that?"

Pausing, I can tell she's contemplating how much she can say.

"I hate those weak little shits the most. But, again, I can't tell you anything specific about the case. I know the paper said she was gang raped, but let me just say that in typical gang rape cases, there is an identifiable leader, and then many willing participants. These are the chicken-shits of the rapist community, in my opinion. They can't even rape on their own. They have to do it with their friends; there is this wolf-pack mentality. Most of them thoroughly enjoy what they've done, and they will never accept blame. When questioned and shown clear evidence, they most often claim their friends made them do it. They are so worried about being part of the group, so worried about what others think about them, they won't stand up to any of the members and say how what they are all doing is wrong. There will always be a dominant male, the leader, and no one else in the group has the balls to stand up to him. But although this dominant leader may rule in that particular group, in the outer world where everyone else lives in reality, he or she is a nobody, and they know it deep down. That's why I say they're all chicken-shits. I find great pleasure in catching these assholes and, if I might say, my success rate keeps getting higher and higher.

"And unless you have the rest of the afternoon to listen to all of this, we won't even come close to having enough time to talk about sporting clubs, and the absolute blight on humanity this is."

"Sporting clubs?"

I don't want to know the answer, but I'm in deep already. The waitress has returned the difference, but Detective Renae seems determined to continue.

"Yep. Where parents rent out their kids – some as young as

six months old – so others can have sex with them. It's how they can make money. We've also seen guys who molested hundreds of children before they were caught because they focused on at-risk kids. These kids were known liars from tough backgrounds. The perverts chose them because, well, who would believe their story? And do you know how many parents take the side of the abusers over their children? Far too many."

I'm beginning to feel nauseous again.

"Or how about this one? My favorite. Human Sex Trafficking. I have my reasons, but this one absolutely makes me sick, really and truly. At the end of my day, I really want to help these women break out of this."

She's clicking to another Internet tab, no smile evident on her face, and machine guns the stats my way.

"One million women worldwide forced into prostitution. Also, who knows how many young boys and children are forced into it, but we know it's in the hundreds of thousands. If they try to run away, their families and friends are threatened with death. They are given birth control injections. Abortions are forced if they get pregnant. Both men and women captors. And here in the United States? Up to 17,000 right now. Up to 300,000 teens are forced into prostitution every single year here. There's a nationwide circuit where their pimps drive them around, all drugged up.

"You said you looked at websites? There are plenty of them where the pimps show off their girls and the customers rank them for the next customer. Many people think these girls are doing this for their own pleasure, by their own choice. They don't have a fucking clue about how bad this is. My question is, in order for this to keep going, there has to be a demand. Customers. Men mostly. Who are they? I'll tell you who they are. They are husbands, fathers, brothers and other 'respectable' men from all walks of life. I wonder if their wives know what STD they may be bringing home to them."

I absentmindedly drink what remains of my lukewarm coffee.

"My second biggest pet peeve? All the women, and now more men, who are sexually molested while serving in the military. My best friend from college went through it. She was raped by her direct report, and eventually kicked out with an 'other-than-honorable' discharge – that's one step below an 'honorable discharge' – so she ended up with no benefits. The prick trumped up charges against her to cover his own ass, and given his level of authority, he was believed over her. She was humiliated; he kept his job. She committed suicide. I'm certain he doesn't believe he really *did* anything wrong to begin with. Just 'boys being boys,' right, Father? If you're into movies, I highly recommend you rent 'The Invisible War.' That'll open your eyes with one perspective of the blight which overshadows all veterans who have served our country honorably over the years. I tell every person I know who has a son or daughter that's considering going into the military to definitely watch it."

She's imploring me to feel the full weight of how bad this is.

"Father," she says, leaning towards me, her voice husky with rage, "last year a Pentagon study found there are an average of 70 sexual assaults every single day in the military. *70 a day.* And that's more than likely only what they can put their finger on."

I hold up my hand, the weight of it all cascading over me. I don't want to hear another thing and try to redirect to an issue I keep wondering about.

"Do you feel sorry for any of them? The sexual predators, I mean? I'm not on their side, I guess I'm just really trying to understand what in the hell is going on."

Her eyes flash anger again, as she replies coldly, the words coming out at a stone cold pace.

"I fully understand some, but certainly not all, of the sexual predators have low self-esteem for a thousand and more reasons. Many come from abusive or otherwise severely dysfunctional backgrounds. I get that. But you know what? If we were to analyze every single person's life who's ever lived, we can safely say *everyone* has had a bad past in one form or another. Some worse than others, I know. But when you really look at the history of their lives, you have to ask yourself why there are *so many* of their brothers or sisters and other family members who are good, decent, law abiding people. I mean, really. How do entire families

136

go through tough upbringings and only one or two do things to end up in prison?"

Strangling her car keys, I wonder if she's going to puncture herself.

"Every moment of every single day, we choose how we live, right?"

I'm not sure if she's asking or telling me, but I nod in full agreement.

"Look, Father, I had a pathetic, nightmarish past, and you don't see me going around raping and killing. And do you know how many children are coming out of abusive and dysfunctional families today all around the world? A shitload of them. But I guarantee not all will turn out to be sexual predators. Unfortunately, statistically, many will, unless things change drastically, suddenly, and quickly.

"Do you know who I really feel sorry for? The abused, right here, right now, because no matter what anyone says, they don't deserve that shit. From anyone. Ever. No matter the predator's pathetic past or present situation. No way."

I interrupt her briefly. "Okay, I hear you. I really do. I'm really not trying to upset you, further, I promise. But from your professional perspective, can they change?"

She nods. "Of course. Like anything else, there's always hope and resources if someone wants to change. I mean, think about it this way. One time, growing up, after I moved in with my aunt, there was this Jetta I wanted to buy. Loved that car. And my aunt had been really working with me on trying to instill some discipline, to do chores and stuff like that. You know, to help around the house. And I balked and made excuses and played games all the time with her so I could get out of it. But *I wanted that car*. She said she wouldn't give me any money for it unless I worked for it. So I worked my ass off. It was all because I wanted something. It was important to *me*. In the end, I got the car.

"But most of these sexual predators? They *enjoy* what they are doing. They like it. They live for it. They don't *want* to change, and until they do, society better watch out. The ones I've seen change, and they are few and far between, found a reason to change – like them not wanting their kids to know how mentally deranged they've become by their own choices. That, combined with the therapy they received, has helped some.

"All the others are just playing a game to get everyone around them to *think* they're fine, that they're 'cured.' The reality is they just want to go on living their lives exactly as they have been. Hell, probably 60% are sure to re-offend if they get a chance to do it again. The remaining 40%? I wouldn't want to be their date to find out. Others are just going to self-destruct, because it just doesn't matter. The only change they'll make is where they do their dirty deeds – they'll find safer zones to operate – but they won't change their preferences nor their activities. And I say the sooner they implode the better. But remember, I'm only talking here about the ones who have been caught. I can't even put a number on the thousands, maybe millions, of rapists who have never been caught, and never will be caught, unless we change how we look at this pandemic."

I nod, understanding much better the magnitude of it all. "I hear you, I really do. So what would you tell all the women out there on how to protect themselves, their families, their children?"

"Honestly? Don't be so trusting. Really. I mean it. Don't be stupid and sleep with a guy the first night or, even better, for a very long time! Wait until you really, truly get to know him. Don't give in if he says he's going to commit suicide if you don't. Don't give in to his guilt trips. Don't meet him just anywhere. Look, there are many things they can do, but before I forget, do you know the type of women or men these perps are most likely to attack?"

"No."

"Christian or other religious. Why? Because they are so trusting and forgiving. No matter what a predator has done in the past, these people will forgive and forget. Always. And that's exactly the type of simple-hearted victim these bastards are looking for."

This comment angers me. I've seen it before in some of the women who have come to me after being raped. And sleep with the guy on the first date? Whatever happened to the concept of abstinence until you're married? "Detective, I'm with ya. God gave us intelligence to use it. Yes, we need to always forgive, but we don't have to be passive victims of pain and abuse, ever. We don't need to be anyone's doormat. And we need to do all we can to help those who have been abused. You really have a special mission in life. Thank you for what you do."

She pauses now, looking down. I can't imagine the last time anyone thanked or complimented her sincerely. She distracts herself by closing down her laptop and places it in her carry bag. Turning serious once more, she continues.

"Do you want to know, Father, how many victims keep silent on sexual abuse, not telling anyone at all, so that it never hits the papers or the news? The majority, that's how many. Then a victim commits suicide, and the world begins to notice, and people are surprised? Really? C'mon! These victims have been living this nightmare every single day, feeling the safety of the world they once knew being ripped away from them.

"People are getting tired of this shit, or, if they aren't, they should be. But my bigger concern is they don't have any idea how bad this has gotten. Justice, that's what I want – no more suicides, no more pain – and I'm going to give my all to help and protect every single victim." I can see she's as serious as serious can be.

"I am embarrassed to admit it" I offer, "but I really didn't know how bad it was until this last week, especially after spending this time with you. All these maggots sharing this crap on the Internet, becoming programmed by it and then taking so many others with them down this sick road. And I agree with you that so many people sit back and wonder, 'Gee, how are they learning it?' I share your amazement at the absurdity of it all."

Like hers moments before, my own voice is now raised. Heads turn toward us but I don't care. Our righteous anger has formed a mutual bond between us. Our Lord felt it every time the Pharisees and Sadducees said one thing and did another. Hypocrites, all of them. And when he saw how the people had turned the temple into a retail store, forgetting what it was all about, He took action. It's time for me to enter the fray. "Will you do me a favor? Will you talk to my youth group about rape prevention when I get back from an overseas trip I'm about to take?"

"After all I just told you, Father, you should know you don't have to even ask. I want and, more importantly, need to get this information out to everyone. And if I were you, I would invite anyone who wants to come. This affects everyone. The victims, their families and friends, the entire community."

"Great idea. Thanks for the information, and know I will always keep you and your work in my prayers."

A courteous, faint smile crosses her lips. If she ever believed in the power of prayer, after what she's seen and experienced in life, she has every right to doubt its value.

I check my watch and she does the same, both of us knowing we need to get back to work. We stand and walk side by side to the door.

"Thank you for the meal, and thanks for the information. I've gotta get back to Vidant Beaufort to see Gina. I've yet to meet her. While I'm there, I'll check in on the sheriff again."

Confused, she queries. "Why? Gina Jerpun is at Martin General Hospital over in Williamston. Has been there since they transferred her, a few days after she was attacked."

Martin General in Williamston? She continues before I can ask anything else.

"If I may, remember that Michele's been through a lot. I'm not sure if she'll speak to you, but she might like company. It's nice of you to think about going over there. By the way, she grilled me about what Cameron Gambke told you that day at the prison, since she saw you driving off with me in my car."

"What did you tell her?"

"Since you didn't tell me what he said, I told her the same thing."

I nod my head. "Everybody needs somebody at different times in their lives, and maybe Michele will feel comfortable getting things off of her chest with me."

Our conversation dwindles as I walk her to her car. We shake hands and she opens her driver side door as I turn and begin heading towards mine. The wind has picked up, a light sprinkle announcing the seasonal storm on its way.

140

"Father?" she calls out.

"Yes?"

"I want to give this to you. You asked me earlier about 'my world,' so here's an example of the type of people I chase for a living. I hand these out when I give presentations, so you can have this copy if you want it. It's an excerpt of the final interview of serial rapist and killer Ted Bundy with Dr. James Dobson of Focus on the Family, the day before he was executed in 1989, at the Florida State Prison in Starke, Florida. He had requested Dr. Dobson visit him for this last interview because he said he had an important message to tell, in part, about how he was very much influenced by pornographic violence. You can read the full interview on the Internet if you're interested.

"Parts of the interview he says he believes he was just a normal person, a good guy, and led a normal life other than this indescribably evil side of him he kept secret and to himself. Said his family and friends didn't have a clue; they were surprised when the truth came out because he had done such a great job of living this double-life. However, this 'exemplary' individual murdered 28 women which may have been as high as 36. They still don't know at this point."

I thank her and turn back to my car, wondering once again why I saw Michele Jerpun coming out of the elevator at Vidant Beaufort. Maybe she was just visiting someone else.

Still bothered by all Detective Renae has just told me about sexual crime, I don't notice at first, that somewhere on my way here, I must have driven over something which cost me a flat tire.

Realizing I will have to postpone my trip to the hospital for another day, I unfold the document she handed me, lean against the trunk, and begin reading.

<u>Excerpts from a January 23, 1989, interview by Ted Bundy with Dr. James Dobson, Focus on the Family</u>:

"We are not inherent monsters. We`are your sons and we are your husbands. We grew up in regular families."

"Pornography can reach out and snatch a kid out of any house today – it snatched me out of my home twenty, thirty years ago. And as diligent

*as my parents were, and they were diligent in protecting their children,
and as good a Christian home we had, and we had a wonderful Christian
home, there is no protection against the kinds of influences that are loose
in a society that tolerates..."*

*"I've lived in prison for a long time now and, I've met a lot of men
who were motivated to commit violence just like me, and without
exception, every one of them was deeply involved in pornography,
without question, without exception, deeply influenced and consumed by
an addiction to pornography. There is no question about it. The FBI's
own study on serial homicide shows that the most common interest
among serial killers is pornography."*

*"I think society deserves to be protected from itself because, just as
we've been talking, there are forces at loose in this country, particularly
this kind of violent pornography where, on the one hand, well-meaning
decent people will condemn the behavior of a Ted Bundy while they are
walking past a magazine rack full of the very kinds of things that send
young kids down the road to be Ted Bundy's. That's the irony."*

January 23, 1989. Almost 25 years ago. Shaking my head, it
suddenly strikes me Ted Bundy was only immersing himself in
print pornography back then because that's probably all that was
readily available, and, granted this must have been a tweaked
individual to begin with, but this was the impact on him before the
explosion of images and videos on the Internet.

I recall the advent of high-speed desktop computers in my
business days and how so much has changed since then. Today
everyone routinely carries technology, such as smartphones,
iPhones, iPads, and laptops, everywhere they go. People of all ages
can now instantly access images – heck, they can download a
virtually unlimited volume of sexually graphic material within the
time it will take me to open the trunk of my car and remove the
spare tire.

"How many more Ted Bundys are out there? Heck, how
many rapists are out there?" I say out loud, kicking the ground in
frustration, both at the flat tire I now need to fix and at all the crap
that is happening around me. I'm outraged at the filth the
detective just described to me. My heart goes out to all of the

victims, and the eternal threat to the souls of the abusers causes me great horror.

I'm emotionally spent. The rejuvenation of a pilgrimage can't come soon enough. The downpour begins, assuring the process of changing the tire will be a struggle.

Chapter 17

It's Saturday morning, and the Weather Channel informs me it's going to be a sunny March day. I'm glad because our parish has agreed to participate, along with the other parishes in the diocese, in a silent vigil at the abortion clinic every Saturday. The purpose is to give hope and options to women and couples in need.

Since we'll begin at 9:00 a.m., I have plenty of time to start my day in prayer with Our Blessed Lady in the grotto. I reflect on the Joyful Mysteries as I pray the Rosary.

- The Annunciation, when Mother Mary agreed to be the Mother of the Son of God
- The Visitation of Mary to her cousin Elizabeth
- The Nativity, where Our Lord was humbly born in a manger in Bethlehem
- The Presentation in the Temple of Our Lord by Mother Mary and St. Joseph, and
- Mother Mary and St. Joseph finding Jesus in the temple after they had lost him for three days.

As I finish up, I offer a final prayer, "Lord, please protect our hearts, minds and tongues as we go to the silent vigil at Planned Parenthood today. And please bless and protect all the mothers, fathers and their unborn children in their wombs. As always, thank you in advance for hearing and answering my prayers as you see fit to do so."

***

"Hello, everyone!" I say to the dozen volunteers gathered in front of the abortion clinic.

The facility looks like any other well-kept office building, with trees and trimmed bushes surrounding the parking lot. Any routine passerby would never know that this facility, along with the other 800 plus locations around the United States, assists with 300,000 abortions each year. Not many know that, globally, there are up to 42 million induced abortions conducted, legally and illegally, each year.

"Let's begin our prayers."

All bow their heads as I lead.

"Lord God, we thank you today for the gift of our lives,
And for the lives of all our brothers and sisters.
We know there is nothing that destroys more life than abortion,
Yet we rejoice that you have conquered death
by the Resurrection of Your Son.
We are ready to do our part in ending abortion.
Today we commit ourselves
Never to be silent,
Never to be passive,
Never to be forgetful of the unborn.
We commit ourselves to be active in the pro-life movement,
And never to stop defending life
Until all our brothers and sisters are protected,
And our nation once again becomes
A nation with liberty and justice
Not just for some, but for all,
Through Christ our Lord. Amen!"

I continue with a reading from St. James, 2:14-18:

"What good is it, my brothers and sisters, if someone says he has faith but does not have works? Can that faith save him? If a brother or sister has nothing to wear and has no food for the day, and one of you says to them, 'Go in peace, keep warm, and eat well,' but you do not give them the necessities of the body, what good is it? So also faith of itself, if it does not have works, is dead. Indeed someone might say, 'You have faith and I have works.' Demonstrate your faith to me without works, and I will demonstrate my faith to you from my works.'"

Addressing the gathered group, I remind them that these are harsh words for anyone that doesn't put their faith into action.

"We can't pick and choose which part of a Christian life we

145

want to live; our faith is a package deal. They go hand in hand, my friends. One cannot exist without the other, as Our Lord plainly showed us by the life He lived. How can we think that we can live in eternity with God if we aren't willing to carry our cross here on earth, just like Our Lord did? Glory in Heaven for eternity means carrying our Cross, and one example of that is what we are doing here today, out of love.

"Given you've all chosen to spend your Saturday morning here with me, I truly thank you for being here and walking the talk."

It's imperative I explain our peaceful plan of action to spread the Good News of Our Lord to all those we come in contact with today.

"Now, for those of you here for the first time, we gather here today in peace. Please stay calm, no matter what. I need to stress that, okay? We are going to pray the Divine Mercy Chaplet and then all five decades of the Rosary. Through our collective presence, we hope to show everyone working at this location, along with whoever is going in and out of these doors, that God loves them and that there is another way, all right?

"Keep in mind that most of these women are afraid, most feel very lonely or very much pressured by their boyfriends, husbands, friends and families, and we are here to provide support. If the Holy Spirit guides them to us, hand out these brochures and speak lovingly and gently to them. This is NOT an 'us against them' rally as these should never be. As the prayer we just said stresses, we are all brothers and sisters in God's family. So let's begin with the Divine Mercy Chaplet."

Rosary beads in hand, we begin the prayer.

Partway through our peaceful prayer, the quiet is broken by the sound of tires on a late model Chevy truck squealing in protest. A woman in her mid-30's passing by whips a quick illegal U-turn, turns into the parking lot, and screeches to a halt. She opens the door, jumps out, marches directly over to me, jamming her index finger repeatedly in my chest.

"Who in the hell do you think you are, you fucking priest! How dare you tell these girls what they can and can't do with their lives! You have no right!"

All prayer stops. Everyone appears alarmed, some are rightfully angered, while others are slightly afraid by the aggressive nature of this woman. Standing my ground, I let her vent her rage.

I learned long ago that this woman has probably closed her mind to anything I, the Church, or fellow believers might try to say to her. Given that her mind is no longer open, I remain quiet, although she would be the first to say that it's the old-fashioned Church's mind that is closed on this and a plethora of other "real life" issues.

Once her vent has spent itself, I tell her she has misunderstood our purpose and invite her to stay awhile longer so I may explain our position. Rolling her eyes, she turns on her heels and strides back to her truck, head held high, clearly feeling victorious for standing up for all the women that she believes we are somehow condemning. The wave with her middle finger is the last we see of her.

I raise my hands to everyone standing around, as their murmuring grows louder.

"I've seen worse than that before. Let's just keep her in our prayers, okay? She needs God's grace in her life to find peace. God will help her in whatever she is seeking if she remains open to Him."

Finishing the Divine Mercy Chaplet, I lead the group in praying the Rosary.

No other confrontations occur. I'm pleased to say that at least a half a dozen women and what appeared to be the father of an unborn child came by and picked up some of the packets we offered. We provided information on the truth about Planned Parenthood and, more importantly, information that described the horrifying deadly process that takes place when a baby in the mother's womb is aborted. In the packet was also a flyer for the DVD, Changing Sides: How a Pro-Life Presence Changed the Heart of a Planned Parenthood Director. A local Christian bookstore is offering a discount for anyone who was interested in picking up a copy. One of the teenage mothers who chose not to go inside, after spending some quiet time on the sidewalk together with one of our elderly parishioners, said she was heading right over to pick up a copy.

One person at a time, another unborn baby, and mother, helped.

***

Parking in the alley behind an old garage on the rectory grounds, I enter the rear of the administrative building, a location I don't routinely use.

"What, uh, what are you doing here?! I thought you were going to be at the demonstration and then go and do some shopping," Mrs. Bellers utters, her head snapping around quickly in my direction. She's standing in the door to my office, with her back to me, positioned in such a way where she can see the front door. I've clearly caught her off guard, her eyes wide and voice pitch a little too high. I'm immediately suspicious.

"I'm, uh, well, for the most part, it was a peaceful rally and went smoothly and now I'm back here to begin getting ready for Palm Sunday tomorrow and Holy Week. I'll do my shopping later tonight."

Why in the world do I even feel compelled to explain myself to this self-proclaimed czarina, as though I've done something wrong?

Suddenly her nephew Dennis appears, hastily leaving my office. I have met him before, but only briefly. A technology genius, or so Mrs. Bellers tells everyone when she introduces him. He doesn't look my way as he heads out the front door. What the heck is going on here?

Noticing my look of surprise, she offers, "Oh, he was just helping me to run some wires for our computer system. Unfortunately, we needed to get into your office to run them through the drop ceiling and thought it would be better to do so on the weekend when the office is closed."

With that, she moves to her desk, hastily placing papers in stacks.

Glancing into my office, I notice nothing out of the ordinary. All ceiling tiles look to be in place. Her story sounds plausible enough. The problem is, I don't trust her and probably never will.

148

In addition, she has a standalone desktop system, a very basic one at that, so why do wires have to be run? She must have forgotten my business background.

I'm really uncomfortable with her having a key to my office, but when I had arrived here there was no available office that I could use. The only possible room was one that served a dual-purpose: the storage of supplies and the break room. It is now my office. My desk is in the corner, with a credenza up against the back wall, along with the office coffee pot and a small refrigerator. My office also serves as the location where the weekly contributions are counted.

Necessary change is on its way, and I'm going to make sure it does. Patience, I remind myself, patience.

Chapter 18

"Father, I would like you to meet the wife."

Jean Luder, a petite, attractive brunette offers me a weak smile and a hesitating, yet courteous, handshake.

"It's nice to meet you," she replies curtly.

"I'll take good care of him and will drop him off tonight when we get done." I smile, not sure at all the reasoning behind her reaction to me.

She quickly nods her head, glances at the sheriff, and returns to her white Lincoln Mark IV.

The sheriff was released from the hospital earlier this morning and can't drive for at least a week, doctor's orders. He insisted he speak with me again regarding his experience after his accident. Mrs. Luder agreed to bring him by the rectory. As long as we can catch up in the car on the way to visit Gina at the hospital, it's fine with me. I hope to speak to Michele as well, just to see how she's holding up.

"You doing all right?" I ask, noticing the sheriff gingerly climbing into the front seat of my car, slowly fastening his seat belt.

"Oh, I'm sorry, you need to sit in the back. Only people on official business with the Church can sit up front here with me." I crack another smile, and he returns it in kind.

"Okay, I deserved that. Yeah, I'm doin' okay. Still a little headache but they said that was normal. Are you sure visiting hours are still open at the hospital?"

It's only 6:00 p.m. and I'm certain the hospital where Gina is will accept visitors until around 9:00. He seems a little nervous we are heading that way. Maybe he just wants to drive around with me so we can talk, and with the way I feel about hospitals in addition to what he just went through, I kind of wish that's exactly what we were going to do. But duty calls.

"Yeah, I'm sure. Are you still okay to go with me? I mean, I know you're not at your best, so why don't you just rest, okay? We can talk about your experience later, maybe even on the way home tonight. I can tell you the Church's stance on what may have been a near death experience, especially where there is no obvious medical reasoning behind it."

"That's probably a good idea. I'm just going to shut my eyes for a bit," he says, which allows me time to think about my upcoming schedule. This is Holy Week, my absolute favorite time of the year. I have a heavy schedule ahead so this is probably the only time I can meet with the sheriff for a while.

I'm sure you remember the Church uses a liturgical calendar which begins with Advent, the time when we prepare for the birth of Our Lord. Within the liturgical year, we observe two major events: Our Lord's birth at Christmas and His resurrection at Easter. The liturgical calendar is segmented into Advent, the Christmas season, Ordinary Time, Lent, the Easter Triduum, the Easter season, and then back to Ordinary Time.

Throughout the liturgical year we honor one or more saints almost every day. And since Mother Mary is so important in the life of Christ and in the history of the Catholic Church, there are 16 days set aside in her honor, some of which are Holy Days of Obligation given their importance.

The Lenten season is coming to a close. Yesterday was Palm Sunday, a celebration of when Jesus rode triumphantly into Jerusalem, while the crowd waved palm branches and placed them in his path as a sign of honor.

Lent will end this Wednesday and on Thursday we'll celebrate the Triduum, three days which consists of Holy Thursday, Good Friday, and Holy Saturday.

Sunday is Easter, when we rejoice in Christ's Resurrection from the dead. This is considered the most holy of all days, and the climax of the liturgical year.

A slight snore emanates from the mouth of the sheriff. I'm pleased he is resting.

I'd like to remind you of the precepts of the Church, spelled out in the Catechism, which are intended to provide the faithful with the minimum requirements for living a sacramental life. In other words, when we follow these precepts we will be nourished with the necessary graces to live a moral life.

There are only six of them:

- Attend Mass on Sunday and Holy Days of Obligation unless there is a valid reason not do so.
- Observe the fasting and abstinence rules for Ash Wednesday, Good Friday, all the Fridays of Lent, and for 1 hour prior to receiving Communion. Exceptions are allowed for the sick, the elderly, or for those in which fasting and abstinence would jeopardize their health.
- Confess any grave sins at least once a year, but certainly before receiving Communion.
- Receive Communion at least once a year, preferably during the Easter season.
- Contribute to the support of the Church, and
- Observe the Church's laws concerning marriage.

So you can see, the "have to's" are all meant to insure we rightfully give due thanks and praise to God. I pray, for your own spiritual health and happiness, you have remained faithful to God and are still following these precepts.

The pothole appears out of nowhere and I hit it square.

The jolt brings the sheriff awake. He turns and looks at me, obvious pain reflected in his eyes, and speaks while still in a daze.

"It was real, I know it. I went through something, okay? I mean, it felt real. Or maybe it was all in my head, you know, my brains just swishing around from the hit. Then, all those drugs. But all the stuff I recorded on the microphone, what about that? I mean, where does that fit into all of this?"

His eyes are wild now. Is it just confusion I see? Or fear?

"You ready to talk about this or do you want to rest some more?"

"Now. I need to know. Anything you can offer. This is driving me nuts, man."

He holds his bandaged skull in his hands, resting it gently once more on the back head rest.

"Okay. I'm not sure how much you kept up with the teachings of the Church, and I'm only saying that to set a base for what I'm about to share with you about near death experiences, okay?"

"Let's just assume I don't remember anything," his eyes tightly clenched closed. "That won't be far from the truth."

"Fair enough. That's our starting point. If indeed you had a near death experience, the phenomenon appears to be thousands of years old. If you've ever read Plato's Republic, you may remember he gave an account of a soldier describing his own near death experience over 2,300 years ago. What the soldier apparently went through sounds strikingly similar to what we hear about today. Things like leaving their body, floating above where their body is or going to other locations, entering a long dark tunnel, traveling at extraordinary speeds, seeing people long since passed, or meeting Jesus or a light of unbelievable beauty and love. And also what's very common is, although it all happens over a small number of minutes, it feels like a much longer time for the one experiencing it."

He has turned his entire upper body towards me, fully engaged in what I am saying.

"The Church teaches that St. Paul, who lived while Christ was on earth, says in second Corinthians he was 'caught up into Paradise – whether in the body or out of the body I do not know, God knows…,' so this may have been a near death experience, or something similar to it. And since St. Paul's time, there have been hundreds of thousands of people who have reported having this type of experience, from every culture and nation.

"The Catholic Church has not issued a formal statement on the matter, although that isn't unprecedented. All it means is that it has not found a reason to do so. God can communicate with His people in any way He wishes. There's no doctrinal concern with a near death experience, per se. The Church will only get involved in cases which question divine revelation. For instance, if someone claims to have had a near death experience and then asserts something that is clearly contrary to what Our Lord revealed while on earth, something which is written in the bible or the Catechism of the Catholic Church, then there is cause for concern.

"Like what?" he asks.

I stop and think for a moment.

"Well, let's say they come back and say God really doesn't exist, or Jesus is just a made up person, or if He did exist, He was just some guy like any other guy, then that would be against the teachings of the Church."

He nods. "What's the Catechism?"

"It's a summary of everything the Catholic Church believes as it relates to Catholic doctrine on faith and morals. To try and give you an example, it would be like the handbook for the pertinent policies and procedures in the Sheriff's Department. For Catholics, this book is indispensable and is the basis for all Catholic teaching."

He stares out the front, eyes a bit clearer.

"I've told you what the Catholic Church's position is on the matter, and I know you've been through a lot, both physically and spiritually but that reminds me – how long will you be off work because of the accident?"

He looks through the windshield at the darkening evening sky. "The doctors tell me at least three or four weeks. So I guess until the first or second week of May."

"Perfect. That gives us time for the trip in addition to some time for you to do your homework on near death experiences. I encourage you to pick up all you can on the topic. Read both sides, but while you do that, I encourage you to pray before, during and after, asking the Holy Spirit to guide you to the truth.

"Read the stories of researchers who have gone through systematic testing of patients in a very organized, detailed way, in highly controlled environments. From what I do know, for the past 35 years, at least, there's been an enormous amount of data accumulated on these occurrences because there have been a great many scientific studies conducted on them. Read what these professionals, most of whom were originally staunch skeptics, have come to believe and the conclusions they've made as to the authenticity of the cases they studied."

He's nodding, seeing the wisdom of doing more research before he comes to any conclusions about what he went through.

"Heck, you can even take the books on our pilgrimage."

154

"What pilgrimage?"

"You promised, remember? If I did the steps you had me take, and remember I already completed each one of them, then you would do something for me. So you're going to go on the pilgrimage with me."

"Well, you know…"

"Hey, no way. You said you would, and you said your word is good, remember? Plus, you just said you have the time off. The timing will be perfect."

"Yeah, I guess. But if something comes up….."

"Sheriff, you're already off of work so you have plenty of time off. Plus, you need a vacation. Just as you insisted I needed to have my eyes opened, yours need to be opened as well. And while I'm thinking about it, thank you for making me aware of the problem. Really. But, you're going, because you really need to see and experience this."

Leaning his head back, he closes his eyes and remains silent until we get to Martin General Hospital. He chooses to sit in the car and rest rather than go in with me to see how Gina Jerpun is doing.

"I'll tell Michele you said hello if she's there and if you want me to."

He looks away out his side window.

"Uh, okay. Sure. That would be fine. Thanks."

***

Returning to the car 10 minutes later I find the sheriff awake, although his seat is fully reclined.

"That was quick," he says, straining to lift his seat.

"They were running tests on Gina. Poor girl. Bandages everywhere. No one else seemed to be around. I'll try again, but will call next time. It was dumb of me not to do so."

A sudden look of sadness fills his face.

"I've done it before, Father. Don't get all worked up about it. But it's good you tried. She's a very special young lady."

As I pull back onto the freeway, he quickly adds. "We never talked about what you thought about your travels down the sick porn highway on the Internet."

I shake my head in disgust. We've got 90 miles to travel together; plenty of time for this conversation. While I've given it a good deal of thought, especially in light of my conversation with Detective Gambke, I hope this will give me a chance to formulate my thoughts into something which makes sense. He leans his head back and I realize he probably doesn't want to do much of the talking.

"I actually felt nauseated as I went through it. It took me quite a while afterwards to get the images out of my head. But I tell you, I was much more concerned about the souls of every single person that came across the screen."

"Their souls?" he asks, frowning.

"Yes, their souls, Sheriff." I can sense his reluctance, his deep seated hesitation about everything and anything related to a reference to God, even after undergoing his out of body experience.

"Look. The Church teaches that human beings are created in the image and likeness of God. That doesn't mean we have physical characteristics like God, but that we have a soul, a spirit, which is immortal, and when we are conceived in our mother's womb, it is intended from that moment on that we live in Heaven for eternity with God when our lives are through here on earth. But it doesn't always happen, right?"

I'm not asking for an answer, and he's immediately relieved when I continue my train of thought.

"Why? Because we have a free will, we constantly make choices which will either bring us closer to or further away from God and the life He intended for us. However, with the help of God's grace, and if we remain open to it, we can avoid the occasions to sin and lead a good life. When we do sin we have the option to return to God like the prodigal son did in the Bible. But God won't force us to do anything because He loves us too much, and love can never be forced.

"Every single one of us is obliged to do what is good and avoid what is evil. We all know this – it's built into our soul; our conscience. Some choose to follow the wrong path; some don't. Anyone can choose, at any point in their life, to turn to God, or not. You can. I can. There is no middle road. We're either with Him or against Him."

His scowl returns. I'm not certain whether he believes this or if he even *wants* any of them to turn back to God. I continue.

"Do you know what I believe those people are seeking, as well as those who are attracted to those sites on the Internet? Well, at least most of those I saw on the Internet?"

"What?" he responds flatly. I don't believe he likes the direction this conversation is going, but since he opened the door, I'm going to walk through it.

"Happiness. It's a natural, God-given desire," I say.

"So, tell me, Father, what does the all-knowing Catholic Church say is the way to happiness? I mean, is there some Heavenly checklist or something?"

He mockingly raises his arms, hand signing imaginary quote marks around the words "Catholic Church."

"Actually, Our Lord told us directly, and it is in a checklist form, if you will. You can find them in the Gospel of Matthew as the Sermon on the Mount and Luke as the Sermon on the Plain. Do you remember them from your religious education?"

He rolls his eyes. I take it this isn't something he has chosen to remember.

"I'll tell you a few of them. You should look them up for yourself when you have a moment. *'Blessed are the poor in spirit, for theirs is the kingdom of heaven; Blessed are those who mourn, for they shall be comforted; Blessed are the meek, for they shall inherit the earth.'* Once you find the rest, ask me any time if you have any questions about any of them."

"You bet," he says sarcastically, looking out his passenger side window.

"So let's tie in the worldly search for happiness via Internet porn and illicit sex with the teachings of Our Lord via one of the beatitudes.

"One of the Beatitudes is about purity – *'Blessed are the pure in heart, for they shall see God.'* Certainly we think of chastity as it relates to the Sixth Commandment, *'You Shall Not Commit Adultery,'* and that is related with self-control and temperance, virtues we all need to control our natural desires.

"But Our Lord tells us we must not only talk the talk but walk the walk. We cannot simply ask everyone else to be pure. Our own hearts, our own intentions, must be pure as well in everything we do. God doesn't like hypocrites, as we read throughout the Bible. Those people that tell everyone to be good but aren't living their own lives in righteousness aren't exactly God's favorite people. Especially when they act like they're better than everyone else. Their lack of humility and 'holier than thou' attitudes push people away from God, not closer.

"Look at Jesus. He ate with sinners, touched lepers and the sick, spent time with pagans – and that really upset the religious leaders of His day. But He told them, and you can read it for yourself in the Gospel of Mark, that evil comes from within man's heart – evil thoughts, fornication, theft, murder, adultery, covetousness, envy, slander, and pride, among other sins. That's what defiles a man, he tells us."

"Father, I really don't even know what you are saying. Tell me again what all of this has to do with porn?"

I can tell the pain medication he is taking is making it difficult for him to focus.

"It has everything to do with porn. It means we were born with pure souls, and we are intended for Heaven. And throughout our life, we have the freedom, by using our free will, to do the right things or not – to either participate in the filth that's depicted on those websites or to choose to look at it for our own self-serving pleasure – or not. No matter if you are involved or just looking; God will see the hypocrisy because He knows what's in our hearts.

"You see, with freedom comes responsibility, and each one of us needs to stop playing the victim card, blaming everyone else for what we ourselves do in life, as though it is always someone else's fault. The truth is, in most cases, no one can make you do anything you really don't want to do."

"You mean like rape? Are you telling me that women who are raped want it?"

"No! That's not what I am saying at all. I'm talking about normal situations. Of course there are times when things are done

158

out of duress, fear, or even ignorance or habit – maybe even a number of other psychological or social reasons – but I'm saying at the end of the day, God knows what's in our hearts.

"So we, you and me, and all those people involved with that smut, have the freedom to sin. To partake in it. To relish in it. To view it. To act out on it. But we also have the freedom to refuse sin and come back to God. He always welcomes us with open arms. At the end of each day we should ask ourselves, 'How does God think I lived my life today?'"

Sheriff Luder shakes his head now, and I see his eyes wincing from the pain as he says "Cameron Gambke chose to travel that road. I hope he goes to Hell, if there even is a Hell."

"I'm not going to try and tell you how you should feel. Really, I'm not. It's obvious, for whatever reason, you have a great deal of anger against him."

"Gambke hurt a lot of people real bad, real bad!" He bangs his fist on his side passenger door.

"Yes, yes he did. And I know none of this is easy. I commend you for trying to do the right thing with everyone involved. I can see that's a great quality in you. To serve and protect."

He looks at me now, not sure if I'm patronizing him. I'm not.

"Have you ever heard of something called 'Legitimate Defense' within the Church?"

"No. Well, if I did, I don't remember. We have the right to defend ourselves. But are you talking about the whole 'turn the other cheek' thing again?"

"Exactly. We certainly need to be humble and patient in our lives, but we also don't need to be fools or to be someone's doormat. What 'turn the other cheek' really means is we need to fight for justice peacefully, for ourselves and our loved ones. Again, it in no way means we aren't to fight at all. I've heard it said that 'Nothing shames evil more than when you can look it in the eye.'"

I can tell from the look on his face he's starting to feel as though we may be able to find some common ground. I'm not his enemy. I'm actually trying to be a friend. He's going through a lot of physical, spiritual and mental pain, and I pray God will guide him through.

"Each victim has every right to defend themselves. And if they were to kill their aggressor while in the act of being raped while trying to protect themselves, I mean, if that were to happen, anyone could see they were only trying to defend themselves. Legitimate defense. In their minds, they might actually think they might be killed by their attackers because, unfortunately, countless have. So, they can and should know they can fight, and fight like crazy, if they choose to do so.

"Every single member of the human race needs to be protected. I need to protect myself, and I also need to protect others. And every effort must especially be made to protect all those who can't protect themselves, like innocent embryos, children, the elderly, the abused – there are so many I can't even begin to list them all."

"Like, the mentally challenged?" he asks. "Like poor Gina and what that pervert did to her?"

"Yes, undoubtedly, and all the others who are faced with mental and physical challenges. Depending on the severity of their disability, they may or may not be capable of defending themselves. For Gina, I would imagine she may not understand clearly what's right or wrong, especially when she thinks someone loves her."

"I'm with you on that, Father. I really hate all the abusers and want them all to go straight to Hell, if that place really does exist, for all the mistreatment, the mental and physical torture, they have put people through here on earth."

"Hang on a minute. I wouldn't be showing you much love as a fellow Christian if I didn't caution you about that. For your own sake, you need to be careful with all the hate and anger you are carrying for all these people, especially Cameron Gambke. It will be on your own soul on your last day, not his."

"You have no idea what he did!" he snaps.

"I saw the file. You showed it to me," I reply.

"Yeah, but, you still...you just don't know what he did. He should have never done that to Gina. Ever."

"I completely agree. And there's probably more to it than I saw in that file, and I'm not trying to put you down here, okay?

Just listen to me for a minute." I'm really trying to help him understand a different perspective.

"The Fifth Commandment tells us 'Thou Shalt Not Kill' and, like the Beatitudes, it means many things. You see, every life belongs to God, and each one of us can be judged by Him alone, not by us. And each one of us knows murder, fighting, quarreling, using injurious words, causing scandal, anger, hatred, and revenge are wrong. All of this can lead to the injury and spiritual death of our soul and perhaps even of our neighbor. In the end, each one of us should want everyone else on this earth to get to Heaven."

"But you just told me about 'Legitimate Defense' and how we are supposed to protect ourselves from the evils of this world."

"Yeah," I reply, not sure where he is heading.

"So if the bastard did what he did, he should die and go to Hell."

"That's exactly what I'm cautioning you about. Yes, he committed evil acts and the investigation and the courts decided he had to be put away and ultimately have his life taken, but as Christians, we are called to forgive. Yes, we need to protect ourselves, of course. And our government needs to protect us, and that's why he was put behind bars. But when all is said and done, if we are truly Christians and want the best for our neighbor – whoever that neighbor is – we really should want to see everyone's soul in Heaven. If we don't feel it in our heart, then we need to pray to God, and ask Mother Mary to intercede for us, to give us the grace to love our neighbor. Never forget Jesus told us to forgive 'seventy times seven,' meaning; this wasn't a suggestion. So, we must always forgive, at all times, for the sake of our own souls and the sake of others."

"Whatever, Father. He doesn't deserve forgiveness," he says, leaning his head back now, waving his hand to dismiss me, and glancing out the window. I persist.

"We are told to forgive, but that doesn't mean we have to forget. But let me ask you this. Have you ever sinned? I mean, let's just look at the seven capital sins: Pride, Covetousness, Lust, Anger, Envy, Gluttony and Sloth. Or as Bishop Sheen used to say, *'our self-love, inordinate love of money, illicit sex, hate, jealousy, over-*

161

indulgence and laziness.' I don't know of any human being, including myself, who hasn't battled this seven-headed monster at some level at one time or another. Are you telling me you haven't done any of these? At all? Ever?"

He pauses now. "Well, yeah, but not like that."

"Like what?" I press.

"Like the way Gambke did it!"

He's angry again, but for his own good I'm not going to let up.

"As I've said, God knows what's in the heart of every person. He knows all our deeds, so He decides, not you. We are all indebted to God, every single one of us, for we are all sinners. We all have fallen short at times and will continue to do so."

Trying to close the conversation in a gentle way as I pull into his driveway, I add: "Look, get some rest this week. If you feel up to it try and join us this Easter Sunday, or if that doesn't work out, maybe the week after for Divine Mercy Sunday."

Struggling out of the car, he looks at me once more with an expression which clearly shows his displeasure, as though I had just asked him to go and find the person who hit him on his motorcycle and thank her for the pain she's caused him.

"You've said a lot on this trip, and I know you mean well, I really do, Father. But all that shit about Gambke and forgiveness and all? It's all real easy for you to say, but he didn't rape your daughter!"

He slams the door, leaving no chance for further discussion. Was Cameron Gambke the one who hid in his house and raped his teenaged daughter years ago?

162

Chapter 19

Prompted by multiple urgent requests left on my voicemail, I'm meeting with Sheriff Luder at his home. I haven't seen or spoke with him since our trip to the hospital.

Mrs. Luder has prepared dinner and has chosen not to stick around. I wave to her when I arrive. She returns my gesture with a strained smile as she darts down the street in their truck, quickly surpassing the 25 mph speed limit. Within a few minutes of my arrival, the sheriff and I sit down to dinner.

"How was your Easter with Mrs. Luder?" I ask. I didn't see him yesterday at Easter services, but I understand. The journey back to the faith is seldom easy, and its length is entirely dependent on the person, if they choose to take the journey at all.

"Uneventful," he says, pouring me a glass of merlot.

"Listen, my time tonight is limited because I need to get back to the parish for a few late evening meetings, but before we catch up on everything, I would like to invite you again to join us this Sunday for the Divine Mercy Sunday. I can hear your confession any time this week if you would like. It's a day of extraordinary graces...."

He holds up his right hand, causing me to pause.

"I, uh, look......thanks for coming over. I've gone through a whole lot, and I'm not sure if I'm ready for much more happening in my life right now, okay?"

"Not a problem. I certainly didn't mean to offend if I did."

"No, no, you didn't, Father. I really just want to talk to you about where I go from here with this whole near death experience. I know you're very busy, so thanks again for coming over."

"Sure, I understand," taking a bite, my mood improving with each fork full of chicken parmesan. "This is excellent. Mrs. Luder can really cook a great meal, Sheriff."

"Yeah, the wife does real well in that department."

I note since I've known him, he's yet to call his spouse by her name, but it doesn't seem like the time to point it out.

"I took your advice and bought all I could find, or I checked it out from the library, or found it online."

He nods his head towards the stack of books and DVD's on near death experiences neatly stacked on the top of the buffet. I catch a few of the names of the authors: Raymond Moody, Elisabeth Kubler-Ross, Melvin Morse, the National Library of Medicine and other institutional journals are boldly printed on the bindings.

"Now with my head feeling better, and sittin' here at home, I was able to devour all of 'em."

He pauses, finishing his mouthful and washing it down with a drink from his glass.

I wait for him to begin and it appears he's formulating his thoughts. After a few minutes of silence, I nudge him forward.

"And, what did you discover?"

Placing his fork and knife down, he sits back and stares at the centerpiece on the table, a baby's breath centerpiece.

"Well, like anything else, it's across the board. The naysayers, who of course, have never experienced anything like I did, claim they are hallucinations, a result of oxygen deprivation, or can be explained by rational or scientific reasoning. In many cases, they dismiss cases simply because they just haven't had enough time to fully examine the evidence. These are the modern, rational thinkers who once were completely convinced their 'science' could and would reveal a fully explainable universe. They were convinced the nature of the universe was random and unpredictable. They could neither accept nor imagine there was a master design to the universe that was simultaneously ordered and at the same time chaotic. They struggle with the fact our world isn't completely random at all.

"And another group seems to think these hallucinations are drug-induced that involve serious distortions of reality normally accompanied by anxiety or disturbance. But that's not even close to what I felt. From what I remember and what I heard on the tape recorder, all I felt was peace, calm, and clear headedness. I think the drugs *after* I woke up made me much fuzzier. Remember how I sounded on the recorder? So clear, so specific about what I went through?"

"Yes, I remember it distinctly." I offer, swirling the red nectar in my glass.

"Some of the stories I read recounted people who had otherwardly, positive experiences, while others experienced what they said was Hell, the actual place. But one thing for sure, a common theme is they were so moved they turned their lives around completely, either right away or not long after their experience. And there's a significant number of professionals with medical, psychological, or scientific training who believe these experiences are real, very real. Heck, many of the people who had NDE's were those same doctors, scientists and psychologists!"

He laughs now, completely amused by the irony, but I'm not certain why he finds this funny. He himself is still obviously struggling. His anger. His hate. His issues with "religion." I don't doubt he had a moving experience, but I just don't know how deep seated his negative convictions are.

"Have you ever heard of Elisabeth Kubler-Ross?" he asks.

His eyes are alive, full of excitement.

"No," I reply, shaking my head.

"She's dead now, but she was a Swiss-born physician who was raised a Protestant but wasn't really active in her faith. She married a Jewish man, and spent a large amount of time with dying children from the world over, recording their experiences. She found the same experiences, no matter their culture, no matter their religion, if any, and no matter their age.

"Your dad is in a nursing home, right?" His leap from one topic to the other catches me off guard.

"Well, yes, a group home in a residential neighborhood," I hesitatingly reply.

"Right. You can borrow that book from Kubler-Ross." He's pointing now. "The one titled On Death and Dying. And, I thought you would really appreciate this, Father."

He reaches for the book on the side, one it appears he had kept out just for me.

"One guy who went through a near death experience in 1943 said he encountered Christ. He said that Christ communicated to him, not by words or anything, which is exactly how He spoke to me, but almost from heart to heart if you will, or mind to mind, heck, I really can't explain it. But, this guy says Christ made him understand that the purpose of life is to love other human beings. And this guy responds back to Him, 'Well, someone should have told me,' and Christ made known to him very plainly that He indeed did tell him – He told him by the life He lived, and by the death He underwent."

We both sit back now, the sheriff closing the book and putting both hands behind his head, leaning back in his chair. This information doesn't surprise me, but I hope beyond hope Sheriff Luder gets the right message. I stare at the stack of books a few feet away.

"Did you actually read all of that? I mean, it's only been a few days and that's a lot of books."

His eyes refocus on mine as his arms come onto the table in front of him, picking up his dinner knife, playing with it. At least he seems much less defensive than before, and I pray it sticks.

"Yes, and I watched all the DVDs. But there are two things above and beyond all that information I crammed into my head which have convinced me more than anything else this was real."

The knife is being held up now, firmly grasped in his beefy fist.

"Do you remember, on the tape recorder, where I said I saw Cameron Gambke in his cell?"

"Yes."

"I called the prison. He's dead." He bangs the blunt end of the knife on the table as emphasis.

I nod. I'm not going to tell him I already know this from Detective Renae.

"Everything I described, every damn thing, is exactly what they saw when they found him in his cell. What he was wearing, the position his body was in when they found him, all of it."

"Wow," I mutter, my interest piquing.

"And, I compared his time of death with the time I was in the hospital. According to the hospital records, it was exactly when I was in the emergency room when my heart stopped!"

We sit dumbfounded for nearly five minutes. I am fascinated at this point, but then it gets better.

Shaking his head in disbelief, he turns to me and continues.

"Do you remember on the tape where I said I floated to my house and saw some kid in my garage?"

I pause for a moment, trying to remember.

"Remember, you know, the kid in my attic?" He's suddenly exasperated, desperate for me to hear this and believe him.

"Yes, yes, sorry…..now I do, yes," I reply, trying to calm him.

"Well, I checked my gun safe yesterday afternoon. I have no idea how the son of a bitch knew it was even there, but sure as shit it was broken into. All I kept in there were pistols, and they were all gone. He was probably snooping around in my house a ways back, heck, we had him and his family over for barbecues for years. I called his dad, and he checked his room. Nothing. Then I checked with the pawn shops in this town and the surrounding area. The kid isn't a dummy. He spread it out. Two in Rocky Mount, one in Greenville, one in Kinston, and the other three in Jacksonville. Trying to cover his trail. Got the photos this morning from each location – that little ass was the customer. He wasn't as smart as he thought. He's over at juvie right now."

Taking another drink, he stares at me, ensuring I fully grasped the weight of what he is telling me.

"I probably wouldn't have even looked up there for months had it not been for my accident, I guarantee you. By that time the video tape of all those pawn shops would more than likely have been erased and the guns long gone. And, I compared the video tapes and saw he went there the very next day after I had my near death – probably didn't want all the stolen stuff in his room. But I needed more detail, so I talked to him with his parents present and he admitted to the whole thing. Said it had happened after he saw me take the motorcycle out and then after the wife had gone out, too. The time matched *exactly* with when I was lying in the hospital bed, while I was flying around everywhere.

"You can see why I now know all I need to know about my own experience, and no one is going to tell me any different. But now I have no idea what to do next. I believe what I went through was real. I have the evidence. But what in the world does that damn message mean?"

I nod. I do remember the message.

167

He stands now, pacing, rubbing his hands through what's left of his brown, receding hair, repeating what he has since memorized since the accident.

"You have to go back now, my little Danny. But remember, both of you – trust God, live as He wills, help your father, and the others. God loves you, my little Danny."

Eyes wild, his hands grasp the top of one of the six oak dining chairs. I notice he's holding a picture in his hands.

"What in the hell does it mean, Father? Who's 'both of you?' Me and my wife? Me and my daughter? Me and Detective Gambke? Me and who? And help my father? He's been dead a long time. Help the others? Who are the 'others'?"

He's begging me to answer his question, as though as a Catholic priest I have the answers to all of the mysteries of God's glorious universe. I don't, nor does anyone else no matter what they may claim. Noticing I'm trying desperately to strain closer to what he has in his hands, he gives it to me. The shock on my face is immediate.

"What's the matter?" he says.

"Where did you get this? I mean, who is this?" My heart races immediately.

"That's my dad's aunt! The one who came to me." He's incredulous, as though I should be in lock step with all he's been experiencing.

Shaking my head, I say, "I've seen this picture before."

"You've what?!" he shouts.

"I, uh, I can't tell you offhand from where. All I know is I've seen this picture before." I've seen it before, but can't immediately place from where. But why does he have a copy of it, too?

"Do you think she's someone famous? Is my dad's aunt someone famous and that's why you've seen it before? How could you have seen this picture before?" At his urging, I hand the picture back. The sheriff needs answers, is begging for them, yet I can only do so much.

Immediately checking my watch for a reason to leave, I stand. He rises with me.

"Sheriff, I really don't know. It's probably nothing. As a

priest, I see a lot of people. Maybe it's something like that."

Heading for his front door, I continue.

"I've gotta go. There's a lot going on this week at the parish. Will you be here for a while?"

"I'll be here. I guess packin' for that pilgrimage I promised." He sits, his head dropping.

"Good. We'll talk in more detail on the trip, okay? I've got a lot to do to get ready for the trip myself. I hope you and Mrs. Luder have a nice week, and, please thank her for the meal. See you at the airport a week from Friday."

Chapter 20

The rain is coming at me sideways as I enter the Martin General Hospital parking lot, the wiper blades straining to keep up, yet losing the battle. Water runs down my back, sending a shiver up my spine as I stand at the elevator. When I called earlier, a hospital aide answered the phone in Gina's room, telling me Michele had just stepped out but would be returning in a moment.

Detective Gambke had given me the backstory on Michele earlier, cautioning me that she's a hard person to figure out. At least I now feel like I know Michele better than when we first clashed in the Central Prison parking lot. What I've grasped provides a likely justification for her acidic disposition, actions, and the words she spoke to me that day. I hope I can help in some way. How she, or anyone, could have stayed in a marriage to someone like Cameron Gambke is hard to comprehend.

As I enter the hospital room, the image of the Pieta immediately comes to mind. You know, Mother Mary holding the body of her Son, Jesus, looking closely at all that had been done to Him. Michele sits in the bed next to Gina, her arm around her, holding her head. As upon our first meeting, she appears very put together – nicely dressed, every hair in place, makeup applied to perfection. I notice again just how attractive she is. There's no wonder Cameron Gambke was attracted to her.

Her tears appear to be real, and her eyes less harsh than during our first encounter. I relax, but only slightly. Our first meeting isn't tucked too far away into my memory bank.

"Thank you for coming," she says, although from anyone else I might believe the words.

"Of course. I want to tell you how sorry I am for what you are going through; what Gina has been through," I offer.

She nods.

"A computer genius, you know,' she begins, looking back at the still-bandaged head of her daughter. "She's a techie wizard."

I raise my eyebrows in amazement, quickly embarrassed by my immediate doubt. I didn't know anyone with Down syndrome could have that level of intelligence.

Catching my look of surprise, she's suddenly defensive. "Yes, seriously. She's won a number of awards at school. She has two laptops, a Kindle, an iPad, and a variety of other electronic gadgets I can't even begin to name."

Beginning to cry a little more, she adds: "The doctors aren't sure if she'll be able to do any of it when she wakes up."

A minute of silence elapses, then she continues.

"You may be wondering about me. About Gina. About her father."

My real purpose is just to see if they are doing okay, but I'm certainly open if she wants to unload. I sit in the only chair in the room, placing my dripping jacket over the backrest.

"That evil thing was not her father," she says, shades of the old Michele returning, her voice rising, yet immediately lowering into a hiss thinking this might wake Gina.

"Her biological father and I didn't want to have kids. He told me he had a vasectomy done years before, and I was on the pill, but things happen. Then we found out we were pregnant."

"Children are gifts from God," I add, looking at Gina.

I note a quick turn of her head, like a dog does when he's not sure what you're up to, but she doesn't respond to my comment.

"Initially he wasn't happy I was pregnant, but quickly came around to the idea. He said he loved me completely. Said he would love her forever," she says, glancing down once more at the comatose young lady in the bed beside her.

"But when we were informed by the doctors she might be born with this condition, he focused all of his fury on me, like it was all my fault. But even though they all tried to talk me out of it, I wanted my baby girl. I just couldn't kill her."

She begins to sob.

"I mean, they all talked like I was deciding on whether I should get a flu shot or maybe my teeth cleaned, they were so methodical and uncaring about it."

"You made a good decision, Michele."

"Of course I made a good decision," she snaps. "I was so happy I was pregnant, but when I got the news about her condition I was crushed. He kept trying to talk me into terminating the pregnancy, and stressed how screwed up our lives were going to be. At first I listened to him, because I was still trying to save our relationship. But when I told him I was going to keep her, he left. Just like that. He slowly came around, but it changed everything in our lives.

"I really had no idea what I was getting into. At first, I didn't know anything about Down syndrome. So I consumed all the books and articles I could find. I talked to agencies everywhere. I mean, it's pretty simple. Her condition is called trisomy 21, and it means she has a third chromosome where most people just have two.

"But the bills! I had read children with Down syndrome could have multiple surgeries because their bodies aren't fully developed at birth, but I had no idea, not a clue. I was on maternity leave and although he would give me some money and offered to pay for different things, he said he was limited because he already had many other financial commitments.

"She was always sick. Her low immune system let her catch everything. Even to this day I have to be so careful who she's around, and school makes it especially challenging. But it's gotten better with medical advances. She had to have three open heart surgeries before she was even two years old. I'm surprised everyone in health care isn't driving Jaguars with all the money we've paid!"

Through intermittent sobs, she continues.

"But one day, not long after she was born, I was sitting in another doctor's office waiting for another round of test results while Gina napped. I was thinking about my life and my future, and realized I hated her. My pity party gained full steam. I thought of all the young bitches out there who get pregnant, assuring everyone they had only had sex that one time and somehow they got pregnant when it's so hard for many other women who really *want* kids, but can't, after trying everything under the sun. Then I thought about all those children aborted by those same shithead girls, and how it really seemed like the best solution for them at the time, and it hit me maybe they were right.

Maybe I should have had the damn abortion, too. Then I thought about her father and all those other little pricks who got all those girls pregnant but are indifferent motherfuckers. And at that point, I began to hate all men, and all those lying little girls, and the piece of shit men and boys. I began to hate the world.

"Then Gina woke up, right at that very moment, and smiled. Then she laughed. I knew that even though people all around me were bailing right and left on their responsibilities, I would never, ever leave Gina. She needs me and I need her. We are alone, together. No matter what, she's definitely been the brightest sun that has ever shone in my world, and I stopped looking back, asking 'what if' questions. I embraced our life together," she pauses, "and then the bastards got to her."

Hugging the listless body tightly, she kisses the bandages on her head. She's quiet for a few moments before continuing.

"You know, on my worse days, when I look at her I can't help but smile. Man, she is determined to survive. Everything has been a challenge for her. Learning sign language. Trying to express her desires to me early on and me not understanding even though I was trying like mad to do so. Falling and getting right back up. But people can be incredibly cruel, and it doesn't matter their age. Pointing, making comments, and looking at me as though I should have done the right, decent thing by aborting her. Our lives are a piece of cake compared to hers, and yet, every morning she wakes up with a smile, happy and looking forward to her day. And every night, she always gives me a huge hug and says 'I love you, Mommy!' before she climbs into bed with her favorite animal, her cat 'Mr. Fatty.' I cry now, but only because I can't believe I almost aborted her."

Holding Gina tighter, her tears flow freely. Five minutes go by in silence and I grab my jacket and stand, preparing to leave. She has more to say to me so I sit back down, not wanting to rush her.

"And then I married Cameron Gambke. He was charming. Intelligent. Witty when he needed to be. He said all the right things all the time. The courtship was right out of the books – wine, dinners, dancing – and the sex was beyond what I could have ever imagined. He didn't believe in marriage, but I wanted the ring and the legal benefits the ceremony would assure for me and my little girl."

She turns her head toward the window as the rain continues to pound against it.

"And he had money, lots of it. I was tired of living alone, afraid of not being able to pay our bills, and he came just at the right time. Her biological father didn't like it one bit, he was incensed. I reminded him a million times he had chosen his path, and I had to choose ours.

"But with Cameron, I should have known early on I should have bailed. I mean, he was nice to Gina, but after he moved in it was all about the sex. Every moment of every day, it seemed. A few times Gina walked in on us, which wasn't really hard for her to do because we would be in the kitchen, in the hallway, even in the backyard on the lawn furniture. She didn't seem to understand so he would just keep right at it."

Her matter of fact tone about this part of her past life gives me an inkling she also doesn't seem to think this was completely inappropriate for Gina to witness. Her focused comments seem more locked on Cameron and his responsibility in all this.

"You met him. You saw him. Hell, you talked to him at the prison. But I'm sure he fooled you, too. I agreed early on to some light bondage play, but the night he whipped me I told him to get out. The next week he couldn't apologize enough, the bastard. And I fell for it. We were finally married two weeks later. And then…" she places her free hand over her eyes, "my entire world exploded."

Turning back to the window, her eyes glaze over as she remembers.

"The whippings continued, and the sexual bondage intensified. One day he ordered me to stand in the backyard in broad daylight and masturbate or else he would leave me. I wouldn't do it. But he knew my financial situation. My insurance was really screwed up. Although he had paid more than $100,000 by then, I still owed over $60,000 in medical bills.

"He locked me up that night in a room he kept in our

basement for his sex toys. I remember Gina crying, over and over, because she couldn't find me. He let me out when I promised I would do whatever he wanted. After that, he rammed so many different things up my vagina, if I had to I couldn't list them all. But he was never happy, always angry, always depressed. He hated his mom and his sister. I really think he hated all women. And the more I tried to make him happy, the worse it got. Towards the end, he made me drink dog urine, and then tried to force the dog's shit down my mouth but it only ended up in my eyes and hair. He beat me then, and peed all over my face telling me I had to sleep like that."

She runs her hand over her face now, absentmindedly trying to wipe away the memory. I wonder if Detective Renae knows about all this.

I'm screaming inside, wanting to ask her why she just didn't leave. But I know the answer. I've spoken to far too many abused women before. Go where? Do what? And will the abuse stop? Ever? Will they always have to live their lives like this? I've heard the questions many times, and am grateful many of them did break out, did escape, and are thriving in life. I wonder if she knows Cameron Gambke is dead.

"It wasn't until much later that I heard of his history – what he did to that poor girl in Idaho and those other two girls. That could have been me, you know."

Remembering what I saw on his favorite websites, I have to ask.

"Did he attempt erotic asphyxiation with you, too?"

She responds without hesitation.

"Once. I told him never again, no matter if he beat me. No, he used me for other things. Like enemas or rape scenarios since it really turned him on, he said."

She was his guinea pig, and when she didn't cooperate or when his interest waned, he ventured out. This absolute beauty in front of me wasn't enough for Cameron Gambke. By the time he was caught, his level of sickness was far advanced. I now share Detective Renae's thought process – how many more victims of his are still out there?

"I'm really hesitant to ask this, and I really do apologize in advance, but did he do any of these warped, perverted things to Gina?" I hold my breath now, hoping her answer is 'no', but for some reason needing to know the real truth even though Sheriff Luder had let me see his "official" file.

Her reaction is quick. "Not that I know of, but if he ever did and I knew about it, I would have killed the motherfucker." Her tone is direct; she means every word of it.

"He did do something much more sinister with her, though. He taught her things she didn't need to know; things she will forever think are appropriate, I'm sure. The night I left him for good, the same night he went on his business trip to Idaho, I had come back home in the late afternoon just about ten minutes after I had left for the store because I had forgotten my checkbook. Gina was home from school because I had picked her up and dropped her off at home – she said she didn't want to go to the store with me, that she just wanted to stay with Cameron. Well, I walked into our bedroom and caught both of them naked in our bed!"

I look at bandaged Gina Jerpun, her Down syndrome features still evident, and begin to feel nauseous, imagining the scene. Michele lays Gina's head onto the pill, and moves to the window, opening it slightly to feel the moisture against her skin.

"This apparently wasn't the first time, either. I screamed and dragged Gina to her room. When I came back, he just sat there, his erection plainly evident. He said they had been doing this for about a year, and he was merely teaching her about sex because she needed to know before any of the boys at school tried to take advantage of her. He tried to convince me he was doing her and me a favor, that this was a good thing, that I should actually thank him for keeping her from getting pregnant from an irresponsible boy. Instead, I belted him, and ended up in the hospital with a concussion. He told the police I attacked him and he was only 'protecting himself.'"

"Did you press charges?"

"Of course I pressed charges! Hell, if there wasn't a chance I would go to prison, I would have killed him then, but there's no way I was going to let Gina lose her mother." She's not

176

whispering now, but Gina doesn't budge.

"The responding officer said it was merely a domestic dispute. I reported what I saw and what I did from the E/R room, but that bastard told them nothing had happened between him and Gina. Denied it all. They talked to Gina, but since he had threatened her if she ever told – that he would never love her again if she told on him which probably really tore her heart out – she also denied it all. So, nothing happened. But, bills or no bills, I had to get us away from him.

"Then I reached out to Sheriff Luder, but it still went nowhere. Oh, he wanted to kill him, but it was Cameron's word against mine, and since Gina wouldn't testify, it would have gone nowhere in court."

It's now beginning to make sense to me why the sheriff has harbored such hate for Cameron Gambke. I'm also beginning to see the connection between him and Michele that day in the execution viewing room. He can't stand people like Gambke because he sees the likes of him every day, and she was manipulated, used, and abused by the same kind of monster.

"At least he's finally dead," she says flatly. So she does know what happened to him.

"I am really very sorry for all of this. I hope they find out who did this to Gina soon," I reply.

"He will. And it better not be who I think it was." Her gaze is distant. Her expression one of steel.

I want to ask for details, but choose not to. Instead, I offer help.

"Is there anything I can do? Do you need anything at all?"

Once more, Michele Jerpun throws me. Gliding from the window, she approaches me as I rise from my chair, the glistening in her eyes rapidly evaporating. I move away from her towards the door, recalling her seductive move the first time we met. She pauses, immediately recognizing my hesitancy.

"You know, there is some Cherry Vitamin Water in the vending machine downstairs. They don't sell any in the cafeteria, but maybe there is some in the machine near E/R. Would you mind?"

"No, not at all," I reply, happy to be of assistance, and pleased to be able to leave quickly.

During the next 45 minutes I discover there are 16 different vending machines throughout this hospital. None of them carry the Cherry Vitamin Water she's referring to. In fact, the staff tells me they've never carried it. Not wanting to make Michele's day worse, I go into the worsening rain and drive about five blocks until I find a convenience store. An hour later, with 15 minutes to visitor closing time, I trudge back into the hospital lobby, hoping Michele is still there.

Quietly pushing open the door to Gina's hospital room, I see her sitting in the chair I had vacated not long ago.

"I finally found it for you," I say, reaching towards her. "I'm really sorry it took me so long. Apparently they don't..."

Without meeting my gaze, she rises and heads towards the window as I blurt out the reason for my tardiness.

"I never drink that shit. It's disgusting."

She waves me away, as though I am a slave who has disappointed her Majesty with my feeble efforts.

Chapter 21

It's Divine Mercy Sunday! For Christians, there is no greater feast in the world than Easter, and the grand finale is the eighth day of the Octave of Easter. Today, every single person is given the opportunity to truly and more completely receive the gifts of forgiveness, salvation, and eternal life in Heaven that Our Lord gave the entire world.

You may recall that the Feast of Mercy has been observed since the earliest days of the Church. St. Thomas the Apostle wrote in the Apostolic Constitutions that:

"After eight days (following the feast of Easter) let there be another feast observed with honor, the eighth day itself on which He gave me, Thomas, who was hard of belief, full assurance, by showing me the print of the nails, and the wound made in His side by the spear."

But it has its roots in the Old Testament when the Lord told Moses:

"… on this day atonement is made for you to make you clean, so that you may be cleansed of all your sins before the LORD, by everlasting ordinance it shall be a most solemn Sabbath for you, on which you must mortify yourselves" [Leviticus 16:30-31]

And the Lord later told Moses:

"The tenth of this seventh month is the Day of Atonement, when you shall hold a sacred assembly and mortify yourselves and offer an oblation to the LORD. On this day you shall not do any work, because it is the Day of Atonement, when atonement is made for you before the LORD, your God." [Leviticus 23:27:28]

But do you remember how and when Divine Mercy Sunday came about? Our Lord appeared to St. Faustina Kowalska on many occasions. She wrote all He told her in her diary. Blessed

Pope John Paul II canonized her on May 5, 2000, the same day he established Divine Mercy Sunday as a feast day for the entire church.

This is what Our Lord told her, as it relates to Purgatory:

"My mercy does not want this, but justice demands it."

Getting back to this great feast day, it is a day when we, like the ancient Jews, are offered the opportunity to prepare for judgment and offer atonement for all our sins. To receive forgiveness we must go to Confession and receive Holy Communion. In order to prepare for the Feast of Mercy, we are asked to pray the Divine Mercy Chaplet as either a perpetual novena or one that begins on Good Friday, as we do in our parish. I pray the Divine Chaplet every day at 3:00 using Rosary Beads and hope you're still doing the same.

Our Lord instructed St. Faustina to first say one "Our Father," one "Hail Mary," and one "Apostles Creed" Then on the large beads, He told her to say the following words:

"Eternal Father, I offer You the Body and Blood, Soul and Divinity of Your dearly beloved Son, Our Lord Jesus Christ, in atonement for our sins and those of the whole world."

On the smaller beads, she was told to say:

"For the sake of His sorrowful Passion, have mercy on us and on the whole world."

He asked her to meditate on the Sorrowful mysteries of the Rosary as she prayed each decade. She was then instructed to say these words three times at the conclusion:

"Holy God, Holy Mighty One, Holy Immortal One, have mercy on us and on the whole world."

Jesus later told St. Faustina:

"Say unceasingly this chaplet that I have taught you. Anyone who says it will receive great Mercy at the hour of death. Priests will recommend it to sinners as the last hope. Even the most hardened sinner, if he recites this Chaplet even once, will receive grace from My Infinite Mercy. I want the whole world to know My Infinite Mercy. I want to give unimaginable graces to those who trust in My Mercy..."

He also told her:

"...When they say this Chaplet in the presence of the dying, I will stand between My Father and the dying person not as the just judge but as the Merciful Savior."

As Our Lord taught St. Faustina this Chaplet, He also gave her 14 revelations concerning the feast He desired, the feast we celebrate today. I would like to make note of a few of the diary entries in case you have forgotten:

Entry 699

"My daughter, tell the whole world about My inconceivable mercy. I desire that the Feast of Mercy be a refuge and a shelter for all souls, and especially for poor sinners. On that day the very depths of My tender mercy are open. I pour out a whole ocean of graces upon those souls who approach the fount of My mercy.

The soul that will go to Confession and receive Holy Communion shall obtain complete forgiveness of sins and punishment. On that day are opened all the divine floodgates through which graces flow. Let no soul fear to draw near to Me, even though its sins be as scarlet.

My mercy is so great that no mind, be it of man or of angel, will be able to fathom it throughout all eternity. Everything that exists has come from the very depths of My most tender mercy. Every soul in its relation to Me will contemplate My love and mercy throughout eternity.

The Feast of Mercy emerged from My very depths of tenderness. It is My desire that it be solemnly celebrated on the first Sunday after Easter. Mankind will not have peace until it turns to the Fount of My mercy."

Entry 341 (The Image of Jesus; The Divine Mercy)

"I want the Image to be solemnly blessed on the first Sunday after Easter, and I want it to be venerated publicly so that every soul may know about it."

Entry 1109; 300; and 699, respectively (Our Lord's promise to grant complete forgiveness of sins and punishment on the Feast of Mercy)

"I want to grant a complete pardon to the souls that will go to Confession and receive Holy Communion on the Feast of My mercy;"

"Whoever approaches the Fountain of Life on this day will be granted complete forgiveness of sins and punishment;"

"The soul that will go to Confession and receive Holy Communion will obtain complete forgiveness of sins and punishment."

Entry 742 (He will grant us His mercy, but we must be merciful to others)

"Yes, the first Sunday after Easter is the Feast of Mercy, but there must also be acts of mercy…..I demand from you deeds of mercy, which are to arise out of love for Me. You are to show mercy to your neighbors always and everywhere. You must not shrink from this or try to excuse or absolve yourself from it."

So on this day, wherever you may be and no matter the year, I pray that you remain devoted to this special feast day, Divine Mercy Sunday. The gifts you receive are the salvation of your soul and eternal life in Heaven. But remember, you must have sincerely repented of all of your sins. God is no fool – He knows what's in your heart. Remember also that you must go to confession, preferably before this day, or as close to it as you can; receive Holy Communion; venerate the Sacred Image of The Divine Mercy; and be merciful to others, through your actions, words, and prayers on their behalf.

It is most certainly "FRESH START SUNDAY!"

Chapter 22

Sheriff Luder is seated next to me on our flight overseas. I haven't slept well the past few nights, and the coffee is only making me jittery. The stress in preparing for the trip, the anxiety wondering if I'm going to get ill along the way, and the pressure of what awaits me when I get back home, are all making me tense.

Before I left, Father Bernard, while supportive of my commitment to the pilgrimage, reminded me of all the work that will be awaiting my return. The largest, and the one that will require most of my time and energy, will be the Capital Contribution Campaign to help finance the construction of the new Church.

During my business days I would grab onto a project like this with both hands and wrestle it until it was properly completed. Now I'm hesitant, knowing that when I dive in I will give it all I've got. And that, I know, will unleash a flood of anxious feelings, high blood pressure, and a range of negative emotions that I'm not sure I'm prepared to re-experience any time soon.

"I leave all this in your hands, Lord," I pray, sitting back into my seat and gazing out the window.

Breaking through the rain clouds that blanket much of North Carolina, our plane levels off as it reaches cruising altitude. We fly towards the welcoming sun. I instinctively relax at the site of this beautiful scene. Distraction is often a good thing, especially when I'm worrying.

I've picked up a copy of "Paideia" written by Thomas Victor, the book that Cameron Gambke mentioned in his letter to Detective Renae, the one he claimed had a powerful impact on his life. I plan to read some or all of it during the trip. I'm hoping it will shed some light on Gambke, and maybe I will then be better able to help his daughter. The sheriff glances at the book, but has other things on his mind. "I need to get something off my chest before we head down this circus of a journey."

"Circus of a journey?"

"Yeah, you know, traveling all around and going to different places where people are all probably praying and trying to save my soul."

"Ah, yes," I say. Here we go. You would think after his NDE he would be fired up to go. How tight are the metal mental chains around his heart? "I hate to break it to you, Sheriff, but I would imagine that although many of the people you meet are kind and loving and want the best for you, they're more than likely thinking much more about themselves and their families and friends. Sure they're praying for you in general as a sinner, but they're praying for everybody else, too. Sorry to disappoint you, but not everyone spends their entire day just thinking about you."

"I didn't say that."

He sure as heck is thinking it, I'm certain. I'm not going to argue, but I can see once more he isn't comfortable with being put in his place.

"Anyway, look, I do believe there is *something* else out there, I just don't know what that is, and the NDE drove that home. But ... oh hell; I'm just going to come out and say this, no matter how stupid it sounds. My problem with all of this is that I just don't believe in organized religion at all. None of it. Men and women telling other men and women how to live their lives."

"But you said you spoke with Jesus," I point out.

"Well, I know I said that on the tape recorder, but maybe it was just an image from my early childhood religious education that was effectively burned into my memory banks. I mean, I know I went through something, something very real. But everyone wants to just say it's 'God' or "Jesus,' and I don't think it's that simple of an answer. I mean, I've seen way too many things in my life to think otherwise. I don't get the religious fanatics, for example. You know, all that's done in 'the name of God.' All it feels like to me is people trying to control other people. And all the pain, suffering and evil. What about all of that?" He shakes his head, the shackles of his old convictions not willing to release his head and heart.

"I agree with you. It irritates me more than you might possibly know. I get attacked by people who simply misunderstand or who have serious misconceptions all the time, especially when I am wearing my clerics."

He seems surprised that I didn't jump on him.

"Look, Father, you seem like a reasonable man, and we have a relatively long flight. May I ask why you believe?"

"Well, sure. Not a problem." I pause, trying to formulate my words as best I can before continuing.

"When I was growing up, I was baptized, attended Catechism classes, received my First Holy Communion, went to Confession, was an altar boy, and attended Mass on most Sundays. But I noticed that not much in the real world seemed to match up with what I was being taught. So I watched. I observed.

"My parents made me go to Catechism, but what I was being taught didn't match with how my parents or other adults around me were living their lives. Even the priests – wow, there were times I was amazed at the things they said about their own parishioners! It wasn't until much later, after I grew up, that I realized everyone sins, that we all fall. I mean, I look at how many times I've fallen in my life, especially now as a priest, and yet I know God still loves me and wants me to get back up and try again."

I sense that I'm getting off track, but he appears to continue to listen attentively.

"As I got older things began to happen around me. In middle and high school drugs were becoming very popular. Sex was a big thing, too. No one ever mentioned God, ever, especially those CCD classmates I knew personally growing up. So, I saw the hypocrisy of it all. I became jaded, kind of numb to the whole 'God and religion' thing.

"Fortunately, as it turned out, my parents' efforts to instill in me an understanding of God, Heaven, Purgatory and Hell faintly stuck with me, so in my high school and college days I kept one foot in Church as a 'good Catholic boy' and the other foot in the world – parties, drugs, girlfriends, fun – playing the odds. Like everyone else at that age, I wanted to be accepted by my peers, plain and simple, and that was much more important than what God thought of me. Plus, I knew He would forgive me, and that was a dangerous thought, because I lived my life as though no matter what I did or didn't do, I was going to Heaven. Repentance? Penance? Living the way He wanted? Please. There was no need as far as I was concerned."

I shake my head, saying a silent prayer that the Good Lord saved me before He decided it was time for my life here on earth to end.

"So what happened?" he asks, obviously still interested in what I am saying.

"Some friends started dropping, you know, dying. Not friends of my family or older people I knew, but my friends. My age. Drug overdoses. Car and motorcycle accidents. AIDS. And it all began to hit home. I started to really look again at Catholicism because I figured all of this bad stuff couldn't be all there was to life. The good, healthy side of fear kicked in, the respect of the Lord."

As I begin to remember those earlier years, the dendrites in my brain begin firing on all cylinders. "You know, let me add to that. What I really remember, and what just hit me, is that I needed God. I mean, I was scared. So I began praying like crazy, making deals with God. 'If you do this for me, I will do this for you' sort of thing. But, sadly, whenever things were good, I would return to my old ways. I actually had the audacity to ask God to bless my sinful activities, you know, to keep me safe as I did whatever I pleased in life. And when things got bad again, all because of me, not Him, then I would pray all the more. I needed God, but only on my terms. Almost like a slot machine. Insert coin, hope to get a jackpot. Insert prayer, hope to get my prayer answered. I had a prayer life, yes, but a very immature one. A personal relationship with God where He was my best friend because He loved me so much and wanted the best for me if only I would listen and see the road He clearly laid out for me? Not even close.

"About that time I 'graduated' into the business world, worked at a million-miles-an-hour pace, and excelled at the backstabbing political games, traveling the golden path that all my college professors taught was the ultimate endgame. Then it all changed.

"I came down with a really bad virus that put me in the

hospital for weeks, and everyone thought I might be paralyzed for life. I'd never prayed so much or so hard in my life. People I didn't even know were praying for me. Eventually I regained my health and came out of it unscathed, but it was my wakeup call. My health was very, very important to me and that was the one sure way God knew to get my attention. I really believe that to be true to this day."

I look at him now, hoping he'll see that maybe his NDE was his wakeup call. He got a message – I'm sure of it – but will he interpret it correctly? Or will his analytical and jaded mind continue to rule his very being? He is silent, but his eyes are locked on mine.

"So at that point in my life I found myself at a crossroad. I believed I had two choices, either the seminary or marriage. I chose the priesthood or, more specifically, it chose me."

I notice him checking his watch. Maybe I'm not getting to the point quickly enough. Or maybe he doesn't like what he's hearing, as though what I went through in my life has nothing to do with what he's gone through in his. If so, then why did he bother to ask?

"As I said, I just knew there was 'something' out there, I felt it. Even though I was fully immersed in the ways of this world, I kept searching. I read St. Thomas Aquinas' Summa Theologiae, in which he postulated five proofs for the existence of God. For instance, he argued that there is a need for a 'prime mover' in the universe. There's a need for a 'first cause' – that nothing begins to exist without a cause. There is a need for a 'Necessary Being' to have put this into motion. There is a need for a 'Supremely Perfect Being' that is omnipotent in order to put our world together as perfectly as it has been. And, ultimately, there is a need for an 'Intelligent Designer.' This really made sense to me."

He's nodding his head, and maybe his recent research on NDE's is seeming more relevant.

"Now bear with me for a moment, but I gotta tell ya, I began to seriously look at these proofs. For whatever reason, *that* clicked with me. More specifically, I remembered from my Catechism days that God revealed Himself to us; He has never, then or now, removed Himself from us. For instance, from my school and college astronomy and geography classes I could see in the material realm all the beautiful things on this earth and in our universe that God made.

"And the natural moral law that He put into our hearts, our 'voice of conscience' also made more sense to me. I knew that no matter how much I lied to everyone around me, I couldn't avoid the fact that I really did know right from wrong.

"Then, I really delved into Sacred Scripture to see how Our Lord gave us the ultimately example to follow – Him.

"Finally, I looked at Sacred Tradition, the wisdom passed down by the Apostles, who were with Our Lord while He was here on earth, the Church Fathers, and their successors. I was amazed at what they knew then, and how it applies now.

"Ultimately I began to see that as our knowledge and understanding of the world around us grew and as new discoveries opened our minds to new ideas – topics on human embryos or euthanasia, for example – the Church's teaching naturally evolved, as well, to address them. So any reasonable person, especially someone like me who isn't the sharpest person around, could see that there was so much more than happenstance going on.

"In seminary, I discovered the harmony that existed between faith and science. I read important pieces by Nobel Prize winners, Templeton Prize winners, Harvard and other scholarly physicists, biologists, scientists, cosmologists – all these learned people – who were leaning towards an intelligent designer because everything they were seeing pointed not away from that, but towards it. So many people were coming to the conclusion that this world had been designed so meticulously in order to support life as we know it. They had come to believe that our existence, on this one planet capable of supporting life like ours, among all the other planets in the universe, was truly miraculous.

"In the end, I was profoundly moved by how these people admit they just don't have the tools – and probably never will – to give solid answers to all of these questions. They have begun to acknowledge that something exists that is much greater, and infinitely more intelligent, than man."

"What about the Big Bang theory?" he asks. "How can you argue that one?" His face remains passive, his tone accusatory.

"The Church has no problem with the Big Bang theory because that event was orchestrated by the Intelligent Designer – God. I mean, science has discovered order in the universe and has identified the intricate and necessary balance that must exist for our world, our universe, and life itself to be sustained. Even metaphysics is showing that the universe could not have created itself out of nothing. I mean, nothing is nothing!

His face is expressionless, so I finish my long-winded response to his question.

"In the end, I finally saw that I was getting right back to where He had been leading me all along – back to Him. I became humble and realized God is God, and I am not."

He's brooding now, struggling with what I've told him.

"I don't know, Father, it all sounds very sci-fi and made up to me. Very controlling."

"Look, you asked me to be open-minded about how bad sexual sin is in this world. No, I take that back, you challenged me. You were right. I had an inkling, but I had no idea the extent of the muck. But by the same token, I now reiterate my challenge for you to do the same thing on this trip. See the bigger world, the bigger picture. God said there would be darkness, but there is also light everywhere that He is shining to give the world hope, guidance, and comfort."

"I know, Father, and I'm here. But tell me this. What about the need for evil and suffering, okay? This 'Great God' you keep talking about that has changed your whole world must only be focusing on you, 'cuz I can't see it."

"It's a very common question, but let me just say a few things that you might want to meditate on. This goes back to man's free will. It's a fabulous gift that God has given us but when human beings misuse it, then we all suffer. But is that God's fault?"

"So why doesn't God protect everyone all the time, all the believers?" He claps his hands on his knees.

"I don't know the answer to that, Sheriff, but someday I may, at the Last Judgment."

A smirk crosses his face. He thinks he's got me in a corner. I continue.

"Just because I don't have the full answer to God's mysterious plan doesn't mean you are right to not believe in Him or His existence. I've already shared all the reasons to believe in Him. And look at all the good around you, and there is great good.

"But back to suffering. Look at the value it has brought in my own life. The suffering I went through actually made me stronger, wiser, and more empathetic to those around me. It's probably had that kind of an impact on you, too."

He's rapidly shaking his head, vehemently disagreeing. "What about all the needless suffering around the world? Is that supposed to somehow mold the character of all those poor people?"

"Sheriff, I'm not going to argue with you because, like I already said, I can't fully explain it, but I most certainly feel the pain of all those around me, just like you. And I do agree with you to some extent – we've both seen things in our lives that we just can't explain. You'll never know how many times I've looked to God, hoping for an explanation, yet unable to find one. But I pray I never lose hope that it's there even though my finite mind can't grasp it. Not meaning to sound trite, but to suffer is to be human. At least believers have hope and answers for suffering through the Bible and Sacred Tradition that help us to understand its purpose, if only dimly.

"Look, we are meant to be the body of Christ – His arms, His feet, His legs, His mouth, His ears – with God's grace, each one of us can do a great deal to relieve the suffering of others. That, too, is part of God's plan. He wants us to love others as much as we love ourselves. Suffering can serve a positive purpose when we learn to turn outward from our own lives and learn to help others. God gave us the ability to be sympathetic and empathetic for a reason so we can care, so we can help those in need."

The flight crew begins their landing procedures, and everyone dutifully returns their trays to their upright position, stowing away anything they took out for the flight.

Looking out the window, I gaze at the New York City skyline, and am reminded of that infamous day of September 11th, slightly over a decade ago, when the horizon of the city looked very different – dark, smoky, and hostile. I remind myself once more – trust God, for He was here that horrific day, and He is here now and forevermore.

Looking towards the same skyline, Sheriff Luder takes a parting shot. "I'll bet you priests and all your religious co-workers had a real challenge talking to your little scared sheep after 9/11."

My eyes lock with his. "We walk by faith, Sheriff, not by sight, and faith is a gift from God if only we ask."

He snorts, laying his head back. I pray God gives him this gift, because my words don't seem to be making a bit of difference.

Chapter 23

It's Sunday morning in Rome. We arrived yesterday morning from the States and spent the past 24 hours acclimating ourselves to the weather and time zone change. I had the opportunity to eat some good Italian food and drank plenty of water to flush out my system just in case any foreign microbes are preparing for an attack.

A short bus ride took us to our first approved Marian apparition site, the Basilica Sant'Andrea delle Fratte. Everyone has disembarked and stretched and now we have regrouped at the rear of the Basilica surrounded by the daily flurry of accompanying tourists. Sheriff Luder straggles in the back, yet I'm glad he's here to hear this story.

I share that Marie Alphonse Ratisbonne was a Jewish man with strong anti-Catholic views. He was an heir to an aristocratic family of Jewish bankers. His oldest brother had decided to not only join the Catholic faith but to become a priest. This caused a great rift in his family and, because of this, he hated the Catholic faith and, quite literally, everything Catholic.

He ran into a Baron while touring Rome who challenged him to a test – to wear a medal of the Virgin Mary, the "Miraculous Medal" – in addition to praying the Memorare every morning and evening. He mockingly agreed to do so.

Most of the heads nod, some reaching around their neck and pulling their own 'Miraculous Medals' out, sacramentals they have probably been wearing faithfully for decades.

The Baron also turned to a great number of his own friends asking them to pray for the conversion of Mr. Ratisbonne.

"Not long after, the Baron saw Mr. Ratisbonne on his knees in prayer in this Church which, of course, shocked the Baron and brought him to tears."

I turn to my own packet of notes that I've developed from previous pilgrimages.

"In his own words, this is what Marie Alphonse Ratisbonne told the Baron what had happened to him:

'I was scarcely in the church when a total confusion came over me. When I looked up, it seemed to me that the entire church had been swallowed up in shadow, except one chapel. It was as though all the light was concentrated in that single place. I looked over towards this chapel whence so much light shone, and above the altar was a living figure, tall, majestic, beautiful and full of mercy. It was the most holy Virgin Mary, resembling her figure on the Miraculous Medal. At this sight I fell on my knees right where I stood. Unable to look up because of the blinding light, I fixed my glance on her hands, and in them I could read the expression of mercy and pardon. In the presence of the Most Blessed Virgin, even though she did not speak a word to me, I understood the frightful situation I was in, my sins and the beauty of the Catholic Faith.'"

A frown starts to form on the sheriff's face. Moving away from the crowd he begins to wander aimlessly through the Basilica.

Unfazed, I share with the group that Mr. Ratisbonne was then taken by the Baron to a priest. He was sobbing a great deal, but he finally pulled out the Miraculous Medal and told the priest that the lady he saw in the church was the lady on the medal. Mr. Ratisbonne gave his confession at that moment to the priest, and eventually was baptized and confirmed into the Catholic Church and received his first Holy Communion. Knowing his entire world of family and friends would mock him, he entered the convent of the Jesuits for a retreat. Under the direction of Mr. Ratisbonne, a canvas was painted of Our Lady by a famous painter in the exact image he remembered. When it was completed it was placed in the spot where the apparition had occurred.

"Over time, there were so many miracles attributed to Mary that the Shrine was elevated to a Basilica, and was then ennobled to a Cardinal's church. This is where we stand today, right here, right now. After a thorough investigation, the apparitions were approved by the Holy See on June 3, 1842. The late Pope John Paul II visited this Basilica on February 28, 1982."

As we leave the Basilica, in the front of a side alcove housing a statue of the Blessed Virgin Mary, a group of pilgrims, led by a Filipino priest is praying the "Memorare."

"Remember, O most gracious Virgin Mary, that never was it known that anyone who fled to your protection, implored your help, or sought your intercession was left unaided. Inspired by this confidence, we fly unto you, O Virgin of virgins, our Mother! To you we come, before you we stand, sinful and sorrowful. O Mother of the Word incarnate, despise not our petitions, but in your mercy hear and answer us. Amen."

Entering the tour bus for the 12-hour ride ahead of us, I see the sheriff, his head buried in the tour book, absentmindedly turning the pages. He doesn't make eye contact with me. I'm struck by how much this grown man is behaving like a spoiled little boy, clearly not wanting to be here but also making sure everyone around knows it.

Chapter 24

Yesterday, the bus ride to the town of Laus, at the bottom of the French Alps, lifted my already buoyed spirits. The surrounding mountainside views were breathtaking. I felt the peace of God within me as we traveled through His beautiful creation. I took in as much as I could before the sun went down and darkness fell.

Gathering outside this morning on a grassy knoll under a clear sky and gentle sun, and gratefully noticing that the sheriff is present and accounted for, I begin.

"For 54 years – from 1664 to 1718 – the Virgin Mary appeared to Benoite Rencurel, who was also known as Benedicta. Briefly, her father died when she was seven, which left her family destitute and in extreme poverty. She could neither read nor write, and the only education she received was from the homilies she heard at Sunday Mass. She was known to be stubborn, ill-mannered and uncivil. When she was seventeen, Mother Mary began appearing to her, forming and instructing her, as a good mother does with her child, preparing her for a special mission. She had been chosen to draw people to conversion through penance, minister to penitents, and exhortation, that is, reading hearts. She received a special charism for this task, and many of you who have studied the lives of St. John Vianney and St. Padre Pio know that these two great saints were also given this charism.

"In regards to the apparitions at this site, Mother Mary told Benedicta that she had asked her Son to set aside Laus for the conversion of sinners, and that He had granted it to her. This site was approved by the Vatican in May 2008. Just recently, Bishop Jean-Michel de Falco of Gap felt that this is the most important approval to take place in France since the apparition of Lourdes, which we'll be visiting next week.

"And since the beginning, just as Our Lady foretold, cures of all kinds have occurred here, and sinners have been converted in great numbers." Looking at the throng around us, I add, "There are about 120,000 pilgrims like us who come here every single year."

Refocusing back on the group, I continue. "For four months Mother Mary visited Benedicta daily, talking to her and preparing her for the mission I just told you about. No one believed her.

"On August 29th of that year, Benedicta asked Our Lady what her name was. She replied, *'My name is Mary.'* She continued to ask Benedicta to *'pray continuously for sinners.'*

"Benedicta was so moved by these visits from Mother Mary that her personality began to change. She went from being stubborn and surly to being happy and cheerful all the time. This got the attention of many, and word spread. Pilgrims began coming to the area. A small church was built. Mother Mary then disclosed to Benedicta that she was the *'Reconciler and refuge for sinners'.*

"Mother Mary asked Benedicta to address certain souls – she would literally tell her by name with whom she was to speak– but told her to do so with kindness and compassion. Benedicta, humbled by the miracles she had seen, was reluctant and even embarrassed to speak to those named by Mother Mary after she was made aware of their sins. But Mother Mary coached her and told her that when helping others, she should take heart, have patience, be cheerful, bear no hatred towards others, and not be upset if people didn't take her advice for conversion and repentance.

"She also told Benedicta not to be disturbed by *'temptations, visible or invisible spirits, or temporal affairs.'* And she told her to *'strive never to forsake the presence of God, for whoever has any faith will not dare to offend him.'*

"She encouraged priests and religious to be faithful to their vows. So you can see," I offer, "that Mother Mary is a loving mother, and she has messages for all of us, no matter our state in life."

I begin walking up the steps towards the Church and beckon everyone to follow me.

"Fr. Antoine Lambert, the Vicar General of the Diocese of Embrun, initially thought the apparitions to be diabolical in nature. He asked for a sign to prove that Mother Mary was really appearing. Mother Mary told Benedicta to tell the Vicar General that *'he can very well make God come down from Heaven by the power he received when he became a priest, but he has no commands to give the Mother of God.'*

Glancing again at my own well-worn notes, I continue:

"A well-known woman of the area by the name of Catherine Vial had been suffering for the past six years from the contraction of the nerves in her legs: they were both bent backwards and seemed bound to her body, and no effort could separate them. Her case had been declared incurable by two eminent surgeons. Having come to Laus with her mother to make a novena, she was a pity to behold, crouched all day long in the chapel. Around midnight on the last day of the novena, she suddenly felt her legs relax and begin to move. She was cured.

The next morning she entered the chapel under her own power while the Vicar General was saying Mass. Her presence caused quite a stir as the people exclaimed, 'Miracle! Miracle! Catherine Vial is cured!' Moved to tears, Father Lambert had a hard time finishing his Mass. Father Gaillard, who was serving, wrote, 'I am a faithful witness of all that occurred.' And the Vicar General declared, 'There is something extraordinary occurring in that chapel. Yes, the hand of God is there!'

"This church was built in four years as Mother Mary said she wanted a *'large church built on this spot, along with a building for a few resident priests.'* She had said that *'the church will be in honor of my dear Son and myself. Here many sinners will be converted''* and told Benedicta that she would appear often to her here, which is exactly what she did.

"Satan wasn't about to let this place become a refuge for sinners without a fight. For twenty years a great deal of hostility surrounded the apparitions and Benedicta. She was placed under house arrest for 15 years, only being allowed to leave to attend Sunday Mass. But God always wins these battles. On March 18, 1700, Benedicta's Guardian Angel told her, *'The Laus devotion is the work of God which neither man nor the devil can destroy. It will continue until the end of the world, flourishing more and more and bearing great fruit everywhere.'*

"Of incredibly important note is that Benedicta had five visions over a ten year period of Our Lord in his suffering. For one of them, Jesus told her: *'My daughter, I show myself in this state so that you can participate in my Passion.'* He wanted her to see what He suffered for all humanity.

"During one of Mother Mary's visits, she asked Benedicta to admonish women and girls about living lives of scandal, especially those who have abortions, the unjust wealthy, and the perverse."

Chapter 25

It's Tuesday, and I stretch my arms high and breathe in the fresh, cool mountain air here in La Salette, France. After a four-hour bus ride from Laus, we arrived at our hotel in time to get a peaceful, full night's rest. This picturesque, mountainous area makes my heart leap for joy.

My morning reverie is suddenly broken by someone in our group announcing that she had just heard on the television that there had been a bombing at the Boston Marathon. Normally on these trips everyone tries to unplug from the world, but the television in the hotel lobby was showing images of what took place yesterday. Apparently a few people have died and many more are injured. The manhunt is ongoing and I pray they quickly capture those who did this despicable deed. I have no hesitancy in saying that I'm tired of this terrorism bullshit, and I'm certain everyone agrees with me.

"Let's begin this morning with a prayer for the victims, the families and friends of those killed or injured in the Boston Marathon terrorist attack yesterday, and for justice and a change of heart for those responsible. Let's also pray for all those working this case, and for healing of all involved."

Sheriff Luder smirks. Our eyes lock. He's probably thinking of the conversation we had on our way to New York a few days ago regarding evil and suffering in the world. I hold his look. God is still in charge, I'm certain of that.

Refocusing on the apparition site, I relay that it occurred in 1846. Two small children were the recipients while tending sheep. A girl fourteen years old, and an eleven-year-old boy. Their parents were not practicing Catholics. They were a very poor family. When they awoke from their nap after lunch, they saw a glowing globe of light they described as being brighter than the sun. They understandably were frightened. They began to run away, but then saw a weeping lady seated with her head in her hands.

"She rose, faced them, crossed her arms, and asked them to

199

kindly come to her. She was wearing a crucifix around her neck, and spoke first in French but then in the children's dialect. She told them they were to repeat her messages to all the people. Except they didn't speak French. So, by the grace of God, these impoverished, illiterate children were suddenly able to speak fluent French!

"The lady told them a secret which they later wrote down and gave to the Pope. Subsequently the Pope summarized the secrets of La Salette by saying *"Unless the world repents, it shall perish!"*

I pause before continuing, letting the message sink in.

"The enemies of the Church, the Marxists, freemasons and free thinkers of the day were all over this. Modernists had been attempting to drive a stake through the heart of God's Church when they heard news of this supposed apparition and accompanying 'secret.'"

I share some of the important messages of Our Lady, slowing my pace accordingly:

"If my people will not obey, I shall be compelled to let go of my Son's arm. It is so heavy, so pressing, that I can no longer restrain it. How long have I suffered for you! If I do not wish my Son to abandon you, I must take it upon myself to pray for this continually. And the rest of you think little of this! In vain will you pray, in vain will you act, you will never be able to make up for the trouble I have taken for you all!"

"I gave you six days to work, I kept the seventh for myself and no one wishes to grant me that one day. This it is that causes the weight of my Son's arm to be crushing. Those who drive carts cannot swear without adding my Son's name. These are the two things which cause the weight of my Son's arm to be so burdensome."

"If the harvest is spoiled, it is your own fault. I made you see this last year with the potatoes; you took little account of this. It was quite the opposite when you found bad potatoes; you swore oaths, and you included the name of my Son. They will continue to go bad; at Christmas there will be none left."

"If you have corn, you must not sow it. The beasts will eat all that you sow. And all that grows will fall to dust when you thresh it. A great famine will come. Before the famine comes, children under the age of

seven will begin to tremble and will die in the arms of those who hold them. The others will do penance through hunger. The nuts will go bad, the grapes will become rotten."

I also share that by December of that year, the crops were indeed stricken with disease, and the following year all over Europe a famine claimed a million lives – one hundred thousand died in France alone. What was said about the potatoes, grapes, and walnuts also came true. The horrible disease of Cholera caused the deaths of many.

"Messages were also given urging everyone to pray at least every morning and at night. Let's now take a look at some of the other messages."

"Only a few old women go to Mass; in the summer, the rest work all day Sunday and, in the winter, when they do not know what to do, they only go to Mass to make fun of religion. During Lent, they go to the butchers like hungry dogs!'"

"The priests, ministers of my Son, the priests, by their wicked lives, by their irreverence and their impiety in the celebration of the holy mysteries, by their love of money, their love of honors and pleasures, the priests have become cesspools of impurity. Yes, the priests are asking for vengeance, and vengeance is hanging over their heads."

"Many shall abandon the Faith and great shall be the number of Priests and Religious who shall separate themselves from the True Religion."

"Voices shall be heard in the air....they shall preach a Gospel contrary to that of Jesus Christ, denying the existence of Heaven."

"There will be murder, hate, envy and deceit with no love or regard for one's country family."

"God will strike in an unprecedented way. Woe to the inhabitants of the earth! The chiefs, the leaders of the people of God have neglected prayer and penance, and the devil has dimmed their intelligence. God will abandon mankind to itself and will send punishments which will follow one after the other. The society of men is on the eve of the most terrible scourges and of gravest events. Mankind must expect to drink from the chalice of the wrath of God."

"The earth will be struck by calamities of all kinds, in addition to plague and famine which will be widespread. There will be a series of wars until the last war. Before this comes to pass, there will be a kind of false peace in the world. People will think of nothing but amusement. The wicked will give themselves over to all kinds of sin. But blessed are the souls humbly guided by the Holy Spirit! I shall fight at their side until they reach the fullness of years."

"The seasons of the year will change...water and fire in the interior of the earth will rage violently and cause terrible earthquakes...There shall be wars until the last war...which shall be waged by the ten kings of the Antichrist...Fire shall reign from Heaven...Finally, the sun will be darkened and Faith alone will give light...then rest and peace between God and man will appear. Jesus Christ will be served, adored and glorified. Love of neighbor will begin to flourish all over...and people will live in the fear of God."

I pause once more, looking around at the hundreds of pilgrims milling about.

After a few moments, I add:

"Think about some of the key historical events that occurred during this period. This apparition occurred in 1846, right? Since we're all from the United States, consider that the U.S. Civil War began in 1861. Over 600,000 casualties; over 400,000 wounded. And what about World War I from 1914 to 1918? Over eight million dead; 21 million wounded; and almost eight million missing. And World War II from 1939 to 1945? Although the Allies won, the cost of human lives was enormous for both sides. More than 48 million military and civilians dead. Close to 300,000 people either lost their lives or were injured right around here. Can you imagine what that did for their families back home? Make no mistake about it. Evil was very present during this war, and the evil had to be stopped. Mother Mary was trying to warn everyone in advance.

"Peace, prayer, penance, sacrifice, forgiveness, love – by all – is what Mother Mary was asking every single person on earth then, and is still requesting now. Her requests are very straightforward and simple, aren't they? I think the real question is, why doesn't the entire world listen? We can only guess at that. Could all this be coincidence? That's what many people have argued and want to believe.

"Was Our Lady specifically referring to these events and results? Only the Good Lord knows. But we have brains, intelligence, the gift of common sense and the ability to read and listen to these messages. It's up to each of us to decide. We'll talk more about the World Wars when we get to Fatima, the last stop on our trip, okay?"

The group disperses for free time collectively deep in thought. A few hours later I find the sheriff on the bus, avoiding my stare but at least making notes.

Chapter 26

"I just got a call from back home. Gina's out of the coma!" It's a new sheriff.

"Yes! Thank you, God!" I automatically say as we stand together in the hotel lobby.

He suddenly turns sour. I'm not sure if it's because of my spontaneous prayer, or what he's about to tell me.

"You'll like this," he says. "It looks like Matt Gambke, the son of your now dead girlfriend, Cameron Gambke, was the one who put her into a coma."

I choose to ignore the verbal shot at my manhood and the inference that somehow I was on the side of Cameron Gambke. His joy at the news of Gina coming out of the coma is eclipsed immediately with the animosity he feels for Matt Gambke, no doubt fueled by his hatred for his dead father. The news of Matt's involvement, however, definitely piques my interest.

"What? What happened?

Given his law enforcement training and the confidential information he deals with on a daily basis, the sheriff searches for some place with greater privacy. We move to a side window and sit down on two empty stools.

"She came out of it around five last night. Detective Gambke went over to see her, and Michele was there."

He stops again. I wonder if I'm supposed to beg him for more information.

"Who did you talk with? Detective Renae?"

"That's nothing that you need to know."

I shake my head at this childish game he's playing, but I'm interested in the details nonetheless. For whatever reason, I am now involved in this unfolding drama.

"So, what happened?" I ask again.

"Can I trust you?" he asks.

"That's a ridiculous question, Sheriff. You apparently felt more than willing to trust me when you told me about your out-of-body experience, telling me you might lose your job if I said anything, and now you ask if you can trust me? Who am I going to tell? Who do I even know that knows you? Detective Gambke? She's already on your team."

He nods. "You're right, okay. But you have to keep this confidential, got it?

"Yes, of course, got it."

"Well, apparently Gina said that she was with Matt Gambke the night she blacked out. He had told her mother he was going to take her to a movie. There was nothing out of the ordinary about that since they are step-brother and sister. He used to take her to the movies all the time before he became a teenager with an attitude. But they didn't go to the movie that night. Her memory is really fuzzy, but she said when she asked what was going on, Matt asked her if she wanted to be in a movie herself. She says, well, 'Sure.' They ended up at some house she didn't recognize but wasn't furnished or anything, and two guys in masks were there.

"In fact, the last thing she remembers clearly at all is the Sprite Matt gave her on the way over to the house. It's her favorite drink, one that Michele doesn't allow her to drink very often, and she was upset because she wanted to drink one at the movie. Everything after that is a blank."

"What do you think really happened?" I ask.

"Well, have you heard of GHB?" He looks over my shoulder, ensuring no one is within earshot range.

"Unfortunately, yes. It's one of the date rape drugs, right?" This had become a real threat to our teens and young adults in the Brooklyn Diocese, so I'm certainly aware of its existence.

"Yes. It stands for 'gamma-hydroxybutyrate' but they call it by a number of names like 'G,' "Georgia home boy,' 'grievous bodily harm,' or 'liquid ecstasy.' There also is something called 'Rohypnol' which does the same thing. They call that by other names too, like the 'forget-me pill.' Oh, and the bastards also use prescription drugs like 'clonazepam' which is sold here as 'Klonopin,' and it's sold in Mexico as 'Rivotril' as well as 'alprazolam,' which is sold as 'Xanax.'

I nod, sadly envisioning where this story may be leading and bracing myself. Some people say knowledge of these drugs only makes it worse or teaches others how to do bad things. But it's a Catch-22 really – I'm of the group that says that knowledge of things that will harm me or others is good if I use that knowledge to help. Burying my head in the sand only ensures the bad guys will have the upper hand.

"When they drew blood at the hospital, Gina's contained traces of GHB. But since she's on six other medications, her blood work was all over the place. Now it all makes sense. Unfortunately, the combination caused her to go into a coma.'

He's silent now, his fists balling into a tight knot.

"It almost killed her," he adds, punching his knee, the anger seething through his clenched teeth, and continues.

"All these punk ass pieces of shit, and probably men of all ages and even women who want to take advantage of people, use this stuff. They are depressants. They are colorless, tasteless and odorless which means that victims never know it's even there. It is usually placed in a victim's drink when they are distracted. Or someone makes or buys them a drink and slips it in before they give it to 'em. It doesn't normally knock them out completely; just puts 'em into a state of semi-paralysis and confusion.

"What these guys are banking on, is afterwards, more often than not, the victim does not remember clearly what happened. Complete and total submission is what they're after, and they usually end up with exactly that. No ability for the victim to fight. No memory and therefore no ability for the victim to pin it on them afterwards.

"Many of them use condoms so they don't leave any DNA evidence. And this is one of the primary reasons these rapists are looked upon so poorly in the prisons – they're candy asses through and through and aren't even man enough to get sex on their own. They have to resort to tricks – they think they're smart because they are getting laid without getting caught. That is, until they do. Their fellow prisoners quickly turn them into lovers and if they say 'no,' it's just a matter of time before they become fuck buddies. Ain't justice sweet?"

We sit quietly for a while, and a creeping feeling of depression begins to come over me. I feel so sorry for all of the victims of sexual assault – past, present and future.

"Sheriff, I gotta ask. I mean, this all sounds so helpless. What in the world can people do to protect themselves, I mean, from the law enforcement side?" I know Detective Renae opened up to me, but I also want to hear this from the sheriff's perspective. The weight of the topic and realization of what happened to Gina lowers my shoulders, and my voice drops in unison as I ask the question.

His eyes flash as he spits his response.

"In Gina's case, with her Down syndrome, I really don't know what she could have done. She trusted her step-brother, as did her mom. But we're gonna bring his ass to justice. And then we'll try to teach her new ways of protecting herself.

"But for others? That's easy. I tell this to school age and college girls all the time. I've told it to my daughter a million times. Only go to parties with a group of friends who promise, and actually follow through, with looking out for each other. They need to stay very well aware of everyone who is around them.

"They need to always watch their drinks from the time it is poured until they have finished it, always! If they leave for the dance floor, a trusted friend must remain; someone who can stay focused on their drinks and not be distracted. This will eliminate the opportunity for anyone to drop something into an unattended drink. If no one is willing to watch the drinks, then throw the drink away and get another one. I know that can get expensive, but that cost is far outweighed if they are raped.

"And if they start to feel strange, or feel really drunk, or feel like they are losing control, they need to immediately tell a friend they can trust and leave! Or call someone to come and get them right away. Finally, they shouldn't place themselves in a vulnerable position by becoming intoxicated, like drinking too much alcohol or taking drugs. I mean, c'mon, why make it even easier for these pricks?"

I interrupt. "But still that doesn't mean they deserve to be raped, does it? I mean, if they are trying to have a good time and maybe have a little too much, shouldn't they still feel like they can be protected?"

He glares at me.

"Of course not! I can't believe you just said that, after all the preaching you've done to me. First of all, these girls are too young to be drinking and doing drugs, so you shouldn't infer that doing so is even acceptable. Second, you keep telling me about our free will. So, they should take that good old 'free will' and not set themselves up for disaster by staying sober and in a safe environment. Or else the 'free will' of the bastards will make their life miserable. I've seen it time and again.

"But, to your point, if for whatever reason they have put themselves in a vulnerable position, of course I'm not suggesting they deserve to be raped. It's a crime! What I'm saying is they need to protect themselves, always and everywhere."

I'm nodding, appreciating the clarification. "I know, yes, I know you're right. This just seems to happen a lot. The whole thing is just very upsetting."

He softens now, seeing that I'm not questioning him, rather, I'm really just trying to communicate, to understand it all.

"Look, let me tell you a story of a situation that has stuck with me through all these years. I think it's an appropriate way for these young women to look at how they should live their lives. There was this school buddy of mine, a football player who was having a great senior year. Four major colleges were talking to him. One night he was out just being a teenager and ended up in the worst part of town and gets shot, right in the gut. They had to take most of his insides out. Did he deserve to be shot? No! But I have to ask, what in the hell was he doing downtown to begin with? I mean, really? When I asked him, he just said he wandered down with some of his other friends.

"Is this a sad story? Of course it is. Did he deserve to be shot because he was where he shouldn't have been? Nope. The guy who shot him was caught and did some time in prison, some drug dealer who thought my football player buddy was from a rival gang. But in the end, my buddy didn't go to college at all and never played football again. Last time I saw him, he himself was in prison for distributing drugs. It was the only way he thought he could make money, because he never made the effort to even go to

208

college after that. Man, I was sick when I saw him in there.

"My point is that if there's a dark alley somewhere, why walk down it? Or, based on what we're talking about here, let's just say there's a college party and some high school girls crash it. They have no idea the tricks those college boys are going to play to get them into that bedroom upstairs. Why are they there to begin with?!?! What the hell are they thinking? That everyone has their best interests in mind, that there are kind and courteous heroes around them, and if they get in trouble someone will come to their rescue and not take advantage of them? They might be book smart and great with technology, but they don't have any street smarts or common sense at all. I mean, do they at least have a plan to protect themselves and their friends if they do decide to make the initial bad decision and go to the party? For me, that goes back to staying aware of your surroundings and making good choices, always, always, always!

"So, Father, another Gambke goes down the road of doom. And he hurts someone, just like his dad did. And now I have his sister working for me and I'm stuck here in la-la land wishing I had a flight out in an hour."

He shakes his head now, growing quiet.

Every time the sheriff has said the word "Gambke" in this conversation, his bitterness slides off his tongue. And that includes Detective Renae.

"Oh man, not good," I say after a few moments, shaking my head.

"Ya think?" he says sarcastically.

"No, no, I mean, yeah, I agree, none of it is good, but it just hit me. If all of this proves to be true, it means that not only was Detective Renae's father a rapist and murderer, but now her brother is also a rapist. And she's the one that's been trying to help Gina, help Michele, help you, help the community. How is she?"

"Yep. Seems like it runs in the family," he abruptly answers, ignoring my question. I don't believe he cares one bit how Detective Renae is with all this.

Looking at the sheriff, I see something I haven't seen before, an all-knowing grin on his face, laced with a new level of spite, and a desire for revenge. But revenge against who? Cameron? He's dead. Matt? If indeed they can prove he was the one who did this, then justice must be properly served, but at what lengths will he go to mete out his own justice on him? Detective Renae? I really believe she's one of the good people here, but does he? If not, then why did he hire her in the first place?

I repeat my question.

"How is she doing? I mean, you talked to her. Is she holding up okay?"

"She'll be fine, Father. She's a professional. However, I did talk to her again and we had it out a little."

I'm really surprised that he's sharing this with me. After all, I can't say that we have the greatest relationship. He seems pretty good at keeping things like this to himself. Maybe he's talking to me as a confidant since I'm a priest. I really can't figure him out quite yet.

"You had it out?"

"Yeah. Detective Gambke is wondering how much reliance she can place on Gina's story. The case is somewhat problematic when you look at the fact that Gina has Down syndrome and the mix of drugs involved. Add to that the fact that she can't remember what happened, and that her story seems to be all over the place with other things that happened days before, and you have a real tricky situation.

"Detective Gambke had already checked Michele's house to see if Matt was still there, but he was already gone. Probably heard it on the police scanner she keeps. I told her to put out an 'All-Points Bulletin' on her brother ASAP, and she better not be trying to cover for him. It was tense, I tell ya, but she said she would do it."

"I thought Matt was out of town," I say, wondering to myself why Matt would have been at Michele's house, why Michele has a police scanner, and how much the sheriff knows that I will never be privy to. My mind is swirling, trying to make sense of it all.

"Yeah, so did I. I talked with her about that, too. She said Michele admitted to hiding Matt at Cameron's request. Apparently, he had gotten in trouble with something in one of his businesses, but the more I asked, the more she shut down. So I called Michele myself. Now that she knows it may have been Matt, she's understandably pissed, very pissed. I've gotta be careful that she won't find him and blow his head off because she probably will if given the chance. But I still don't know why she didn't tell me."

The sheriff's voice trails off, a hint of sadness and hurt evident. Michele hated Cameron Gambke yet agreed to take Matt in? What? I'm still defensive of Renae, though, because I've grown fond of her and really believe she's trying to do the right thing.

"With all due respect, Sheriff, maybe Detective Renae is making a good point. I mean, at least it's something to consider until this all works out."

"Look, I don't miss much. I know you two are pretty chummy. And that's fine, because you seem to be chummy with all sorts of people. Someday I may even shed some light for you on your new little friend, Detective Gambke. You will be amazed at what I know about her."

Should I remind him that Our Lord also met with sinners, prostitutes and all the outcasts offering them guidance, assistance, and hope? Probably not the best time to do so, although I can't imagine Detective Renae is a prostitute or outcast.

"But you should know that since Detective Gambke may have a serious conflict of interest and may not be able to stay on the case, I've also assigned one of my lieutenants to work it. I just got a call from him. He told me there was a report last night, around eleven o'clock, of a person in hospital scrubs posing as a hospital employee, matching Matt Gambke's physical description, in Gina's room. When the suspect entered her room, Gina screamed and a nurse came running. The nurse saw him exit the room and run out the nearest exit door. This same nurse swears she saw him once before hanging around the lobby but he left as soon as she made eye contact with him. All Gina could tell her was that he was messing with the tubes feeding fluids into her body. She said it was Matt Gambke all right, and the videotape they just reviewed proved it."

"How could and why would Matt Gambke have access to hospital scrubs?" I ask.

"Yeah, I asked that too. In the video they were able to focus in on the small logo on his left shoulder. They can make it out clearly as he walked down the hallway. It read 'Serenity Lane,' an old folks home in the town you live in. We verified he worked there as an intern last summer but they fired him. Seems some of their guests were complaining about him doing inappropriate things. We haven't been able to confirm it because their attorneys have told them not to communicate with anyone on the matter. Whatever he did they've kept it quiet. Probably wanted to avoid bad press, so they just let him go."

He stands, and I do the same.

"Well, that's the update, Father. Chew on that while we all hide here in the Wizard of Oz."

He takes his last verbal shot – at least for now – and exits the building into the warm French day, leaving me alone with my racing thoughts.

Running my hands through my hair I say out loud, "Serenity Lane," and recall that's where mom was located. Inappropriate things? What in the heck does that mean? As with the realization a few moments ago of Renae's Gambke family connection, it dawns on me that Matt Gambke and my mom were probably at Serenity Lane at the same time. Dad had complained to the management about what mom had told him, but they had done nothing. Was he right? Was it Matt Gambke? If so, what did he do to her?

When I think of what might have happened to mom, I feel sick. My stomach churns, the gag reflex begins deep down inside, and I rush back to my room. My thoughts turn to rage. If this is true, Sheriff Luder and I will have another thing in common – our revulsion of Matt Gambke.

"Lord, help me now, please, because I'm slipping fast!"

Chapter 27

I notice the sheriff is at least asking questions of those around him and not ignoring them as he was at the beginning of the pilgrimage. Unfortunately, his agenda for doing so is disappointing.

One of the members of our group informed me that the sheriff was heard muttering disgustedly how he couldn't believe all the people "flocking like idol worshippers" to me as a Catholic priest asking for blessings, or for me to hear their confession, or merely just to talk.

"What, does he think he's a rock star or something?" he has been overheard saying more than once. He's missing the point entirely, and my patience is waning. I'm beginning to wonder if his NDE was even real to begin with.

I must admit, though, the distraction of Sheriff Luder's antics are welcomed. I know if I find out that Matt did anything to mom, the urge for revenge will be very strong. I'm a priest, but also human, and she meant the world to me and my family.

The trip to Paris puts me in a melancholy mood. My prior visits bring back vivid memories of the culture and food, the architecture and the city life.

We checked into our hotel last night. We travel to the apparition site, and to the surprise of the first-timers after we disembark the bus, we meander through the crowds and down a fairly empty side street until we arrive at a rather nondescript address, "140 Rue du Bac," the location of the Sisters of Charity. There are many visitors and inhabitants of the city hurrying to their destinations or checking guide maps for places to see on their tours, but they all seem completely oblivious to the great events that occurred at this location 182 years ago.

The sheriff is in the front of the group now, with a pen and paper in hand. I have no idea what he's up to, but it looks like he has reengaged in the process. I begin highlighting the events that occurred here.

"At the time of this particular apparition, the world had been

213

changing rapidly, and the epicenter was right here in France, the cultural center of Europe. Significantly, what happened here, in all likelihood, would impact the rest of Europe, and that is exactly what eventually happened. The thoughts, politics, and general upheaval that began here spread throughout – some of it good and necessary, but much of it very evil.

"The 'Enlightenment' period began in the eighteenth century. In short, it was a period in which the 'intellectuals' rejected traditional religious principles and argued that everyone and everything could be figured out through human reason and strict scientific methods. Yes, science was determined to be the end all, be all, and was going to solve all the answers to absolutely everything. The results of that movement still envelop the world today.

"The 'great' minds of the time got together, men like Denis Diderot, Francois-Marie Arouet, who was better known as Voltaire, Berkeley, Hume, Descartes, Condillac, Rousseau, and others, to spread their ideas. They compiled all of their ideas into a book with the title of <u>Encyclopedia</u> which was actually a total of 35 volumes. Their ideas spread rapidly. To help their cause, the printing press was already alive and well and worked overtime to promote their revolutionary ideas.

"But here's really what they were espousing. I've already mentioned science to be the end all, be all for all the questions in the world, and there was a real belief in human progress and unlimited freedom for man with no restraints. As such, a hedonistic reality kicked into high gear and, guess what institution was standing in their way? That's right, traditional religion. The Catholic Church was still the preeminent religious institution, and even though the Protestant revolution had taken hold, the Catholic Church became a very real, tangible target.

"So, at the time, intellectually, all of this is happening and, unfortunately, given how poorly so many of the common people were being treated at the time, there was a huge demand for change. As such, in 1789, the bloody French Revolution began. The express goal of its leaders was to overthrow the governments of Europe and put new administrations in place – their

214

administrations, of course, were to be run by 'enlightened' thinkers. Eventually Napoleon Bonaparte became the dictator of France. Up until his defeat at the Battle of Waterloo, he and his army pretty much dominated Europe, which included defeats in Italy and even a push into Egypt, in addition to taking Pope Pius VII prisoner, and putting their 'Enlightened' Administrations in place all over the continent.

"With that backdrop in mind, in 1830, Mother Mary chose to appear here, smack in the middle of all the chaos, just fifteen years after Napoleon lost at Waterloo. The concepts and ideas of the Enlightenment remained firmly entrenched and hatred for the Catholic Church was at an all-time high.

"Make no mistake about it. Mother Mary is full of love, care and concern for all her children, but she's no wimp. Why should she be? She's the Mother of God. All the intellectuals, free thinkers, and military bullies who railed against the Church didn't scare her one bit. And for those of you who can connect the dots, you'll note that she always appears where she is needed the most. When the world is in great need, she appears.

"It was here that a young Catherine Labouré, whose mother died when she was only nine years old, came to this religious order at the age of 23. Although she lacked a solid education, she was accepted anyway. Upon her mother's death, she had embraced a statue of the Virgin Mary and said, 'Now, dear Blessed Mother, you will be my mother.' When she was 18 years old, she had recurring dreams in which an old priest would come to her. She later saw a portrait of the old man from her dreams in a hospital where she was working – the priest who had been in her dreams was St. Vincent de Paul – the founder of the very same Sisters of Charity that she was soon to become a member. She took it as a sign and that is how she ended up here.

"Before she experienced the apparitions of Mother Mary almost immediately after joining the order, she continued to have apparitions of St. Vincent de Paul showing her his heart while she was at prayer in the chapel. It was the colors of white, red and black representing what would happen, in the future, to France and Paris in particular: Peace, fire, and charred remains, respectively.

"She also saw Our Lord Jesus Christ in the Sacred Host. She later said that she saw Our Lord in the Blessed Sacrament all of the time, except for the times when she doubted.

"It was on the eve of the feast of St. Vincent de Paul, July 18, 1830, after falling asleep, her guardian angel, in the form of a little four or five-year-old child appeared, dressed in white. He told her to follow him as the Blessed Virgin was waiting for her in the chapel. Catherine followed, and Mother Mary was sitting in the Father Director's chair. She flung herself at her feet on the steps of the altar and put her hands on Mother Mary's knees. She later said that she didn't know how long she remained there but that it was the sweetest time of her life. The Holy Virgin told her how she should act toward her director, and confided several things to her.

"Mother Mary told Catherine that God wished to give her a mission, but she wasn't told the nature of this mission at that time. It appears that Mother Mary, as she did with other visionaries, needed time to prepare this soon to be canonized saint for her mission. She told her she would have much to suffer, but that she would rise above it all by knowing that what she would be doing would be for the glory of God. She would know what the 'good God' wants of her, and that she would be tormented until she told her director what she needed to say. She would be contradicted, but that she need not fear as she would be given the grace to do what needed to be done. She was told to do all this with confidence, to tell it with simplicity and, again, to have confidence and not be afraid.

"She was also told that the times were very evil, that sorrows would befall France, and that the throne would be overturned. She was told that the whole world would be plunged into every kind of misery, but that for everyone, the great and the humble alike, who came to the *'foot of this altar,'* graces would be poured out on all those who *'ask for them with confidence and fervor.'* Mother Mary told her again that grave troubles were coming, that there would be great danger for all religious communities, including hers, but that God would protect this one in particular but not all of the others.

"Then Mother Mary said, with tears in her eyes, that *'Among the clergy in Paris there will be victims – Monsignor the Archbishop will die, my child, the Cross will be treated with contempt, they will hurl it to the ground and trample it. Blood will flow. The streets will run with blood. Monsignor the Archbishop will be stripped of his garments'.* She told her that some of these events were to take place very soon, and others 'in about 40 years.'

"Mother Mary assured Catherine that her eyes would be ever upon her, that she would grant her graces, and that special graces would be given to all who ask them, but that people must pray."

I reach into the collar of my shirt and pull out the Miraculous Medal that I wear daily.

"For those of you who wear one of these, it all began here."

Heads nod.

"It has become the most popular sacramental devotion since the introduction of the Rosary.

"This was the mission, given to her by God, which Mother Mary had been preparing her for since the first apparition in July. A globe of the world being held by Mother Mary suddenly turned into an image of what we now see on this Medal, with the words *'O Mary, Conceived Without Sin, Pray For Us Who Have Recourse To Thee.'* On the reverse side were the letter 'M' intertwined with a cross, and two hearts below it. You can see by looking at it closely that one of the hearts is crowned with a crown of thorns, and the other is pierced by a sword. She said that those who wear it will receive great graces; that abundant graces will be given to those who have confidence."

"Father, what does the M, the cross, and the two hearts symbolize?" asks a member of the group.

"If you look, you'll see at the base of the Cross a bar, and that symbolizes the foot of the Cross. The intertwined 'M' reflects Mother Mary's intimate involvement at the foot of the Cross with her Son's Redemptive Sacrifice, and it stands for 'Mary' as well as 'Mother' to us all. It's at the bottom of the cross because it shows Mary's subordinate role to that of Jesus, all in line with Church teaching. The first heart represents the Sacred Heart of Jesus encircled with a crown of thorns, and the other heart reflects the sword of sorrow for Mother Mary. These two hearts reflect the prophesy of Simeon which were fulfilled when he said a 'sword will pierce your heart' – remember this is the first mystery of the Devotion of the Seven Sorrows for those of you recite this prayer. We'll see these two hearts together again at Fatima next week. One of the children, Lucia Santos, said that 'The Sacred Heart of Jesus wants the Immaculate Heart of Mary to be venerated at His side.'"

I return my attention back to the group at large.

"Catherine told her spiritual director, Fr. Aladel, about both apparitions when they occurred, and the request for the medal, specifically, after the second apparition in November. Now, understandably, Fr. Aladel was hesitant because Catholics were being murdered. They had many confrontations over the matter, and finally in 1832, two years after the apparitions, Catherine put into writing three full accounts of her visions – her common sense and attention to detail impressed Fr. Aladel. But it was only by comparing her visions with the actual occurrences that caused him to be even more convinced.

"For instance, only eight days after the first apparition on July 18, the 'Second French Revolution' began, which is also known as the 'July Monarchy.' It lasted three days, July 26 through 29, 1830. Riots broke out all over Paris and churches were, indeed, desecrated. Fr. Aladel met with Archbishop Hyacinth de Quelen of Paris to bring the entire matter to his attention, although the name of Catherine Labouré was kept confidential to the public until after her death. The Archbishop, who was very devoted to the Immaculate Conception of Mary, approved the request, and asked for some of the first medals made.

"On June 30, 1832, the first 2,000 medals were delivered and spread like wildfire. Stories of conversions, cures and other miracles began immediately by many who wore the medal around their neck, just as Mother Mary had requested. In 1832 and 1833, 50,000 were made and distributed, and millions have been made every year after.

"Within the next 40 years, as Mother Mary predicted, King Charles X was indeed overthrown. As predicted, mobs desecrated churches, destroyed statues and threw down crucifixes and trampled them underfoot. Also as predicted, this very Sisters of

Charity convent remained untouched although angry mobs came right by here. Bishops and Priests were imprisoned, with 30 of them beaten and executed, including Archbishop Darboy. Archbishop Hyacinth de Quelen of Paris, who had approved the production of the Miraculous Medal, had to flee into hiding twice to save his life.

"In 1836, the medal received Canonical approval. In essence, it was determined that the medal was of supernatural origin and the miracles reviewed were, indeed, authentic."

I lead the group in front of the incorrupt body of St. Catherine Labouré located under a side altar. Her body, as is common practice for the beatification process for saints in the Church, was exhumed 57 years after burial in 1933 and was found to be completely incorrupt and supple. Sheriff Luder pushes his way to the front where he remains for a long time, seemingly entranced with what he is seeing while making an occasional note on his notepad.

I approach him and ask, "Pretty amazing, isn't it?"

He stands up straight and faces me.

"This is the best plastic version I've seen of a human in a very long time. Looks just like some of those Ripley's Believe It or Not mannequins, only better!" he says loudly, not caring about the heads that snap his way.

I immediately put a finger to my lips, imploring him to quiet down out of respect for everyone around who are deep in prayer and contemplation.

"It's very real, Sheriff, well, most of it. Her body is incorrupt."

"Incorrupt? What does that mean? And what do you mean by 'most of it?'"

I lead him outside so I don't have to whisper.

"Incorruption is a supernatural mystery in which God has granted certain individuals a special grace whereby their body does not go through the natural process of decay like everyone else's. So even hundreds of years after their death, they still look like they did the day they died.

"And this isn't like the ancient Egyptians who embalmed bodies. Even though that culture got very good at it, when archeologists unburied their embalmed bodies, they still didn't look at all like the physical bodies that must have existed the day they died.

"Admittedly, it has been determined that nature has preserved some bodies to a certain extent – like very hot or cold climates that are dry or have levels of radiation, lead, or other substances – but even those preserved bodies don't look as though they recently died, like the one you just saw in St. Catherine.

"For the incorruptibles recognized by the Catholic Church, some have sweet fragrances, healing oils, or even flowing blood emanating from them. It's truly remarkable. Unfortunately, today there are fewer incorruptibles than there could have been, because during the French Revolution, and even earlier during the Protestant Revolution, many of them were destroyed as part of the 'Destroy anything related to the Catholic Church' mindset.

"But for St. Catherine Labouré, as part of standard procedure, because the Church has a tradition of venerating relics from saints, some of her body parts were removed and stored elsewhere. Her hands were removed and kept in a special reliquary in the novitiate cloister of this order's motherhouse. The hands that you see wrapped around Rosary beads are made of wax. So, to your point, there is some wax on her incorruptible body but only in that instance. Her heart was also put into a special reliquary made of jeweled crystal and gold and is kept in the chapel at Reuilly where she prayed during her later years while working at the hospice."

He's shaking his head and rolling his eyes.

I press the issue, just as he did with me when he shoved the Cameron Gambke file into my lap on our way to the Community College not long ago.

"Are you seeing the world any differently now, Sheriff? The places we've visited, the miracles? I strongly encourage you to consider that reality."

He snorts.

"*My* world is real, Father. My world is reality. Yours is a bullshit fantasy. For a while, you seemed like such an intelligent man. Don't even hint that *I'm* the lost one."

He turns abruptly towards the door leading to the bustling

City of Light, a name earned during the infamous age of Enlightenment. I realize that those errant teachings from long ago still permeate the very being of the man whose figure has just disappeared from my sight. I've seen hardened hearts before, but his may be at the top of the list.

Chapter 28

"Father Jonah, this is Susan Bellers."

"Hello, Mrs. Bellers," I say, grinding my teeth. We're just loading up on to the bus, and I stand off to the side with every intention of making this a quick call.

"I only have a few minutes. How can I help you?"

"I have Sex Crimes Detective Renae Gambke here, and I need to know what approval has been given for her to give this Rape Education class here at the parish."

Did she actually just say that to me?

"Mrs. Bellers, I have spoken to Fr. Bernard about all of this. Is this the reason why you are making such an expensive international call, or is there something specific you need from me in order to help Detective Gambke?"

"This unauthorized seminar is the reason I am making this call, Father Jonah. We have very specific procedures to follow within our parish before we move forward with an event like this. Apparently, you want this class but you haven't told me anything about it. And now, I'm sure I will have to do all the work while you're traveling around the world. You have no idea how much I have to do here every single day just to keep up with things. The copier is broke, I have meetings all the time, and I can't get any help!"

I listen patiently to her repeat rant. It is the same discourse I've heard before on multiple occasions. It's time to wrap this call up.

"Mrs. Bellers, what exactly does Detective Gambke need from you?"

"Well, she says she needs to do a site visit. She needs to check out the place before she gives this presentation."

"All right. Can't you just open the door and show her the hall?"

Ignoring my question, she continues in her infamous snappy way.

"And I'm sure she'll need copies made of her materials to

give to everyone. That's going to take my time and the church's money."

"Have her go to a print shop. I'll pick up the tab."

"You?" Her laugh is abrupt and sharp.

"Yes, me. What else, Mrs. Bellers?"

The bus driver glances down at me and I make a move towards the open door. The entire group has already found their seats and all the luggage is loaded. I'm the holdup. Rather, Mrs. Bellers is the holdup.

"She also was asking about refreshments. How much is this going to cost?"

I am done with this conversation.

"Mrs. Bellers, listen to me clearly. As I've said already, all of this has been approved by Fr. Bernard, and we have already spoke about the details, understand? Please open the hall for Detective Gambke and let her see the facility. You don't have to do anything else, okay? But before you hang up, I need to speak with her."

Click.

"You've got to be kidding me," I say out loud, punching the redial button.

"Our Lady of Perpetual Help, Susan Bellers speaking," a charming voice welcomes me, forced in every way.

"Mrs. Bellers, please put Detective Gambke on the phone for me."

"Oh, sorry, Father. The call somehow dropped. Here she is."

"Uh huh," I reply, needing her to know I'm on to her game.

"It's for you," I hear her say, envisioning the phone being thrust towards Detective Gambke with an accompanying terse attitude.

"This is Detective Gambke."

"Hey Detective. Sorry about that. We really do appreciate you helping us out with this."

"It's okay, Father. Not a problem."

I'm certain she wants to say a few more things about our illustrious parish employee, but she holds her tongue.

"Is there any way that you can step outside?" I ask. "I want to call you back on your cell really quick."

223

"Sure," she replies.

I give her a few moments to make her way outside, telling the driver I will just need a few more minutes. He's in no rush and smiles understandably.

"I just wanted to say that that's great news about Gina! How are she and Michele doing?"

"Yes, it is great news. From what I've gathered it's an understandable emotional rollercoaster with Michele. She's thrilled that Gina is out of the coma so that goes without saying, but she's furious and rightfully so. She wants someone's head, but now, well, she's not really talking to me since one of the suspects is..."

"The sheriff told me about it. Any updates?"

She pauses, probably wondering the extent of what I know about the open investigation.

"He told you about the case? About the suspect?"

"Yes. Well, about the supposed night at the movie with Matt and Gina, about the guys dressed in black at some undetermined location, about a probable date rape drug used, and about the hospital video of a guy going into and then running out of Gina's hospital room when a hospital employee came in."

I pause, feeling awkward, and then continue.

"If it is Matt, I mean, if he did it, I'm really very, very sorry."

I don't mention the possible connection with her brother and my mom. I don't want my rage to infect her – she's already got enough to grapple with.

"There's a great deal that still needs to be proven, Father. But, well, thank you."

Detective Gambke's tone turns serious.

"I can tell you that our office now knows that once the pictures were distributed, a man came forward from a neighborhood not far from town. Said he lives next to a distressed home that was abandoned when the bottom fell out of the economy. Said he sees kids coming in and out once in a while late at night. He notices the flashlights shining off the walls because the power has been cut by the utility company. Said he's called to have something done about it, but nothing has, so the kids know a good thing when they have it and keep coming back.

"The night Gina went into a coma, he saw something at that house that he's never seen before. Normally the people are just drinking and partying. He says he saw three guys and a girl, through an upstairs window, but the window was covered by a white, sheer curtain. Two of the guys were dressed all in black and they dragged this girl onto a bed. They raped her continuously and the other guy videotaped it but didn't take part in the actual raping, at least from what the witness can remember. The witness says it seemed to him the third guy was directing it, as he would periodically go over and hand them different things to place into her vagina or anus, or things to pinch onto her nipples. He said even though the sheer curtain was in place, the room was lit up so much he could still see bodies but no specific facial characteristics on the girl or the third perp.

"Our office has been there and taken DNA samples but nothing matches up in our system yet. However, I need to say that we have no DNA in our database for Matt to begin with so we can't make that connection if indeed it was him. Plus, the witness can't positively ID Matt as being one of the guys, nor Gina as being the girl. The only thing for certain is the inside of the house has been beat to crap so has probably been a 'party house' for some time.

"There's a very good chance that this group didn't include Matt or Gina at all. I mean, the timing of it may be pure coincidence, especially if they've been to this house on multiple occasions and nothing has ever been reported to us like this from any other supposed 'victim.'"

Before she continues, I blurt out a question.

"If I can ask, why so long for this witness to come forward? I mean, I know you said the pictures just came out, but when he saw this the first time, did he really just think it was normal teenage activity so he didn't feel he needed to report anything to the police?"

"You'll love this," she grunts. "He didn't really have a reason that we could get out of him. When we asked, he got nervous and kind of danced around the question. All he offered was when he recently saw the picture of Matt that was shown on the news and heard the accompanying story, he thought he should at least say something. The kicker came when we talked to his wife to see if she had seen or heard anything, and when she found out why we were there, she was not pleased at all. She wasn't mad at us, she was disgusted with her husband. She flew into an absolute rage. She claims the most likely reason he never told the police about what was happening at the house next door is because he probably enjoyed watching it and was hoping they would come back and do it again. To make matters worse, I guess a week after he filmed it he confided in her what he saw, and asked her to watch the video of it with him, like a real 'live' porn show. She flipped then and he never said anything else about it, until now."

"What video?" I ask.

"His own. Apparently he videotaped them with his own I-Phone. However, the upside of Mr. Pervert-Sick-Bastard's voyeurism is that we now have copies of it at our lab. I understand the female was face down most of the time, and even when she was on her back the angle might not have been the best, but you would be amazed at the technology we have to assist us.

"We just need to find Matt. Unfortunately, as I told you before, he left town not long ago but now that we're actually trying to find him, he's disappeared completely. No one has seen him. He's still the prime suspect and we need to either clear his name or charge him, along with the other two. The sheriff's tying my hands on this. I'm not stupid – my connection with Matt – if it is him – makes him nervous. And I can see his point. He needs to ensure objectivity and independence because the press is all over him."

Maybe she doesn't know Matt was hiding out at Michele's. Maybe the sheriff chose not to tell her that tidbit of information, and now it makes more sense. He's trying to be very careful about what he tells this third member of the Gambke family.

She sounds frustrated when she continues.

"What the sheriff needs to understand is that if Matt was part of this, I want more than anything to bring him to justice. I really mean that. I don't care if he is my brother; if he's guilty, he's done something very wrong and, worse, it almost cost Gina her life. I've said this to the sheriff, but I'm not sure he's listening. At any rate, I need to take a few days off to clear my head and get out of town to take care of some business, but I'll be back for the presentation, I promise. And...I really do thank you for listening. First Cameron, and now, maybe... "

"Possibly your brother," I say, ending her sentence.

"Maybe you and I can just talk at length someday, if that's okay," she says.

"Absolutely. Anytime. Just let me know where and when."

Chapter 29

Our pilgrimage group arrived yesterday in Pontmain, France after a four-hour bus ride from Paris. Last night, I celebrated Mass in the old barn above where the Marian apparition occurred.

I'm sitting on the steps just outside the beautiful Basilica of Our Lady of Hope, built subsequent to the apparitions that occurred here in 1871 and visited by more than 200,000 pilgrims each year. No train service is available, so anyone interested in visiting the site must travel by car, bus, or taxi – and there are plenty of each all around. It's one o'clock and, as I had requested, the group has gathered around me at the barn. Even Sheriff Luder, pen and paper in hand, is here as I begin.

"This was a time of great turmoil throughout Europe, especially in France. It was in the midst of the Age of Enlightenment, and all around this area people were caught up in the mindset of the day. However, this particular town remained staunchly Catholic in both word and action."

I stare across at the famous barn above where the apparition occurred, sharing with the group that during the evening of January 17, 1871, Mother Mary appeared to two young boys, 10 and 12 years old, whose older brother had just been enlisted to fight for the French army.

"The boys saw a beautiful woman in the sky over this barn, smiling down at them. She was wearing a blue gown covered with golden stars, and a black veil under a golden crown. She wore blue shoes adorned with gold ribbons. Three other young children, aged six, nine and 11, all came by at various times and also saw the apparition. Even a two-year-old baby looked up and saw the Virgin Mary. Some adults noticed the infant's reaction to what was happening above the barn, but couldn't see her themselves – only the innocent, young children who reacted quite naturally to what was occurring above them in the sky.

"About 60 people eventually gathered for about two hours. Then, a nun who had been with the group from the beginning, encouraged everyone to begin praying the Rosary. The local priest was quickly notified and also joined the group. As they prayed in unison, the children relayed that the figure became twice the size and the stars around her began to increase in number and attach themselves to her dress until it was entirely covered. They all prayed the Magnificat and sang 'Mother of Hope' and litanies of the Virgin Mary, and during this time, as the children were transfixed on the apparition in the sky, letters began appearing one at a time over the barn, forming words. And each of the children on their own, but in unison as the letters appeared, repeated them for the adults to hear. Amazingly, the appearance of the letters was predicated on the prayers the people were saying. As they prayed, letters appeared. When they stopped praying, the letters stopped appearing.

"After all the letters were spoken out loud by the children, the adults were able to decipher the messages.

"But pray, my children."

"God will soon answer you."

"My Son allows Himself to be moved."

"After giving the children this last message, the children said that Mother Mary's smile changed to one of extreme sadness and that a large red cross suddenly appeared before her, with a figure of Jesus on it in an even darker shade of red. Then the cross vanished, and candles in an oval frame were lit by a star, and when Mother Mary lowered her hands, two white crosses appeared on her shoulders. A white veil rose from beneath her feet and covered her until she disappeared.

"Mother Mary informed her children, which obviously meant everyone who was present – not just the young children – that *'God will answer you.'* So what were they all praying for at that time? What were they asking for?

"Right at that exact moment, the Prussian Army was rapidly advancing toward this area, and was only about 30 miles away."

With the group's full attention, I again share that while the world around them was moving *away from* God, this village had remained steadfast in their belief. They had a special devotion to Mother Mary and prayed the Rosary faithfully. They also attended Mass and had been praying at length for protection and safety, not only for their village, but also for the 38 local men fighting in the French army.

"The Emperor Napoleon had been captured by the Prussian army, and they were quickly advancing through France, making a beeline to this village. Mother Mary appeared to tell them that their faithfulness would be rewarded, that they would be protected, that God had indeed heard and was answering their prayers. *'My Son allows Himself to be moved','* she had said to them.

"Right at the time the apparitions began, the Prussian army actually stopped moving forward. The commander, General Von Schmidt, had received orders from the Prussian High Command to halt his campaign and withdraw. Some of the Prussian soldiers reported seeing an image of a 'lady in the sky' at the same time all of this was occurring! Of course, scientists would later argue that what was actually seen by the Prussian Army was an aurora borealis, or 'northern lights.' At any rate, 11 days later, Prussia and France signed a treaty, and all 38 men returned to Pontmain, safe and healthy!"

Unbeknownst to me, Sheriff Luder had apparently moved from our group, and is in a verbally aggressive argument with an Italian priest. As the sheriff stomps away, I see the priest make the sign of the cross towards his retreating frame.

Chapter 30

It's Tuesday morning as I type this on our flight to Lourdes, which is only about an hour by air, but much better than an eight-hour bus ride which was our only other option. Although I've approached the sheriff on yesterday's verbal outburst, he clearly doesn't want to speak with me. Incredibly well-documented apparitions abound for him to research, but will he?

On the way to the airport, I had provided the group a light blue bookmark titled "The Fifteen Promises of Mary to Christians Who Recite the Rosary" – I mentioned these promises in this journal earlier. The bookmark had received an *"Imprimatur"* from Patrick J. Hayes, D.D., the Archbishop of New York. I explained to the group that the word *'Imprimatur'* is Latin for "let it be printed." An *'Imprimatur'* is granted to a printed work by a Roman Catholic bishop to assure the reader that nothing therein is contrary to Catholic faith or morals. I stress to them that this *'imprimatur'* is not given lightly and only after a thorough review process.

We've heard, at each of the apparition sites we've visited, how Mother Mary has implored the faithful to pray the Rosary. So, for the benefit of our first-time pilgrims, I told them the history of the Rosary. For instance, how the Rosary grew from the early Christian practice of reciting the 150 psalms from Scripture into what it is now. That tradition has it Mother Mary appeared to St. Dominic showing him a wreath of roses – her favorite flower – which represented the Rosary. St. Dominic, who died in 1221, was the founder of the Order of the Friars Preachers, widely known as the Dominicans. The Dominicans wore Rosary beads as part of their habit, after becoming discouraged over fighting against heresies of the time. Our Lady told him to pray the Rosary daily and to teach all who would listen so that the true faith would eventually triumph.

Unfortunately, after a relatively short time, devotion to the Rosary declined. In 1460, a preacher of St. Dominic's order, Blessed Alan de la Roche, was visited by Jesus, Mary, and St. Dominic chastising him and urging him to revitalize the practice.

***

This morning, I reminded the group we have all day today and part of tomorrow to tour the vast grounds on their own, to experience firsthand the history, beauty, blessings and grandeur of this famous site.

I will become a pilgrim once more on my own. My sojourn takes me to the baths where many healings have taken place, the Rosary Basilica, the Immaculate Conception "Upper" Basilica, the Shrine Museum, Saint Bernadette's Chapel, and the Way of the Cross up the mountain, marveling again at the bronze life-sized statues of Our Lord and other figures, each representing a different event during Jesus' passion.

I sit for a long time, gazing at the Pyrenees Mountains.

I catch a glimpse of the sheriff, his muscular 6' 4" frame towering over what appears to be a group of Romanian pilgrims. He spots me and, to my surprise, chooses to quickly walk my way.

"Where's the incorrupt body of St. Bernadette?" he implores.

"Well, unfortunately, it's kept in a sarcophagus at the Convent of the Sisters of Nevers – a seven-hour ride north of here – where Bernadette was accepted after the apparitions and where she later died, after a long illness, at the young age of 35."

A look of anger fills his eyes – based on our previous experience in Paris with the body of St. Catherine Labouré, he probably just wants to look closely to see if he can find any evidence of fraud.

Pointing to his left, he says: "You see that youth camp over there? How sick is it that the Church is brainwashing all these poor kids, just like Hitler tried to do with his young German protégées."

Turning quickly, he heads back towards the grotto. "This place is just a propaganda spouting, money making machine," I hear him say. I drop my head, hoping to return to my peaceful silence. He needs his time, his space and I have no problem admitting that so do I at this moment.

I am moved by the large number of ailing people dutifully lined up, row after row, in wheelchairs or hospital beds. I speak personally to quite a few, offering hope, care, compassion, and my time. As I move from one fellow soul to another, a battle rages inside me, just like it always seems to do, as I see the evidence of their sicknesses – the open wounds, the scars, the pain. All the while I pray that I, not now nor ever, become afflicted with what they have. I'm embarrassed by this reaction that always seems to come over me whenever I am around people who are sick, even with the common cold. I try hard to make the extra effort to listen to their stories and those of their loved ones who have brought them here. As I wander through the throng of sorrow, I pray for all of them and the grace for me to get over my irrational health fears.

At the fountains near the grotto, thousands of pilgrims drink and wash their faces with the waters, and I see the sheriff standing off to the side, shaking his head in apparent disgust.

He's on the outside of this group of believers, and he knows it. Back at home he could stand up in a crowd in the middle of town and scream his opinion quite easily, or write a column for the local paper doing the same. And many would cheer in agreement about the horrible, backwards, gullible, and misguided Catholic Church and its members. Oh, a few might stand up against him and argue on the side of the Church, but any backlash against him would undoubtedly be subdued. Unfortunately, he's in the norm. Recent statistics show that belief in God continues its rapid decline throughout the United States and that only 24 percent of the population still claim to be Catholic.

I think about the rest of the world as pilgrims from many different nationalities mill about in prayer. Even though Catholics represent only about one percent of the total population of Russia, China and India, in other countries such as Mexico, Peru, Brazil, Argentina, Spain and the Philippines they are in the majority, with the percentage in the high 70's or greater. Poland, the homeland of Blessed Pope John Paul II and St. Faustina, the saint intimately tied to Divine Mercy Sunday, claims that 92% of their population is Catholic. And as a continent? North America claims 85 million Catholics; Asia 130 million; Central America 162 million; Africa 186 million; Europe 285 million and South America, 339 million. Sheriff Luder would be hard pressed to voice his disbelief in some of these devoted areas of the world.

Visiting the Medical Bureau where reported cures are carefully examined, I see him well in front of me. Maybe, just maybe, he'll begin to see.

"Open his heart, Lord, please remove the scales from his eyes," I pray silently.

Reviewing my tour guide book, I glance over the highlights of what transpired here in 1858.

Bernadette Soubirous was the oldest of four children from a prosperous family. Shortly after her birth, misfortune struck and her family was plunged into extreme poverty. She was frequently ill, contracted cholera as a toddler, and suffered from severe asthma her entire life. She received little education and many who knew her believed that she was illiterate, most likely because she spoke French poorly, speaking primarily in the native Basque tongue common to Southern France and Northern Spain.

When she was 14, Bernadette, along with one of her sisters and some other girls, was out gathering firewood to sell for money to assist her impoverished family. The other girls had gone ahead and Bernadette was alone at the river when she had her first vision. She later described what she saw:

"I came back towards the grotto and started taking off my stockings. I had hardly taken off the first stocking when I heard a sound like a gust of wind. Then I turned my head towards the meadow. I saw the trees quite still: I went on taking off my stockings. I heard the same sound again. As I raised my head to look at the grotto, I saw a Lady dressed in white, wearing a white dress, a blue girdle and a yellow rose on each foot, the same color as the chain of her rosary; the beads of the rosary were white."

Her mother forbade her to return but, while normally an obedient young girl, after attending Mass on Sunday she returned to the grotto where she once again experienced a vision of the "Lady in White." The following Thursday, she went to the grotto for the third time, accompanied by a few adults. This was the first time the lady spoke to Bernadette, asking her to come to the grotto for the next fortnight and she also told her that *"she could not promise to make me happy in this world, only in the next."*

Over the following two weeks word quickly spread and

hundreds of people began to follow Bernadette to the grotto. The lady looked at the crowd and her face saddened. She told Bernadette to *"Pray for sinners,"* and also asked for *"penance, penance, penance."* She asked Bernadette to kiss the ground as an act of penance for sinners, and when she did, many in the crowd mocked her. However, some of the more pious followed her lead and began kissing the ground.

Witnesses said they felt as though they were in a place of great reverence. A priest and witness, Father Desirat wrote:

"What struck me was the joy, the sadness reflected in Bernadette's face ... Respect, silence, recollection reigned everywhere. Oh, it was good to be there - It was like being at the gates of paradise."

Bernadette was subjected to enormous pressure. She was interrogated multiple times by the local police and required to undergo medical testing to determine whether she should be committed to a mental asylum. Despite all the criticism and disbelief, no one was ever able to find flaws in her story.

During the 9th apparition the lady asked Bernadette: *"Would you kiss the ground and crawl on your knees for sinner?"* And, *"Would you eat the grass that is there for sinners?"* Finally, the Lady said, *"Go and drink from the spring and wash yourself there."* No spring existed in the Grotto at that time so Bernadette began to dig in a muddy patch and drank a few drops of muddy water. The lady also asked her to eat some grass *"for sinners,"* which she did. The onlookers were disgusted and thought she was insane. No one believed her and began to call it a fraud. Yet in the days that followed, water flowed from the spring and people began to speak of miraculous healing experiences.

The Lady asked Bernadette to go to the parish priest, Fr. Peyramale, and request that a chapel be built at the grotto. The priest, while initially skeptical and even hostile, told Bernadette that he wouldn't do anything until the "Lady" revealed her name. While the lady had only smiled when Bernadette had asked her before, she finally told Bernadette that "QUE SOY ERA IMMACULADA COUNCEPCIOU." *"I am the Immaculate Conception."* The Priest was absolutely amazed. He knew that Bernadette was not well-schooled and totally unfamiliar with the

Immaculate Conception, which had only recently been declared a dogma of faith by the Vatican. Fr. Peyramale knew there was no way Bernadette could have known this.

Bernadette saw the lady for the final time on July 16th. By this time the bishop and the local authorities had stopped anyone from entering the grotto. Bernadette stood across the river but felt that the lady was as close to her as if she was in the cave.

Closing my book, I walk through the Bureau, reviewing the documentation available to the public, and look at the pictures of those apparently having received a "miracle" healing.

I stop to listen to a well-informed host of another group explain the process required for a miracle to be officially recognized. She explains that a dedicated group of doctors and scientists, consisting of both religious and non-believers, are assigned to each reported miracle. This group is tasked with determining whether a medical or scientific reason, as opposed to a supernatural cause, exists that would explain the cure. My spirit is buoyed once more.

"The local Bishop then has to approve it," the young female Swiss host says, smiling towards the 30 or so pilgrims trailing behind her.

She continues.

"To date, there have been 66 officially declared miracles through the intercession of Our Lady of Lourdes, and around 40 new ones are reported as potential miracles each year that need to go through extensive review. To date, about 7,000 cures have been attributed to Lourdes that haven't been officially recognized. The reason so many aren't officially labeled as a 'miracle' is that the doctors have to be 100 percent certain of the supernatural nature of the cure, which requires multiple return trips to the Medical Bureau, located here in this very distant, yet picturesque countryside. Returning here multiple times is a financial hardship for the majority so they just don't come back. They thank God for the gift given and move forward with their lives."

She looks towards the Pyrenees, her smile broadening.

"There are a number of accounts of atheists and agnostics, doctors and scientists alike, who converted to Catholicism after seeing firsthand the cures and healings that have occurred here at Lourdes. These accounts are available in a number of books and publications readily available, here or online, and at many bookstores, for anyone that's interested. There have been so many cures and so many visitors over the years to this site, that there is a plethora of readily available material."

Chapter 31

At dinner, I get word from one of our group members that a miracle appears to have occurred here earlier in the day. Dolores Saltzinger, a member of a parish in upstate New York, who had been born with a deformed left hand, had bathed in the healing baths. A few moments after, as she explained to everyone around her, her hand became very warm, and within 20 minutes she could move it normally. This was witnessed by four other members of the group, and she was rushed to the Medical Bureau for the doctors to perform their initial evaluation of her case.

Paying my bill, I head towards our tour bus where I asked those in our group to meet so we could experience the evening torchlight procession together. All pilgrims walk together, praying the Rosary and singing Marian hymns and other religious songs. The sheriff is there, listening to the two women excitedly tell me the details of what they witnessed. I see confusion more than anger on his face, far different than when I saw him at the fountains earlier in the day.

Smiling at the ladies, I share in the joy of this gift from God if, indeed, that is what has occurred. I will leave it to the Church to make their determination after thorough testing, but since I don't doubt that miracles have and still happen all the time, I'm delighted all the more.

An African Catholic priest begins the celebration of the Mass on an elevated stage, with the use of a sound system that would make any rock band manager proud. It's a necessary expenditure – the crowd is in the thousands. A large crucifix hangs behind the altar, supported by thick black cables that hang from a prodigious, black apparatus that covers the stage, all invisible to the masses whose eyes are trained on the lights shining specifically on the altar, the crucifix, and the faces of the choir members singing with angelic voices off to the right. His introduction is powerful, and appears to hold great meaning to those present, as the priest articulates well Mother Mary's messages of penance, prayer, and sacrifice for the love of God and, thus, for the love of our neighbor.

The sheriff has now positioned himself to my left, just a few worshippers away from our group. I'm pleased for his sake that he has chosen to be here.

Before the Mass is celebrated, we spend time before the Blessed Sacrament, exposed upon the altar in a monstrance. All surrounding lights have been turned off, save the spotlight affixed on Our Lord. The wonderful smell of incense fills the air, the chords of the *Tantum Ergo* still softly in my mind as we kneel in prayer.

A few minutes into the tranquility of our adoration, I detect the seductive smell of perfume. An exquisite American brunette saunters between the two members of the faithful that separate the sheriff and I. She looks directly back at him. The corners of her mouth raise slightly, a tantalizing smile sent to him personally, I'm sure. She is wearing an alluringly short, pink sundress. She stops a few feet in front of him, along with the other four members of her group. Glancing at the sheriff, I notice he can't seem to keep his eyes off her. His gawking made blatantly apparent by the movement of his entire head as he attempts to visually consume her entirely – from the back of her long hair, down to her bronzed, shaved, and shapely legs, to her ornamental Cleopatra-like thongs adorning her pink pedicured toes. Admittedly and in his defense, it's hard for anyone not to see her, including me. She's stunning. I make a concerted effort to refocus on Our Lord and pray for the grace to continue to do so.

Disappointingly, as the entire group is in prayer, kneeling in unison out of respect for the actual presence of Our Lord, she and her friends continue to stand. She doesn't seem to understand nor care that the adoration is for Our Lord; maybe she thinks it's for her. Many heads are shaking now, and a woman from our group whispers harshly for all of them to kneel before Our Lord. Her directives are ignored, and the young lady tells her to keep her mouth shut, that she chooses to kneel to no one, especially Him. So she *does* know who He is. My prayers before Our Lord now focus on her and her companions because she just doesn't get it. I'm reminded of the number of people over the years – especially "practicing" Catholics – who I've witnessed entering a Catholic

Church where Our Lord is exposed and acting disrespectfully, too – talking on cell phones, speaking loudly with whomever is with them – as though they're shopping for groceries in a store and not in the presence of the Lord of Lords.

After a short while, the priest, a humeral veil covering his shoulders, takes the monstrance into his hands and, with it, makes the sign of the cross in silence over the vast gathering.

Rather than returning Our Lord to the tabernacle, however, the priest decides to take Our Lord into the congregation, and exits the stage heading slowly, yet methodically, directly toward us.

Something that I've seen occur only one time before is about to happen again. I'm not prepared for it. It is as frightening now as it was the first time I saw it a decade ago on a night very similar to this, at Fatima, at the close of Benediction.

On each side of the African priest are two others gently swinging thuribles filled with incense. These priests will concelebrate the Mass after this "salut," this "segen," this blessing over the crowd.

The priest makes his way through the crowd, holding the monstrance high above his head, back and forth in a calm, methodical manner, proclaiming loudly "This IS Our Lord Jesus Christ!" He's only 10 feet away now and I can see the whites of his glaring eyes. I hear the choir singing with redoubled energy, the crescendo building, their pace quickening.

The noises begin. Preternatural utterances, cries of torment, fearful screams, and what appear to be howls of pain erupt in front of me at the approaching monstrance. As with the first time at Fatima, I'm reminded of the coyotes I have heard on hiking trips and campouts along the Appalachian Trail. Except this chorus of shouts and yells are much harsher and more desperate; emanating with infuriated and hysterical voices. For a brief moment I think it's feedback in the audio system, a combination of the multiple speakers battling the empyrean music resounding from the choir. I bow my head again and redouble my efforts to concentrate on my prayer, when the detestable commotion finally shows itself. My head shoots up, capturing the scene unfolding in front of me.

The priest is standing in front of the brunette, swinging the monstrance back and forth. Her companions try to move away but are packed between kneeling believers, yet she continues to stand defiantly, proudly, as the harsh roar exuding from her body continues. She begins gyrating, back and forth towards and then away from Our Lord in the towering monstrance.

"You motherfucker, Jesus! Fuck you, fuck you, fuck you!!!" scream from her mouth in various languages. Latin appears to be the predominate language used in this defamatory tirade. Many heads turn now in horror, the commotion so intense it's effectively countering the voices emanating from the choir. It appears that everyone is alarmed and offended by this open display of disrespect and vulgarity, except for the priest. He defiantly stands his ground, holding the monstrance above her head as foam begins to stream from her snarling mouth.

From this physically self-absorbed and self-proclaimed goddess, who only a short time ago was assured of her own beauty and self-importance, comes a multitude of low, guttural, infernal, masculine shrieks and wails. Coughing violently, she continues to twist and bend, her back arching as though caught by a series of seizures. What we witness is real and not special effects generated for a Hollywood movie. No computer-generated magic is being used to make her body contort in these completely unnatural ways. I've seen a fair number of seizures over the years in hospitals and even in the pews, and this is definitely not of that category.

The priest continues to hold the monstrance high above her, remaining unfazed by her actions and blaspheming.

She flops hard to the ground, her back slapping on the concrete, her head bouncing with a gruesome-sounding thud. The surrounding crowd instinctively shift away, some trying to stand and flee – the majority fall into each other. Without warning, her middle torso shoots up toward the night sky, balancing herself on her heels and head. Her mouth continues to foam as she spews forth obscene outbursts of rage at the monstrance. This surreal scene, illuminated by nearby torchlights, eerily emphasize her eyes rolling up into her eyelids. Finally, with a last, horrendous tortuous gasp, she collapses.

I join those around her, including her companions, who look more alarmed than the rest of the group, as the priest moves away. Sheriff Luder is by my side, his caring instincts, at least for the moment, overtaking his reluctance to be on this trip.

The smell suddenly hits us. My memory bank hasn't let me easily forget that stench from the first time I was in a similar situation. On cue, I'm overwhelmed once more. My head and those of the people around instinctively snap back when we reach her side as the rancid, putrid, rotten odor escapes from the body of this now very disoriented woman.

Helping her to her feet, we gently pass her to her friends. They walk the exhausted woman through the crowds towards a bench. I feel sick to my stomach. I have no doubt that Satan and his demons are at work spreading evil throughout the world. I have complete faith that Our Lord will protect me as long as I don't venture down roads that I clearly know I shouldn't travel. I'm sick over this entire scene. I can't help but despair once more over the number of souls who just don't get it, who willingly accept the evil that Satan promotes, and ignore or refuse His love, His constant desire to help us through this life – His Church, the Sacraments, Mother Mary, the Saints, the Angels, and various Sacramentals, among other gifts.

The sheriff is staring at me, stupefied. I can tell his world is metamorphosing once more. The tomb around his heart that was cracked and opened slightly with his near death experience has now opened wide with what he has just witnessed. But will it stay that way, I wonder? How hard is his heart? How locked in to his way of thinking is he? As I ponder these thoughts, he immediately leaves for the hotel.

I watch him go, and lo and behold, I see him making the sign of the cross. Conversions come in many forms. Many are from physical or mental healings, but I think the greatest are conversions of the heart. Because when all is said and done, when our life here on earth is over, I firmly believe it will be the latter that matters the most to Our Lord. Did we make the effort to change? Did we humbly return to Him? Did we repent? Did we follow what Our Lady has told us and keeps telling us at these apparition sites? Or do we remain firmly entrenched in our belief that we are our own God, and He isn't?

My senses are on high alert, and it's been months since I've been this happy and full of optimism.

"Thank you, God," I say out loud.

Chapter 32

Sheriff Luder looked ragged yesterday on our bus ride to the airport for our trip to Fatima, Portugal, our final stop on this pilgrimage. Our eyes have met a few times and although he has appeared on the verge of speaking, I don't believe he quite knows yet what he wants to say. I hate to admit it, but I'm glad he didn't speak, as I had a much more compelling issue to deal with – my health.

There is always someone in every group who can't seem to leave home without bringing it all with them. JoAnn Mazzitrius, a repeat pilgrim, is infamous for bringing multiple changes of clothing and far too many beauty products. Her heavy bag weighed well over 100 pounds, so much so that one of the zippers had snapped, leaving a jagged edge. As our driver struggled to lift her luggage into the storage compartment of the bus, I instinctively reached down to help. My finger caught the edge, and I received a slice in my index finger for my efforts. Blood began flowing immediately, and lightheadedness soon followed as I saw my life fluids where they weren't supposed to be. Embarrassed and agitated by my reaction, I boarded the bus and field-dressed the surface wound with a band aid and Neosporin, a first aid antibiotic, from my spit kit. To individuals who aren't obsessive about their health, that would have been the end of it. Lucky people.

Unfortunately, I could think of nothing else. A constant heartbeat pounded from the wound, the area became numb, and a tingling sensation moved through my hand. The more I stared at the bandaged finger, the more I became convinced that a red rash, the sure sign of infection, was overtaking my hand. A low level of panic quickly ensued.

Within seconds I became flushed, and a pain hit my chest. I knew this was stress driven by irrational thinking, so I reminded myself to relax and breathe deeply, looking out the window so those around me couldn't see the look of terror on my face. Did I work myself up so much I was having a heart attack? What if there was something in the air that got into the wound before I cleaned it properly? My mind raced back to everything I touched from the moment I was cut. What if the zipper that cut me had been touched by someone who had a deadly disease? Did *that* get into my system?

All I wanted, at that moment, was to be home in Gardensville, where my doctor is located. I've already visited him seven times for various minor ailments since I came to town, but since he is compassionate and now knows my tendency to overreact to my health, he always takes the extra time to try and make me feel better. I am grateful, but it's humiliating. I'm a grown man, a Catholic priest no less. I trust God with everything, except my health. How goofy is that? He's assured me I'm far from the only person who has irrational health-related concerns.

Looking around the bus, it all began to feel weird, very surreal. I couldn't stop the negative thoughts from overwhelming me. I was detached from myself, and I couldn't explain the feeling even if I tried. The fear that I was going to die hit me hard and fast, and I buried my head into my hands, begging God to help me, to end this trip, to get me home. The anxiety attack took me then, and I was terrified. When it finally subsided, I was exhausted and slept the remainder of the trip, just barely holding back a torrent of fearful, frustrating tears.

Chapter 33

Fatima, Portugal. If you've forgotten the miracles of this blessed place, let me remind you that the apparitions that occurred here in 1917 included a spectacularly visible miracle that was witnessed by tens of thousands. Over four million pilgrims from around the world travel to Fatima each year. Pope Benedict XVI, while still in office, encouraged all the faithful to entrust ourselves to Our Lady of Fatima.

I'm still a little exhausted from the anxiety attack I experienced on the bus, but am determined to tour the facility, reviewing the images and accompanying captions and documentation. I've changed my bandage multiple times, and haven't seen any of the redness I was certain meant impending death. Still, as I move from one historical picture to the next, I can't help but look forward to the plane trip home.

In the first picture that I come upon, I see the three children who were the central focus of the apparitions here at Fatima. Six-year-old Jacinta Marto is on the left, her left hand on her waist, defiant in the face of all the attention and the accusations. Her older brother, eight-year-old Francisco, stands in the middle holding a crutch under his left arm, an almost bored look on his face. And their cousin, nine-year-old Lucia dos Santos, stands on the left holding her hands in front of her with a scowl on her face.

As foretold by Mother Mary during one of her apparitions, Francisco died at age 11 and Jacinta died at the tender age of nine, enduring excruciating pain during her final months. She displayed surprising strength for one so young, offering her pain and suffering for the conversion of souls – especially those being consumed by the influenza epidemic that had decimated parts of Europe during that period.

After the deaths of her cousins, at the request of Mother Mary, Lucia entered the Sisters of St. Dorothy in Spain in 1925, transferring in 1948 to the cloistered convent of the Carmelites in Coimbra, Portugal. She died in 2005 just one month before her 98th birthday. She saw Mother Mary three more times throughout the remainder of her life.

Another picture shows the three children, hands steepled in prayer, and wrapped with Rosary beads. All were from poor Portuguese peasant families, and all were relatively forgotten once the controversy and excitement surrounding the visions and apparitions of 1917 subsided.

An important side note is that, as we've seen at the other sites we've visited, Mother Mary chose to appear to poor innocent children, located in remote places, in order to lend greater credence to her messages and to remain above suspicion from the "learned" people of their day. When the Church decided on the authenticity of these apparitions, all of the seers were proven to be above reproach.

"The World During This Period" is the next section, reminding pilgrims that World War I was raging and Communism was entering the world stage. Portugal had become anti-Christian, so much so that nearly 1,700 priests, nuns, and monks had been murdered. All public religious ceremonies had been forbidden.

It was during this dark period that Pope Benedict XV sent out a plea to all the faithful of the world to pray the Rosary and ask for the intercession of the Blessed Mother in bringing the war to an end. Eight days later, on May 13, 1917, Mother Mary appeared to the children at Fatima, letting the world know through them of her own "peace plan from Heaven." She chose to communicate these messages in Portugal, right in the midst of all the hatred being directed at Christianity.

The next section contains a painting of an angel with the three young children. The narrative explains that an angel appeared to the children on three separate occasions in 1916, the year before the apparitions from the Virgin Mary began, preparing them for what was to come. He would later tell them he was the Guardian Angel of Portugal. The angel appeared to the children as a young, transparent, light-filled man, and by his voice and manner made the children very comfortable with him. The two girls could see and hear the angel, but the boy, Francisco, could only hear him.

On the first visit, the angel said:

"Fear not. I am the Angel of Peace. Pray with me."

While kneeling on the ground, he recited this prayer three times:

"My God, I believe, I adore, I hope, and I love you. I ask pardon of You for those who do not believe, do not adore, do not hope, and do not love You."

Rising, he said:

"Pray this way. The Hearts of Jesus and Mary are attentive to the voice of your supplications."

During the second visit, the angel told them:

"The Hearts of Jesus and Mary have designs of mercy for you. Offer unceasingly to the Most High prayer and sacrifices. Offer up everything within your power as a sacrifice to the Lord in reparation for the sins by which he is so much offended and of supplication for the conversion of sinners. Thus bring down peace upon your country. I am the Guardian Angel of Portugal. More than all else, accept and bear with resignation the sufferings that God may send you."

On the last visit, the angel prostrated himself and said this prayer: *"Most Holy Trinity, Father, Son, and Holy Ghost, I adore You profoundly and I offer You the most precious Body, Blood, Soul, and Divinity of Jesus Christ, present in all the tabernacles of the world, in reparation for the outrages, sacrileges, and indifference by which He Himself is offended. And by the infinite merits of His Most Sacred Heart and the Immaculate Heart of Mary, I beg of You the conversion of poor sinners."*

He then offered Our Lord in the Eucharist to the children saying: *"Take and drink the Body and Blood of Jesus Christ, horribly outraged by ungrateful men. Make reparation for their crimes and console your God."*

Even though I've been here several times, a surreal feeling returns. Although much of the world has either forgotten what took place here or has chosen to ignore it, I pray that it will eventually take heed. You see, throughout 1917 there were six apparitions, and Fatima was the first apparition in Church history in which the Virgin Mother announced a miracle beforehand. This same thing occurred in Kibeho, Africa, in 1981 – only 32 years ago – when Mother Mary foretold the "River of Blood," the pilgrimage I will be leading next year.

So a year later, in 1917, after having been prepared by the Guardian Angel of Portugal, Mother Mary began appearing to the children. Each apparition has its own dedicated section; designed so that pilgrims can absorb the full impact of each one.

I spend the next few minutes reviewing the messages from the first three apparitions.

The next placard tells us that the Fourth Apparition did not occur on the 13th of August because the children were kidnapped by a cruel civil administrator who was against the Church. However, approximately 18,000 people were present who witnessed a sign of Heaven's displeasure at what was happening to the children. There was lightning and thunder, the sun turned pale, and there was a yellowish haze in the atmosphere. A white cloud settled on the oak tree where Mother Mary had appeared since May on the 13th of each month. It rapidly changed colors, taking on all the colors of the rainbow.

As this was occurring, the civil authorities were threatening the lives of the children with boiling water and other pain and torture if they didn't change their story and tell the truth. Even under the threat of severe torture and having no reason to not believe that this wasn't going to happen to them, the children held fast to what they had seen and heard, to all they had experienced during the apparitions. Whether answering questions from their families, the Church, or civil authorities – together or separate – their stories held true from the beginning to the end. Mother Mary appeared to the children six days later.

After reviewing the messages from the fourth, fifth and sixth apparitions, I move to the next section and lean in to look more closely at the pictures taken the day of the miracle, foretold in advance by Mother Mary. There are photos of pilgrims, prior to the event, holding umbrellas, seeking protection from the pouring rain, the ground having turned to mud. During the actual miracle, there are photos of pilgrims looking into the sky with horror on their faces, some crouching down as though protecting themselves from being hit by an unknown object from the sky, others lying prostate on the ground or kneeling in prayer. And then pictures taken immediately after the Miracle of the Sun, where the ground was completely dry. The placard reads as follows:

DEFINITION: THEOPHANY – A direct communication or appearance by God to human beings. Instances: God confronting Adam and Eve after their disobedience (Genesis 3:8); God appearing to Moses out of a burning bush (Exodus 3:2-6); Abraham pleading with Yahweh to be merciful to the Sodomites (Genesis 18:23).

In front of 70,000 witnesses which included at least 30 journalists, many of them believers but also a large percentage of skeptics, the Miracle of the Sun occurred as promised by Mother Mary, lasting about 12 minutes.

Suddenly the rain stopped and the clouds, thick all morning, dissipated. The sun appeared at its zenith, like a silver disk. Suddenly it began to turn on itself like a wheel of fire, projecting in all directions a shower of light whose color changed several times. Streaks of yellow, red, green, blue, etc. tinted the clouds, the trees, the hills, lending a strange aspect to the countryside and to all that landscape, bizarrely transformed by its Creator. After several minutes, the heavenly body halted, blazing with a light that did no hurt to the eyes; then it began its stupefying dance again. This phenomenon occurred three times and each time a little faster, with a brighter and more colorful light. And during the twelve unforgettable minutes that this impressive spectacle lasted, the crowd was held in suspense, watching open-mouthed this tragic and captivating phenomenon, which could be seen for 40 kilometers around. Abruptly, the spectators had the impression that the sun was tearing loose from the heavens and falling on them. A formidable cry rose simultaneously from every watcher. Some genuflected, others cried out, still others prayed aloud ... Meanwhile it stopped in its tracks, then slowly returned to its place; then it resumed its normal brightness. There were no more clouds and the sky was a limpid blue. The crowd's clothes, soaked through by the rain an instant before, dried immediately. The enthusiasm was indescribable.

People then began to ask each other what they had seen. The great majority admitted to having seen the trembling and dancing of the sun; others affirmed that they saw the face of the Blessed Virgin; others, again, swore that the sun whirled on itself like a giant Catherine wheel and that it lowered itself to the earth as if to burn it with its rays. Some said they saw it change colors successively....

Witnesses, such as Maria Carreira, testified to the terrifying nature of the solar miracle: "It turned everything different colors, yellow, blue, white, and it shook and trembled; it seemed like a wheel of fire which was going to fall on the people. They cried out: 'We shall all be killed, we shall all be killed!' ...At last the sun stopped moving and we all breathed a sigh of relief. We were still alive and the miracle which the children had foretold had taken place."

Other people witnessed the solar miracle from a distance thus ruling out the possibility of any type of collective hallucination. Many of the lame could suddenly walk, and the physically blind could see. Conversions and reconversions abounded.

As the people were witnessing the dancing sun, the children were seeing something completely different. As foretold by Mother Mary, St. Joseph appeared to them, holding the child Jesus and Mother Mary clothed in white with a blue sash and veil. St. Joseph and the baby Jesus blessed the world. The apparition then changed: Our Lord and Our Lady appeared, blessing the world. Finally, Our Lady of Carmel appeared with the brown scapular in her right hand while holding the Child Jesus.

Stories of the Miracle of the Sun were sent back with the pictures by the journalists present, but were mostly unheeded by their respective editors-in-chief, most thinking their correspondents were irrational, delusional, incoherent. Some were printed, however, but the majority of the world completely ignored the miraculous event. The Greenwich Observatory, 1,200 miles away, didn't report any unusual activity that day but this fact was offset by the one voice of all those present that stated they saw the same whirling, multicolored, descending sun – an atheist who was present to mock the entire event ended up being hospitalized for three days given what he saw with his own eyes, being taken away from the scene in shock.

The Catholic Church, via Bishop Correia of Fatima, approved the apparitions in 1930, as follows: "In virtue of considerations made known, and others which for reasons of brevity we omit; humbly invoking the Divine Spirit and placing ourselves under the protection of the most Holy Virgin, and after hearing the opinions of our Rev. Advisors in this diocese, we hereby: 1. Declare worthy of belief, the visions of the shepherd children in the Cova da Iria, parish of Fatima, in this diocese, from the 13th May to 13th October, 1917. 2. Permit officially the cult of Our Lady of Fatima."

A Shrine, as Mother Mary had requested, was built which is now the Basilica you see on the grounds today. On July 7, 1952, Pope Pius XII consecrated the Russian people to the Immaculate Heart of Mary, as requested by Our Lady at Fatima, but not in conjunction with the bishops of the world as she had requested. However, on November 21, 1964, Pope Paul VI renewed the earlier consecration by Pope Pius XII, this time doing so in the presence of the bishops of the world, when they were all gathered for the Second Vatican Council, which group worked tirelessly on what is now known as the Catechism of the Catholic Church publication.

Wars are caused by sin, according to the Fatima message, and so Our Lady is calling all people back to her Son, Jesus Christ, in the daily living of an authentic Christian life. But the message is not pessimistic but optimistic, an answer to wars and hate around the world, if only the people throughout the world LIVE the message of Fatima by accepting all the teachings of the Church and loyalty in obedience to the pope, the Chief Vicar of Jesus Christ, upon earth. True happiness requires sanctity on earth.

As I enter the adjoining room that marks the end of this self-guided tour, I hear a fellow priest remind a group that praying the Rosary is a very powerful tool against Satan. Mother Mary has clearly reminded the faithful of this, time and again, during her apparitions.

As with the other rooms, this one is filled with pilgrims, quietly reading and studying the exhibits. Moving to the next station, I inadvertently bump into another pilgrim. "Sorry about that," I say, motioning for him to go before me. I thank God once again for this peaceful place, these like-minded people, and the charity that exudes from all who open themselves to God.

Standing side by side, we gaze at a painting Sr. Lucia saw in a vision from Mother Mary, a copy of which I found on the DVD titled "The Call to Fatima" located on an adjoining table. I pick up a copy for the parish library back home.

My newfound companion and I shuffle slowly, side by side, down the line of pictures while reading the accompanying verbiage on the displays, until we reach the section that discusses the secrets Our Lady gave to the children.

The Secrets

At different times during the apparitions, Mother Mary told three 'secrets' to the seers. The first and second parts of the "secret" refer especially to the frightening vision of Hell, devotion to the Immaculate Heart of Mary, the Second World War, and finally the prediction of the immense damage that Russia would do to humanity by abandoning the Christian faith and embracing Communist totalitarianism.

The First Secret – The Vision of Hell,
per Sr. Lucia's Memoirs
written by order of Bishop of Leiria
and with Our Lady's permission

"Our Lady showed us a great sea of fire which seemed to be under the earth. Plunged in this fire were demons and souls in human form, like transparent burning embers, all blackened or burnished bronze, floating about in the conflagration, now raised into the air by the flames that issued from within themselves together with great clouds of smoke, now falling back on every side like sparks in a huge fire, without weight or equilibrium, and amid shrieks and groans of pain and despair, which horrified us and made us tremble with fear. The demons could be distinguished by their terrifying and repulsive likeness to frightful and unknown animals, all black and transparent. This vision lasted but an instant. How can we ever be grateful enough to our kind heavenly Mother, who had already prepared us by promising, in the first Apparition, to take us to Heaven. Otherwise, I think we would have died of fear and terror."

Jacinta Marto, the youngest of the seers, upon her deathbed had asked Lucia, "Why doesn't the Lady show Hell to everybody? Then nobody would ever again commit a mortal sin."

The Second Secret – Devotion to the Immaculate Heart of Mary

"The message therein was the same given by Mother Mary during the July 13, 1917, apparition that he had read from that section in the previous room."

The Third Secret

"The third part of the secret revealed at the Cova da Iria-Fatima, on July 13, 1917.

I write in obedience to you, my God, who command me to do so through his Excellency the Bishop of Leiria and through your Most Holy Mother and mine.

After the two parts which I have already explained, at the left of Our Lady and a little above, we saw an Angel with a flaming sword in his left hand; flashing, it gave out flames that looked as though they would set the world on fire; but they died out in contact with the splendour that Our Lady radiated towards him from her right hand: pointing to the earth with his right hand, the Angel cried out in a loud voice: 'Penance, Penance, Penance.' And we saw in an immense light that is God: 'something similar to how people appear in a mirror when they pass in front of it' a Bishop dressed in White 'we had the impression that it was the Holy Father.' Other Bishops, Priests, men and women Religious going up a steep mountain, at the top of which there was a big Cross of rough-hewn trunks as of a cork-tree with the bark; before reaching there the Holy Father passed through a big city half in ruins and half-trembling with halting step, afflicted with pain and sorrow, he prayed for the souls of the corpses he met on his way; having reached the top of the mountain, on his knees at the foot of the big Cross he was killed by a group of soldiers who fired bullets and arrows at him, and in the same way there died one after another the other Bishops, Priests, men and women Religious, and various lay people of different ranks and positions. Beneath the two arms of the Cross there were two Angels each with a crystal aspersorium in his hand, in which they gathered up the blood of the Martyrs and with it sprinkled the souls that were making their way to God.

Sister Lucia responded by pointing out that she had received the vision but not its interpretation. The interpretation, she said, belonged not to the visionary but to the Church.

The recently retired Pope Emeritus Benedict XVI, has stated that the third secret alluded to a moment in history when the entire power of evil would come to a head in the major dictatorships of the twentieth century, and a belief that said evil is still present in the world today. He urges the faithful "that full and complete transformation can only come not via grand political actions, rather, it must come from a conversion of the hearts of all – through 'faith, hope, love and penance' in a spirit of humility, which are the essentials of the faith, and the culmination of the messages to the seers by Our Lady of Fatima in 1917."

Chapter 34

"Can I ask you a question?" the gentle elderly man with the kind smile asks, as we turn away from the last Fatima exhibit. I'm wearing my clerics, and I am pleased that he feels comfortable enough to approach me. He reminds me of my spiritual advisor, Fr. Jack back in Brooklyn.

"I really do apologize, Father, but this is my first pilgrimage here or, well, anywhere. I really just came because my wife always wanted to go during her lifetime. I don't deny the existence of God and Heaven, but I just don't know for certain whether or not anything like this exists. She calls me an agnostic. I spent my career as a physician and I struggle with much of this."

Smiling broadly and uncontrollably, I feel like I could hug him. I've always loved physicians because they never seem to worry about the small things like I do when they get bumps on their skin, or strange sensations in their body, or little cuts from damn snapped zippers on luggage.

"It's okay. I understand. Faith is a gift from God. How can I help you?" I ask, wondering for the millionth time how I can say this to someone so confidently, while I stand here with my finger wrapped with so much gauze it looks like I've just had major surgery. I know, I know, this is a mental issue, not a mental illness. It's just my own weird way of thinking and I know I really need to address it for my own sanity. But I need reassurance *now* from someone else. This kind physician, specifically.

Becoming more at ease, he says: "Well, uh, let me just ask this and I know it sounds dumb since you're a priest and all, but…" he shuffles back and forth now, embarrassed. "Do you believe in all of this?" sweeping his hands around, trying to encompass all of the grounds of Fatima, I would imagine. "You know, all of this? The whole thing?"

He looks towards his wife who is waving to him hurriedly so they won't miss their tour bus, pointing to her watch. Putting his finger up to her motioning for just one more moment, I try to rapidly crystalize my thoughts.

"Yes, I do. I really do. Oh, throughout my life, on occasion I've fallen away from God. Ran from Him, if you will, but He never stopped chasing me, blessing me."

Gesturing to the pictures, I say, "I firmly believe those people saw a miracle right before their very eyes, and I really do believe that. They could see that the world was larger than they were, and that what was happening in their lives, and the way they were living, really meant something, whether for good or for evil. Mother Mary was giving them a loving warning. Very lucky people I would say, that is, if they paid attention and changed their lives accordingly."

He looks back toward his wife. I continue before she arrives, not wanting him to leave as I have my own favor to ask of him.

"All of us who haven't had a chance to witness a physical miracle live by faith, and not by sight, my friend, but we can come to apparition sites like these and see glimpses of what they saw with their eyes, or even see it on our own through pictures or documentary videos."

I smile at his wife and she returns the welcoming gesture. He reaches out his hand and we shake awkwardly as I hide the big, goofy bandaged right hand behind me.

"God bless you, my friend. I'll keep you in my prayers as you continue your search. But remember, He's not a mystery, at least not the mystery you're making Him out to be. He's here, He really is, and He really does love you. Perhaps you should think about it the way Blaise Pascal did, the 17th century French mathematician, physicist, inventor, writer and Christian philosopher, of which I will very roughly paraphrase: If it's all false but you change your life, what have you got to lose? A better life for yourself and everyone around you? But if it's all true, look what you have to gain. Eternal happiness. That's a pretty solid bet, don't you think?"

He smiles again, turns to his wife and they begin to walk away. It's now or never.

"Excuse me," I call out to him. "Can I ask you something? It will take less than two minutes, I promise."

Squeezing his wife's hands, he returns to me, and I guide him to a corner that has ample lighting, yet enough privacy for me to ask my question.

"I, uh, look, can you check this for me really quick?" I ask sheepishly.

Do I tell him I'm afraid for my health, that ever since I got this cut, even though the people around me think I'm perfectly fine, I have been torn up inside worrying about nothing else? That it's become so bad that I've suffered an anxiety attack? That I really wish I could just go through life like him, unconcerned about these stupid cares that choke my world? No, I won't, I'll just hold up my right hand, feeling like a child, allowing him to inspect the cut, and be silent.

Taking my hand, I am incredibly thankful and at once at ease as this gentle, learned man undresses the bandage.

"Looks fine to me. In fact, it's already starting to heal," he assures me.

At this moment, I could cry. The relief I feel is immediate and immense, the 10 ton worry that has been hanging over me instantly disappearing.

Choking up, I offer meekly, "Thank you."

God has answered my prayers for assistance. This gentle soul, who undoubtedly has seen many patients just like me, offers me a few words of wisdom.

"You know, can I share something with you that might help? Do you mind?"

"Not at all, please, I welcome anything you can tell me." I am elated.

"In all my years of treating patients, I really believe that the vast majority of them came to me *not* because of actual ailments, but because of what they *thought* about those ailments. I became convinced that if they could learn to control their minds, then in large part, they could learn to control their bodies. I would recommend to them that they should think, but not worry and obsess, about their bodies. When they got ill, I encouraged them to take one or even two weeks treating themselves, using simple remedies like proper rest, diet, pain relievers, or whatever they felt they needed, and allow their body to heal itself. But, of course, if it got worse to then come and see me.

"So many would feel a sensation early in the morning and

then rush into my office early that afternoon, and I felt bad for them, I really did, because they were so worried that it was a major sickness that had pounced upon them. They were so afraid of getting sick, of catching that strange disease that they had just read about in the paper, or heard that someone else had caught, and that caused them to get all worked up about it which made even subtle sensations worse, much worse. So I would always recommend they learn to slow down, to relax and take it easy and get out of the way of their body and mind's natural healing process. To not make something worse than it really was, and to not make something up that didn't exist. Our minds are very powerful forces, and they can help us reach great heights, or they can take us down very deep to frightening lows."

I nod. He's just described me perfectly. He finishes but adds a final piece of advice as he begins to turn toward his wife.

"Father, slow down, okay? Especially with your breathing; you can never slow it down enough. You may just have a tendency to worry about your health like millions of others, but that habit is very manageable with the right tools. You may have to live with this quirk, but you can minimize it if you really try. Check out the Midwest Center for Anxiety. They have an incredible program that some of my past patients have gone through and raved about. And there are a great many books available and many fine therapists out there who can help, okay?"

I give this wonderful man a warm embrace. I am so very tired of being like this.

Thanking him, I start to follow he and his wife out of the building to get some fresh air and to thank God profusely for His kindness in sending this man to me, but I recall one more section that's off to the side – the final story regarding what happened to the other two children – Blessed Francisco and Jacinta.

Poking my head into the room, I see the sheriff. He's leaning in closely, scribbling furiously onto the notepad he's been carrying. Not wanting him to see me and perhaps cause him to walk away, I step back into the main room until he leaves. Within a few moments, he exits, moving at a rapid pace. I remember the look of horror he had that night at Lourdes during Adoration, and now his tortured face matches that memory. He moves outside, right hand on the back of his head, rapidly rubbing it, clearly bothered. I enter the room he just left; hoping to see what has alarmed the sheriff to this degree.

Standing at the beginning of this section which starts with Jacinta Marto, I recall how she was a sweet but stubborn soul, and would fight with her brother as siblings often do. When she didn't get her way, she tended to sulk. Before the apparitions, she was capricious and vivacious. After the visits from Mother Mary, however, she was much more serious and generous. She offered everything in her life for the conversion of sinners, even giving her lunch to the animals she was tending.

It was this change in her that her family, and all those that knew her well, recognized as the most convincing sign that what she said had occurred, did indeed happen. Although very young, Jacinta possessed a solid inner strength, which became necessary when people would make fun of them. People in the town where they lived would throw rocks at them, sometimes even as they were on the way to the *Cova da Iria* for the scheduled apparitions.

Her diagnosis was *"purulent pleurisy of the large left cavity, fistulous osteitis of the seventh and eight ribs of the same side."* In short, her chest membrane was inflamed and discharging pus. Also, her bones were inflamed and an abscess had formed, which was very painful and required daily changing.

Mother Mary had told her of all the hospitals she would be visiting and that she would die alone. She also told her that she would come for her soon and that when she did her pain would leave her. Jacinta relayed all of this to the mother of the orphanage who documented what she told her and it all occurred just as she had said – she visited each hospital foretold, she died exactly when Mother Mary had told her, and was indeed alone and far away from her home when it happened.

I move to the final station of this section where the sheriff had been standing when I saw him, no more than 20 minutes ago. It's a photo dated September 12, 1935, of a priest bending over the uncovered face of Jacinta Marto. I scan the caption for the words that must have been read by the sheriff just moments before.

261

During a transfer of her remains....Perfectly preserved........Had been buried in a standard grave and coffin due to poor family.....intense heat of Portugal after being buried for 15 years....No perceptible odor.....same state of the body during a subsequent transfer in 1950. Although her body had been eaten away by the disease before she died, none of the effects of the infection could be found when they exhumed her body. St. Catherine Laboure and the Miraculous Medal – Incorrupt; St. Bernadette Soubirous of Lourdes – Incorrupt. Jacinta Marto of Fatima – Incorrupt – the only case of an incorrupt body of a child in Church history.

The plaque above the photo reads as follows:

In her last days when the Blessed Virgin appeared to her and told her she would no longer suffer, Jacinta related (to Lucia) that Mary looked very sad and told her the cause of her sadness:

The sins which lead the greatest number of souls to perdition are the sins of the flesh.

Luxurious living must be avoided, people must do penance and repent of their sins.

Great penance is indispensable.

Chapter 35

It's the weekend and we're on our 21-hour trip home.

"Father, may I speak with you?"

Sheriff Luder stands before me, beckoning me to join him. We make our way to the last row of the half-full 375-passenger Boeing 767, and I can see that he has commandeered the last three seats with only two people seated two rows ahead. We have privacy, and by the sheriff's whispering, I gather this is what he wants.

Sitting in the window seat, a couple of notepads resting in the middle seat, he respectfully motions for me to take the aisle.

He's bothered, but I can't pinpoint the exact reason why.

"You believe in 'the sins of the flesh and going to Hell' and all that other stuff."

His eyes stare intensely into mine, begging me now for the truth.

"Yes, I do. The faithful may choose to believe or not what occurred there. I choose to believe," I reply.

"Why? I mean, what makes you believe? I guess there's a governing body, or whatever, in the Church and they tell everyone what they have to do, how they have to live, but why do you really believe, deep down?" His gaze is tense, and he's leaning towards me in his seat.

"First of all, the 'governing body' that you are probably referring to is called the Magisterium. When you have time, I strongly recommend you obtain a Catholic Bible and crack it open to Matthew 16:13-20 where it will tell you that Christ founded his Church upon St. Peter, the leader of the apostles and the first pope, giving him the Keys to the Kingdom. Second, the Church doesn't force itself on anyone. However, she's a good mother, and like a good mother she informs her children as to what's best for them, guided by a special charism given by God. Think about it this way. Growing up, did your mom ever warn you not to play in the street, put your hand into a campfire, or to not point your rubber band gun at anyone's eye?"

He nods his head, his eyes never leaving mine.

"Well, you could have done any of those things if you really wanted. Your mom told you those things out of love, not because she was some tyrant wanting to control you. This is how we should look at the teachings of the Church."

I'm encouraged as he continues to nod his head, making notes as I speak.

"As far as your question about if I really believe in all of this, why wouldn't I? I mean, it's amazing what people will believe, even without seeing it, just because an 'expert' says it's true. For instance, do you believe that Christopher Columbus discovered America in 1492?"

"Sure, yeah," he replies, shrugging his shoulder to reflect that there's no reason *not* to believe this obvious fact that we were all taught in grade school.

"Okay, well, why do you? Because you read it in a history book? Because a teacher that you had no reason not to believe told you this was true? I mean, no one who was living then is alive today. There were no pictures taken, no videos, no Youtube to show that he landed on the eastern shores of America.

"Granted, on the one hand, being naïve and accepting everything as a miracle serves no good purpose. But let's consider these Marian apparitions. There are people alive today who actually saw them firsthand and so many more who have experienced miracles at Lourdes, like possibly Dolores. And you were right there with me, right? But nonetheless, people choose *not* to believe. So why is that?"

"Well, I guess since everyone is different, there are many reasons why people might not believe. We've been let down by authority way too many times. Maybe we've all learned to be distrustful," he says, shrugging his shoulders.

"Fair enough, yes, I'll give you that, Sheriff. But, let me now ask you, do *you* believe?"

He turns to gaze out the window, and eventually turns back to meet my inquiring gaze.

"Well, I'm beginning to. And…" his eyes lower now, his hand running through his hair, "for me, what has hit me so hard is that if this is all true, I mean, if it's really the way I should have been living, then I'm really in deep shit."

Rubbing his face with both hands, he stares back at his notes, but his mind is somewhere else. He continues.

"I gotta ask this question because it's confused me all my life. Why did God give us sexual desire if, according to his big 'master plan,' He knew we were going to be humping like rabbits, or in the very least, wanting to do so?"

I've been asked this many times before. "This goes back to the topic of original sin. You told me that you were baptized, so that means that the stain of the sin committed by our first parents, plus any sin you might have committed up to that point in your life, was forgiven by God. You then began a new life in Christ and the Holy Spirit and became a member of the Body of Christ and the Church."

Eyebrows furrowing now, I can tell he's trying to process this information as he writes at a furious pace. What inner battle is raging, I wonder? I continue my explanation, and slow my pace for his benefit.

"As an infant your parents chose to have you baptized and you received the grace that the sacrament provides. You can only be baptized once, but the grace you received is with you the rest of your life. Our Lord told us baptism is necessary for salvation. But baptism is only the beginning; you must continue to grow in your faith throughout the rest of your life.

"There are many who, after their baptism, spend their entire lives accepting God's graces, through the sacraments in particular. They are, you might say, inoculated from the temptations of the devil by the sanctifying graces they receive. They understand that although original and personal sin were washed away at baptism, their human appetites or desires still remain disordered due to the consequences of original sin. But with God's help, they are able to overcome or subdue their inclination to sin or 'concupiscence.'

"Concupiscence doesn't mean we can't control ourselves, it just means that we have a 'tendency' toward sin. So, in other words, yes, we have a desire for sex, but there's no way we have to give into it. We also have desires to eat, to drink, to drive fast, to say things we shouldn't – but it doesn't mean we have to give in to those desires, either, and for some people, they can be just as strong, yet they remain steadfast."

He continues to write now, and I pray that I explained it well.

"But others don't get this. They 'live like every day is their last day,' which is sound advice if you wish to always be prepared to achieve eternal life with God. But that isn't what many have in mind when they use that term. They say it to mean 'do whatever you want to, every day, in any way, just don't get caught, enjoy all the pleasures life has to offer.' And their souls, which were originally white at baptism, if they even did get baptized to begin with, end up being very dark, soiled, and stained from sin."

"Is that why the Church is so down on sex?" he asks, sounding exasperated. "Because it can send us to Hell?"

"That's a common misunderstanding," I reply. "For the record, the Catholic Church has no problem with 'sex,' none at all. I mean, God *created* sex. It's a holy, life-giving act. Granted, some people within the Church have, often with the best intentions, produced a lot of misinformation on the topic of sex, which has resulted in great divisiveness and confusion among many of the faithful.

"But the reality is that the Church fully appreciates, supports, and condones the goodness and beauty of sex between married couples. Man and woman. Husband and wife. Sex is an absolutely beautiful thing. God created it so it must be good, if partaken in as He desired. With the sexual revolution that occurred a few decades ago, Blessed John Paul II saw the absolute need to publish his monumental work, 'Theology of the Body,' which talks about love, life, and human sexuality."

He's nodding his head again, pointing his pen at his yellow notepad. "I actually made some notes about the sexual revolution."

"Really? Might I ask of what?" I'm most certainly curious.

"Yeah, but, I'll get back to that in a minute. I didn't mean to interrupt you but, before I forget, did you know that Pope John Paul II had an immense porn collection, and he himself struggled with sexuality issues his whole life?"

The bile in my throat rises and I feel the anger rising with it. I attempt to control it with only minor success.

266

"What?! And where did you find that out? I mean, how did you validate it? On the Internet? From a post of a sick mind out there? And you choose to believe it at face value? Really, show me specifically where you heard that, and then how you validated it."

"Well, uh. Yeah, it was a blog. But how do you know it's not true?" His jaded outlook and defensive attitude flare up in response to my outburst. Obviously, his deep-seeded negative views regarding God and the Church remain.

I've been hearing disparaging things about the Church for too long, and I'm going to tell him straight up what I believe, whether he likes it or not.

"Let me tell you something, Sheriff. Now you may not believe any of what I'm about to tell you, and that's your choice – your free will. But you sure seem smart enough to at least consider it.

"First of all, you appear to have been very blessed in your life. Your wife, your daughter, your career, your beautiful home, all the material things you might ever need, but you still seem to hate everything and everyone around you.

"Then, you have what very well could be a near death experience, which rocks you, knocks you off balance, and shakes you to the core of your beliefs, hurts your pride, and dings your ego. And, quite honestly, that was a good thing, because it needed to happen. You've been blessed with a wonderful gift from God, a glimpse into what lies ahead. But you probably don't want to see it that way."

He drops his head quickly. "Yeah, well, about that….." I cut him off.

"And here you are, traveling from Europe, and all that you've seen, right? The stories, the miracles, the evidence at each Marian site, and even a glimpse of Satan. But after all that, you still want to stick hard and fast to your old, untested and lazy way of looking at your spiritual life?

"You know what you are? You're a 21st century unbelieving Pharisee."

I immediately feel bad, and say a quick prayer once more for the gift of patience. He puts his head down, and I quickly rub my face out of frustration.

"Look, I guess growing up in this day and age, what else is to be expected? There's so much pressure against the Church on this topic, so much hounding to try and force the Magisterium and other Church leaders to give in, to say that everything and anything with sex is just fine, as long as people are happy and consenting adults.

"And you want to know another reason why I personally have no issue with the message of the 'sins of the flesh' from Mother Mary to Blessed Jacinta? Because God gave Moses the Ten Commandments; and by the way, they are commandments, not suggestions. And two of those commandments deal with sex – the sixth, "Thou Shall Not Commit Adultery," and the ninth, "Thou Shall Not Covet Your Neighbor's Wife." Even the tenth Commandment, "You Shall Not Covet Anything That Is Your Neighbor's" ties into it, too, because it completes the ninth. So if three of the Ten Commandments deal with sexual impurity, I think it's pretty dang obvious that God has an issue with its misuse by His creation.

"And do you know why Jesus only talks about chastity four times in the Bible? Once with the woman at the well who had five husbands; once with the woman caught in adultery and was to be stoned; once with the woman with the jar of alabaster; and as one of the Beatitudes, 'Blessed are the pure in heart, for they shall see God?' Because the people of his time understood that this type of activity was wrong, very wrong. They didn't question it. They didn't flirt with it. *They got it and lived their lives accordingly.*

"But not today. Satan has made huge inroads into our lives; we see evidence of this all around us. Just look at the growing number of people that say God does not exist, so what does any of it matter? Or consider how many truly believe that no matter how they act, no matter what they do here on earth, they never have a need to repent, ask for forgiveness, or even try to amend their lives, because when they die they are going straight to Heaven. Really? Where does *that* come from? Certainly not from God, nor His Church going back to the beginning. Where does it say *that* in the Bible? I've never found it there.

"I mean, think about that community college class you and I attended. Do you remember how that instructor was pushing the "just be happy and do whatever you want in your life" mentality? Certainly the students could choose for themselves, even after being in his class. But what if their own moral compass has been skewed before they came to his class?

"C'mon, Sheriff, we always need to fight the good fight. But we need to understand that, without the grace of God, through Jesus, through his Church, and his Sacraments, we simply can't live a chaste, virtuous life. But with His grace, all of the grace He has freely given us and offers us all the time, we *will* win the battle, we *will* win our individual and collective war! I've said it before and I'll say it a million times again, God has never nor will he ever leave us. But the truth is, so many people have *left Him*, turned their backs on *His Church, His truth, and His love*. But still they wonder and accuse, *'Where is God?'* Are you kidding me? Even one of Michael Jackson's song partially addressed this concept when he sang 'Man in the Mirror.'"

We sit in silence for a moment.

"Hey, I'm sorry that I jumped on you like that. It's just that sex, and all of its disordered variations, is the number one topic heard in the confessional and sexual sin is at the top of the list of sins confessed."

Giving a moment of silence to reign, I change course.

"Do you have any idea what has happened to the two of us in the last month or so?"

"What? Who? You and me?" he asks, caught off guard by the question.

"Yes, you and me. The scales have dropped from our eyes. Me, thanks to your challenge. You with a clear vision of the path you can now take if you want to turn your life around.

"But I implore you – you can't stop now. The fight will get tougher, not easier. The last road Satan wants you to travel is back to God. But you don't need to fear that, okay? Satan is all about despair and depression. God is all about light, love, forgiveness, understanding, and mercy. And justice, too. Turn to him. Go to him. If you haven't gone to confession in a while, do it. I can hear your confession right now if you want. I'm not forcing you at all, I'm just offering it. It's one of the most beautiful sacraments God offers. His mercy is waiting for you."

He shakes his head, but only tentatively this time.

"Okay. The offer stands. I'm not the only one, you know. You can always have any priest hear your confession when you get back home, but I wouldn't wait too long. Once you do, receive Our Lord in the Eucharist as often as you can. Get back to going to Mass every single weekend. He really is there in the tabernacle, in the Eucharist. His Body. His Blood. Spiritual food for our journey here on Earth.

"And ask for Our Lady's help. Buy a little book or even get a brochure on the Rosary and pray it daily – even a decade – just as Mother Mary has recommended so many times.

"Make full use of the sacramentals – like wearing a Miraculous Medal and brown scapular around your neck. Have holy water in your house, and ask me or any other priest to bless your home. There are many accepted spiritual weapons you can make use of. Also, get a copy of the Catechism of the Catholic Church and also a solid, Catholic Bible – I recommend the Navarre Bible but there are other good ones – because you must maintain absolute fidelity to the teaching of the Magisterium of the Church. They're there to help you, to help us all, to light the path that we should follow and to keep us from the darkness.

"I'm going to go back up to my seat to pray and maybe take a little nap. But if you need me, just let me know, okay?"

He nods almost absentmindedly, and then quickly grabs the notepad that has been resting in the middle seat separating us.

"So, let me get this straight," he says, looking up at me with worried, furrowed eyebrows. "In 1917 – almost 100 years ago – Mother Mary allegedly tells Jacinta Marto that more people were going to Hell because of sins of the flesh than for any other reason. Since then illicit sex has become a mainstay, right? So much so that when the majority of industries took a dive during this past recession, the sex business actually grew?"

Reaching for his notepad from the middle seat, he hands it to me.

"Look, I scratched this out over the last few weeks and I just wanted to show it to you."

He reclines his chair and folds his arms in frustration.

***

Returning to my seat, I read the Bible quote the sheriff had included at the top of the first page.

"Thomas said to him, 'Lord, we do not know where you are going; how can we know the way?' Jesus said to him, 'I am the way, and the truth, and the life; no one comes to the Father, but by me. If you had known me, you would have known my Father also; henceforth you know him and have seen him." (John 14: 5-7)

Continuing to the rest of the pages, I read his somewhat organized, chronological notes, as follows:

1917 – Fatima, Portugal – Message to Jacinta Marto: "The sins which lead the greatest number of souls to perdition are the sins of the flesh."

• *During that same period and certainly before, prostitution abounds in Europe, the United States, and other select parts of the world.*

• *Slaves as sexual tools in early United States.*

• *Homosexuality being banned, then accepted, back and forth in the eyes of the public.*

• *Sex only for procreation and not pleasure during the Victorian period.*

• *The age of the photograph leading to pornography. Cheap printing process. Porn pamphlets readily available and distributed.*

• *1839 – Paris, France the epicenter for pornography. Eventually, not only the elite have access to it, but also the masses. Church fighting it. Police fighting it. Porn doesn't die out, it just goes underground.*

• *1880's – Diaphragm developed and introduced to the general public.*

• *Early 1900's – France exporting tens of thousands of porn pictures outside of the country. NOTE: 1917! Fatima, Portugal!*

- *Families selling their children for money to become brothel workers.*
- *World War I and II – Women becoming independent. Many men overseas. Women having affairs or exploring their sexuality with other women.*
- *Many single men who were not enlisted preying on women.*
- *Porn magazines and mass distribution of the same.*
- *Roaring 20's in the United States. Very sexual period. Condoms.*
- *1905 – Sigmund Freud's Three Essays on the Theory of Sexuality.*
- *1910 – Freud's writings on sex. The term "Sexual Revolution" is coined.*
- *Sexual topics and scenes making their way into the movies.*
- *Gay and Lesbian clubs very popular.*
- *1948 – Kinsey Report.*
- *1953 – Hugh Hefner – Playboy magazine*
- *1960 – Birth control pill into mass production. Sexual Revolution begins en masse due to a lack of fear of getting pregnant.*
- *1962 – Sex and the Single Girl book published, is highly successful, and is made into a theatrical movie in 1964.*
- *1965 – Bob Guccione – Penthouse magazine*
- *1966 – Nearly 5 million women on the pill.*
- *1972 – Deep Throat porn movie in theatres. Enormous crowds.*
- *1972 – Behind the Green Door porn movie in theatres. Box office hit.*
- *1973 – The Devil in Miss Jones porn movie in theatres. Another box office hit.*
- *1975 – VCR units made for mass market; People owning porn movies to watch in the privacy of their homes and not having to go to theatres or adult book stores. As of 1998, approximately 19,000*

272

new video titles are produced every year. Ninety percent of all those made are done in Silicon Valley, California. A billion dollar business with trade magazines, conferences, and awards. Annual revenues are now in the multi-billion dollar range.

- 1981 – Centers for Disease Control and Prevention first recognize AIDS and its cause, the HIV infection. In 1985, 12,000 Americans died from AIDS; worldwide, as of 2009, up to 30 million deaths from AIDS. As of 2010, approximately 34 million have contracted HIV around the world.

- Late 1980's – Camcorder provides a boon for home porn videos.

- 1990's – World Wide Web created for the military makes its way to the general public.

- 2000's – Interactive sex CD's; approximately 567 niche porn magazines in production.

- 2012: "Adult Entertainment" industry: A range of sexual options are routinely available like prostitution, call girls, adult movie theatres, pornography on the Internet, sex shops, strip clubs, magazines, movies, and a variety of other vehicles to satisfy any conceivable sexual appetite which includes: Bestiality, exhibitionism, fetishes, BDSM, swinging, human sex trafficking, child pornography and prostitution. The down side: STD's, drug abuse, divorces, at least 16 million people battling sexual addiction and Internet pornography earning the title of the "crack cocaine" equivalent for sex addicts.

For online pornography specifically, men become the common users, although more women are moving towards this form of sexual entertainment; Mass production of erotic novels with the predominate user being females.

NOTE 1: The "Seven Deadly Sins": LUST, Envy, Gluttony, Greed, Pride, Sloth, and Wrath.

Chapter 36

"Father?"

The sheriff is standing beside me.

He leans into my ear, speaking as quietly as he can. "Can I, well, can I take you up on that offer for confession?" I follow him back to the same seats where we visited before.

"You may have to help me with this. It's been a long while," he says as he settles into his seat.

"Not to worry," I say, incredibly pleased he's asked me to hear his confession.

"Okay. Well, uh, forgive me Father, but it has been, uh, heck, I don't even know. Let's just say since I was in high school that I had my last confession."

I nod, silently yet gently urging him to continue.

"And since that time, wow..." He's holding an Examination of Conscience booklet in his hand, staring at it intently. "I don't know how many of these things I've done since then so, I want to confess every single time I've sinned in the ways mentioned in this book."

Waiting a moment, I say: "Good." Before I can continue speaking, he says:

"But I really also need to confess...." he hangs his head, the weight of the shame making it hard for him to hold it upright.

"Take your time," I say. "Keep in mind that you are speaking directly to God. He knows you, He loves you, and He wants you to confess your sins. I'm standing in His place, but He is here, He truly is. And whatever you say will remain between you and God. I face very grave consequences if I ever repeat what you confess. So, unburden yourself."

I see hope, however slight, beginning to flicker in his eyes. Jumbled, some melded together, all sincere and painful memories begin to come forth.

"Well, okay. I've been having an affair with Michele Jerpun for years, over a decade, at least. I'm not sure if I'm a sex addict, but I do know I'm addicted to sex with her. I mean, I'm addicted to her in my life and the sex with her is a huge part of it. She makes me crazy, yeah, but I've never, ever had sex with my wife as I've had with her. Ever."

"Do you know about how many times?" I ask.

His head snaps back, his eyes looking up to his right as he tries to calculate.

"Shit, I, damn, I don't know. Since my last confession in high school? Maybe a hundred. Yeah," he pauses, calculating, "at least a hundred. But since I got married, only about 13 or 14 times with different ladies, maybe more, I don't really know at this point. I mean, my life with the wife was bad, really bad. The sex was nonexistent. And whenever we made love, she made me feel like she was doing me such a big favor.

"When I married her I had absolutely no intention of sleeping with any other woman, ever. And I didn't for a long time. But when we had our daughter, something changed in her. She was no longer interested in sex. Then she went back to work and more changed, she became even more distant. Then she got breast cancer, and, well, it was all over after that. Our romance ended, our fun together ended, and the job of living life, paying bills, and doing all the right things in order to make a living just overtook us. But when she started to make me feel inferior to every man around, comparing me to other guys – well, let's just say that not only did it feel like she didn't love me, it felt like she didn't even like or respect me. *That* hurt me to the core.

"So I started looking for women. Father, there are so many unhappily married women out there it was easy, so easy. Most of them were one-night stands which is what we both wanted. Their reasons were all across the board. One woman just wanted to be a bad girl. Another wanted to pay her husband back for his own affairs. A few had no intimacy in their lives and were feeling neglected or underappreciated; it only took a few well spoken words from me for us to melt into each other's arms in a hotel room where nobody knew us – just wanting to be held, desired, cared for, if only for a night. I tell ya, there were some close calls with suspicious husbands and some whacked out girls that I should have never messed with to begin with. I'd gotten myself caught up in a major spider web with all my lies. But, heck, I'm a saint compared to many other guys I know.

"Then I met Michele and, wow, I can't even explain how hard I fell for her. It was intense right from the very beginning. She was single and heavily into the swinging lifestyle. She said she would end it, promised to focus everything on me, on us and she did. But when the wife got breast cancer, I knew we had to break it off. So I did."

I wonder if Michele Jerpun was the one that Detective Renae said I knew who was into the swinging lifestyle. If that's the case, the sheriff seems to think she ended it.

"That's when she married Cameron Gambke, for her and Gina. We saw each other, on and off, for years. Then they divorced and we got together again. You see, Michele became my reason for living. I didn't want to get a divorce and hurt the wife or our daughter, and I didn't want to toss away my life, all that I had worked for in my career. I was tired of running around trying to find the right partner. I just wanted to be loved and appreciated. It was that simple.

"Living this double life actually was pretty easy once we got into a routine. When we got back together we just clicked, and before long it was like we were the married ones; the wife was just someone with whom I shared a house. Shit, Father, I've had sex more times with Michele than I ever had with the wife. And many times it was just crazy sex, like any place, anytime, anywhere kind of erotic stuff. Just a few weeks ago I went to visit her and Gina in the hospital and we made love right there. She insisted. Said it made her so horny since there was a chance we were gonna get caught."

"In the same room with Gina?" I blurt.

"Yeah. Well, I mean, I made sure we pulled the curtain, just in case she woke up from the coma, so she wouldn't see. But she would sure have been able to hear us. Michele didn't seem to care one way or the other. Man, she must have had two or three orgasms, and she's loud! And all I can focus on is this damn tattoo she got when we first started the affair. Really, all I wanted was to be done. It seemed so wrong, doing it with Gina right on the other side of that curtain."

He's not smiling. He actually looks horrified, remembering

what had no doubt given him a high before.

"That damn tattoo. 'EBYT' are on her lower back, a gift she gave to me right after we first met. She told me that the initials were for her favorite song, 'Every Breath You Take' by Sting. She said it meant that if she died before me, she would always look out for me from Heaven. But in our rough moments, like when I decided I wasn't going to leave the wife after everything was going wrong with our daughter...."

Stopping, he stares at me intently.

"Our daughter was raped, Father, and it really threw me for a loop. Well, anyway, the real meaning of the title of the song came crashing into my life when I said we needed to end it. My new truck had its tires slashed and the entire car keyed with the same initials, 'EBYT' all over, front and back, side to side. I called her right away. She said, 'Never, ever walk away from me. I will be your worst fucking nightmare and will stalk you until you're dead. Prick.' A little while later I found out this may be a stalking song, when one lover leaves another."

"But you're still together?" I ask.

"Well," he fidgets with his hands, "yeah. You see, we're tied together. Plus, I'm in love with her. I can't seem to break away."

"You can't or you won't?" I prod.

He doesn't reply, choosing instead to deflect.

"But I can swear the wife was having an affair, too, maybe a few, hell I don't know. I mean, she began saying her job and then her studies to become a substance abuse counselor were so important, and she also wanted her independence, so we literally just stopped doing things together. We were together for Sheri, plain and simple.

"It was all clear to me. She wanted a lot of free time away from me. She literally quit needing me. No more nagging, after a while she wasn't even angry at me. She was always so damned secretive, too, with our money or whenever she was on the Internet. Whenever I would question her, she would deflect even the simplest of questions. And when she would go out with friends of hers, she would dress sexy. But she never dressed like that for me when we went on a very infrequent date. Right now,

I'm about as irrelevant to her as a man can be to his wife. She hasn't said it, but I can damn well feel it."

"So you know for a fact she's having an affair? I mean, have you followed her or had her followed?" I have to ask; he is the sheriff, after all.

"Well, no, I haven't been able to prove anything. I mean, yeah, I've had her followed when she's gone out with friends, but nothing has come up. I've tracked her calls, too. She seems to go to the park a lot, or just on long drives to nowhere."

His thought process has brought him full circle. Since he's been having an affair, he wants to convince himself that she is, too. It allows him to let himself off the hook, to rationalize his own adulterous behavior. I've seen it happen before, but more often than not, the wife is just trying to find things to stay busy, or ways to find enjoyment in life since her marriage is so hurtful, nonexistent, and psychologically damaging. More than likely, Mrs. Luder is merely trying to survive and get some normalcy back in her life. Could she be having an affair? Yes. Only God and Mrs. Luder know the answer to that question.

"I did catch her masturbating once. I found out later that she went to some sex toy party. I found a bunch of dildos and stuff in her chest of drawers."

I say, "You know, there is a chance there really is no other guy. I've had some women tell me that with all the new sex toys out there, they don't even need a man anymore which makes masturbation a very big issue. Of course, that doesn't make it right," I emphasize.

He looks at me now, aghast that I would even know about these things.

"In confession, Sheriff, that's where I have been told this. I'm not breaking my seal of confession by telling you this at all.

"Extramarital affairs are all too common in our world today, so it's something I hear a great deal about. But the fact I am hearing it in the Sacrament of Reconciliation is a very good thing, when seen through the eyes of this healing sacrament. But know that maybe she's fine now without having an orgasm at all. That's pretty common, too. Not everyone's world revolves around sex."

He nods, encouraged once more as he continues.

"I really think that the biggest reason I began cheating was because of the wife. I mean, no matter what I did, no matter how hard I tried, nothing seemed to matter. She was convinced that I wasn't good enough for her. I knew then I couldn't win. So I said, 'To hell with it' and the affairs began. It was that simple, and I didn't look back until, well, until that damn girl hit me. And that, of course, occurred while I was talking to Michele on the cell phone."

The hospital. Michele coming out of the elevator. She was probably the one visiting him that the nurse referred to; not Mrs. Luder.

I hold up my hand.

"Let's focus on you. Your world. Your choices. Your sins. Your confession. Not hers or what you perceive to be what she has done, even if you may be right in any or all of what you have said. Part of your healing is going to be recognizing that Mrs. Luder is a real person, created by God, whom He loves dearly. So I want you to begin referring to her by her name. Jean, or Jean Luder, or Mrs. Jean Luder, or maybe 'my' wife, or something much more personal. 'The wife' just isn't going to cut it anymore. Okay?"

He nods his head again, absorbing my comments.

"Are you sorry for what you have done? I mean, really, genuinely sorry for what you have done? Because if you are, in your heart, know that God will immediately respond to your repentance."

"Yeah, yes, Father," his head slowly nodding, his eyes glazing over, "I really am sorry for all of it. Every single thing. I know I need to change. I have so much hate inside of me, anger towards my wife, things that have happened in my life, Gambke, and the world that I bought into. But mostly I can't stand myself. I mean, I've been so full of myself, so arrogant, I thought I was right in everything I did. Justified. 'Woe is me and feeling sorry for myself' kind of thing."

"Well, remorse and humility are your first big steps. Realizing that God is God, and we are not. So...what are you going to do about it?" He needs to take some action steps, and I'm here to point that out.

"What am I going to do about it?" I've caught him off guard. He's forgotten that there are different elements to a sound confession.

"Let me tell you a quick story to help you understand this better. In my old parish, there was a nice young lady who came to me for confession. She told me that the following day her parents were going to renew their wedding vows and she wanted to be able to receive Holy Communion during the celebration of the Mass. She at least knew that if she was in a state of mortal sin, she couldn't. However, she was afraid that she would disappoint her parents if they saw her not receiving Communion. When I asked her the same question I just asked of you, she said, 'Well, nothing.' You see, she had been living with her boyfriend for about six months and they were constantly engaging in premarital sex. That's called 'fornication,' which is sexual intercourse between an unmarried man and an unmarried woman. It's also a serious violation of the Sixth Commandment. With that knowledge, I couldn't give her absolution because she was not truly sorry for her sins; she was just going through the motions, there was no true contrition in her heart.

"In order for someone to make a good confession, the penitent must be sorry for their sins, truly hate or detest the sins they've committed, and resolve from sinning again. It's the most important act of the penitent. Now, they actually may slip up and sin again after their confession, that's human nature. But what is important is that when they confess their sins they really do hate their sins, they don't intend to repeat them, *and* – this is a critical component of a sound confession – they plan to make a sincere effort to *not* sin again.

"The Sacrament of Reconciliation is a great gift that God has given us. No one should ever make a mockery of it, or think they are fooling God when they are confessing to an ordained priest."

He ponders this for a while.

"Well, I already know I need to take some sexual addiction classes. To be honest, I'm really happy that Detective Gambke is our Sex Crimes Detective because I don't want to be exposed to all those pictures. The porn, I mean. Not the violent ones, because those disgust me. But when I see the regular porn stuff, I just want to have sex with Michele. I don't want to see any of it."

"Okay, well, that's a good start and very wise of you at work. What else?" I press.

"I suppose I need to end it with Michele, but I've tried so many times." He looks down, shaking it in defeat.

"Yes, certainly," I say. "You're committing adultery, and that's a sin against the Sixth Commandment. So you need to pray for the grace to end it with her and also for the wisdom to know how to do that. In addition, you need to make sure it happens."

His look of despair remains, and we sit quietly for a few minutes.

"Here are some practices I highly recommend you do. We've talked about some of this before, but I believe they're that important. It's not exhaustive, but it's a wonderful start. Again, get a good Catholic Bible and study guide. Then, read through the Catechism of the Catholic Church; there are even study guides for that if you wish. Next, pray the Rosary. Every single day. This is of huge importance for you to come out of the darkness where you've been living. And remember that it's not a race to pray it; the prayers are meant to be a soothing background mantra while you meditate on the specific mysteries for that day."

He nods.

"Good. Also, study the lives of as many saints and mystics as you can. You will be amazed at the challenges they faced, many battling sexual temptations like St. Augustine, St. Benedict, St. Jerome, St. Margaret of Cortona, St. Philip Neri, St. Charles of Sezze, or St. Clement Mary Hofbauer. Pray to them for help and guidance.

"And, the week after Easter next year, consider taking full advantage of Divine Mercy Sunday. Maybe read about the life of St. Faustina Kowalska who Our Lord visited in a convent in Poland in 1931 regarding this great, merciful gift to mankind."

Nodding his head again, he's happy to have something concrete to do.

"And, like I said, when you see temptations, run, don't just walk, away. Do these things and you won't have to worry about Satan. And, most importantly, when you fall — not if, but when — get back up and try again, every single time. It took you years to get where you are now, so don't get discouraged, okay? But don't give in, ever again. Don't give up! The state of your immortal soul is banking on it. Always trust in God, for Our Lord says, 'Come to me, for my yoke is easy and my burden is light.'"

He's holding his head higher, and his breathing has relaxed a bit.

"Now, would you like to confess anything else? If not, you can say your act of contrition and I will give you absolution and your penance."

He runs his right hand through his hair again, pauses, then shakes his head.

I assist him with his act of contrition and then say the prayer of absolution.

He manages a tentative smile realizing he has finally gone to confession after many years. Yet, he still seems bothered. Maybe he doesn't believe God has forgiven him.

"It is extremely important that you understand what has just happened," I say. "God just forgave you. He really did. And because He forgave you, *you need to forgive yourself.* It's done. Over.

"And for your penance, I want you to begin immediately to stop all communication with Michele. End it. Recommit yourself to your wife. Remember the wedding vows you made, the promises to her in the presence of Our Lord and those witnesses who attended your wedding. Take some marriage classes, or attend a retreat with Jean. There's a great one called Retrovaille. "

Still looking very forlorn, he says: "I will most definitely do that with my wife. But, well, I don't think I'll ever be able to get Michele completely out of my life."

"Why's that?" I ask, wondering why after this in-depth discussion and wonderful confession, combined with what he's seen on this trip, he's still reluctant.

"Gina's our daughter."

Chapter 37

After saying our goodbyes to the rest of the group in New York, the sheriff and I sit together on the five hour flight to New Bern, North Carolina, with a stop in Atlanta.

"Do you think it was Cameron Gambke who raped your daughter, Sheri?" I ask.

"What? Why would you say that?" His eyes are wide, eyebrows now furrowing.

I immediately regret asking. "You had inferred that Cameron Gambke raped your daughter during one of our visits before this trip."

"Gina, I meant Gina. He forced himself on her, someone that couldn't tell right from wrong. And if I find out he ever did that to Sheri, I...I guess I don't know what I would or could do."

He leans back, and I attempt to change the subject, by telling him the book I have been carrying around with me is the one that Cameron Gambke had said was the most instrumental to him in his life.

"Cameron's a perfect example of someone who read the wrong thing and lived his life accordingly," I say.

"Huh?" he says, not recalling the book I was reading on the flight to Rome.

"This book. Paideia by this guy," I reply, showing him the author's picture, Thomas Victor, on the back cover jacket. He shrugs, not recognizing the face.

"What kind of a title is 'Paideia', anyway?" he asks.

"Well, in Greek, it means the 'upbringing of a child.'"

"Hmm. Okay. So then what does that mean for that twisted grey mass that Gambke had between his ears?" He smirks, and my expression matches his as I continue.

"Let me give you an overview of what I've read so far. This author meshes together a potpourri of philosophies, with a big focus on reincarnation; a concept absolutely incompatible with Christianity, yet believed by about 25 percent of Christians. And then he includes portions of 'Gnosticism,' an ancient heretical theology that believed there was secret knowledge concerning the 'real' truth about life, a sacred truth that is only available to a certain few. So this guy believes everything is One and the One is God, or whomever we want the One to be; that nothing we see is real, it's all just an illusion. Thus, we are God, he claims. He talks about some Universal Energy, a Universal Force that we are all a part. Reincarnation is the way for us to try, time and again, to get to this higher level so we can ultimately become God.

"His skewed philosophy stresses how it really doesn't matter what we do here on earth. According to his theory, there's no real ultimate consequence to anything we ever do because we can correct it in the next life.

"Now, this is where I thought it was interesting because I understand that Cameron Gambke had this thing with wolves."

"How do you know that?" His tone changes, the strictly professional Sheriff Daniel Robert Luder persona has once more arrived.

I'm not in a position to share the letter to Detective Renae with him. I will leave that up to her to tell him if she ever desires to do so.

"Let's just say I do, okay? It's not important right now. This life theory espoused by Mr. Victor is that wolves are the highest form of beings on earth. They were once humans, and now they are gods protecting this world. People that are not enlightened try to kill the wolves – they're the ones at a lower level of consciousness from pre-world dark karma experiences – and they want to do so because they are jealous of them. So we need to look to the wolves for answers."

His laugh is quick.

"Father, I gotta tell you. Remember the morning you were riding with me to Central Prison?"

"Yeah, that's a tough one to forget." I hope I don't have many days like that again.

"And remember seeing the red animal carcasses on the side of the road tied up, almost as though they were crucified?"

"Uh huh." The thought hits me immediately. "Were they wolves?"

"No, they weren't wolves. They were coyote skins that we got our hands on and then dyed them red. We knew for a long time that Gambke had this thing for some red wolves that live near the prison, and we wanted to show him that on the day he was going to be killed, his furry friends were going to be killed, too."

"Did you feel better after that?" I quip.

"Much." We both laugh again. The release from the tension between us is very welcome. I continue my Reader's Digest summary of Cameron Gambke's favorite read.

"Part of Victor's theory is that yoga helps us to grow closer to our ultimate earthly reality so that when we die and are reincarnated, we come back even better and can immediately jump into higher levels of consciousness. Genius children, the author claims, are actually adults who died in a past life that were yoga masters and that's why they start their new lives well ahead of the curve.

"He writes that we have no control over ourselves, that it's all driven by karma. The wolves may help us by taking the form of humans, or spirits. These spirits are what he says this world calls 'angels.' So we can only live by our gut instincts. At any given moment it's what our heart and mind tells us to do, not what the uninformed world says is right or wrong, and it is this that allows us to pay our debts and to grow further. So, whether what we are doing in life is good or bad doesn't matter, we get points for just doing what we feel we should, because in following our hearts, we are doing what the Universal Force has intended all along. His rationale? Since everyone around us is doing the same thing, it all balances out.

"His summation of this supposed brilliant line of thinking is that this should be great news for everyone because we have no need for guilt, no need for remorse. Everyone is doing whatever they feel is best for them anyway, so they all cancel each other out and if they don't, when we die in this life, we pick it up during the next and this goes on until, well, until it's all designed to end. By whom I don't know and he doesn't say. He just closes with saying that all of our realities then morph together in a beautiful rainbow, until we individually know that our own reality is actually determined in our own minds."

"What the...?" Sheriff Luder catches himself.

"I know, right? And do you want to know how even more twisted this gets?" I ask.

"Sure." He smiles, the absurdity of the book's content not lost on either of us.

"I googled this guy, Thomas Victor. Last year he goes clean. Says he has prostate cancer, never got it treated, and now only has a few years to live. He wants to right some wrongs so he admits that he made this whole thing up." I finish with a flourish, shaking my head as I relay the author's public admission.

"He made it up?! You have *got* to be kidding me." He chuckles. I continue.

"Yep. He was in college when all this New Age stuff was still in its infancy, and he was trying to get some grant money for a project he had proposed. One of his professors was all into this way of thinking and he believed that if he got on his good side, he would support him. He says the mind-altering drugs he was experimenting with during this time – the glorious 1960's – had a lot to do with it, and that his dealer was this same college professor, who later died of an overdose of heroin. So he wrote this book, saying all the things that were popular at that time. He got the support and they thought he was a genius – really, one of 'them.' The professor published his work. No one knew the difference."

"You mean this whole time Cameron thought this was real stuff? A genuine philosophy to live by?" His amazement now matches mine.

"Yep, he became what he thought about most," I add.

We both laugh again, but then his anger returns as he makes a chilling comment.

"I wonder how many people had been negatively affected by Gambke because he believed this Victor guy and lived his life with this twisted mindset. Or how about the number of people that read Victor's book and lived their life in this distorted, narcissistic way with no guilt whatsoever, because there aren't really any consequences to their actions? That it doesn't matter in the overall scheme of things? I'll bet Gambke didn't even know that the guy admitted to making it all up. Obviously, Victor never considered the ramifications, only how he could achieve his own self-centered goals."

"I don't think Cameron knew any of this before he was killed in prison. If he did, I didn't catch it when he was telling me how awesome of a book it was," I say.

I make a mental note that I need to share this information with Detective Renae.

Pulling out the notebook with the sex dateline that the sheriff had put together and given to me earlier, I place it on the drink tray in front of me, returning the Paideia book to my travel bag.

"Eye opening, isn't it?" he says, pointing over the empty middle seat at the document as he stands to stretch. Long overseas flights are never easy on the body and his back has suffered from the trip.

"Very much so. What are you going to do with it?" I ask.

"Well, nothing really. It was just for me, to put my thoughts on paper. But all these people are really screwed up aren't they? I mean, they're all going to go to Hell, right?" he says, more of a statement than a question.

Sitting back down, he sees that I have circled in red a few items that I want to talk about in detail. But first, I share with him a story.

"Do you recall the story in the Bible from the Book of John about the adulterous woman and Our Lord being asked to judge her activities?"

"Kind of," he says.

"He was at the temple in the early morning, and the Pharisees brought a woman to him who had been caught in the act of adultery. They said, in essence, 'She's been caught committing this sin. The law says she should be stoned but what do you say?' They were trying to trip him up, to see if He would stick to the law and show justice or if He would stick to mercy and say she should be let go. Either choice would get Him in big trouble with them. Do you know what He did?"

He shakes his head. I continue.

"He did both, by saying *'Let him who is without sin among you be the first to throw a stone at her.'* And, beginning with the oldest, they all walked away. However, and this is very important, he said to her, *'Woman, where are they? Has no one condemned you?'* She said in return, *'No one, Lord.'* And Jesus said, *'Neither do I condemn you; go, and **do not sin again.'***

"Remember I've told you that only God decides, only God can judge? For the woman in the story, He didn't condemn her. Why? Because, although she had sinned, Jesus saw her as a flawed human being, and He knew that she would go through a personal judgment on her last day on earth, but not before. So she had time to change her life. But, and again a very, very important 'but,' the last thing He said to her was, 'Do Not Sin Again.'"

He slowly nods his head, but I'm not sure if he's making the connection.

"Let me put it this way. I'm not judging you or any of these people. That's not for me or you to do. But am I concerned about their souls? Yes! That's why it is so important I share the Good News with everyone in any way I can, to give them a chance to hear it, and a chance to change their lives. And, as a baptized and confirmed Christian, you have the same obligation. But neither you nor I can force them to do anything. I said it before and I'll say it again – love can't be forced on anyone, okay?"

"Father, I gotta ask – why doesn't God just come down and *make* people see Him, *make* people believe?"

I need to correct his thinking. "For one thing, if He did make people believe, where would our free will be? Either we are free to believe or we are simply automatons, only capable of doing His commands.

"He has come to you, Sheriff. I'm absolutely certain that He has come to you many times throughout your life. God is always with you and He is always available to help you whether you ask Him or not. But you need to be willing and ready to accept His help.

"You have now been given an incredible gift through the Sacrament of Reconciliation. This is a great opportunity to rejoice, for your soul has been cleansed and your sins forgiven. And for all those who haven't, all the people we've been talking about, there is always hope. I understand. I get it. I mean, we've all been seriously misled with regard to human sexuality."

I see no need to tell him of my own challenges with porn in my pre-priest years, but I would like to find some common ground for us to continue our dialog.

"Do you know much about the Kinsey Reports? You have it listed here as a line item for the year 1948." I hold it up for him to see.

"Yeah. The Kinsey Reports were some books that really changed how Americans looked at sex. They were a clear reflection of the sexual habits and behavior of Americans at that time. It really opened people's eyes. I remember seeing a copy of it in my dad's home library," he replies.

"Well, kind of," I state. "But what is most interesting is that today, many reputable experts have called into question many of the underlying assumptions and the validity of much of Kinsey's research. Alfred Kinsey was an American biologist, professor of entomology and zoology, turned 'sexologist' who was apparently not pleased with the lack of 'scientific' material on human sexuality. So he decided to use his 'research skills' to do it on his own. He was a fan of Darwin and was fascinated with the evolution of human sexuality – especially as it related to homosexuality.

"He also had a big axe to grind with the Catholic Church. I understand his father was a strict Methodist who was very intolerant of other views – maybe this is where he picked it up, I don't know. Unfortunately, as a child he was taught that all sexual urges were fundamentally ungodly, that he would go crazy if he masturbated, etc. This misinformation and bias undoubtedly had a huge impact on him growing up.

"I know it sounds like Dr. Jekyll and Mr. Hyde. On the one hand saying I'm concerned about souls caught up in sexual sin while, on the other, saying that it might be all right. But what I'm really trying to say is that it all has to be within reason, there has to be some balance, and understanding. Some people masturbate due to mental disorders – are they going to Hell? Again, only God knows that answer, but why would we think they would?

"At any rate, this is not a cut and dry topic, although some things are obvious. If this activity is done with the full knowledge of it being wrong, and if they make no attempt to stop it although they have the capacity to do so, then certainly that falls under the category of sexual sin."

He nods, allowing me to continue.

"I've seen so many who have walked away from the Church and their faith because all they felt was guilt – much of it again driven by well-meaning parents or Church leaders who made them feel bad about their God-given desires. The lack of proper information on these matters can be and is very damaging."

He interrupts. "Are you saying that Kinsey was a murderer?"

"What? No, no, that's not what I'm saying at all," I reply quickly. "I'm just saying that people need to be very careful about what they tell young people, that's all. Look, I'm getting off track here."

Readjusting in my seat, I turn completely towards him, well at least as much as is humanly possible while sitting in an airplane seat.

"So, Kinsey began talking to people about their sexual habits. Over time, he collected a massive amount of porn and thousands of hours of interviews, all in the name of 'science.' His 'research' required a ton of money, which he got from grants. And when his reports were published, they immediately topped the best seller lists. Copies of *The Kinsey Reports* went flying off the shelves. Husbands told their wives that this was how sex *really* was, inferring that their spouses were prudes if they didn't join everyone else in the sexual revolution. Boyfriends were telling their girlfriends the same thing. Hugh Hefner was so inspired that he created 'Playboy.'"

He looks back at me, still trying to figure out where all this is heading.

"Here's the problem," I point out. "One of the biggest, most important hurdles to overcome in any scientific study is validation. It's imperative that your results can be replicated and then authenticated by independent, outside reviewers. All scientists, or in this instance, 'sexologists,' must be prepared to defend and prove their results. But it's been said that Kinsey wouldn't allow anyone to review or validate his research, at least in an open, cooperative manner. Not then, not now. And why has that been an issue? Because his findings had been in question from the very beginning from reputable researchers, at a minimum.

"What is known is that the people he interviewed, the population he used in his reports, were for the most part homosexuals, prostitutes and prison inmates. He spent over seven hundred hours with one specific homosexual asking him about his sex life. But when he published his findings he reported it as a true representation of the *general population*. Every man and woman. Do you know the name Abraham Maslow?"

"Uh, yeah. He was the guy with the 'hierarchy of needs,' right?" he says.

"Yep. He was a psychologist, and he expressed his concerns to Kinsey. Do you know what Kinsey did? He ignored him."

Catching me off guard, he asks, "Did you have sex in high school?"

Since I've been ordained a priest, I always get stuck on this question when asked, and have a hard time admitting it, but I feel compelled to do so, and he's asked me a direct question. "Yes, twice. You?"

"Uh huh. Only with Jean when we were dating, and then with one other girl when we broke up for a while, before she and I got back together again. I was so afraid I would get a girl pregnant that it kept me at bay. We weren't about to use birth control because we might get caught by our parents so we just risked it. Come to think of it, that fear of pregnancy did force me to keep it in my pants."

I join him on the trip down memory lane. "I hear ya. Well, when I graduated from high school, MTV hit the air. With my love for music and the fascination with videos, I was hooked. I remember watching Madonna during the first ever Music Awards sing 'Like a Virgin' as she rolled around in sexual ecstasy on the stage. And she was hot, really."

He laughs. "Madonna. Wow, is that even her real name?"

We are probably both thinking the same thing. We've just

spent a few weeks on a pilgrimage to Marian apparitions and one of the titles for the Blessed Virgin Mary is "Madonna."

"I understand it is," I say. "I guess she came from a very strict Catholic home, and one time I read her parents always had priests and nuns in her house. Then her mom died of breast cancer at the age of thirty, when Madonna was only five years old. She had a stepmother but admitted she didn't grow up with the teaching you would normally get from a mother who taught rules and manners. Understandably, I'm sure that affected her a great deal. She had so many good songs, such a talent.

"So I'm listening to her with sex songs like 'Justify My Love' and watching her seductive videos and it all seems so right, so good. Then you see all these girls starting to dress like her and I'm like, 'Yes!' I mean, I'm 16 or 17, with hormones raging. While the girls were dressing like her, I became fully entrenched in the yuppie scene. It's amazing what we will do without question, wanting glory, notoriety, to be seen by others, admired by others, accepted by others. I was no different than anyone else back then."

I tell the sheriff about some of the popular songs that had sexual connotations, if not direct sexual messages, that I heard back then. Songs like *She Bop* by Cyndi Lauper which is about girls masturbating, *Orgasm Addict* by Buzzcocks, *Freak Me Baby* by Silk, *I Want Your Sex* by George Michael, *Relax* by Frankie Goes Hollywood just to name a few. Great performers, great songs, all of them. Heck, I was a big Billy Joel fan, and his song *Only the Good Die Young* really impacted me, too. I effortlessly remember the tune, and the accompanying words and inferences encouraging a more reckless life, as I type this.

"And, man, I let them screw me up; they primed me for the porn that was come." I said, shifting gears to another form of influential media.

"Then there were the movies. Tons of 'em. The sex scenes were all I needed to put me into overdrive. *Altered States, Videodrome, American Gigolo, Fast Times at Ridgemont High, Porkys, All The Right Moves, Bachelor Party, Private Lessons,* even that fake orgasm scene in *When Harry Met Sally, Pretty Woman, An Officer and a Gentleman, Top Gun, Saturday Night Fever, The Blue Lagoon,*

Blue Velvet, Risky Business, Flashdance, Dirty Dancing, Fatal Attraction. All of 'em and so many more."

He picks up my lead.

"Yep. I remember *Dangerous Liaisons*, the nude scenes in *Nightmare on Elm Street* and the *Friday the 13th* series, all the Bo Derek films, *The Hollywood Nights, The Last American Virgin, Star 80, Body Double, Purple Rain...*"

Pausing to remember his own youthful past, he continues.

"I remember thinking back then that it would be impossible to stay with just one woman all my life, like Jean, because I kept seeing all of these naked women and these love scenes. Heck, I just wanted sex. And that was how I thought when I began my affairs. If they were willing, so was I."

Leaning forward now in a barely audible whisper, he offers:

"I gotta tell you, Father. I remember a time when Michele said Cameron had hit her, and she's calling me on my cell phone asking if we could meet somewhere, begging me. I felt so bad for her. I'm sitting at home, because Jean had gone out to a movie with a friend. It was at a time when I knew I should stop the affair, but I really couldn't decide what to do. I mean, Michele needed help, right? And if I love someone, I should love her like this, right? All this stuff is going back and forth in my mind. And, I had Journey cranked on my stereo singing 'Faithfully' and in my mind I don't see Jean, my wife, I see Michele, my best friend and lover. I believed I should be 'faithful' to Michele, not Jean. So I switch off the music and turn on the TV because I'm really trying to fight this, I'm actually praying to God to show me a sign, to do the right thing, right? And do you know what commercial came on?"

I shake my head as I have no idea.

"It's a 'Just Do It' ad by Nike. And I take it as God giving me a sign to just 'Do It." I knew then and I know now how stupid that sounds, but it's all I needed to hear. I grabbed my keys and met her at a motel outside of town and we made love like never before. It was that simple – some lame commercial telling me what I wanted to hear. It's okay. Just 'Do It.' That's messed up, isn't it?"

I can sympathize but, again, his thought processes are skewed. "Yes, but I hear what you're saying. Doing something evil to make something right is still wrong. In your situation, at that moment, what God wanted was for you, as a friend, to listen to Michele, and get her out of danger. He certainly did not want you to 'make love' to her, that kind of love was reserved for your wife Jean, to whom you were already committed.

"Look, Sheriff, I'm not going to blame the musicians of the songs I heard, or the producers and directors of the movies I watched, or even the authors of the books I read. Why? Because as my mom once said, 'No one can ever make you do something you don't want to do.' And I *wanted* to do it. I really was old enough to know better. Cameron *wanted* to read that book, and he actively chose to do so a number of times, per his own admission. And with your own acknowledgment, you yourself wanted to travel the road you did, and you kept looking for signs to allow you to rationalize your own behavior. So every day now, I ask the Holy Spirit to give me His gifts – fortitude, piety, counsel, fear of the Lord, understanding, knowledge, and wisdom. With all that, how can I lose?

"Coming home to God is a gift that we should always accept. We've both seen how bad things can be just by living in the world every day, and we have received gifts from God, the messages from Heaven, and even miracles beckoning us to change our hearts. He changed mine long ago, and if I may, by listening to you talk and seeing your own spiritual transformation, your heart is being transformed as well. And if hearts can be changed, so can this same world we live in."

He smiles now, closes his eyes, and leans back in his seat. I sense he's feeling a hint of the peace he hasn't experienced in quite a long time. I believe we are finally connecting as two human beings.

Chapter 38

I should have expected it. I was not at all surprised to find my In-Box overflowing upon my return two weeks ago. It was easy to see that Mrs. Bellers had worked extra hard at not assisting me with anything while I was away.

I'm seated in the grotto once more, unwinding. The peace of the French mountains and European landscapes is fading, rapidly becoming a distant memory.

"Father, excuse me, but may I speak with you for a moment?"

Jean Luder stands behind me. I didn't hear her approach, probably because of the Kentucky Bluegrass that surrounds the grotto.

Surprised to see her, I stand up and offer my hand.

"I won't take much of your time," she says.

As she shakes my hand, she glances at the administrative building behind her. We notice an elderly couple exiting the parish office, holding the door for another elderly couple.

"Would you like to go inside?" I ask.

"No, this is fine," she says, taking a seat on an adjacent bench.

A few moments pass as she gathers her thoughts, her oversized black purse leaning up against her sharp dress slacks and high heeled, open-toed shoes. She most likely is on her lunch break, and has taken a good portion of it driving here. It is my understanding from Sheriff Luder she works a good 20-30 minutes away. In fact, it's the only time he complimented her, saying she's the best Substance Abuse Counselor he knows. If that's the case and she has only an hour lunch, we'll need to speak quickly.

"How may I help you?" I say, hoping to move the conversation along. I don't mind her coming here unannounced, but I also have a prior commitment, a 12:30 p.m. appointment.

"My apologies for not calling ahead…." she begins, and I wave my hand to dismiss her concern.

"It's fine, it's fine."

"Well, it's about Daniel. My husband."

I nod. "Okay. Is everything all right?"

"Yes, and well, no. It's strange, and I'm not sure how to accurately describe it. I, I guess I'm just hoping I can ask you some questions about your trip. I mean, he's changed, really changed. First he had the accident on his damn motorcycle and was acting really weird after that, and now he gets back from this pilgrimage that you made him go on and now, well...."

"No one can make anyone do anything they don't really want to do, Mrs. Luder, and in the end, your husband decided to go on the pilgrimage all on his own. He's a grown man." I'm not going to tell her about the challenge we gave each other, but what I'm saying is still on the mark.

"I know, I'm sorry. I just mean that he said you talked him into it and he didn't even want to go but, yeah, I know, he decided on his own. You're right, he's a grown man."

I patiently wait for her to continue.

"He's, well, what happened over there? He can't do enough for me. He's always around. He's trying to hug me or hold me constantly. He's told me he loves me about 25,000 times.

"And this 'God' thing. All he talks about is God, with all due respect, Father. He's handed out a thousand Bibles or brochures that he picked up from some church. He talks on the phone all night to all our friends and relatives. He's upsetting almost everyone and probably pushing them further away from God – at least that's what he's doing to me. He talks to people in stores, or when we're out together just driving around, telling them about how the Lord can save their souls.

"He even drags me along to the prison to 'save' the people there; the prisoners just laugh at him. Here is a guy who helped put them away; probably told them to their face just how worthless they were. That's the kind of guy my husband is, or was, I guess, and now he wants to save their souls? I am completely embarrassed, mortified even. I don't even want to go out of the house with him anymore in case he wants to lay his hands on people and heal them of something."

Her hands are flailing, so much so her cell phone slips from her hand, making a soft landing in the lush green lawn surrounding us.

I can't control my chuckle.

"Seriously. The other day we're shopping for, oh, I don't know, steak for dinner and there is this poor woman wearing a scarf. It looked like she'd been undergoing chemo treatment and just trying to look normal, you know, inconspicuous. She was in the store hoping to do some shopping without everyone looking at her. And here comes my husband. He marches right up to her while she is in a long checkout line, places his hands on her head, and says, 'Woman, be healed!' Her scarf comes flying off exposing her bald head and little patches of hair that are trying to regrow. She marches right out of the store, leaving her groceries, and my husband just stands there, looking all victorious yet confused. It was as if he couldn't figure out why she reacted that way. Really?

"And when he introduces me, he keeps calling me by my name, 'Jean.' I guess I've graduated from 'the wife' to an actual, living and breathing person."

"Jean is your name, isn't it?" I gently interrupt. "Look, it sounds like he is full of zeal, wanting just to tell everyone about the spiritual transformation he's gone through. But I will talk with him. There are wonderful ways to evangelize, and some that fail even though the evangelizer's intentions of sharing the Good News of Our Lord are good."

She nods, thankful.

"Mrs. Luder, a pilgrimage like the one your husband went on can be a very special time for many people; not all, but certainly most. It sounds like he was positively impacted by the event, but you don't seem at all pleased."

She stares at me, with no indication of agreement or denial.

"What did he tell you, Father, I mean, did he say anything? I'm asking because I'm really confused. This is very unlike him. He told me he had this major freeing experience since he went to confession with you, and now he feels like an unchained man. Unchained from what?"

She's obviously fishing now, wanting to know if her husband spilled his greasy beans to me. I've been through this before with both husbands and wives or even boyfriends and girlfriends. They try to trick me into telling them what may have been revealed in the confessional by the other. I understand and I really do feel for her, but there's no way this conversation is going much further in this particular direction.

"Mrs. Luder, are you Catholic?"

"Well, I guess. I mean, I was baptized and confirmed and all of that, but, I'm not really practicing. I just believe that if you have a good heart and don't do anything really bad, then you will go to Heaven when you die."

I nod my head slightly, merely reflecting that I am paying attention. I don't agree with her philosophy nor does the Church teach this, but I need to address what I believe is her sole reason for coming here.

"I ask because, as a Catholic, you must recall that every time I hear a confession I am bound, under very severe penalties, to hold in absolute secrecy anything told to me. It's called the 'sacramental seal,' because whatever a penitent makes known to me will remain forever 'sealed.'"

"I understand, Father, I do. I was just hoping...." the tears now begin to flow, her voice cracking as she clumsily reaches into her black handbag, retrieving a package of Kleenex.

My heart goes out to her.

"He's just changed so much. Like I said, he's around all the time. I can't stand it. He used to be gone all the time, I mean, *all* the time. He always blamed work. But now, although he has the same job and I know he's got to take it slow because he had that damn accident, he hasn't said he has to go back into work once.

"Wherever I go he wants to go with me. And before all this, everything was my fault, everything! He blamed me, criticized me for the house, the way I was parenting, the bills, the food, the inside, the outside, you name it, he wasn't happy about it. And now? I could light the damn house on fire and he would probably compliment me on how well I lit the flame."

Her tears have stopped, but she's wringing her hands now.

"Do you know what the biggest problem is?" Her focused stare grabs my attention.

"No," I reply.

"It's that I don't trust him. I just don't trust him. I haven't for years. And all that he's trying to do now is fine if it makes him happy, I guess, but it's way too late for me. He just wants me to act like nothing has happened, that I'm stupid. That it's all 'okay.' That everything in our past means nothing, that we just simply need to move on. But you know, Father? I know what he's done. I know who *she* is."

She's searching my eyes now. I don't flinch.

"Michele Jerpun. That's who. Whenever I asked him why he always talked about her, he would say he just felt sorry for her because all Cameron Gambke did to her, whatever that was. He would just leave late at night after we had gone to bed and would say he had to go on a ride to clear his head, or into the office to look at the file notes again, or on the weekends he would say there was a new lead on the case and he just had to go in.

"And you know what? After a while, I just didn't care anymore. I got used to just me and Sheri spending time together, and since all we did was fight when he was home, it was probably better. Sheri said she liked the peace around the house when her dad wasn't there.

"He rarely, if ever, accepted any responsibility for his part in any challenges or issues we had in our relationship. He's been such an ass, Father, really and truly, and that's me being nice because I'm sitting here in front of you.

"I should have known that marrying him was going to be a nightmare, but I was just too much in love, I guess, or maybe I just thought I was in love with him. Getting married just seemed the right thing to do. All of our friends were doing it, so why not?

"Then one Saturday morning, and I know I'll ever forget this, he was in the shower. He had always told me very specifically that I was never to check his cell phone. It was 'official company property' and he could get in big trouble if it was ever found out that his wife was reading confidential information that was sent to him.

"Oh well, I thought, because I knew something was going on. So a text comes in, and it says *'It's naptime and I'll be free for two hours.'* I mean, I didn't know who sent the text, but I wasn't really surprised. The sad part is I guess I still loved him then, or maybe it was a woman-ownership thing, but I was mad, really upset. He hops out of the shower and I just go about my business. But I'm watching him. Still dripping, he goes right to the phone and reads the text. He couldn't wait to check his messages. Within ten minutes he's dressed, cologne is on, and he's out the door heading 'to work.' I was going to follow him, but I needed to pick up Sheri from a friend's house and our plan was to drive over together to get her and then go to a movie as a family. Heck, we had just made love that morning and now he's off to his lover. But I had a plan. The prick had taught me a few things along the way from law enforcement, and now I put what I learned into action.

"That Monday I knew he would be in meetings all day. That's when they catch up on the weekend's criminal and administrative activities and prepare for the upcoming week. So I went to his office. His secretary and I have known each other for years. I brought some flowers, telling her it was a surprise for him.

"She let me into his office and I go through his In-Box. I find the phone bill he had submitted and approved for payment by the department. I quickly scan the bill and see quite a few brief calls from and to her number, but what really catches my attention is he had texted that number over 1000 times that month. He had written a note on the bottom of the bill stating it was part of the 'Gambke Case' to justify the expense. Heck, he's the boss and most people are afraid of him in the office, so who's going to question it anyway? Since it was a company cell phone he probably figured I would never see his cell phone bill. He was wrong.

"I called that number from one of the phones in the office, not his, though. I didn't want him to get mad at me in case it really was for "official" business. Guess who answered? Michele Jerpun, that's who. I mean, really! What in the world about this damn Gambke case could require my husband to call or text Michele Jerpun over one-thousand times in a single month?! Does he think I'm stupid? I didn't say anything because I hated him already, but I really didn't want to leave him because of Sheri. My own parents divorced when I was young and it was ugly. Their divorce really affected me and I vowed to never do that to my daughter."

"I'm sorry to hear all that. I really am," I say in earnest.

"I just don't know what I'm supposed to do. He's a liar. When I confronted him, he denied it, and he has continued to lie about it. Over the years I have created my own space, away from him. At night, when I can't sleep and he's gone, I go on random drives. When Sheri was younger, she was so involved with sports and school activities that I could hide behind her activities. But now she's moved out and it's just him and me. Now he's all excited to start over. But I'm not sure if I can, or even want to."

She's crying again. I'm deeply saddened by the situation that has evolved between her and the sheriff, and angered by another prime example of ultimately how damaging sexual sin can be.

"I'm going to suggest something to you, Mrs. Luder. I've offered it many times before to women who are hurting, no matter the cause. The peace that you have found on your drives is a good thing. In your life, what is of paramount importance is your personal health and well-being. You need to find positive things to do to keep you above it all, things like hobbies, music, long walks, warm baths, healthy foods, or exercise. These help those who are burdened with the challenges that life brings. They definitely help you keep a clear conscience. Looking for revenge or ways to pay him back, such as through alcohol, drugs, or even extramarital affairs, are not only detrimental to your health, they will also damage your soul.

"People seem to think that love is an emotion. That's why they claim to fall in and out of love, why they don't *feel* love for another person. But love isn't an emotion, love is a choice. In any relationship we choose to be in love, because relationships can be challenging, very hard, right? It sounds like you're a living example of that. But if you do choose to love him, to stay and make this work, I really encourage you to find ways to appreciate him again, to pay attention to him, to even thank him – you know, the kinds of things you did long ago when you were in love with him.

"Taking care of yourself is important. But I strongly suggest you never forget that God loves both of you – not just you, but Daniel as well. He never promised you an easy life, but He did promise He would always be with you."

She furrows her eyebrows and glares at me in anger. What did I say to upset her?

"Be nice to him?" she snaps. "For what? Folding the clothes after I took the time to wash them? Thank him for what? Mowing the lawn? If I do that why would he have any reason to change, ever? Give me a break! He's *supposed* to do those things. It's called being a 'husband,' just like I'm expected to do all the things that I do. You have no idea of all the things I did raising Sheri, mostly on my own."

"I know, I hear you. I really do," I say, holding up my hand. "But everyone likes to be appreciated, even for things we're supposed to do. No one wants to be taken for granted. Not you, not him, not me. Always tearing someone down is dehumanizing. He did it to you, as you just told me, and you didn't like it, right? Well, you're both human.

"Let me ask. Were you two married in the Catholic Church?"

"Yes," she says more calmly.

"Okay, the Church recognizes that there are times when a marriage can be harmful or even dangerous, such as with spousal or child abuse. The Church does not believe that abusive relationships should continue. Just because they were married in the Church does not mean that battered wives have to suck it up and stay in a relationship. No way. That is a huge misunderstanding.

"Where there is stress and difficulties in a marriage, such as what you have experienced, the Church recognizes that separation may be for the best. If civil divorce remains the only possible solution, the Church may recognize it."

She shakes her head, no doubt needing time to process what I've told her. Given all the time invested in a relationship, the act of leaving someone, even for a separation, should never be taken lightly. I can only hope that in the future, since the seed has been planted, that she will feel free to contact me for any answers she might need.

Standing suddenly, she grabs her purse, forcing a smile and extending her hand. Quickly turning, she struggles through the grass in her high-heels to the parking lot. I join her as we cover the

30 steps to her car and I offer, "If you and the sheriff would like to return to the Church, or if you want to take advantage of some classes we are going to be offering for couples who are struggling in their marriage, just let me know."

"Father," she says, stopping abruptly and facing me, blurting what she had been holding in the last few minutes. "Just so you know, I never had an affair like him, but I did have one of the heart. What my husband carved out of me I found again in someone else. Neither of them ever knew, my husband nor my fantasy lover, because I kept it all to myself. I fell in love from afar. It did make me feel alive again, even hopeful. But I never would have an actual affair. I couldn't do that to myself, my husband, or my daughter. And I wouldn't do it to the man I fell in love with, nor to his wife and children. I know how much it hurts and they don't deserve that pain just because I have been betrayed and selfishly want to pay my bastard husband back."

Pausing, her breathing slows and she continues.

"I want a happy life again, I want peace. I really was in love with Daniel at one point; I know that for a fact. He was my entire world. But the whole thing is dark and sad now. I don't want it to be like this anymore."

"I completely understand, I really do," I offer. "But you need to know that all too often all we see or hear about are the marriages that have failed. I think you also need to know that I've had the immense pleasure of seeing them when they do work out, when they succeed. And this happens a whole heckuva lot more than people know. And those marriages end up being stronger, more open, and both spouses have greater respect and appreciation for one another."

No smile comes my way as she gets into her car, only a curt nod of her head.

Chapter 39

"Good afternoon, everyone. If you can take your seats, we'll go ahead and get started."

The detached hall that we use for special events is full to capacity – 250 persons. Most are seated but the walls are lined, shoulder to shoulder. A local news station has a camera in the back of the room and a reporter ready with her notepad. I'm certain that Mrs. Bellers had something to do with their presence, hoping to find a way to trip me up. However, this might work to my favor, as I believe this important information needs to get out to everyone.

"I would like to welcome you to Our Lady of Perpetual Help Catholic Church. We are very fortunate to have Sex Crimes Detective Renae Gambke with us to talk about Rape Prevention for the next hour.

"After much thought, we've opened this up to the general public because we believe this is a societal problem that needs to be better understood by everyone. I respectfully request you give Detective Gambke your full attention since our time with her is limited.

"I must stress, before we begin, that certainly not all men, and even women, are like the predators she is about to describe. I've had the pleasure of spending enough time with Detective Gambke to know she also knows this to be the case. However, it is imperative that all of us, our entire community, know what to look for to help one another, protect each other, support the victims, and prosecute the abusers. Please now join me in welcoming Detective Renae Gambke."

All high school Confirmation students have been required to attend, at a minimum, and are receiving service hours for doing so. Over this past week I have spent time in the appropriate classes discussing the Church's position on the topic of sex to ensure they have a proper base before this presentation.

Turning to Detective Renae, we shake hands.

"I have the green light to run this any way I want, right?" she asks for the third time in a lowered voice, as I lead the scattered applause.

"Certainly. But if I feel a need, I will also interject." I don't know what she's after, but I have confidence she knows what she's doing.

"Good afternoon, everyone," she begins, standing behind the podium. A power point presentation with the title of the seminar is projected on the screen behind her:

Rape Prevention: The 'Y.E.S.' Approach

"As Father Jonah mentioned, my name is Detective Renae Gambke and….."

"Hey, aren't you the one whose father was convicted of killing that poor little girl in Idaho after sexually molesting her and also a few more, at least from what they've found out so far?" A voice conveniently located a few feet from the camera booms from the back. The same irate, grizzled, and slightly overweight troublemaker wearing the same *"Life Is Shit Unless You're the Shitter"* yellow and black baseball cap that was spouting off at Detective Gambke at Central Prison the day of Cameron Gambkes' scheduled execution is present, glaring at her. His moment of fame is within his grasp. I have an urge now, as I did then, to protect her, but I instinctively know she'll handle it as well as she did then, if not better.

"Mr. Buzel, what you've mentioned isn't new news to anyone here. But let me remind you that this evening we've set aside time to speak on the topic of Rape Prevention."

I didn't know she knew Mr. Buzel. He's just getting started.

"Rape prevention. Whatever. This is just another attempt by all you feminists to blame all the men for your problems. Do you want to know what you and your fellow police people need to be working on? See that black guy standing up by you? He's probably trying to see who is here in this room today so he can call his buddies and rob their house sure shit as we're all sittin' here. See that Hispanic woman sitting there? She's probably got 18 kids and should be home watching them in case they're out spraying graffiti around town. And see that suspicious Muslim-looking dude? I would check his bag – there's probably a bomb in it. Those are the real problems of this world, and you're going to stand here and tell us about something called 'rape,' a highly-questionable problem, when so many women are either begging for or selling their bodies for sex? But let me get back to my original point before you try to avoid the subject altogether. You also have a brother named Matt Gambke, don't you?"

Detective Renae eyes the sheriff, who is standing near the back door, slowly moving in the direction of Mr. Buzel. Calmly turning her gaze to me I can sense she is very much in control. I nod. It's your floor, young lady, kick ass and take names, please. Before she can respond, lugnut unwisely continues.

"I heard rumor that your brother now may be involved with what happened to poor Gina Jerpun. So you, with your illustrious family background, want to sit up there and tell all of these folks how to protect themselves? From who? Turds like the Gambkes?"

Another glance back at the sheriff and he nods to her. Finally, her direct report seems to support her. I know I have complete authority to throw him out as this is private property, however, I want to see how this plays out. So far he has a hand that he doesn't deserve, the upper. He started it, and I need to give Detective Renae a chance to end it, in full public view. The crowd begins moving away from Mr. Buzel, trying to distance themselves from his venomous comments. All eyes turn toward the detective, tensely awaiting her response.

"Mr. Buzel, do you really want to travel down this road with me? Right here? Right now? In front of everyone? Is that really what you want?" She's standing arms akimbo. Her tone reflects how insignificant she considers this man's opinion and that she evidently knows much more about him than probably anyone else in the room, save Sheriff Luder. I can't wait to see what happens next.

"Everyone knows about you, Detective Gambke, and you should be mortified to even be up here in front of everyone this morning, showing your face as some expert in crime prevention. Give me a break. And you ain't got nuthin' that you can say to these good folks that will make one ounce of difference. Us Buzels are saints compared to you Gambkes, and you know it."

She moves to the front of the podium, crosses her arms, and stares him down. He's at the back of the room sitting in the last chair in the last row, probably planning to quickly exit once he has unleashed his vile venom. He certainly doesn't have the guts, nor the active brain cells, to participate in an equal exchange. He's a sniper attacker, a bully until someone stands up to him.

"You know, Mr. Buzel, you must be under the mistaken impression that I fear you or can be intimated."

His eyebrows raise and a smirk suddenly appears – fear from others is what he has longed for, and probably gotten, his entire life. It's what makes him feel important, in control, on top of his world. But his tactics aren't having the desired effect.

"Yes, my father Cameron Gambke was on death row. And there you were, spitting obscenities my way. That interaction caused me to do some research. Do you really want me to tell these 'good folks' here about you, Mr. Buzel? About the hellion you were growing up? How your dad had a lot of money from owning the only pharmacy in town and all you did was drink and party and destroy things and he got you off, every single time? Or about your son who went into the military and was kicked out for being a chip off the old block, you know, acting the same way you did in life, just the way you taught him through your daily actions of being an asshole? Or how about your grandson who holds the illustrious title of Registered Sex Offender? You must be so proud of all you've accomplished with your offspring, Mr. Buzel."

He stands hastily, his metal chair clanging to the floor. The deep redness in his face evident even from 15 yards away, accented even more by his white hair. All eyes are on him now, and he peers a little too anxiously at the back door.

"Oh, don't go yet, Mr. Buzel. That 'black man' you just accused of being a burglar? His name is Cory Johnson – he's an intern in our department, has the highest GPA in his college, and if we're lucky enough, we can talk him into staying on after graduation because he's the best I've ever seen. And that 'Hispanic' woman you disparaged? Her name is Maria Gonzalez –

she runs our Crime Lab. Last year she won Employee of the Year, has a degree in Business Management, is working towards her MBA, and has three young children, all with honors in their respective schools. And the 'Muslim bomb guy' you just demeaned? His name is Aaban Hasan. He's our Systems Administrator and has done an incredible job with getting our department up to speed. You don't want to know how many degrees he has. He has the nicest family I've ever known, and I trust him implicitly.

"And if I put the combined results of their individual background checks up on the screen behind me and put the total score next to yours, your sons and your grandsons, everyone would plainly see that you and your backwards, uneducated, emotion-laden opinions and lifestyle are the problem, Mr. Buzel, not those you've publicly stereotyped and vilified.

"But getting to know them would be too much work for you, wouldn't it, Mr. Buzel? You'd rather just talk smack about everyone based on whatever opinion you've formed without ever doing any homework, because research would be too difficult for you, wouldn't it, Mr. Buzel? You would have to actually put down the remote control for your big screen, pull your hands out of your pants, and make an effort at something productive, maybe read or study. Haven't done that in a while have you?"

Heads are turning his way, as is the camera. The sheriff is making no effort to quiet her, and Mr. Buzel once more leans towards the door, no doubt trying to think of the words for his last parting shot, as Detective Renae lays bare his indiscretions.

"Oh, one more thing before you leave, Mr. Buzel, I will give you this. Cameron Gambke did do some horrible things and has paid for them. And if my brother, Matt, is proven guilty, I will do everything in my power to bring him to justice. But my philosophy in life is that everyone has a past, that's a given. You. Me. Everyone in this room, for that matter. And for my father, yes, his was a very horrible past. But I offer another question since we all have a 'past.' In which direction are we headed? Are we trying to live our lives now to help and not hinder? To heal and not harm? Clearly, you're no better now than you were a teenager. In fact, by all indications, you've gotten worse. And you want to point fingers at all of us? Doesn't that embarrass you, Mr. Buzel? If not, it should…"

Furious now yet ill-equipped for a verbal exchange, he offers a weak rebuff as he turns to leave.

"I'm sure there's a whole lot more these people don't know about you, Gambke."

"You've probably always tried to make people think you know more than you do, but you really are just an ignorant old man. And the worst part is, you know it to be true, don't you?" She's slowly moving his way. He's walking backwards to the door.

His head snapping towards the sheriff, Mr. Buzel barks: "You gonna let your employee talk to me like that, Sheriff?"

"Well, looks to me like she just did, Bobbie. Can't handle the firestorm you started? If you want to push this even further to a physical level, I suggest you prepare yourself. Maybe she can show you her finely tuned combat skills, you know, for when she has to subdue a loudmouth troublemaker."

The sheriff knows him too, I see. The door slams open as Mr. Bobbie Buzel exits, the audience applauding loudly as they stand facing Detective Renae. If she didn't have respect from the crowd before this presentation began, she sure has it now.

Chapter 40

"My apologies to all of you. Now, let's get on with the presentation.

"We've already burned ten minutes, so I'm going to need to move quickly through this material, and there's a lot of it. Please bear with me, all right? This information is extremely important."

With a click of the button and a quick glance towards the screen to ensure the first slide is correct, Detective Renae begins. She doesn't repeat the words that are displayed – they change every three minutes – but focuses on the handout she holds in her hand instead.

MOOD SWINGS / DEPRESSION / EMOTIONAL OUTBURSTS

"How big of a problem is this? Numbers and statistics vary, but let me throw some your way. I encourage each of you to check out www.rainn.org periodically, at a minimum, as these are available to the general public. Here are some of the numbers they provide, but keep in mind the exact extent is unknown because this is a crime that is routinely unreported.

"Rape has decreased 60 percent since 1993. There are varying opinions on this, but my belief is that this is due to a combination of increased awareness and self-protection measures being employed which is fantastic, but also due to many women – and more and more men – still not reporting it.

"Every two minutes someone in the U.S. is sexually assaulted. This includes date rape, stranger rape, acquaintance rape, jail/prison rape, marital rape, etc.

"There is an average of 207,754 victims ages 12 and older each year. Anyone can become a victim at any time, no matter your age or how you look.

"54 percent of sexual assaults are never reported to the police. Approximately two-thirds of all assaults are committed by someone known to the victim. 38 percent of rapists are a friend or an acquaintance."

The second slide appears on the screen, yet she continues reading from her handout. Clearly, and intentionally, the information behind her is not the same she is sharing with the group from the handout.

FEELINGS OF HUMILIATION / FEELINGS OF DEGRADATION / GUILT

"Sadly, from 1957 through today, I've seen studies which reflect that the same percentage of women are still suffering attempted or completed rape so the efforts at educating men to change their ways haven't been entirely effective. Either the rapists aren't listening, or they don't care about what they're hearing – that rape is a *crime*.

"And, most unfortunately, 97 percent of rapists never spend a day in jail. What's worse, a majority of sexual predators continue their assaults until only one thing happens – they are stopped. The longer they are allowed to do this activity, the more confidence they get.

"This is also not just a problem here in the United States. India has really been struggling with this issue as of late, because the people have had it. The 16-year-old Indian girl who was raped by 40 men over forty days. She had been kidnapped and forced into human sex trafficking. The men just had their hands slapped. The focus was squarely on the girl's "character." She may now be forever stigmatized in her culture.

A HORRIFIC LIFE CHANGING EXPERIENCE

"Let's knock out some of the myths about rape that, in my opinion, Mr. Buzel and so many like him probably hold near and dear to their hardened hearts.

"Top of most lists from the experts. 'The victim deserved it.' This has been a line of thought for the last 60 years. Specifically, the victim *did something* to cause the rape or allowed it to happen, or what they were wearing brought it on, or maybe they egged a guy on and he just couldn't help himself.

"Let me repeat a very important point – rape is a crime, just like any other crime! Understand? And rapists choose to rape, got it? And this is the only crime where the victim is routinely not believed, and even blamed, for what happened!"

She's angry now, her memories of assisting rape victims and listening to the pathetic responses from the rapists themselves rushing forward.

PURPOSELESSNESS / HIGHER THAN AVERAGE THOUGHTS OF SUICIDE

"How about this myth? 'Rape is a crime controlled by an uncontrollable sex drive.' There is absolutely no evidence to support this. How idiotic is it to think that you men can't control yourself?"

She looks at the sheriff and back at me, a wry smile crossing her lips, as she proceeds to remove her blue business suit. Standing nonchalantly in high heels and a two piece bathing suit, she continues with her presentation. Murmurs, laughter and some gasps spread throughout the room which she dutifully ignores.

"Keep in mind that many sexual predators are married or have girlfriends or partners willing to have sex with them. So this clearly reiterates a point I just made earlier – rape is a choice they make, and for many, it reflects a pattern of living and lifestyle they've followed for a long time. What ever happened with practicing self-control? Temperance? If they don't learn how to control their urges when they're young, when will they?"

Walking slowly up and down the middle aisle, she turns in the back and up the side, then back to the front to the other side aisle, returning finally up the center aisle to the podium, swishing like a walkway model in New York City, talking all the while.

"Another myth. 'A woman can really resist rape if she truly wishes.' Not only are men typically stronger and more physical, but rapists have one big element on their side – surprise. A woman does not control whether or not she will be raped; the rapist does.

"'All women want to be raped' is another myth that drives me nuts. Really? Do people actually believe this? The romance/erotic novel genre and many movies and songs make us believe this, but it just isn't true.

"And, finally, here is a myth that continues to be very prominent – 'most women falsely report rape.' This has been proven to be grossly false. Major studies have shown that the range is between two to eight percent of the total of those women who were brave enough to even come forward.

"But here is a point that I cannot emphasize strongly enough. Many rape victims recant their claim for a variety of reasons. They were indeed raped, but they just want to move beyond it. They never wanted it to happen to begin with, and they just want and need to move on, especially when they see that no one is supporting them. It's tragic. And no one has the right to assume this proves they filed a false report, ever. I implore you, don't go there or else you'll end up with the same outlook as Mr. Buzel, all right?

SILENCE TO PROTECT THEMSELVES, FAMILIES AND FRIENDS

"Now if these myths don't sound insane enough, let me throw this concept out to you.

"How many of you moms and dads raised your child to be all they could be? I mean, you birthed them, clothed them, and took them to school, to plays, on vacations. You tried to teach them right from wrong. You cared for them, loved them, held them, many of you prayed for and with them. You helped them with their homework and tried to ensure they did well in school. You cried with them and for them; and most of you have never loved more deeply than you have for your children. With that being established, how many of you ever raised your child to be some sexual predator's piece of ass, used for their selfish pleasure, many discarded as though they were mere take-out food, valueless? If that doesn't burn you, I'm not sure what will."

She pauses a moment to let the last comment settle in, taking the opportunity to put her clothes back on over her bathing suit. Turning another page in her packet, Detective Renae continues her presentation.

"Over the last few minutes I've been speaking up here with just my bathing suit and high-heeled shoes on. There are many men in this room, along with women. If the sexual urge is so strong and uncontrollable as so many people – especially men with a vested interest in the topic – want all of us to believe, why didn't anyone attack me? For you rapists in this room – and statistically I know you're in here – even *you* were able to control yourself. You certainly aren't going to make a move in front of this crowd, and in front of that camera back there, so if you can control it in this environment, there goes your bullshit argument that you just can't control yourself anywhere else. You can whenever you want to, you just choose not to, and you know very well that's the honest truth.

SHAME / EMBARRASMENT / SELF-BLAME

"Now, what are some of the other primary reasons why victims don't report rape? All types of fear drive it. Certainly of not being believed. Maybe of being mocked by others. Some are afraid that the investigation may victimize them again and again, believing that if it goes to court the District Attorney will attack their character and make them look like a whore, a slut, a willing participant – just like they did in India. Plus, they will have to prove that the attack was against their will.

"Now, who are these sexual predators? I mean, can't we clearly identify them? Everyone stand up. Yes, men and women. It looks like we have all ages, races, and gender covered."

She allows time for everyone to stand; some taking the opportunity to stretch in relief from sitting for the past 20 minutes on the metal chairs.

"Look around. These are the faces of rapists. Oh, wait, these are the faces of non-rapists. No, wait again. Maybe some are, maybe some aren't.

"Okay, go ahead and sit back down.

"My point is that there is no set profile for a rapist. You need to learn to watch for what people *do*, not what they *say* or what they *look like* in order to pinpoint trouble, but I'll get to that later.

"One of the primary ways of protecting ourselves and others is through education. Buy some books and get on the Internet, where you'll find many useful sites covering this topic. I've listed some in the back of the handouts to get you started.

"Here's a sampling of what the experts have pinpointed over the years so you can get an idea of what to look for.

"Pedophiliacs. These people focus on prepubertal children. There was a bust not long ago of an international online group that had over 70,000 registered members, including school teachers and police officers. 70,000. Disgusting, isn't it?

"Then there are the hebephiles. They prefer children roughly between the ages of 11 and 14.

ANGER / REVENGE / NIGHTMARES / SCREAMING OUT IN SLEEP

"An angry rapist has been identified as someone who is just flat out mad at the world, including his boss, wife, girlfriend, his car, his dog, whatever or whomever, and he vents that emotion at a helpless victim. Any victim will do.

"The sexual sadist may be the most dangerous. These are the people who merge their sexual fantasies with their aggression and can't seem to get off without inflicting psychological or physical pain on their victim. In their twisted world, they may even think the victim is enjoying it. They may have what we call a 'rape kit' with handcuffs, duct tape, silk scarves, or rope in their possession – we've seen them in car trunks on routine stops – which is a big red flag for us.

"Lust rapist. These folks just want to have sex. Like all rapists, they can control themselves, they just don't want to. They do things like look at porn to fuel their fantasies over and over. In my experience, this is the type I've seen the most.

"The righteous rapists are the ones who believe they are 'owed' sex. By their spouses, their partners, whomever.

315

SORENESS / DECREASE IN APPETITE / FOOD DOESN'T TASTE RIGHT

"The rage-filled rapist. This person is really pissed off, even more so than the angry rapist. They truly hate women, or gays and lesbians, for instance, and their primary objective is to commit an unnecessary level of violence to them, far above and beyond any desire to have sex with them.

"The Power-Reassurance rapists. An example is someone who can't get a date with someone they want, so they force them.

"The exploitative rapist is very impulsive. If the opportunity is there to rape, they'll take it.

CONTINUALLY TRYING TO BLOCK THE MEMORIES

"Here are some common characteristics, but it's not an all-inclusive list, alright?

"They *may* be very attractive men – gregarious, charming, caring, and warm – which often allows them to get close to their targets. Most likely in their late teens to mid-thirty's, but that's just a parameter. They may have children at home; likely believing they are not getting enough sex from their wife who is working her butt off to keep the kids happy and fed, him content, and the bills paid. He may have a job that requires periodic travel which is a built-in excuse for his escapades. Many rapists are generally intelligent. He may have had a rough childhood which may be why his wife or partner won't leave him, because they've ensured their partner feels real sorry for them, but that isn't always the case at all. He may very well be a loner; or could be very sociable and liked by many. No matter what, like so many criminals out there, their friends and neighbors would never think they could be a rapist because they are so good at managing everyone around them.

"For males, in your dealings with him, he may very well exhibit a hostile attitude towards women and may feel very entitled to things around him, including you.

"He may be very indifferent to others, rude or even mean, and almost always self-serving.

INABILITY TO TRUST ANYONE / FEAR OF STRANGERS / FEAR OF MEN

"But I'll tell ya, he'll be very good at reading people. Non-verbal cues are his specialty. He smells fear, apprehension, and naïveté and will jump all over it if given a chance. Most of the time he will be unarmed, but if he does have a weapon, it will probably be a knife. A few may have a gun, so you should be prepared for that.

"He may suffer from paraphilia, a mental disorder where he prefers unusual sexual practices. And like a drug addict, when rape doesn't get him what he wants, he will rape again. The problem with this kind of thinking is that he will never get what he wants because his life revolves around distorted thinking and fantasy, fueled by masturbation, and supported by ritual. No act of rape can satisfy that fantasy. None. Ever. That's why he will continue to rape, over and over.

"He will threaten to return and get you, although he seldom will. He just wants to scare you into thinking so. I'm not saying you shouldn't be prepared. Don't be paranoid, be prepared.

"Many will blame their victims, rationalizing their behavior and never taking any responsibility for the act. Nothing is their fault, ever. Know any guys like that? I sure do."

She aggressively turns the pages of her handout. While trying to hold her emotions in check, old memories probably from past cases are causing her to speed up and the tone in her voice to rise.

"He will plan his attack in advance, and will be successful because most women live in fear. And many of these rapists will not just grow out of it as they get older, so keep that in mind.

"However, there are many victim success stories out there today, and many wonderful people and groups who are making tremendous strides in combating this blight on our society. So let me state this clearly, right here and now: There is no need to live in fear, just in a consistent state of awareness, okay?

"Remember, no one can ever, with 100 percent certainty, identify a rapist in their midst. As I told you, a complete list of traits simply doesn't exist. And even if it did, our ever changing human nature and culture virtually guarantees that the fantasies and rituals of sexual predators will change along with it. Although I assure you that doesn't mean we need to feel helpless nor lose hope. Not at all. Not even close.

"So let's get to the heart and soul of this presentation – what can you do about it?

"First and foremost, and it sounds like I am regressing from what I just finished saying, but I have to apologize and tell you I'm sorry. Why? Because I *cannot* give you any easy solution. Nor am I going to give you a foolproof plan of action, because there isn't one. Rather, I'm going to give you some solid guidelines, based on what I and other professionals who do this for a living, recommend. Like anything else, it's up to you what you do with it.

"Before I get into the 'Y.E.S' system, let's talk about something very important – PREVENTION. Never forget that *if there is no opportunity*, the chances for this heinous crime go way, way down."

Detective Renae takes 20 minutes to cover the minefield called "dating," explaining in detail the points already made by Sheriff Luder to me on the topic during our recent pilgrimage, while adding her own helpful points based on personal experience.

DREADFULLY SELF-CONSCIOUS

"Again, I'm not suggesting you be obsessively distrustful; just always try to be smart. You'll be amazed at how accurate your instincts can be. I've worked so many cases where the victim said she should have done just that and trusted her instincts, but she overrode her own senses by berating herself for being silly or overly cautious.

"Now let's talk about the character of your date. I am speaking from experience here, ladies, and so are the hundreds of victims I've met. I'm not saying that what I'm about to describe means that your guy is a raging rapist, however, don't ignore these proven red flags. They come from hundreds of thousands of women who dated these types and paid dearly for it. For you men, in many respects, you also need to keep what I am about to say in mind. This could also apply to that woman who you think might become your girlfriend or wife someday.

"Never assume you know a person better than you actually do. Time and again people are convinced they know how to spot a liar and time and again they are proven wrong. This is an incredibly important point for you to never, ever, forget. People like this – sexual predators and criminals of all types – are expert liars! As I said before, never listen to what people say, just watch what they do – their actions speak louder than their words, okay?

"If you know the man or woman is prone to violence, don't go down that road. Truly and seriously. As soon as you find this out, get out right away.

"More often than not, they will be on their best behavior while you're courting. It's really hard to pinpoint whether this person is a scumbag or not at first. That's why I strongly encourage you to check them out beforehand with background checks and trusting your instincts.

"If that doesn't raise any red flags, then give the relationship enough time *before* you make any commitments, like sleeping with him. Or telling him or her you love them. Why? Because I firmly believe that once they get what they want and hear you say those magical words, they know they have you. So give it time, and then watch for their true colors to come out before committing long-term or giving in to sex.

TRYING TO WEAR A "HAPPY" FACE

"If they emotionally abuse you through insults, ignoring your opinion or making you always feel stupid, watch out. If they are always trying to control you and telling you how you should dress, who you should hang out with, what you should eat and laying out all the things you have to do during your day, and also keep you from your friends and family, beware.

"If they get jealous easily for no solid reason at all, if they talk badly about women in general, if they're always on you for not wanting to do the things they want to do – like getting drunk, getting high, having sex – head for the door.

"I know this one sounds obvious, but when you say 'no' and they really become frustrated and angry with you, sometimes lashing out at walls, couches, animals or other material things, be prepared to bail. And this one goes without saying, if they are physically violent with you – even if they apologize afterward – run. If they are violent with you and blame you, go into an all-out sprint away from that relationship.

"When he or she makes you feel like you are not their equal, that they are superior in many ways and you are a dumb shit, think twice. If they have a fascination with weapons and enjoy being cruel to animals or children, if they are a bully to others, look out because you may be next. Why? Because it's how they've learned to deal with problems in their life, and when you become a problem in their distorted minds, chances may be very good that this is how they will then react to you. It's not your fault, you didn't cause it, and you can't control them, but you can control how you react to it.

CHEMICAL CHANGE: CHRONIC DEPRESSION

"If they are hypersensitive, or if they say they will hit or kill you if you ever decide to leave, already have an action plan and implement it, fast. If they have sudden mood swings that catch you completely off guard, stay alert. If certain events trigger changes in behavior, events that you can't fathom would normally cause such radical changes, and if they blame everyone for everything that has gone wrong with their poor little 'sorry for me' lives, including you, be very, very careful about staying in that relationship.

"If they have a quick and violent temper and/or a history of abuse, go into that relationship with your eyes wide open. You think they won't do it to you? Really? Do you really think you are so different from their past girlfriends or wives even though he has assured you that's not the case? What else is he going to tell you? The truth? The truth doesn't get him what he wants from you. Statistically, when things go wrong in their lives, you will be the one to take the first blow, just like the ones before.

"If they are socially immature but act as though they have all the answers to everything, and everyone else is stupid, strap on your seatbelt if you want to stay in that relationship because history has proven it's gonna be an incredibly rough ride.

"Now, outside of dating, if someone shows up on the street, in a store parking lot or other private or public area, and starts giving you a bunch of unnecessary detail about, well, anything – the weather, what's in his shopping cart, etc. – he could be distracting you for a reason. Be alert, be aware, pay attention, and, again, trust your instincts! If he's offended as you march away, too bad – men in today's world need to understand what women are up against and deal with their fragile ego accordingly. If they are good, mature, caring boys or men, they'll understand. If not, why would you consider dating them in the first place? Do you think so poorly of yourself that you can't find someone else? Or are there just too few good guys out there who will treat you with love and respect you rightfully deserve?"

She laughs. "Maybe you shouldn't answer that question, because I'm trying to find them, too."

The women burst into laughter, as do many of the dads present.

"Let's take a quick 10-minute break, okay?" An appreciative sigh exudes from the group.

Chapter 41

Detective Renae gathers the assembly back to their seats or standing places, continuing on the topic of stalking while the next slide emanates behind her on the screen.

ADDICTION TO ALCOHOL OR DRUGS

"If you feel you are the object of someone else's obsession, get out of that relationship! Make it very clear to that person that you are not interested. Tell your family, tell your friends, tell whomever you need to tell. Do not worry about hurting that person's feelings, okay?

"Stalking, just like rape, is a crime. Remember that. In fact, professionals will tell you that *stalking is the one crime where we know, in advance, who the perpetrator is!* Think about what I just said. The bastards are literally telling the world they are up to something, planning something that may cause great harm to you. Stop it cold turkey immediately. I encourage you to be the biggest bitch or asshole you need to be in doing so. Sure, start out nice but if they don't stop, give it all you got. Protect *you* – that's your primary obligation. If you have children, protect them. The two go hand in hand! Do yourself a favor and don't be flattered by it. I mean, do you really want to date and then marry a stalker? Seriously? If they're stalking, they're not 'getting it.' That derelict is not operating on all cylinders so don't treat them like they are. Respect their feelings? Why? They're not respecting yours.

"And my personal favorite, something that I stress over and over again when I give these presentations: when his orgasm is always, time and again, more important than anything else in your life, get the hell out! Got it? They're showing you they clearly care mostly about themselves, and not about you, plain and simple.

"Now, for those of you who are here today and stuck with people like this, always remember, and actively practice, the self-protection measures I am going to talk about. Also remember that you can get a protection order issued by the court, and if someone breaks it that's a prosecutable crime. Further, I encourage you to make some backup plans for help if you need to get out, because a protection order is only part of your multi-faceted solution that you should have in place. I know this isn't easy, but there are safe houses for you and your kids, if you have any, where no one will know where you are, ever. I'm not saying any of this lightly. My heart goes out to you; it really does, but know that you have options, okay?"

Moving behind the podium, she places the packet on top, while quickly stretching her own back.

HATRED OF LIFE / PROFOUND SADNESS / SELF-DOUBT / PARANOID

"Let's get to some general stuff regarding prevention: Be assertive – many women who successfully thwarted a rapist projected clear signs that they were not to be screwed with. Most rapists look for soft, mild-mannered, overly apologetic girls or women – especially religious ones – because they are so damn easy to manipulate, control, and frighten into submission.

"Be observant. Keep your head on a swivel! Know what's going on around you. Don't always be looking at your cell phone for that text that you just can't wait to answer! Don't walk alone after dark; don't pick up hitchhikers; don't hitchhike yourself; don't go through public parks where there are bushes that sexual predators can hide behind. And if you're waiting for a bus, be alert and ready to run – don't be a statue. If you have to catch the next bus until it's safe, so be it.

"If you are a college student, be especially cautious. Sexual predators are there, ready to take advantage of you. They know that you are in a new environment, away from mom and dad, thinking that you are on your own and can do whatever you want now. They will routinely try to ply you with alcohol, use date rape drugs, and then either individually or gang rape you. I'm not saying all college boys will do this, but you should see the stuff I have to investigate. Find out what protection programs your college has in place immediately and take advantage of any protection services offered."

323

She shares the webcam and spy application information she relayed to me not long ago.

"For your home, make sure you put deadbolt locks on all your doors, and even reinforced strike plates. Put wood dowels with a rope for fast removal in your sliding window and door frames, too. You can go to any local hardware store and buy clips to easily secure your doors and windows.

"Buy a gun. But this is critically important, get trained on how to use that gun and store it safely and properly, okay? Get a home alarm system. Most of them these days are very affordable. Install a video system that ties into your home alarm system, too, or even a separate system. These shitheads do not want to be seen and identified, I guarantee you that.

"And get a dog, big or small, it doesn't matter. These assholes don't like dogs either, any dogs. Doesn't matter the breed or size. They bark and bring attention, and might bite them, and they can be very unpredictable, especially when protecting their owner. But if you do get a dog, please be prepared to take care of it.

"For your car, here are some basics to think about. Don't park close to another car; leave a buffer zone around your car if you can. This is so a perp can't hide and jump you from between cars that are parked next to you. As you walk up to your car from a distance, use your eyes to look underneath to see if someone is hiding under there. Before you get in, look in the backseat of your car to make sure no one is in there.

"As soon as you get in, before you even start your car, lock your doors! I'll repeat that, lock your doors immediately so that as you fumble for your keys, a perp can't just walk up, open your door, and hop in!

"As you're driving, make sure you are paying attention to your rearview and side mirrors to see if anyone is following you. Make sure your car itself is in good working order, has a full tank of gas, has a working spare tire and jack, and that people know your schedule – this is where texting really can come in handy – so if you don't show up on time, someone is looking for you. Have a first aid kit in your trunk. Have a baton and a taser gun, too, because these are legal in almost every single state.

"If someone bumps their vehicle into yours, don't get out! Instead, drive to a police station or another high-traffic area to pull over and have them follow you there to exchange insurance information. This is not 'leaving the scene of the accident,' it's an accepted, and solid protection measure. Be smart and use your common sense.

FEAR OF UNWANTED PREGNANCY / SENSE OF INFERIORITY

"This is where the 'Y.E.S.' system comes in.

"Let's take the first letter, 'Y.' It stands for 'You.' You know yourself better than anyone else, right? You know if you're a fighter, you know what you can do and what you can't. Let me give you an example.

"In my old precinct, there was a hundred pound mom who was heading out to work one day. Her husband was in the house and she thought her toddler was in the backyard. The gate was left open, and he was actually behind the car as she pulled out. She felt a bump, got out, and realized her son was under the rear tire! She screamed for her husband to come, but he didn't hear her right away as he was inside and upstairs. She continued screaming in panic hoping for a neighbor to come out. No one did. Reaching down, she single-handedly lifted the four door sedan up off her child, just as her husband arrived to remove the baby. The baby wasn't critically injured and has healed completely, by the way, but my point is that in any other state of mind or normal situation she wouldn't have been able to do it because her mind would have convinced her body to say 'You aren't strong enough to lift that car.' But the motherly instinct kicked in – her absolute love for her baby – and she lifted that car.

"I offer that story to you because you have more strength inside of you than you realize.

FEAR OF PHYSICAL INJURY / MUTILATION / DEATH

"In the end, you need to save yourself, to protect your

physical and emotional well-being. If that means giving in to survive, then so be it. Never, ever forget that, if you are a victim of rape, you have done nothing wrong. It's the rapist who has committed the crime. It's the rapist who has crossed the line of what's acceptable in society, plain and simple. He or she knows it, and you need to know it, too. And no one has the right to tell you, after the fact, that you should have done this, or you should have done that. Not even me. So with that out of the way, let me hit the high points.

"No matter what you choose to do, I urge you to learn to defend yourself; take some self-defense classes. You can find them here in the local community; you can find them online; you can order DVDs for it.

"So let's say you have decided to fight. There is a common saying, that *"If he can't see, can't breathe or can't stand up, he can't fight."* Learn to take care of yourself. Don't rely on others to take care of you, especially if they aren't always around like a loving father or mother, husband, brother or sister, or boyfriend.

"Also, as one expert says, your legs are to run with and your mouth is to scream with, and I know us girls can scream long and loud when we need to. You may think you'll be so scared that you won't be able to utter a sound, but you will if you are prepared. Prepare yourself in advance by mentally stepping through a potential rape scenario.

SENSE OF INFERIORITY / DEVELOPMENT OF FEARS AND PHOBIAS

"Your best defense is to get the hell out of there as quickly as possible. Run to where there are people, where you see lights, for instance – and yell words like 'FIRE,' 'HELP,' 'RAPE,' or any other emotional word because that tends to make other people listen up. But keep running. If you are approached, do all you can to not get into their car. Statistically, you are more than likely to be harmed, even killed, if you do. Again, not always, but make every effort to avoid this. Scream, fight, kick, punch, all the stuff that you will learn in a self-defense course, and then move it out of there.

"You should also know this. Statistically, if the rapist has a gun and you run away, 98 percent of the time they won't shoot. I know, it's not 100 percent, but in the minds of many victims, they think they will be shot right on the spot. Remember, the rapist does not want to get caught. Shooting at you will be very noisy and bring attention to him. Besides, he more than likely just wants to have sex with you; if he fires his gun, his twisted plan will be foiled and they will pay dearly in prison. Again, it's your call on how you respond but keep your composure, focus, and with a bit of training, you will be able to avoid becoming a victim. But, as I said before, it's your call; do whatever is comfortable for you.

"If you can't get away, try to establish a personal connection with your attacker so they see you as a person with a life, family, friends, hopes and dreams and not just a piece of ass. This may not always work, but it has on occasion. Remember, your goal is to stay alive!

"Some advice should you get into it with your potential rapist, even if they are your so-called 'friend.' If he has a knife, I recommend that you don't try to fight him off unless you have been trained to do so. And know that if you do, you may get hurt. Once you do start fighting back, *do not stop*. Go at it with all you've got. Break their fingers, stab their eyes, butt them with your head, kick them squarely in the nuts, stomp their feet, kick their shins, drive their knees backwards so they are hyper-extended, spit in their face and eyes, attack them with anything you've got – pen, pencil, key ring – taze them, put them into a coma with the pointed end of your high-heeled shoe; grab their tie and choke them with it; grab their hair and yank it completely out; if you have a bat or other weapon, use it; if you have a pin, stab them."

She looks up as a few snickers come her way, a few in the group finding humor in her comments.

"Look, I'm not joking about any of this. My point is that *there are no rules here*. You are fighting for your safety and possibly your life. If you've ever fought like a wild person, this would be the time. You are protecting yourself, and you have every right to do so. The law calls it 'self-defense.' If you think that's being mean to your attacker, then you aren't fully understanding the gravity of this topic. Your attacker sure doesn't care about your health and well-being, so why, in the end, spend time caring about theirs?

"And guess what? A government study showed that three out of four potential victims successfully stopped their attackers. This goes to show that you have an excellent chance of surviving and preventing a rape attempt if you are prepared. So, although the number of rape attempts may still be incredibly high, three-fourths have been prevented, and that is encouraging. But *any* rape is one too many, don't you agree? So, constant vigilance, training and practice are necessary.

HARD TIME GETTING TO SLEEP / HARD TIME STAYING ASLEEP

"The 'E' in 'Y.E.S.' stands for EDUCATE yourself. I've already talked briefly about the different types of attackers and their characteristics, but I really encourage you again to buy some books to study them.

"The 'S' stands for the SITE. Is it in a private area? Know your surroundings and plan what you would do. Yelling and screaming, when there is no one else around, may not be your best option. In that case, fighting back may be your best and only choice. Again, you have to decide.

"If you are raped, know there are a number of fantastic organizations that are available to help. I have had the pleasure of working with some phenomenal victims' advocates; they really do care for and about you, and know what you've been through, and they understand. There are agencies that will provide you with financial support. *You don't have to suffer alone.*

"Help is also available for the secondary victims, those family members and friends who feel in many ways the pain and agony that you went through because they love you so much.

"There are so many rape survivors that have gone on to do great things in this world – so much so that no one even knows they were raped to begin with.

A STRONG DESIRE TO GET AWAY /
ROUTINE OF LIVING COMPLETELY DISRUPTED

"For everyone who came here to learn more about this topic of rape, know that social injustices and criminal behavior can and have been stopped and eradicated.

"As a society, we must stop tolerating it. You need to know there are many cultures around the world with very low rape statistics where women stand up and scream when they are raped or sexually abused. And they are fully supported by their husbands and boyfriends, friends or strangers, to the detriment of the rapists. Why not here in this great country we call home? I mean, when we stand up, when the abusers know – not by our words but by our legal deeds – that what they are doing is not acceptable and that there is a price to pay, then things will change for the better. I really believe that to be true.

DULL LOOK IN THEIR EYES /
THINK THEY CAN GET THROUGH IT ON THEIR OWN

"And, I would be remiss in this presentation if I didn't add that I have no idea what the future holds in store for you, but if you find yourself a victim of a sex crime, you undoubtedly will be contacted by a Sex Crimes Detective. I can't promise you your experience working with one will be always be positive. I'm sorry to say that. Most that I know of are very good at what they do and take their jobs seriously. However, I've also personally met a few who believe that every victim should just kick the shit out of the perpetrator, and if this occurred, rapes would never happen to begin with. That mentality is just another way of blaming the victim as though it was their fault. It's just not reality. Maybe it gives these other detectives a sense of security in their own mental world; maybe it makes them feel safer. In any case, if you ever run into this type of insensitive member of law enforcement and they make you feel like it was your fault, call me personally, all right? They obviously don't have the right empathy or compassion, nor the proper training, to work with sexual assault victims.

"Now, although it's no excuse, keep in mind it truly may be a resource issue. A police force has limited resources to fight not only sex crimes but all crimes. It's not like the Boston Marathon bombing where an amazing number of agencies were pulled together to find the suspects in an incredibly short amount of time. That's not what normally happens. To be completely honest, and it's probably no surprise to anyone in this room, the law enforcement community is often extremely short-staffed. And I just have to add that because of our limited numbers, the criminals often win the battle.

"That's why I stress time and again the critical importance of active community involvement in fighting crime, all crime. Never forget that sexual predators truly fear getting caught. If they didn't, they wouldn't do their crime in the shadows. They must fear that action will be taken against them. Without a hammer, a nail has no purpose."

Detective Renae checks her watch, a signal to all present that she realizes her time is almost up.

"And, finally, if you ever have doubts about reporting a rape, please know that technology has come a long way in helping to prove that a crime has occurred and who committed it. Properly trained personnel can now look for abrasions, tearing, and other types of trauma or irritation and friction in the vaginal or anal canals that would be consistent with forced penetration. You see, for sexual intercourse specifically, the female body prepares itself automatically when aroused and ready. Without that, anything forced is evidenced – even if a condom is used by the assailant when he's worried about DNA evidence.

A SHATTERED SOUL

"Together, with enough like-minded people, we can and will put a stop to this. We all have to weigh the odds and throw the dice. How we go about preparing ourselves for what may happen in the future is important."

Holding the finished packet in her hand and glancing at her watch, she moves to the front of the podium.

"That's the presentation, and I hope you found it insightful. I will stay here for a few minutes to answer any questions. But even though I'm out of time, I would like to say one thing to all of you who came here today hoping to get turned on or find ways to better commit your ugly sex crimes."

She crosses her arms and takes a long look, scanning the sea of faces.

"If you are a rapist, I now speak confidently for every victim and secondary victim out there. You need to understand something very clearly no matter how you rationalize your pathetic actions – you *are* a piece of shit. No ifs, ands, or buts about it. Really, truly, seriously. Always know that, always remember that. And more importantly, I'm comin' after you. Got it?"

As she returns to the back of the podium to begin gathering her notes, a spattering of claps are offered as the attendees realize the presentation is officially over. The tension from her last verbal jab hangs in the air.

Seeing a raised hand in the back of the room, I stand quickly before everyone leaves.

"Detective, you have a question."

"Yes?" she says, looking from me to a man in his forties, sitting next to whom I assume are his wife and teenage daughter.

"Detective, thank you for this information." Pointing up to the screen behind her, he continues. "I take it all those sayings that were projected onto the screen represent what victims go through?"

Pausing, she considers the proper response.

"Well, I don't know if every victim of sexual assault has gone through each stage of the Rape Trauma Syndrome, because some haven't and might not ever. But first let me say that what I find incredibly sad is that many people are real good at looking at people they personally know have been raped and have gone through these trauma stages, but when they find them laughing or actually healing from the assault, they surmise that, well, 'maybe the rape wasn't all that bad for them to begin with', or, "maybe they didn't get raped after all." And that's so incredibly wrong and way off base – they clearly don't understand the devastation it can cause to the mind, body and spiritual connection for victims, nor the healing power of the human spirit.

"But to your question – I only listed what I went through."

Chapter 42

It's early August, and it's hot. 90 and 90 as they say around here. Actually it's 90 degrees and only 82 percent humidity, but who's counting.

Unfortunately, I haven't been able to update this journal the entire summer. The week after Detective Renae gave her presentation on rape prevention, we had a break-in at the parish office. I could see where the side window of my office had been pried open, but strangely enough, only a few things were missing – a stapler, some printer cartridges, and my laptop.

I reported it to the Gardensville police, who were a little surprised that it had been stolen because it was an older model. Plus, guns seem to be the hot item for burglars. The market for personal protection had skyrocketed after the shootings earlier this year at Sandy Hook Elementary School. But, then again, so has Identity Theft. Fortunately, I didn't have any personal information on my laptop like my social security number or bank account information.

To make matters worse, Fr. Bernard said there wasn't enough money to purchase a new one due to the new building fund needs. So I saved money over the summer and just got a new one yesterday over the Internet. At least I had everything backed up on an external hard drive.

This won't be a surprise to you by now, but Mrs. Bellers has not slowed her efforts to wreck my world. After the training, she told Fr. Bernard she had received multiple complaints both during and immediately after the Detective Renae spoke. When I pressed him on the nature of the complaints, he said three people stated they were disappointed the coffee ran out, and another that the toilet overflowed.

"Offer it up, offer it up," I keep repeating to myself in all my interactions with her. Our Lord had to deal with much worse while here on earth.

Outside of the aforementioned complaints, the presentation was very well received. As such, Detective Renae's work load has increased exponentially. A number of women, and some men, had immediately come forward to talk to her, and they keep coming. Because of this, I haven't had a chance to see her much. Surprisingly, to everyone, the sheriff has approved a part-time person to help her. Although he believes in fighting this type of crime, he also believes the current staff should absorb the duties. Like Susan Bellers, he too would rise to the top in Corporate America quickly.

I had asked the detective about her brother and the investigation. She said no one has been able to track him down. Multiple agencies are working on it, an upside to new technology. He may have traveled internationally or he could still be here in the States, but no one knows for sure, she had said.

In May, the nation was shocked and nauseated when it was discovered that a 52-year-old former school bus driver allegedly had abducted, and repeatedly tortured and raped, three young women for over a decade. One of them gave birth to a child from the self-centered deviant. All three experienced a total of five miscarriages – one in which the abuser would starve and punch her in the stomach until the babies inside her womb died.

One of the victims was 14 years old and the best friend of the predator's daughter. She was abducted on her way home from middle school. Another was 16 years old and went missing after finishing her shift at her place of employment. The third was 21 years old and was last seen at her cousin's house. All lived within a short distance from where they were held captive.

It came as no surprise to me to learn from media reports that neighbors and many who knew him thought he was a very nice, outgoing man; they were shocked to learn of his secret life. From what I've learned over these past few months about sex crimes, it all makes perfect sense. Much of his life was hidden from the public eye because he projected this nice guy persona to distract everyone from looking too closely. He was even such a good citizen that he "helped" the community with the search for the lost girls. He had *everything* to lose if he was caught, which is what's about to happen now that he has been, I'm sure.

A few knew that he had had run-ins with the law in the past, a pattern of behavior completely at odds with the man they knew.

It had also been previously reported that he was a very aggressive person with previous run-ins with neighbors. Further, a 2004 self-written letter that they found in the house where he had held them captive, he claimed *"I'm a sexual predator who needs help."*

He also had the audacity to blame the victims for their circumstances, writing, *"They are here against their will because they made the mistake of getting in a car with a total stranger."* You betcha. Not taking responsibility in his life is apparently something he has mastered.

On a better note, when I last saw Detective Renae, she told me Gina is doing well. She had homework to complete for the time she had missed, but luckily she had the summer break to work on catching up. She is enjoying the sunshine, swimming in the ocean, and doing little serious activities except to concentrate on healing.

She said Michele had been all over her when she found out Matt is the primary suspect.

Detective Renae told me she completely understands and empathizes with how Michele feels and her rage. She said she herself is frustrated; all she can do at the moment is focus on the cases in front of her and wait for a break to come in Gina's case. She and the sheriff have come to terms, at least temporarily.

She also told me she had spoken briefly with Gina over the phone but that their conversation was cut short when Michele grabbed the phone and hung up on her. Before she was cut off, Gina told her that she and her mom were going to take a three or four day driving trip somewhere towards the end of July. I myself haven't seen nor spoken to Michele since that rainy spring day at the hospital. You can only imagine how pleased I am.

Remember my mention of Matt interning at Serenity Lane, the same time mom was there? According to the sheriff, once their attorney took control over all communication, the progress slowed even more. Then the records suddenly "disappeared." Thanks to the Good Lord, dad seems very pleased living in the group home we found.

My phone rings, the sheriff is on the line.

"Father, you got a second?" Sheriff Daniel sounds concerned.

"Hey there! Haven't spoken with you in a while. Sure, yeah, what's up? You sound a little stressed."

"I got a couple of things I wanted to tell you about. First, Michele just left here, and this thing may be getting out of control."

"What 'thing'?" I ask.

"Her. Me. Our past. As I told you before, ever since the end of the pilgrimage back in April, she's been all over me. She wants me to find Matt, and I want to find Matt, but he's done a great job at disappearing. So that ticked her off. Then she claimed that because Matt is Detective Gambke's brother, that she's intentionally slowing down the investigation. I explained to her *again* that multiple people are on Gina's case, *including* myself – not just Detective Gambke. I mean, c'mon, she's *our* daughter and I definitely want to bring justice to the little bastard, but she won't listen."

"Well, that sounds reasonable. I mean, I know no one is faulting her for being upset and wanting him caught – heck, we all want whoever did this to Gina to be caught – but you can only do so much, right?" I try to console him.

"Right, but only sane people think like that, Father, and I'm seeing that side of Michele come out that I really never liked. I'm trying to help her, both with the case and her personal life. Her personality has many layers. I suggested she get some professional help, and like many times since we went on that pilgrimage, I told her she really needed to get back to Church. I reminded her of Mother Mary's messages – especially at Fatima regarding 'sins of the flesh.' That's when she threw a picture frame at me that busted in my face while at the same time telling me she never left the swinging lifestyle, just to piss me off, I'm sure. I just got back from the hospital where I got stitched up."

"What?" Isn't anything ever simple when it comes to Michele Jerpun?

"Yep. She came over right before 5:00 as I was just finishing up for the day. I've been making every effort to get to work on time and leave on time, to get home to Jean. I've also done all I can to delegate and make sure I have that 'work-life' balance that my therapist says I need, right? Well, here she comes marching into my office. She walks in, closes the blinds, and sits down at the chair opposite my desk."

"Okay."

"At first she was calm, then she snapped. She said all the stuff I just relayed to you about Detective Gambke and Matt, then accuses me of ignoring her. Says she lies in bed all day and is having withdrawal-like symptoms since I don't love her any more. I tell her I do love her but I can't have this relationship with her; that I've recommitted myself to Jean and that she needs to move on. Then to make her feel better, I tell her we got a small lead on the case."

"You got a lead? On Matt?"

"Yeah, just yesterday. We busted one of his friends on a shoplifting charge. This is the second time we've caught him so he knows he's in a lot more trouble this time. Hoping we'll go easy on him, he tells us he heard from a friend from a friend kind of thing, that Matt was in Nevada but now he's in San Francisco and has been since he left this area."

"What's he doing all the way out on the West Coast?" I ask.

"He doesn't know, but says it has something to do with Burning Man," he replies.

"What the heck is Burning Man?"

"Some 'hippie, spiritual, all freeing, whatever makes you feels good' tribal event out in the middle of the Nevada desert. I'm going to go there in a few weeks to see if I can find him. I'm sure the douche bag is fitting right in. Their organization is headquartered in San Fran. We called them and they said they have no one by that name working for them, but he could be part of the hundreds of volunteers that help out each year."

"Did you tell Michele?" I ask.

The sheriff is understandably frustrated as he continues. "Well, sort of. I said we had a lead but gave her no specifics and she calmed down right away. It's weird with her – like turning on or off a light switch. She can go from calm to insane to gentle to wild in an instant. So, she got up and sauntered over to my side of the desk and proceeded to massage me. Her hand moves to my crotch and tugs my zipper partway down, while her tongue is trying to part my lips and teeth. I mean, she's all over me, taking off her clothes and touching me everywhere. At that point, I'm backing up, trying to get away from her. Then she flips.

"Like I told you before, this ploy has always worked for her. I know I shared with you in confession that after I got back from the pilgrimage I gave in a couple of times, but now, with all the prayer, therapy and really making some inroads on becoming sexually sober, somehow I found the strength to move away. She flipped out, shaking her head and saying weird things I couldn't hear, whispering as though she's talking to someone, but it's not directed at me. Well, I didn't think it was. Hell, who knows sometimes with her? When she goes, she goes.

"Then I realize she's asking me where he's at. 'Where is he?' 'Where is he?!' she keeps saying, louder until she's screaming it. I won't tell her because I'm tired of her shit at that point. I've told her way too many times we're over, and that she needs help. I look back and am embarrassed to even think about the number of times she pulled this ploy on me to get information about something I was working on. Plus, I had told her too much already, and I knew it.

"As I look down to zip up my pants and put myself together she hits me with the picture frame. It was on the side of my desk within reach of her hand. Knocked me to the side. Blood was pouring out all over the place.

"I tell her she's a sex addict, just like me, and all I want to do is to help her or make sure she gets over this because I'm not gonna be there for her anymore, we're through. I mean, I'll help with Gina and all. I still haven't told Jean about either of them. But Michele wasn't listening to any of it. She grabs a note of paper I had on my desk, storms towards my office door, and lets out this bloodcurdling scream when she reaches it. She slammed it and was in her car before I even realized what she had taken."

"What was on the note?" I ask.

"The addresses where we think Matt has been. San Francisco. Nevada. Burning Man. She now knows, or at least she knows the direction we're heading to try and find the little bastard."

I wait to see if he wants to add anything else. He doesn't.

"Well, as it relates to you and Michele, it sounds like you're heading in the right direction. You're trying to get away from her, you're working on your marriage, you're going to therapy, and you're trying to right the ship," I say, encouraging him on his progress.

"I just feel so bad for her, Father, I really do."

"Yeah, I can see that. Since you have feelings for her you don't want to see her going through all of this, especially with all that she has gone through with Gina. But remember what I said before, sheriff, you can only work on you; you can't change Michele. In the end, she has to be willing to change herself. She's fully capable of heading in the right direction if she believes she needs to."

"It's more than that. I never told you this, but there's a reason she really does need help. She was sexually molested for years by her father when she was just a little girl."

"What? Has everyone been molested? Or is everyone a rapist?" I'm shaking my head. The summer has flown by and I've been busy, distracted by the normal routine of parish life. And yet, the acrid distaste for sexual sin still rises like bile in my mouth; it disgusts and angers me that much.

"Yeah, I know, I know," he says. "But what happened to Michele is true. Early on in our relationship, we fell very hard for each other. She opened up to me after I opened up to her. I mean, I loved her. Heck, I still love her. Every emotional comfort that I didn't get from Jean I got from Michele. She adored me. Where I felt like I could do nothing right with Jean, Michele made me feel like I could do nothing wrong. If anything good happened to me at work, Jean would act as though it wasn't a big deal, but Michele would shower me with praise as though I had just won an Academy Award. She celebrated big and even little victories with me all the time, so how could I *not* fall in love with her?

"It was during that falling head over heels period that she started trusting me, and she told me some things about her past. Her father was a child molester through and through. I mean, clinically. She can't remember how many times he raped her when

339

she was little, but when she grew up and became an adult he wouldn't even look at her, hug her, anything. That's because she no longer turned him on. He was apparently only interested in blonde girls between the ages of seven and nine. Seriously. When they finally caught him and put him away, they discovered that was the age range of all his victims."

His voice quiets as he continues, clearly impacted by what Michele has gone through.

"Worse, she came to equate sex with love, the healthy, father - daughter love she never got from her dad. She was so angry at her mom for never protecting her. Both are dead now, yet she has to live with this. She told me she had gone to inpatient therapy, but it didn't 'take.' Truth is, she confessed later that she never stayed through any of the programs because she thought she was handling it all just fine.

"She was married once before to a man, but said that sex with him became very boring, very routine for her. It didn't have the excitement she got from one-night flings or affairs. Plus, it got her away from the mind-numbing pattern of day to day life. And that's when she met Cameron. She told me that addicts find other addicts quite naturally. In other words, they find people who will support them in their addiction. And apparently, Cameron Gambke shared in his desire for sex along with her, except she ran into a very dangerous man."

"I know, she told me," I say.

"What? When did she tell you?" Suddenly upset, the sheriff peppers me.

"I talked to her in the hospital. Remember back in April when I went to see Gina and Michele? She told me then about how bad her relationship was with him."

"You didn't tell me that," he snaps.

"*Why would I tell you that?* I assumed you knew. Why would that even upset you?" He's as flighty as Michele.

"I, uh, well, yeah ...okay." He gathers himself once more, and continues.

"She had learned over the years that what she really feared the most was losing whatever man she was currently 'in love'

340

with. She was convinced that the only way she could hold onto a man was to do whatever he wanted her to do, especially sexually. She thought that if whatever relationship she was in was routinely intense, it must be love. If it was risky, then that meant normalcy for her. That sex was her nectar, her elixir, her potion keeping her alive in every sense of the word. And all along she's been full of shame and embarrassment.

"What no one knows, well, maybe just the lovers before she met me, is that underneath those clothes are cut marks. When I asked her about it, she told me she can't control the men who promise to marry her, who say they will love her forever but don't, and routinely leave her once they get what they want from her, but she can control the pain she feels when she cuts herself."

Shaking my head silently, I picture Michele doing this to herself. Searching for love. For family. For someone to stay true to her, just her, and she thought she found it in Sheriff Daniel, a married man. The sheriff continues his train of thought.

"It wasn't until she asked me to take digital photos of her naked or with different sex toys that I began to wonder just how deep her issues might be. She never wanted me to take them with my own camera, just hers, and she wouldn't really let me know what she was doing with them. Until one day. Gina was taking a nap and Michele had run to the store. I had a few hours; Jean thought I was working a case on a Saturday. I checked her computer and I saw that Michele had been posting pictures of herself onto a site where people, mostly men, would rate her. This was her way of seeing if all the work she had been doing on her hair, her body, her sexuality, was turning other people on. It satisfied her relentless need for the approval of others. It made me sick, horny and insanely jealous all at the same time, but I had to be careful because I couldn't act like that at home or else Jean would catch on. I didn't talk to Michele for a few months, which resulted in her being severely depressed, she told me later.

"One day we were talking about my job and I was talking about all the predators out there, whether they be sexual or not, and she said something that I will never forget. She said, 'I'm a predator, too.' I believe she was trying to tell me she was using predatory practices to lure others in with her body so she could feed off of their approval."

I wonder to myself if that's what she meant. I don't trust her, but he could be right. Unless his heart is blinding his common sense.

"Father, I discovered something important about me. When I started going to treatment for my sexual addiction in May, I began to see so many of these tendencies in her and I would try to share them with her, just to help. I realized that I wasn't addicted to sex with everyone; I was just addicted to sex with her. And as I said, I believe she is addicted, too. She told me I was the only one in her life, and I committed myself to her – in reality and in my fantasies."

How stupid does that sound? He's married, and yet he was trying to stay faithful to his mistress!

"What are some things you told her from your sessions?" I ask.

"What do you mean?"

"I mean, help me to understand, too. Think of me as someone you are trying to teach about sexual addiction. I am very curious. Maybe it will help me to help others down the line."

A pause, as he gathers his thoughts.

"Well, to begin with, sex addiction is a disease, a bona fide issue that has caused many people an immense amount of pain for eons. And like other 12 step programs, it must start with us addicts realizing that we are powerless and that we need help. The addiction is one way we try to soothe ourselves, comfort ourselves if you will, to deal with the pain of other people around us wanting to control, or hurt, or dismiss us as though we aren't even human. But it's not the right solution, like any other addiction.

"We also have to realize that sexual behavior releases a chemical that has a heroin or morphine-like effect; that this is the reason the pleasure centers of the brain are so powerful. Unfortunately, we then want more and more of it, and our addiction will get worse over time. That's why my life has been consumed with Michele, really.

"Like any other addiction, there are plenty of negative side effects, everything from the destruction of marriages and families, to STDs, and even suicide. Case in point: Me with Jean. It almost destroyed everything I, we, have worked for.

"For all addicts, it may not be our only addiction. Mine is work – I really am a workaholic. Although for the most part, I hate the nature of my job because of what I have to deal with all day. So my life has been partitioned off between the duties of my job, Michele and Gina, and then Jean and Sheri, in that order. We think we are using sex to cope with the stressors in our life. There are plenty of different paths we can take if only we make the effort and apply it to our lives.

"We have to change our 'stinking thinking,' as though we think we deserve this sexual release and activity, like we've earned it for a variety of reasons. We have to fully comprehend that the horrible habit *of 'wanting what we want when we want it and not stopping until we get it no matter who we hurt to do so'* is incredibly damaging on multiple levels to us and those closest to us. We need to realize we can't use this crazy sexual activity for a reward. We need to know the power that we feel from it is false – it's just a fantasy.

"And we're all about fantasy – it's the only thing we can rely on because we can control it – and it's also about danger. It makes us and our mood swings toxic to other people, and I feel very bad about how I affected Jean and even Sheri. It opens us up to be drawn to other toxic people. Before I thought Michele and I were destined to be together, that we really helped each other in life. Now I am seeing more and more how we were like fire and ice, or oil and water.

"So, all of us addicts need to aim for honesty with ourselves and everyone around us, safety in all we do, and certainly sobriety. Because when we're sober and not numbed out, we can really find out who we really are, and then be open to becoming emotionally intimate with our mates – all in a balanced, trusting way. The barometer in our life is out of whack, but tens of thousands of people have successfully shown us that we can get it back in balance. All addicts are capable of change, but like anything truly meaningful and lasting in life, they have to want it."

"Your heart is good, Sheriff, I know. But just like I said a moment ago, you can't change others, you can only change yourself. My trusted spiritual advisor tells me that all the time."

"I know. It's just, well, sad. Hey, I gotta go, but thanks again for listening."

Standing up from the wooden rocking chair I have been sitting in, I stretch my lower back and legs.

"Oh, I almost forgot," he says. "What was the name of the guy who wrote the book that Cameron Gambke thought was the best book ever written but was really a farce?"

"Thomas Victor. Why?" I ask.

"You're not gonna believe this, but I got a letter. It said there is a reading of his will in New Mexico a day before Burning Man begins. I'm going to stop by on my way but I have absolutely no idea why it was sent to me. Weird, huh?"

"Hmm. Why would you get something like that?" I wonder out loud.

"Have no idea, Father. Well, I'll talk to you later."

"You bet."

Reaching for my own in-basket to see what surprises Mrs. Bellers has left for me, I'm pleased that she has at least stopped opening my mail.

I notice the official looking 8 ½ X 11" manila folder labeled "From the Law Offices of Sturgeon and Bailies."

I have just received my own copy of the same letter for the reading of the will of Thomas Victor on Sunday, August 25, in Albuquerque, New Mexico, at the address of the very first letter Cameron Gambke asked me to mail for him: #3 Monstrabilis Court!

Chapter 43

"Sheriff, Fr. Jonah here. How is your face tonight?"

"Sore. Kind of busy here. What's up?" he brusquely replies.

I've already told him about the letter I received from the attorney representing the estate of Thomas Victor which has piqued our collective interest.

"It's been crazy around here. The diocese has been performing some random audits around the state and apparently has found some concerns here within our parish. They just left so I thought I would take a few minutes and give you a call."

"I never liked auditors. They ask too many questions about things they don't understand to begin with. So, what can I help you with?" he says, rushed.

"Are you working late again?" I ask.

"No, I'm at home. We just finished dinner and I was just planning on calling Jean's nephew on the West Coast to talk to him about God and this girl he's been seeing. She's bad news."

"Sorry to hear that. I think it's great you're trying to stay involved and help him out if he's willing to listen. But that's what I was hoping to talk to you about. Look, I'll just be direct so I don't hold you. I heard from one of our parishioners today that you stood up in Gabbie's Café during the lunch hour and was talking about God, and I thought we could chat about it a little."

"Yeah? Is there a problem with that?" His defensive tone tells me this will be a challenging conversation.

"Well, she said you were talking about hell, fire, and brimstone and the end of the world coming our way."

"Yep. It's gonna happen. You heard what Mother Mary said," he snaps.

"Sheriff, that's not exactly what Mother Mary said. I think it's wonderful that you are taking the time to try to help others. But do you remember our conversations on the return flight from the pilgrimage and right after we got home? I recommended some things for you to do before you went out and tried to educate the entire world about your resurrected faith?"

"Of course I do, Father. Well, for the most part."

"Good. So you picked up a Catholic Bible, not a Protestant Bible, since it has the seven books that Martin Luther decided to remove, unless you're trying to understand the Protestant faith a little better?"

"I got what I needed to get, Father."

"Good. Did you buy a copy of the *Catechism of the Catholic Church* and go through it, and even a copy of one of the great study guides that support it?"

No reply.

"Okay. Are you at least attending Mass once a week to hear the Word of God spoken and to also receive the greatest Sacrament, the Eucharist – the actual body and blood of Our Lord Jesus Christ?"

"Well, yeah, of course we're now going back to Church. We found this great little one called 'Eternal Salvation Community.'"

He stops now, realizing he's just informed me that he's not going to a Catholic Church.

"Well, that's good you're hearing about the Word of God, but I have to tell you that you need to be very careful with where you choose to go, who you choose to open your mind to for your spiritual growth. Have you been reading the lives of the saints and mystics?"

"Some," he offers meekly.

"Very good. And, are you praying the Rosary every day?"

"Look Father, I'm not a child. I got a Bible and looked through it, and I bought a copy of the Catechism but it's really long and hard to read. After trying out a number of churches, I found this pastor I like and agree with what he's saying, plus they have nice chairs and a great band. I really feel the spirit there, and everyone is very friendly and welcoming. We feel right at home. I have spoken to that pastor a number of times on the direction I should go. And yes, I have read some of the stories of the saints and I have prayed the Rosary. But what I really found is that if I place my faith in God the Holy Spirit, He will impress upon my heart what I need to say when I need to say it. It says so right in the Bible."

"Look, Sheriff, I'm not on you, okay? I really am trying to help you. And don't take this wrong, but I love you and if you love someone, you tell them the truth, even if it hurts."

"What?" he grunts.

"No, I don't love you like that, Sheriff. Calm down. What I mean is that I really consider you a friend, a very good friend at that, and you've helped me with a great many things. But I don't love you because of that. I love you because you are a brother in Christ, and I feel I need to tell you the truth so then you can make up your own mind, not after reacting emotionally, but after sound research on your part. Now, you may ignore all that I tell you, and that's certainly your prerogative, but just give me a moment, will ya?"

"Yep."

"Thank you. Now, did you read the story of St. Paul during your studies?"

"Of course. He was the first one I read about because you told me he may have gone through a near death experience."

"And what did you learn?" I press.

"That he was a fanatic about his Jewish faith and a persecutor of the Christians, even responsible for many of their deaths. Then he was knocked off his horse, saw God, and was completely transformed. He went out and started talking to everyone about God."

"That's a pretty good high level summary. Now, what else?"

"What do you mean?" he replies.

"Did you read how he came to realize, after speaking with the early disciples, that he didn't have a solid foundation in what Jesus taught, what He was all about? He had a strong emotion driving him to help people, and he had the gift of being a skilled orator, but he just didn't know what he was talking about. He was risking doing much more harm than good. So he went to Peter, James and John and the other apostles who actually spent time with Our Lord, and they told him that he really needed to, well, in essence, do his homework before he preached the wrong stuff and took people down the wrong path. Did you then find out that he then went on a minimum three-year hiatus with the primary objective of really learning our faith *before* he began to preach the Gospel? That it was only *after* that time that he was sent forth by Peter, our first Pope, in consultation with the other apostles, and began his three famous journeys to the Gentiles?"

He knows where I'm going but is still defiant.

"God speaks to me, Father. I know this because I was given the Holy Spirit during Baptism and He was sealed within me during Confirmation when the Bishop anointed me with holy oil. So I have all I need to speak about Him to others."

"Sorry, Sheriff, but that's not the whole story. Yes, those were important initial steps, but you have a responsibility to learn our faith, to make an effort, to have a well-formed conscience before you try to change the lives of others. This process of learning and reaching out is life-long. You know, it's been aptly said that *'There is nothing wrong with the Catholic Church, it's just the Catholics within the Church that mess it up.'*"

"Are you saying I'm messing everything up?" He's angry.

"No, I'm just saying that you can if you're not careful. When you speak authoritatively for, and about, Our Lord you need to make sure you have done your homework. You need to learn your faith as well as St. Paul did. Catholic priests have to spend seven or more years of intensive theological study at seminary before they are even qualified to preach the word of God. Even lay people who speak with authority, theologians and apologists, have years of theological study behind them. You see, Baptism and Confirmation are just the beginning of our faith journey; not the conclusion. It takes extensive study and preparation. As I said, it's a lifelong process.

I pause for a moment, then continue. "Let me ask you something, Sheriff. You've heard of the cardinal virtues of prudence, justice, fortitude, and temperance?"

"Well, I guess." He sounds suspicious.

"A quick reminder. Prudence enables us to choose the right course of action inspired by moral law; Justice enables us to render what is due to God and neighbor; Fortitude enables us to perform good actions amid obstacles and difficulties; and Temperance enables us to control our passions in order to maintain a clear mind and a strong will. We receive these graces from God when we are baptized."

"Okay. So what's your point?" he challenges.

"I'll get to it. Please be patient, Sheriff. Now, we also receive what's called the 'theological virtues' of faith, hope and love, or charity."

"Heard of those, yep."

"Perfect, so let me bring it closer to home. Do you recall the popular saying of 'An eye for an eye and a tooth for a tooth?'"

"Uh huh. Do you have a point with all of this, Father?"

"What do you think it means?" I press, ignoring his poor attitude for the moment.

"It's in the Bible, Father. It means revenge. Payback. If someone screws you, screw them. I wish everyone in the world had that mentality, because then no one would be messed with and no one would mess with anyone else."

"You're right about one thing," I reply. "It is in the Bible, in the Old Testament. But what does Our Lord have to say about that? You seem to have conveniently skipped the point that Our Lord made on this important issue. That's in the New Testament and can be found in the Navarre bible. What He said, and what the Church clarifies, is that while it might have been necessary in Old Testament times it isn't necessarily true for all time. Look, as the nomadic peoples grew and evolved, it became necessary to incorporate laws – laws concerning homicide, violence, slaves, restitution – things like that. Their lives were harsh, therefore their laws often dealt harshly with those who committed wrongful acts. The concept of 'revenge' was based on the idea that in order for anyone to be made 'whole' again, payback was necessary, and the exact retribution or revenge factor was based on what the victim thought was right and just."

I pause to let him absorb this before continuing.

"Now fast forward to the time of Jesus. If you read the Gospel of Matthew in the New Testament, Jesus abolishes this harsh law and introduces a new law of 'charity.' Jesus teaches us that we must love God above all things, and that we must love our neighbor as ourselves. Our Lord showed us the way. He loved us so much that he laid down His life for us. He showed us the meaning of charity with his death. He calls us to show our love for him by loving others, not necessarily by what we say, and certainly not by hitting them on the head with the bible, but how we live our lives. There must be justice, yes, but above all there must be charity or else the cycle of hatred, violence and paybacks never has a chance to end.

"We sin against the virtue of charity when we are indifferent to all He did for us, all He taught us, all He gave us. Maybe we aren't grateful for what He's done by how we live or the things we say that we shouldn't; or when we are lazy in learning about and living our faith, in our service of God; or maybe we're lukewarm like always showing up late for Mass or maybe never even going at all; or in the extreme, when we just hate God and truly detest the life He wants us to live. In short, when we aren't doing the things in life that are good for our spiritual life, the things I'm trying to help you with."

A long silence follows, so long that I thought the call had dropped.

"Are you still there?" I ask.

"Yeah. Okay, so I didn't realize all of that." He sounds depressed now, defeated. It's not what my objective is in this conversation, and I make sure I tell him that.

"Again, I'm not trying to bring you down. I just want to see you on the right path. This was never meant to be a solo process, so ask God to open up your heart and mind to His word, okay?

"Sheriff, that's why he gave us His Church – to guide us. The Catholic faith is not just the faith for you – it's for all of us. The word 'Catholic' actually means 'Universal.' We should take advantage of this vast, rich, in-depth storehouse of knowledge to learn all that we can. Some of the most important resources available to us are the writings of the early Church Fathers. That's why we need to read and study a good Catholic Bible. That's why we need to go through the Catechism. That's why we need to listen and obey the leaders of the Church, especially the Pope, in all matters of faith and morals. This three-tiered approach is organized, in-depth, complete and time-tested.

"As a Catholic priest, I too am here to help, because with the example I've given about an 'eye for an eye,' I hope you can see that you can't take everything in the Bible literally. You have to understand the culture and the time in which it was written and then how it relates to today. You need to look at biblical typology, studying how the many events and persons in the Old Testament pre-figure and predict the coming of Our Lord as written in the New Testament. And then you have to be able to tie it all together. By the gifts of the Holy Spirit, if you continue to ask for them, they will be made available to you so you may understand as He wishes.

"Now, when you get to that point, I mean, when you really know your faith, there is an effective way to go and spread the Good News."

"Okay," he says, a hopeful tone returning to his voice.

"Just a few things off the top of my head, since I know you have to go. First, do it for God, not for you. This isn't about you proving your knowledge to one-up everyone. As St. Paul said, 'He must increase, and I must decrease.' Next, learn to listen to the people you meet because you don't know where they are on their faith journey. We have two ears and one mouth for a reason. Continue to pray for God's help, of course, but also use some common sense. Don't try to force your faith down anyone's throat, you know, like you're smarter than everyone else. Then if they resist, back off, leave it for another day. Most importantly, live your faith, really live it, so that when others see you, they see the face of Jesus. But, anyway, when you're ready, just call me, okay?"

"I hear you, Father, I do."

"Well, thanks for at least listening to me and not arguing the entire time. I do appreciate it. I hope it goes well with your nephew. The sex talk and all." I laugh.

"Right. On that point, I really have been meaning to ask you something. Let me just cut to the chase. God made us to love one another, right? So what's the big deal, I mean, really, about sex? Biologically we're programmed to be attracted to each other, to have sex in order to produce offspring for the survival of the human race. We want to walk a certain way, smell a certain way,

351

look a certain way, take care of ourselves in a certain way so we can be noticed and, well, score as big as we can. Look at how we use sex in all our advertising to attract customers to buy the right perfume, body spray, soap, hair shampoo, eyeliners, sports ads, heck, you name it. Women pick men based on all these variables and men do the same for women. In the end, though, what's even wrong with all this? Why do we have these feelings of love, these feelings of lust, and all these chemical reactions? What are we supposed to do with all of it? I mean, flirting, adultery, hooking up – all of it – what does God expect us to do?"

Dr. Chaffgrind asked me a similar question in his community college class, challenging me to tell him and his students what the big deal is since biologically we have been designed to have these sexual urges.

"Well, what you're asking is a very volatile, yet easily understandable, subject," I begin. "However, any answer I could give you would require more time than we probably have available right now. If you and Jean ever want to attend a marriage counseling class, you can learn a whole bunch more about this topic. But knowing that, I would be happy to discuss it if you want to hear it all now."

"Do you have a Reader's Digest version? You know, a summary?" he persists.

"Not one that will do it justice. However, let me put it this way," I offer. "Picture the woman you love."

"Michele or Jean?" he unhesitatingly asks.

"I want to focus on Jean, Sheriff, your wife. Other than your parental obligations with Michele for Gina, and certainly in treating Michele with the courtesy she deserves as a fellow human being, the love of your life needs to be your wife. Let's go back to when you were deeply in love with Jean. What is the one thing you wanted the most for her? Let me back up. You still love Jean, don't you?"

A pause. "Yes, in certain ways, I do."

"Good. That's a start. Now back to the question. What is the one thing you wanted for her then, and I'm hoping now?"

"Her happiness?" He is slowly getting it. I continue.

"And what did you believe would make her happy? I mean, when it's all said and done, when the cows come home, when the dust settles, when her life is over, what would make her happy?"

Silence. Either the clichés have confused him or he thinks this is a trick question. I interject before I lose him altogether.

"Heaven, right? Eternal happiness with God, right?" I say.

"Oh, yeah, yeah. Sure. Sorry," he says.

"Good. So, since you have feelings of love for her, you should want her to reach Heaven. Fair enough?" I hope he's understanding the analogy.

"Fair enough," he replies.

"So you should be doing all you can to get her to Heaven, right?" I state emphatically.

"Okay." His response sounds drawn out, more a question than a definitive agreement.

"And since you need to love your neighbor as yourself, remember we just talked about that – you should want yourself to get to Heaven too, right?" I'm imploring him to understand now.

"Yes, certainly," he says.

"Recognize that you are on the right path. I mean, you've stopped your adulterous affair with Michele, and recommitting yourself to your vocation as husband to Jean. You recognize that you need to love God more than you and what you want out of life. You are learning to live and make it work with Jean, to the best of your ability. Well, that's one example of love. And it's in that wonderful, beautiful, sanctified, and committed relationship of marriage – you and Jean as husband and wife – where you practice the holy gift of lovemaking, of sex. Not adultery with Michele."

"Ah…" I think he's getting it now.

"Hey, hold on a minute, Sheriff. Someone is coming in the front door. I gotta put you on hold."

Chapter 44

Leaning to my left to glance down the hallway, I notice Mrs. Bellers heading towards my office, with another female a few steps behind.

"I came in to get something from my desk, and this woman pulled up right behind me. Said she really, really needs to see you. What's your name, ma'am?"

"Michele Jerpun."

"Jerpun? The mother of Gina Jerpun who was in that coma?"

"Yes," the ice-queen replies in an eerily pleasant, well-practiced tone.

"Oh, I am so happy she came out of that! And I'm so happy I was here to let you in – I'm sure you really need to speak to Father Bereo with all you've been through."

Looking back at me, I note the Cheshire cat smirk plastering Mrs. Bellers' face as she ushers Michele into my office.

If Mrs. Bellers isn't aware of Michele Jerpun's flirtatious reputation, I'm sure she soon will be after a few well-placed phone calls. Juicy information that she can share, whether truthful or not, always gives her a thrill.

As Michele moves past me to the back of my office, I move to the office door but can't reach it before Mrs. Bellers securely shuts it. Fortunately, the door has a glass window. I catch a wink from Mrs. Bellers as she picks up what appears to be a brown bag and some old-fashioned ledger paper, leaving promptly. I find this odd, since everything we do is on the computer.

My mind returns to the immediate problem I have standing ten feet away, leaning against the credenza with her jealous ex-lover waiting on the phone.

As I walk back to my desk to finish the call, she gracefully moves to the door, her gaze moving between me and the flashing light on the telephone. I am very hesitant to tell the sheriff she's even here to begin with. This is a bad situation for me all around, and I need to rectify it immediately.

"Hey, Sheriff, sorry about that. I need to take care of

something. Look, before you speak with your nephew, it would really benefit you and him if you did some homework before you called him on this topic, okay? So pick up a copy of anything from the late John Paul II on his 'Theology of the Body' talks. That information will really help you ...' I intentionally lock eyes with Michele as I finish my sentence, ".... and your wife, Jean. I'll talk to you later."

I detect a flash of anger in her eyes, but she controls it quickly.

"I have an appointment I need to make, Mrs. Jerpun," I say, grabbing my coat from the back of my chair. "We can talk on the way out."

Deftly moving closer to me while still blocking the door, she strategically eliminates any chance I have of getting out without forcibly pushing her. So far, I'm not sure what she wants, but instinctively recognize this is a situation I need to get out of quickly.

"Father, I just wanted to apologize for how I treated you at the hospital back in April. I was just, so, well, upset and all."

Uh huh. With what I've experienced with her already – beginning with the Central Prison interaction to what occurred in the hospital when I went to visit, and now with what the sheriff said she did to him with the glass picture frame –I most definitely will remain on guard.

"That's fine, Mrs. Jerpun. No hard feelings. How is Gina?" I ask, trying to buy time as I strategize for my exit. If I push her out of the way, I'll probably be sued for roughing up a defenseless woman or whatever claim an attorney can talk her into making.

"She's fine. And, well, I just wanted to say how much of a change I've seen in Sheriff Daniel since he came back. He seems to really be committed to, well, turning his life around. You know, his wife, his life...all that. And he sure is trying to be a man of God. I commend you for all you're doing for all of them."

Her voice is soft, seemingly genuine, but I notice she's clenching her hands. Her lips are slightly pursed; a forced smile emanating my way. Her words tell me the sheriff has probably shared that I now am fully aware of their past long-term affair.

Do you ever remember the time I was riding my motorcycle

as a kid, went off that dirt jump, and ended up rolling into some barbed wire that someone had dumped into the hills? At that instant, it seemed to evolve at tortoise-like speed. This next moment with Michele Jerpun is slow-motion covered in sticky molasses.

As I put my jacket on, giving her a clear indication I am fully intending to leave my office, she slips hers off, letting it lay on the floor. At some point she apparently had removed her high heels, and is now standing with bare feet on the tile floor, completely blocking the door. Oh shit.

"Look, I am going to leave the office now. You can make an appointment with me at any time during normal office hours, all right?" I say this as sternly as I can, leaving no doubt of my intentions.

"Oh, Father, what are you afraid of? You look like you're going to pee your pants or something. I just really wanted you to know something, that's why I came here to talk with you personally. That little secretary you have that let me in told me on the phone earlier today that sometimes you come here late at night so I took my chance. In fact, she even encouraged me to do so. Here you are, and here I am. Two healthy human beings, one of whom probably hasn't made passionate love in an awfully long time, if ever."

She takes a few seductive steps towards me and begins to remove the red belt that's tied around her thin, black cocktail dress, holding it softly in her hand. She continues, her voice low, in a barely audible whisper. She's aroused. I need to get the hell out of here.

"I know something you don't know. About you. About the sheriff. Cameron Gambke told me a very personal, deep, dark secret. And I just feel so sorry for both of you. And with the lifestyle you lead, I can't imagine the pain you've felt over the years. I just want to give you comfort."

She reaches for my face talking all the while, and I can smell the titillating perfume wafting my way.

"But before I tell you, I just want to see if great sex skips generations. So far, I don't think it does, but I need validation through this timeless experience I want to share with you."

In my younger days I don't know how I would have reacted to this unfolding nightmare in front of me, but I imagine I wouldn't have labeled it in the negative light I fortunately cast on it now. No, at this very specific point in my life, all my senses are screaming at me to leave, *now,* as I clearly recognize the evil this is! As she pulls up her dress to remove her thong underwear, she moves slightly away from the door to balance herself on the coat rack, giving me the opportunity to escape. She tosses her red belt my way, and I instinctively grab it before the buckle hits my face.

In one motion I open the door, brush her aside, and sprint out. Yes, Catholic priests can run, very fast and very far when panic sets in – and I need to get away from Michele Jerpun and the game she's playing as fast as possible.

Closing the distance between the administrative building and the main street within seconds, belt in hand, I run past the wide-eyed Mrs. Bellers, sitting in her car with the headlights off and cell phone to her ear, talking with who knows who. I slow to an awkward jog, knowing how suspicious this must look, ascertaining immediately that she's thinking she has me now. In the world of Mrs. Bellers, I'm certain this scene unfolding in front of her can only be classified as "fabulous!"

Chapter 45

"You doin' okay?" Detective Renae has come by the rectory, escorted by Fr. Bernard.

"I take it you heard," I say defensively. "Why weren't you there this morning with everyone else? The sheriff was there. He grabbed my arm as I left and told me he knew I would try to seduce her one day. If there weren't others around, I'm certain he would have thrown a punch or two. Are you going to need to ask me your official questions now? If so, do I need my lawyer?"

She and Fr. Bernard look understandably concerned. She puts up her hand, trying to calm me, but I'm already on a roll.

Emotionally, I'm a mess. My accusing questions to Detective Renae only serve to heighten the tension inside my room here at the rectory. I'm angry, confused, and afraid, all at the same time. I feel the early onset of a panic attack threatening to overwhelm me if I don't focus on my calming techniques. Although uncalled for, lashing out at my friend, along with Fr. Bernard standing beside her, seems like a natural response to the evil that has attacked me. There's an internal battle raging within my body causing dizziness, confusion, heart palpitations, feelings of nausea, hot flashes, and discomfort as the beating of my heart goes into overdrive.

I tried deep breathing exercises throughout the night, so much so that I hyperventilated multiple times. I tried closing my eyes and searching for a safe fantasy place, but peace eluded me. In my mind I kept having visions of prison, of being out on the street, de-frocked, no job, branded a sexual predator, with a stick shoved up my anus. I'm hurt, depressed, and now utterly exhausted.

Supposed "experts" tell us that if you are innocent of any wrongdoing, you shouldn't feel any emotional distress over being wrongfully accused. Upon reflection, these experts apparently have never gone through anything very trying in their lives. I am living proof that these same "experts" are clueless about this topic.

The sexual abuse scandal involving Catholic priests has

forever changed the concept of 'innocent until proven guilty.' The public perception now is that if you're a Catholic priest, you're most likely guilty of *something* sexually deviant because you're a man who is sexually repressed. Even if you are accused but eventually found to be innocent, your reputation will be tarnished for life and your career as a priest destroyed.

Around noon today, Fr. Bernard called me into his office. There I was met by his pained expression and members of the Sheriff's Department. A representative from the Diocese in Raleigh was there as well, so Fr. Bernard definitely wasn't having a good morning. Ever since the break in, he had taken the advice of a local security company to change the building alarm every month. He did it at five this morning because he couldn't sleep, and was intending on telling myself and Mrs. Bellers the new building alarm code when we arrived for work this morning. However, a 6:00 a.m. siren in the administrative building when Mrs. Bellers decided to show up much earlier than usual ensured Fr. Bernard was not going to have a good day.

Fr. Bernard told us he first got wind of the "incident" from Mrs. Bellers, after her original shock about the alarm going off and Fr. Bernard's immediate appearance from the rectory, fully dressed for the day's activities. She tried to call him late last night – he slept thru the call. She wasted no time relaying her version of what had happened the night before.

Then at 8:00 a.m., when the parish office opened, Michele Jerpun called Fr. Bernard to lodge an official complaint of sexual molestation. She said she had proof of a red belt that would be in my possession, and that my fingerprints would be on it. I, of course, immediately turned the belt over to the investigator when he arrived and gave him my full statement of the event. The investigator said they were waiting to receive the "torn dress" from Michele. However, by the time I left the office, Michele had yet to arrive and produce this additional "evidence."

Fr. Bernard had said it was best if I stayed close to the area but moved out of the rectory. As I left the administrative building, I saw Mrs. Bellers in the parking lot being interviewed by the local news media. Yep, she had called the media again, and I could tell the representative of the diocese was not happy about it. At his urging, Fr. Bernard took charge and sent them off private property. Unfortunately, quite a few parishioners were there, too, undoubtedly tipped off by Mrs. Bellers.

This surreal scene felt strangely familiar. Images of Jesus carrying the cross with only His mother and a few friends offering what little support they could enter my head. I was able to make my way past the reporters and the parishioners to my room without uttering a word and had begun to pack when Detective Renae and Fr. Bernard arrived.

At least my trusted spiritual advisor, Fr. Jack, was available, except he's not here but back in New York, a place I miss very much at the moment. Sheriff Luder, someone who I thought was becoming a friend, has apparently turned on me. At least Detective Renae is here, but given the circumstances, her presence is due to "official business," I'm certain. I doubt she brought her "friend" hat along. And why is Fr. Bernard standing here with her? On second thought, I'm glad he's here. The last thing I need is for the press, under the guidance of dear sweet Mrs. Bellers, to allege I was in my own room at the rectory alone with a female.

No matter, the word is out. I'm waiting for a call back from a lawyer that Fr. Jack has recommended, and five others have already tried to contact me to offer their services. For a fee, of course, a hefty one at that; money that I neither have nor can gain access to. Unfortunately, all of my dad's money is tied up in his long-term care, and my brother is mortgaged to the hilt putting his oldest daughter through college and his youngest just a few years away. I wouldn't be surprised if the tailgating bloodsuckers from Central Prison months ago showed up to make this into one heckuva celebration, with Mrs. Bellers waving pom-poms at the top of their human pyramid – that is, if she could even get her badunkadunk up there. I know, that's not nice, but at the moment, I really don't care.

I meekly offer an apology to both of them, but only for my sour mood.

Detective Renae motions for me to sit down on the bed, and smiles. I remain standing.

"Actually, that won't be necessary. I don't have any questions for you, just some good news," she says, too cheerily for my mind to wrap around at the moment.

"What?!?" I reply, my head moving quickly between her and Fr. Bernard. He's staring at her but remains serious.

I stop packing my suitcase. Detective Renae continues.

"Well, as quickly as this began, it is going to end, at least as far as our agency is concerned. When Michele Jerpun came in to file her complaint this morning, about an hour and a half ago, I was there, along with another detective. We have it all on video. The sheriff had headed here as soon as he got the call early this morning so he wasn't in the office at the time, but I just got through updating him. He's still furious, which confused me, but he didn't try to stop me from coming over to tell you this. She described how you lured her under some guise that you needed to speak to her about her 'spiritual health,' and that your secretary let her in because you were on the phone and couldn't hear her knocking."

"I never said any of those things. It's been a long while since I've even spoken to Michele Jerpun, and she knows that to be true. Susan Bellers let her in because she said she needed to see me. She opened the door to the building and then marched Jerpun right into my office. Before I could get her out, Bellers shut the door and then headed out the front door!" I'm justifiably ticked. "Have you guys spoken to Bellers?"

"Yes," they reply in unison.

"Did she tell you it was Michele Jerpun who came to the parish and wanted to see me? That it was *her* request? That I wasn't the one who asked her to come?! That I didn't even touch her?!"

"No, she didn't say that," says Detective Renae, "but she claimed she couldn't remember all that had transpired as she was busy getting something from the office and then heading home."

"So she didn't back me at all? No surprise there." I glance at Fr. Bernard, my eyes pleading for him to finally open his own and fire her.

"No, but…." Detective Renae holds up her palm, trying once more to calm me down, "you need to hear the rest of the story. We

361

informed Michele she needed to produce the dress as evidence. We also told her, given the seriousness of the allegations, she needed to stay in town for a week or two in case we needed to talk to her again. At that point, she blurted out she can't stay around for that long, that she absolutely has to leave town soon, but wouldn't tell us why. The interview went downhill from there.

"We asked her what time this alleged activity occurred here last night. She said around 9:00 p.m. which is what both you and Mrs. Bellers confirmed in your statements. What's inconsistent is that one of our deputies ran into her at the local Food Market here in Gardensville around 9:15 last night, which is fine, except that she's as cheery as ever. She doesn't say a word about you, this event, nothing – acting as though yesterday was the best day she's had in a while. You would think she would tell a member of law enforcement immediately, if not right after it occurred, but she didn't. Again, I know all too well myself that victims of sexual abuse can go into shock, so her telling a member of law enforcement right away isn't all too out of the picture. However, not surprisingly, there's more to the story."

Detective Renae sits down on the chair next to my small desk in the corner of my room. Fr. Bernard leans wearily against a side wall. I am still too wound up to sit.

"She's dressed in that black evening dress she claims was torn. The deputy can't recall if it was torn as she later claimed, but our review of the video from the Food Market shows that nothing looked out of the ordinary at all. I mean, she claimed you yanked at her so roughly that the strap on the right side of her dress was literally torn off and a rip the length of her arm down the side resulted, but that's not what the video shows. Her dress looks completely intact, and the store she was at has multiple cameras so we got a very good look from different angles. The only thing that matched up is that she didn't have the red belt which all three of your statements reflect she wouldn't have. It's just how you ended up with the belt that was originally in question."

"I already explained…" I offer, and she instantly holds up her palm again, telling me to wait, that she's not finished.

"I know, I know. But when I asked her about her mood at the

Food Market and not reporting it to the deputy at that moment or at any other time last night, she became very angry and asserted she was in shock at the time which is why she was in a good mood. But that still didn't match up with the description of her torn dress that she gave us originally. When I asked her about that particular inconsistency, she became even more infuriated. When I asked her if she would be willing to go to the hospital for a rape test, she abruptly ended the interview and walked out of the building!"

Sitting down, I realize once more that no matter how this plays out, public opinion will be that I attacked Michele Jerpun. Yet I'm slightly placated by the thought the evidence is mounting against her. Detective Renae continues.

"When I updated the sheriff within the last hour, he called Michele. She told him that since we were so unprofessional and didn't believe her, she just wants to drop it all."

"Drop it? Can she make allegations like that, get everyone stirred up, and then just drop it?" I'm incensed.

"Well, she's not cooperating and we can't force her to continue with the complaint, but you may want to ask your attorney about that. As such, it's over as far as law enforcement is concerned. The case is closed."

Fr. Bernard, who had been standing near the door to my room, begins speaking.

"Understandably, that's not the case as far as the diocese is concerned, Jonah. The new protocol is that the diocese will have to conduct their own extensive investigation given the allegations, especially since one of our own trusted employees, Susan, confirms you were here alone with Mrs. Jerpun late last night and that you exited the building with her belt in your hand."

"I admitted to both of those things! *She* let her in and I was trying to get out and away from here!" As I say it I know how bad it sounds. Sure, since I'm innocent, I can easily argue I was getting away from the trap that was being laid for me. But if I'm guilty, it looks like I was trying to escape the scene of the crime.

"I know, Jonah," Fr. Bernard continues, "but there's more to it. Susan also said she has proof that you've been looking at pornography on your laptop."

"What?!!" My head is spinning.

"I already told you I did that, remember? And I also told Detective Renae the same thing and the 'why' behind it all as part of the challenge Sheriff Luder threw at me!"

Detective Renae nods her head in agreement.

Before I can argue my case further, Fr. Bernard cuts me off. I can tell by the look on his face that he's experiencing information overload and merely wants to let the investigator from the diocese handle it, allowing the process to run the proper course. I'm furious, but I can't blame him. If I'm innocent, which I certainly know I am, God's grace will help me through it. He finishes what he came here to ultimately tell me.

"Look, you need some time off. You being here will be far too distracting for everyone. Take a few weeks. We have your statement and we know where to find you with your cell phone, all right? You're already packing, so just make sure you take enough clothes for at least two weeks. We'll work through the details on our end, and if you're innocent then it will all be fine."

"*If* I'm innocent? I *am* innocent!" My shout has them both alarmed. Neither of them have ever seen me like this. Heck, I haven't seen me like this since I was the CFO dealing with a lying, cheating, backstabbing Board President.

I finally sit on the bed, holding my hands in my head, my elbows supporting the weight on my knees. I need to get away, far away.

"Can I leave the area? Does the diocese require I have to stay here?" I ask.

"Yes, you can. The diocese investigator is not like an official police force, however, your priesthood is at stake if you don't fully cooperate with everything they need from you if and when they ask for anything. Understand?"

"Of course," I say. Why wouldn't I?

A loud knock on my door adds to the tension. Who now?

"Fr. Bernard, I really apologize, but, well, we really need you to come back to the office." The auditor from the diocese that has been here the past week stands at the door.

"What may I help you with? We're in the middle of an

important meeting," a weary Fr. Bernard replies.

The auditor looks from Fr. Bernard, to me, and then to Detective Renae.

"I would really like to speak with you in private. I'm really sorry to ask, but how long will you be?" His tone is serious, and he seems a little winded. He must have jogged over here.

Exasperated now, Fr. Bernard says. "What could possibly be so important? Just tell me. You can trust these two people," he says, his head motioning our way.

"We are going to arrest Susan Bellers on the charge of embezzlement. However, we think she is aware of this and is wreaking havoc in her office. I'm afraid she's going to attempt to destroy evidence. Before this gets out of control, we really need you to come and settle her down. Please." He's pleading.

Turning towards me, Fr. Bernard rubs his face. He actually looks more exasperated than I did just moments before. If true, his own sister-in-law who he has trusted implicitly and supported through thick and thin has put him in an incredibly difficult position. I'm not certain how many more days like this his body, or psyche, can handle.

"I'll take care of this, Jonah," he says. "Head out soon, please, and I'll be in touch. Please just make sure you go somewhere where we can reach you on your cell."

He moves quickly to the door, surprisingly agile for his age.

Chapter 46

I must admit, it was very pleasing to see Bellers handcuffed and stuffed into the back of the sheriff's car. I was very tempted to ask if I could help. The news cameras that were there earlier in the morning filming my apparent demise had decided to hang around, albeit off church property. As such, they easily captured the sheriff's hand on her head as he lowered the stout frame of Bellers into the back seat of his official vehicle. They were probably expecting me to be the one experiencing this humiliating event, and I could see the confusion, and might I say, disappointment, plainly on their faces as the scene unfolded before them.

Completely out of character for her, she kept her mouth closed. I was tempted to fall back to my pre-priest days and wave goodbye to her with my middle finger, but wisely refrained and settled for just a wink. I know this isn't how Our Lord wishes me to handle this, and I know He is incredibly saddened if Susan Bellers is guilty. When we, His children, act like this, He feels the pain and agony all over again that He felt during His Passion – everything that I meditate on when praying the Rosary for the Sorrowful mysteries. Why do we do this to Him time and again? Why do I? I mean, I *get* this stuff and still I fall.

Fortunately, during the commotion I was able to slip out the back door to my vehicle, and agreed to meet Detective Renae at our old restaurant in Swan Quarters. She seems to feel real empathy for me at this moment and has forgiven me for my prior attitude just a short 90 minutes ago.

The same waitress as before takes our orders. Fortunately its mid-afternoon so only two other patrons are present. Even so, I'm also grateful the television is turned to a weather channel.

We talk over the specifics of Michele Jerpun's allegations once more. I feel a little better knowing that Detective Renae will go to bat for me with the diocese given all she knows about Michele and her legitimate sordid history.

How can I type that here with confidence? Well, what I didn't know before, what Detective Renae just told me, is that Michele

Jerpun has claimed allegations of sexual abuse twice in the past – something the department found from another agency. I wonder to myself how the sheriff reacted to this new information, or did he know it already?

Once our meals arrive, I change the subject. "Can I ask you something?"

"Sure," she replies, absentmindedly sipping from her glass of water with a lemon slice.

"We've both been so busy since your rape presentation, but did I understand your parting comment correctly – you were a victim, too?"

She trusts me much more now and begins to open up, if only hesitatingly.

"Yes." She's moved beyond the shame, I can tell, yet her gaze doesn't waiver. I thank God she's been given the help she needed to do so.

Looking out the window, she pauses. I automatically follow the direction of her stare, noticing billowing clouds that begin to darken the landscape, with just enough sun still shining through to highlight the blue skies.

"19 years ago I was only a ten-year-old girl. I was a lot like my mom, compassionate and unassuming. Most people didn't even know I was around. I had learned to be nonexistent, because Cameron Gambke controlled all of us in the household. Mattie was just five at the time, and my mom and I did all we could to protect each other and him by staying off Cameron's radar screen.

"He was a drinker, well, at least socially I guess, but every night he and Mom would knock back a few. He just seemed mad all the time and would complain constantly about what was going wrong in his life, and how it was my mom's fault, or even mine. Stupid things, like a broken door handle, somehow in his mind became this big conspiracy theory fully intended to wreck his world, and surely mom and I were behind it. He never blamed Matt for anything, but the blows would come quickly to Mom and, once in a while, to me."

Her voice trails off, her brow furrowing as a distant memory comes to mind. Shaking the thought aside, she continues.

"As I said, I had learned to stay low and watch for the danger signs, constantly ready to run for cover. One night I heard him screaming about how he was going to leave Mom and us if she didn't comply."

"Comply with what?" I ask.

"Sleeping with other people," she continues. "He said he wanted a freer relationship, that he should be able to sleep with anyone he wanted and she should feel free to do the same. He tried to convince her that 'everyone was doing it.' I remember Mom actually standing up for herself and said she wasn't going to do it; that she didn't feel comfortable with it. So he shoves her aside, packs a bag, and leaves for a hotel. Mom cries all night, but I'm thrilled. I have Mattie under my arm, and we played games that night and laughed really hard. But the next day the dickweed was back, and he and mom were all loving and drinking again, just like it never happened. And that same night, a couple comes over, and our lives would never be the same.

"Right before that, when mom put us to bed, she leaned over to both of us saying, 'It will all be all right. I'm going to make everything better.' I followed her out and sat by the master bedroom door, and from what I can put together now in my head as an adult, they were screwing like rabbits.

"It happened again the next weekend with a different couple, and every weekend after that for I don't know how long. Cameron seemed so happy, but mom, I could tell, resented it. She kept trying to make excuses or dreaming things up for the weekend – like family getaways – but good old Dad didn't want to have anything to do with it. The arguing got worse between them, as did the beatings.

"One night a man came over – Cameron said he was a business associate, a 'Dark Angel' investor who was very important for our family's financial future and protection – and the next thing I know, I'm being held down on the kitchen floor by Cameron while this guy is tearing off my clothes. He rapes me, and when he's done, Cameron and this guy go into the other room and have a drink together – a toast of Jack Daniels to 'seal their deal,' whatever that meant.

"I mean, I trusted my parents, my own parents! I'm screaming for Mom, and I can hear her crying in the other room. Mattie's crying too, he's just so scared at all the commotion. I run outside and my Mom comes after me; she keeps saying how sorry she was, but encouraging me to just keep doing what Cameron asked so we could all have peace, and be happy.

"I had never known real peace, and I couldn't even define the word 'happiness' at that time in my life. Cameron told me since I was his daughter, it was my duty to help out the family like this and if I didn't like it, then I could just leave. Go where? Where does a ten-year-old girl go, anyway? And who was going to believe me even if I did? If I left he said he would kill me, or he would kill Mom or Mattie. I never thought he would touch my brother, but I didn't doubt he would kill Mom. So I stayed and never even tried to run away; I just tried to get smarter.

"Fast-forward two years. This guy comes over about a dozen times each year, and it's the same routine. For a while, when I figured out he was coming over I would run from the house, but Cameron would catch me and beat the shit out of me. So I just learned to stay, close my eyes, and go to a far-away place."

My nerves are already on edge from what I've gone through today. I'm speechless, and barely form a question.

"Do you think Matt was abused?" I interrupt.

"Yes," she says coldly.

"By the same man?" I am persisting, now feeling compelled to know.

"No, and I don't mean that he was sexually abused, at least not that I know," she continues. "I just know he was allowed, well, actually encouraged, to watch Cameron and Mom in these orgies. I heard Cameron telling Mom it was good for him, so he could see it for himself. If Mom argued, Cameron would hit her. So she stopped arguing and he kept watching. It had to really mess him up. I know this sounds stupid, but Cameron never asked me to watch. It was like this guy tribal thing – Mattie was the boy in the house and needed to learn what sex was all about. My role was clearly the giver; Matt was taught that he was the taker. My grades in school took a dive, I had a hard time concentrating on anything;

369

I was really messed up."

"I don't see how you could not have been, Renae. But I have to ask - didn't anyone notice anything abnormal? The school? A counselor? Anyone?"

"I wondered that myself over the years," she says. "They came over a few times, but like all seasoned criminals, Cameron knew exactly how to keep the law at bay. He made sure we appeared to be the typical All-American family – everything in order, everyone dressed respectably, two cats and a dog – and no one ever noticed. I wasn't about to tell, either. Towards the end, because I was a little older and wiser, this same guy began threatening to kill me if I exposed him. He also said he would kill Mom and Mattie if I ever did, and I believed him. I had absolutely no reason not to. Either way I thought that was going to be the course of my life. A sex toy who would end up dead, either by that motherfucker or Cameron – nice adult role models for me, huh?

"On my 13th birthday, he takes me away to his house. My mom is so full of grief that she's curled up in a fetal position in her bedroom. I think they sent Mattie to a friend's house to play because I don't remember seeing him at all. Cameron marches me out to the guy's car which he had parked in our closed garage. None of the neighbors could see or hear me if I put up a fight, which I wasn't about to do anyway. Cameron puts me in the car. He and the guy blindfold me, and force me to lie on the front seat with my head on the guy's lap, probably so he can put his hand over my mouth if I try to scream. I hear the doors lock, and then he drives me out to some place; it seems like forever until we get there.

"I don't remember the next two or three days very well. It was a house, I know that much. And that guy was there. I was locked into a room where the one window had a black sheet over it. He rapes me a few times, then says 'Welcome to your new life.' I know I was drugged repeatedly, with what I don't know. It must have been in the water he kept giving me and ordering me to drink, or maybe the food. I lost count of all the guys that came over and raped me, one at a time. Some were older, some my age or even younger. I pleaded with each one to help me, but none of them did. Not a single one. I don't know whether the guy told them who I was, but they didn't even blink. Some even beat me when I fought. And that's when I ended up with a slew of STDs."

I'm shaking my head now, holding it with both hands, her grief now matching mine. Yet she remains firm, intent on finishing her unspeakable story.

"What would the guys say to you when you pleaded with them?" I ask, amazed at their complete lack of compassion for a fellow human being.

She pauses, and I see her squeezing her napkin harder, slight tears forming in her dark brown eyes.

"At first? Well, let's see. 'Bitch,' 'whore,' 'cunt,' 'sleeze,' 'you like this,' 'you're getting rich off this anyway' – that kind of stuff. Most of 'em, though, they didn't say a thing. They just screwed me, completely ignored my pleas, and then walked away. Some hit me with their fists just for the fun of it. One of them told the 'Dark Angel' guy I was asking for help, and he beat me until I thought I was going to die. At that point, I wished I had. I knew I needed to help myself; that I couldn't rely on anyone else to do so.

"So one day I was able to get out of the room after a guy screwed me and forgot to use the outside lock to keep me in. I saw they were both out front laughing and shaking hands like old friends, and my captor walked him out the front door. I quickly checked out the rooms – the place seemed massive – and I found a bunch of cash on a bedroom nightstand. I thought I heard other people behind some of the doors, but never saw anyone else. I had been naked since I got there, but grabbed some women's clothes from an open bedroom closet and shot out the back door. For the most part it was dark inside the house, and definitely the middle of the night on the outside, and I walked a few miles through the cold, hilly desert, everything surreal from the drugs, the beatings, and pure exhaustion. I grabbed a ride from a trucker, a genuinely nice guy. He didn't take advantage of me at all; he just let me sleep. He dropped me off eight hours later at my aunt's house in Arizona.

"To this day I have no idea where that house was located. I had nightmares of weirdly shaped rooms for years after. I couldn't give a solid description of the place even if I had to.

"My aunt wanted to go to the police after I told her the whole story. Then she told me my mom was dead."

"Dead?!?" I can't help myself, and blurt out the question.

"Yeah, said my mom had called her in hysterics saying I was gone but didn't hear from her again for a week. She kept trying to call back but no one would answer. She called the police and they went over there to check. Cameron played it up good, seemed very sorrowful. Said my mom fell down the stairs and broke her neck. Mattie saw Mom at the bottom of the stairs – no doubt orchestrated by Cameron – but no charges were ever filed.

"My aunt told him she knew everything and that if he ever came after me she would make sure he got what was coming to him. My uncle was an undercover narcotics agent – a mean son of a bitch – and neither he, nor anyone else in the family, ever liked Cameron. Cameron said I was a slut and he didn't want me back anyway, that he and Mattie would survive just fine. My aunt said my mom was such a wonderful person growing up, but everything changed for the worse when she met Cameron Gambke."

"Couldn't your uncle go after him with all of his police contacts?" I'm still trying to wrap my head around how so many criminals like this can get away with what they are doing to others and still have their freedom.

"He tried. But he got stonewalled everywhere. Cameron's story held up. He was a master liar." She says this matter-of-factly, the moisture previously forming now completely gone.

"My Mom and Cameron never married since he didn't believe in the 'institution of marriage,' but Mom stayed with him anyway. They turned their back on the rest of the family because mom knew no one would approve of their lifestyle, especially the drugs which she had admitted to my aunt the week before she heard she was dead. He always kept control over her anyway, so any effort she made probably wouldn't have mattered. No Christmases, no Thanksgivings, no family get-togethers, nothing, ever. He reigned over her and completely dominated me."

She stares at me, the hard shell she's formed over the years returning in full as she continues.

"I told you this before, but my aunt and, well, certainly my uncle, saved me. They took me in and protected me. She became my mother; he my father. They loved me, cared for me, listened to me, helped heal me. Since my aunt was a trained psychologist, she helped me the most, though. And I told you before about the EMDR – my aunt has been working with me for the past eight years. Had I known about it right after it happened, I'm certain I would have gotten a handle on these feelings a long time ago. When I went to college, I decided I just wanted to help others. I was going to become a psychologist, but I wanted to go after all the rapists in the world, all the Cameron's and Sir Walter Raleigh's.

"Sir Walter Raleigh's?" I ask.

"Yeah, you know, the pipe tobacco. I tried to find this guy afterwards, I mean, years later, but I never could. I most certainly can remember his face, but he was never in any of our criminal databases. But it's the smell of the tobacco he smoked that will never let go of me and since I never knew his name, I just gave him that one. His clothes and mouth reeked of it. The house I was held captive in reeked of it. I found out the name of the tobacco years later, and even though I've healed a great deal from the therapy and practice, when I would get a whiff of it, I would experience raw, uncontrollable fear that almost immobilized me.

"Like I said, I was going to do something, anything, in the helping field – maybe be a psychologist like my aunt to help all the victims – but then I read a case where a child who had been sexually abused for years by her stepfather and his brother got a hold of a gun in the house and shot them both. She was put away. Everyone had ignored her pleas for help for years and she finally just lost it.

"Everyone was just shocked. The dense nature of some people's brains continues to floor me. What, do they think she just woke up one day and decided to shoot these people? If they had been loving and caring, protecting of her, why in the world would that thought have ever entered her mind? Obviously I'm not saying they should have been shot and killed. Of course not! I'm just saying they blamed her for all of it. Are you kidding me? I

373

mean, this poor little girl was begging, even screaming for help and was routinely ignored. So when she pulled the trigger, she became the problem that everyone focused on. I was pissed, still am, at the injustice and stupidity of it all. Again, I'm not saying at all that what she did was right, I'm just amazed at how people are so blind at the root causes of real problems in this world.

"Well, right then and there I decided to become a member of law enforcement, and to focus on sex crimes specifically. My focus is two-fold – to help the victims by putting them into contact with all the people they can talk to – the therapists, the advocates, all the great people who can help; and at the same time go after the abusers, because they deserve to become the quarry, the game, the target. You said one time that you found your calling in life as a priest, Father. Well, I found my calling in life, too. I'm now the hunter, and I'm sorry to say, but I have to thank Cameron Gambke for training me to be damn good at it. I guarantee you, I hunt with absolute precision."

"If I ever met that man, I think I would kick his ass, even if you wouldn't." My inner instincts to protect her rise to the surface once more.

She smiles and cocks her head, amused at my bravado.

"He would be in a wheelchair now, Father. And isn't that against your religion or something?"

"Well, righteous anger is something we all have a right to feel, but it's how we go about dealing with that anger that we need to keep in check." Pausing, I smirk, "But I still want to kick his ass."

She shares my humor and then becomes serious again.

"Father, you need to know that I'm not the same person I was back then. Sure, I hate what Cameron did to me. But he's dead. I hate him for having the nerve to deny everything, for calling me a slut, inferring that I caused all my own problems. And then he gives me that whacked letter about wolves and goofy names, like some kind of secret code. What an idiot.

"And I hate what I truly believe he did to my Mom. And I hate how he probably has warped my brother, Mattie. But I got to the point where I didn't want to give him that much control over my life anymore. I needed to let this go – and therapy has been helping me to slowly travel the road to forgiveness – but I will never forget. Never forgetting will always allow me to protect myself.

"All those things I said in my presentation at your church I practice day in and day out. But emotionally it gets even better. I'm not just a survivor, I now make a point of trying to make a positive difference every single day for victims everywhere. I acknowledged my feelings long ago. EMDR and my aunt were, well, God-sent. I have taken back control of my life, and I heal every time I reach out to others, every time I help another victim, just like all those who reached out to me. I have come to realize that I am a helluva lot stronger than I thought I was. I've gained strength from every victim I've met who has shown me the incredible strength that lies within each of us. And it's empowering as hell!

"I am no longer ashamed. I am no longer embarrassed. I no longer blame myself – those bastards did this to me – I didn't do it to myself. My freedom is back, and so is my health. I do all those things that make you well and happy, you know, diet, exercise, meditation, therapy. And the pain that could have lasted a lifetime, if I hadn't received the help that I did? It's a distant memory now, and instead of frightening me, it energizes me to make something good come out of it. Most of all, I'm incredibly cautious with who I allow into my life."

For the first time since I've known her, I see the best, most beautiful smile beam across her face. Her eyes are shining.

"Father, I finally figured out and accepted the fact that I am a wonderful human being. I know that I have a great deal to offer those who are suffering, those who have been through, or are going through, the pain of a sexual crime. And it frees me!"

With the bill paid, we gather our things and head to the parking lot.

"So what are your plans, Father?"

"Fr. Bernard said I should get away from here for a while and let the Diocese do what they need to do. I think I'll head west. Take some time to hit old Route 66; see the sites in Tennessee,

Arkansas, Oklahoma, and into New Mexico where I am going to hear the reading of a will."

"A will?" she asks, intrigued.

"Yeah, some guy I only know from reading a book he wrote. I have no idea who he was, how he knew me, or what the will is about, but now that I have time I can drive across the U.S. and see places I've never seen before."

"Funny, I also went to the reading of a will right about the time you and the sheriff were traveling over in Europe," she says. "And, what's even stranger, I was supposed to go to Albuquerque to hear the reading but I wasn't going to spend money doing that since I figured it was for Cameron's will. So they made arrangements for me to fly to Charlotte and hear it, so I did."

"You did? So it was Cameron's will?" I ask.

"As a matter of fact, yes on both counts. Yes, I went to the reading of the will, and, yes, it was Cameron's. I'm now very rich, Father, very rich. But it's dirty money, I'm certain of it. I'm still trying to figure out what to do with it. At first I refused it all, then I thought, 'Wow, how many people can I help with this? But how? And you remember that damn, weird letter from Cameron?"

"Yes," I reply.

"There was a reference in the will that if I figure the story within the story, there's much more wealth awaiting me and Mattie. Even at the end, good old Cameron is playing his games. But now I'm wondering if that's true."

I nod. Now so am I. I continue my response.

"As far as the rest of your question about my immediate future, I guess after my trip to Albuquerque I'll head up to Burning Man in Northern Nevada and see if I can help track down your brother. Maybe we can begin to put the pieces of this puzzle together. The only problem is, the sheriff was going to be my ticket in, as I understand they are really hard to get, unless you are law enforcement or a registered volunteer."

She smiles. "Well, guess what? I will be there with him and you can be my guest. I think you deserve to meet up with my brother if, indeed, he's there."

I have a confused look on my face. Her smile leaves as quickly as it formed.

376

"Father, did the sheriff tell you what we found about Matt at Serenity Lane?"

I shake my head. She elaborates.

"Well, the investigation has been fully cracked open again and, well, um, it looks like my brother was probably into a number of things, but one for certain was something called 'Gerontophilia.'"

"What's that?" I'm unfamiliar with the term. She explains further.

"The use of an elderly person as a sexual object. Worse, it appears he also fits the model of what is labeled 'sadistic gerontosexuality.' That means he has an obsessive personality, an inability to control impulses, and a violent and sexually aggressive personality. What is unknown is whether he had a hard time controlling his urination through his twenties which is another official component of this disorder, although it's not absolutely necessary that all exist for someone to have a desire to force sexual contact with an elderly person."

Her demeanor is direct and to the point, but she seems ashamed.

"Is this the Matt you remember? I mean, these characteristics? Was he like this growing up?" I ask.

"I really don't remember," she replies, shrugging her shoulders. "What I just shared with you is how his school counselor described him because he was in the principal's office a couple of times when he was younger, along with information from his probation officer after he was arrested a few times for stealing cars. Since he is a suspect in this investigation, we had every reason to do this additional research, and I'm not pleased at all about what we've found."

She looks down at her car keys, absentmindedly fumbling with them before finishing.

"And I am really sorry to tell you this, but we've confirmed your Mom was one of the individuals he molested."

Chapter 47

I've spent the past week driving across the southern half of this great nation, hoping to clear my heart and head. When I left Detective Renae at the restaurant in Swan Quarter, I was at my emotional ground zero. I didn't bother to call Fr. Jack – this was between me and God.

Heading west out of North Carolina, I drove nonstop until I reached Memphis, screaming at God the entire way. For a better part of the rest of the trip, I periodically pulled over at random spots to sit, yell, cry, and wonder for hours. What did I ever do to Susan Bellers that caused her to try to ruin me? What prompted Michele Jerpun to try to destroy my reputation as a Catholic priest? I had only been trying to help her and her poor daughter, and she wants my head on a platter? And why in the world did my mom, the most loving, caring person I've ever known, have to experience sexual molestation, and who knows what else, by twisted Matt Gambke? As importantly, what does God want me to do about all of this?

As the miles on the odometer racked up, I was given the grace to remember that when asking such questions, I needed to remember Our Lord's passion and death. Why did God allow this to happen to His only Son? I sat back then, letting the miles roll on, and my only solace came as I focused not only on Our Lord's death, but more importantly, His resurrection, because something so good came out of something so evil. Because of His sacrifice, I and everyone else now has a chance to live in eternity with Him, if we only accept His grace, and then live our lives accordingly. I know He will never give me more than I can handle. I still wondered, though – what "great good" is supposed to come out of all this? Alas, I realized there is so much more for me to know.

I kept trying to distract myself by staying in the present moment, by experiencing all of the incredible sights, sounds and smells of the south, but it was a useless struggle to do so. What had been impossible for me to suppress, to forget, were all the dark images and unpleasant memories that were crowding my brain ever since I moved to Gardensville.

I slammed my hand hard on the steering wheel then as the Albuquerque skyline drew near.

"Why do I give a shit? Heck, God, why do YOU give a shit about your pathetic creation?!?" I yelled as loud my weakened system could muster. My tears were done, my rage finally spent. I was merely numb.

Pulling into an old western-motif motel off the highway just inside the city limits, I had reminded myself over and over that God's ways are not my ways and that He has it all under control. My role is to do my best to follow Him, to live my life according to what He has in mind for me to do. At a minimum, I know and understand that He wants me to help the poor, oppressed, abused, the meek, and the helpless. I'm just not sure what else He has in store for me, what new crosses He will ask me to bear.

Sitting in my room, disappointed that a soccer channel in any language wasn't one of the channels $39.95 would buy me, the calm finally arrived. I realized then what my rage had blinded me to – certainly Matt Gambke needs to be brought to justice – but he has clearly lost his way in life if he ever even had it to begin with, and I would like to help him find his way back to God. He's on the road to perdition, whether he knows it, believes it, or accepts it. In the end, I hope I can have the opportunity to help him refocus his life on God's mercy, forgiveness, and love, as well as His justice. It's a package deal, not a la carte.

***

This morning, I'm eating breakfast at a Denny's somewhere in Albuquerque. The weather – 89 degrees, arid, with sunny skies – has really buoyed my spirits. The bookmark in "Paideia" – Thomas Victor's infamous tome which I'm agonizingly trying to finish – contains a quote from Blessed Mother Teresa. Between bites of ham, pancakes, eggs and coffee, it speaks volumes to me.

People are often unreasonable and self-centered.
FORGIVE THEM ANYWAY.
If you are kind, people may accuse you of ulterior motives.
BE KIND ANYWAY.
If you are honest, people may cheat you.

BE HONEST ANYWAY.
If you find happiness, people may be jealous.
BE HAPPY ANYWAY.
The good you do today may be forgotten tomorrow.
DO GOOD ANYWAY.
Give the world the best you have, and it may never be enough.
GIVE YOUR BEST ANYWAY.
For you see, in the end, it is between you and God.
IT NEVER WAS BETWEEN YOU AND THEM ANYWAY.

A lighter mood and a half-hearted attempt at whistling – something I have yet to master – enliven me as I make my way to #3 Monstrabilis Court. The map reflects that the city is approximately 180 square miles, and Thomas Victor chose to live on the fringe of this majestic valley, very much away from everyone else. As I climb into the hills of Sandia Park, I can see why. Well above the valley, the downtown core looks like miniature Legos.

It's clear right away that Thomas Victor had managed to accumulate a significant fortune in his lifetime. Pulling into the long circular driveway, the 6-car garage looks downright puny compared to the main structure. Can someone earn this much money writing books? It's a southwestern styled sprawling estate, masterfully cut out of the surrounding forest. From my present vantage point, I can't tell how many levels exist. It drops to the left, rises to my immediate right, and then drops again in what appears to be additional levels that slope around to the back. Perfectly manicured Xeriscape landscaping covers every bit of the 20-acre site, and the house must have at least 20,000 square feet of living space.

A butler, attired in a traditional black outfit, answers the door. I find this funny; a New York City butler in a Southwestern deco home. I smile; he doesn't. Taken to a sitting room, I notice 30-foot ceilings and a myriad of side rooms, all tastefully adorned with Native American art. Slate tile flooring is all I can see – only expensive area rugs catch my eye. The sheriff and Detective Renae have already arrived.

"Hello," I say to the both of them. She looks nervous. The sheriff ignores my hand and me, for that matter. "Grow up," I think of saying, then remember Mother Teresa's words of advice. "How was the flight?" I ask instead.

"Good," Detective Renae replies anxiously, abruptly standing while rapidly massaging her hands.

What's up with her? Maybe it's her boss, who's acting like a three-year-old. I'm sure he was a joy to travel with, but I'm thankful she wasn't with me on the road. I wouldn't have been good company, either.

"And your drive?" she offers, trying to be courteous. Her smile is strained, yet her eyes tell me she's on the verge of panic.

"Good. I needed the time to clear my head. You okay?" I'm getting concerned.

Before she can reply, the sheriff drops the Architectural Digest magazine he's been holding back into the rack, the smacking sound mirroring his infantile mood.

"The attorney will see you now." A young woman with too much cleavage showing, dressed in a sharp, indigo and charcoal grey business suit, grabs our attention.

As a courtesy, I turn to Detective Renae, motioning for her to walk in front of us.

"I'll wait out front, if you don't mind." It's a firm statement. Even if I had one, she isn't waiting for a reply.

We're lucky we have a guide. It takes us nine minutes and three separate elevators to get to the library, plenty of opportunities for us to lose our way without the assistance of our quiet, yet professional, chaperone.

"He will see you in a few moments," our busty escort says pleasantly.

The sheriff and I are now the only ones in the cavernous room.

"Have you found out anything else as far as what this is about?" I ask, trying to open doors to conversation. We're two grown men, aren't we?

"The guy was killed here in this room a few months ago. That's all I know. But even if I did, I don't believe I would tell you.

Seems like when I confide in you, you seem to take advantage of the situation."

"What?" I ask, my anger that I thought dissipated returns quickly.

"You knew she was a sex addict! You knew you could take advantage of her! All that talk about changing my ways, reading the Bible, reading the Catechism, studying the lives of the saints, and that whole trip to Europe you dragged me on, and then you go and try to screw my girl?"

I'm shaking my head now, close to laughing at the insanity of it all.

"How old are you, Sheriff? Ten? I mean, seriously, are you okay? Listen to yourself."

He sulks without immediately replying, but I'm not going to let this go.

"I didn't do anything! She's the one that came on to me. I got out as fast as I could!"

"That's not what your secretary said!" he snarls.

"My secretary is a liar and a thief! And you want to believe her? Seriously?! What's your real problem, Sheriff?"

He stands now, slightly towering above me, finger pointing in my face.

"You and all the damn priests like you are the problem. You say one thing and do another. You are supposed to be held to a higher standard. You say all the right things, then you do shit like this. You are the reason people leave the Church!"

I'm now seriously and righteously pissed. I know I will regret this later, but not at this moment. I stand my ground, only a few feet keeping us apart. I've had it with his tirade, his self-loathing view on life, his role of victim, his bullshit. I have no intention of beginning a physical altercation, but I'm not about to back down should he revert to the only way he probably knows how to deal with his emotional problems – through his muscle.

"Open your ears and your eyes, Sheriff. *You* are *your own* problem, not me, so quit trying to make me your scapegoat! I am a Catholic priest, yes, and I do have a high standard to uphold, but I'm innocent. God will take care of those religious who abuse their position of authority, no matter the denomination they belong to. But He guarantees that He will help them if they change their ways. But in the end, stop blaming the priesthood for your problems, got it?"

He opens his mouth to reply, but it's still my turn.

"And I didn't make any move on 'your Michele.' Do I need to remind you she isn't your wife? And you want to tell me how I'm supposed to be held to a higher standard? How about you? Let's look at your own vocations in life. First, you're a husband. You stood before God in an official wedding ceremony and vowed to God to be true and faithful to your wife, yet you have committed thousands of acts of adultery over the years. Fortunately for you, you've gone to confession and trying to turn your life around, but don't act like you're better than anyone else around, understand?

"Second, you're a father, and yet you became a workaholic and gave up the role of parenting to your wife. You told me these things yourself; I'm not making them up, remember?

"Third, you're serving in the role of sheriff. How many times have you done things in your career where people who should have looked up to you walked away disappointed? How many times were you an absolute jerk to all those who are employed by you? Do you think God isn't paying attention? 'To those who are given more, more is expected' I apparently need to remind you. And, by the way, was the fact that Cameron was murdered in his own jail cell just a coincidence, or was it just a fellow law enforcement 'favor?'"

He looks away, but I'm just getting started. I'm rambling, I know. I've had a lot to say to the good sheriff since I've met him, but it doesn't seem to have stuck. At any rate, I would have a difficult time stopping my tirade right now even if I tried.

"What, do you actually think that when I was ordained a priest it causes some spiritual reaction whereby I will always be perfect? Yes, some priests have fallen down on the job and the Church is finally recognizing and dealing with it to the best of their ability. But we're all part of the family of Christ. Every single human being no matter what role we play in life. So we *all* need to step it up, wouldn't you agree? How dare you make me feel like because I'm a priest I'm somehow supposed to be superhuman.

"If I've broken the law, then I need to be dealt with accordingly; justice needs to be done, no if's, and's or but's about it. Of course. But stop pointing your finger at me as though *you* decide if I'm worthy to be a priest. You've got to be on some kind of a drug, or maybe you just haven't slept in weeks, because you are seriously deluded. Get that damn tree trunk out of your eye so you can see yourself more clearly!"

For the first time since I've met him, he doesn't know what to say.

Sitting now, he takes his wide brimmed hat off, tossing it to the ground, and runs his hands through his matted hair. His arrogance slightly humbled, he replies.

"It's all screwed up. I don't know what to do. I don't know where to go. Everything made sense to me before you came into my life, and everything I knew to be true changed. And this whole 'God' and religious thing? No one cares. Hell, I realized that I don't care, it's just too much hassle, too hard, too much work. The little ounce of peace I had before in my life is gone. And what does it matter who or what we follow anyway, and if we follow anything at all? Who cares???"

Somehow I bite my tongue.

We sit in silence, and thankfully it appears our desire to one up the other has left us, at least for the moment. But I do love him, and I have to tell it to him straight.

"Look, Sheriff, I don't know how to say this to you in any more of a direct way.

"Let me paint a picture for you of how 'bad' this world would be if everyone had the audacity to actually follow the teachings of the Church, to actually live their lives as Christians. Hmm, let's see, people would be putting God first and realizing that they aren't the center of the universe, He is. People would honor and respect how He told us to live and wouldn't put all of their own selfish needs, desires and false gods in front of every important person in our lives. No one would curse using His name in vain.

"Everyone would go to Church once a week to thank Him for all He's done, to receive nourishment from His Word, and food for our souls from His body in the Eucharist. They would then go out to the world and do all they could to love others, to help and not hurt them. They would honor their father and mother unless they asked them to do something that they knew was wrong. They wouldn't kill, commit adultery, steal, lie against their neighbors or make up stories to wreck the lives of others. Everyone would be happy and thankful for all that God has given them, not upset with what others have, or act like little children because they don't have what is not theirs.

"Oh, wouldn't our world be just a crappy place to live if everyone lived these Ten Commandments? Wouldn't you just hate to go to work and have a slow day because all the criminals were actually living a good life as God wishes, actually *following* the law?"

I'm mocking, but before he replies, I continue.

"What if everyone was actually sorry for their sins and took responsibility for the wrongs they have committed? What if everyone did penance and tried to make amends when they did screw up? I mean, can you imagine how horrible this world would be if everyone was charitable, humble, diligent, joyful, at peace, patient with everyone, mild, modest, chaste? If we all tried to feed the hungry, give drink to the thirsty, clothe the naked, bear wrongs patiently, forgive injuries, and prayed for the living and the dead? And, oh, wouldn't it be downright appalling if we tried to convert sinners, instruct the ignorant, give hope to the doubtful, and comfort the sorrowful? Gee, Sheriff, I don't know, I would *really* hate to live in a place like *that*, how about you?"

"No, you're right. We're much better off with how our world has become. I'm with ya. People full of pride, coveting everything around like this world is all that matters, full of lust and anger, envious and full of spite and jealousy, and outright hatred for our fellow brothers and sisters, eating and drinking whatever we can get our hands on without any effort to control our desires, and physical and spiritual laziness. Impulsive, sarcastic, jaded, materialistic people who don't give a shit about anyone other than themselves?

"You betcha, let me just sit back with you and do nothing, trying all I can to *not* change myself, making every effort to not improve the world around me. Uh huh, sure. Sign me up for that. Oh, wait a minute, it's all around us right here, right now, isn't it, Sheriff? *That's the world we live in this very moment!"*

He picks up his hat and rolls his eyes. At that moment, I realize God has just answered my own questions, the ones I screamed at Him somewhere between Tennessee and New Mexico. What I'm supposed to do about all this. It's not only to help Matt, it's to try and help Sheriff Luder, too.

"For the umpteenth time since we've met, Sheriff, let me go through this whole 'God and religion thing' as it relates to your life once more. This time, listen up. Your loving parents baptized you, sent you through religious education classes, and then you were confirmed. You have been blessed with a wonderful wife, a beautiful daughter — make that two beautiful daughters — and a solid career. You have your health, a great home, and money for your immediate and future needs. I even imagine you have friends and family who care about you, to one degree or another.

"But that hasn't been good enough for you – so you went in search of more 'happiness' because poor you was miserable in life. Then you had a motorcycle accident that could have been much worse – you could be paralyzed for life right now – and you more than likely experienced a life-changing out-of-body experience that showed you the possibility that this world, this reality, which is all you had known before then, isn't all there is. Then you had the blessed opportunity to travel on a pilgrimage and hear and see things that have been researched and tested exhaustively by the Church. You've had every opportunity to come to believe what has been said by Mother Mary and how, through these events, Our Lord is telling you and all of us to 'wake up!' You have been given a chance to turn your entire life around, to get it back on track, and you want to sit here and tell me you're still confused, hopeless, and depressed? That nothing really matters? Are you kidding me?!!!!! *EVERYTHING IN YOUR LIFE MATTERS!!!!!!"*

He's looking out the window down into the forest below, but I continue with what he may believe is another worthless diatribe.

"I really don't care if you listen to me; you're going to do what you want to do anyway. I'm not your father or your mother.

386

The Church is not *making* you do anything. She's not some indiscriminate burden-making institution, as so many incorrectly think. As Pope Emeritus Benedict XVI once said, *'The Church offers Him.'* God Himself is not *making* you do anything; He's only offering you the way to eternal happiness with Him. The gift of the Catholic Church exists to guide you; to show you how to live a sacramental life here on earth, with the aim of spending eternity with God. So heed the Church wisely. She's a good mother and wants the best for you. But you have free will and can choose to believe it or not. But you already know that, don't you?

"So I warn you once again, choose your next course of action well. You can take it or leave it. But never *ever* say, somewhere down the line, that you weren't told. What else does God need to show you? *'Blessed are those who haven't seen yet still believe.'* But you've seen! You've been given clear instructions on how you should live your life. No one is forcing you, but stop blaming the world for your lot in life and start taking responsibility for the choices you clearly made on your own accord. Your story is damn old by now."

I rise and walk to the same window. He turns and we face each other.

"Don't *ever* blame me again for anything in your life. Got it, Sheriff?"

Chapter 48

"Um, excuse me. Am I interrupting something?"

A well-dressed, somewhat surprised attorney pauses at the door, distracting the sheriff and myself from our stare down. I'm not sure how much he's heard, but I really don't care at the moment.

"No, it's fine. Come in." I say.

Shaking hands with us, he sits behind the desk and we take ours on the opposite side.

"I am the attorney for Mr. Thomas Victor, William Greenberg. It was somewhat of a challenge tracking both of you down on such short notice. Although I already had your names on file from Mr. Victor, he didn't have your recent addresses to give to me. Thank you for coming."

Why would he know our names? For the first time since entering the library, I take a moment to focus on my surroundings. The panoramic views that I saw on the drive up can be seen through a wall of windows behind where Mr. Greenberg now sits. A portrait of a much younger Thomas Victor posing with a woman hangs majestically next to the wall of windows to my right. At least I assume it's Thomas Victor, due to the likeness to the photograph from the back jacket cover of his book. For some reason, the woman also looks vaguely familiar, but I can't immediately place her. The chemical reactions from my venting at the sheriff, and now my curiosity about why we're even here to begin with, wrestle my brain for control.

As Mr. Greenberg goes through his standard intro spiel before reading the will, I look up to see the plaques and diplomas on the wall. Biophysics. Cosmetology. MIT Institute.

"Mr. Victor had an extensive background. He wore a number of hats, if you will, and had varied tastes and interests. At a minimum, he was a very successful investor, so much so that it allowed him to work on his real passion. Inventions."

"I thought he just wrote books. What did he invent?" the sheriff asks, his breathing still fairly rapid from our verbal exchange.

"Actually, he only wrote one book – one that he deeply regretted later in his life – but he became quite a prolific inventor as he got older. Initially he invented household items, like an improved vacuum system, then he moved onto projects that focused on the design of better telescopes. He dreamed of making a better Hubble. Fortunately, due to his investment prowess, whatever interested him he had the means to pursue it with vigor and finances."

The attorney sits back and allows this information to sink in, then slowly looks from the eyes of the sheriff to mine before continuing.

"But his pride and joy was a 'sex suit.'"

"A 'sex suit'?" we reply in unison.

"Yes. Once he stumbled onto that project a few years ago, his energy in life was completely rejuvenated. In fact, I hadn't seen him that excited in quite some time. He was convinced that all the agonies in the world men and women face, all the crime surrounding humanity's insatiable desire to love and be loved, could be solved if he could only design a suit that made full use of all of the human senses – taste, touch, sound, smell, and sight. He had envisioned through the use of advanced computer programs that a user could call up whomever they wanted to make love to, from a database he was intending to create, and never have to actually be with another human again. He was on the verge of a major breakthrough when he was killed, right here in this office. A lethal injection from a needle we never located was his last memory."

We are both trying to process this information.

"But he had only one overarching regret in his life, he was never able to share it with those whom he loved the most," he adds.

My head turns back towards the portrait hanging on the adjacent wall. This must be his wife to whom the attorney is referring. Maybe she died young.

Mr. Greenberg follows my gaze.

"No, that's not who I'm referring to, Father Bereo. That was his first wife of four, Janet Victor. He once told me he loved her more than any of the others and missed her terribly when she passed, a long time ago. After marrying and subsequently divorcing the other three, they all went their separate ways. As such, he died without a spouse. But the relationships with his wives are not what caused his greatest sadness and deepest regret during the latter period of his life."

Turning to the sheriff, I notice he's gawking at the portrait. He must have missed it when we came in, which isn't a surprise given the enormity of the library.

Turning to me without saying a word, the sheriff stands to get a closer look, pulling a picture from his wallet. After a few moments of comparing the two, he turns back, holding the same small photo of the woman he showed me the night he had me over for dinner. It hits me suddenly that this is the same picture I pulled out of my own storage of photos, but only glanced at briefly before I rushed out of town a week ago, completely distracted by my own recent life events.

Our eyes lock and he strides over to me, leaning into my ear.

"That's my aunt who came to me in my near death experience," he whispers, "so what is she doing in the picture with Thomas Victor?"

The sheriff's face turns pale, his breathing intensifying. My heart jumps. I notice Mr. Greenberg eyeing us intently with a smile forming on his lips. He clearly knows something of great importance that we don't.

"Mr. Greenberg, what does all of this have to do with me? With us, I mean?" I ask.

Standing now, he turns to the same picturesque windows that moments before the sheriff wanted to launch me through. Rotating his head back over his shoulders, he delivers the message that causes me to shake my head uncontrollably multiple times, instinctively rejecting the message.

"Gentleman, she was your mother, and Thomas Victor was your father. You two are brothers."

The next 30 minutes are a blur. Mr. Greenberg reads a letter written by Thomas Victor that was prepared a while ago to be read with his will.

My mind is racing. I attempt to focus on my breathing. The lawyer's words are bouncing in and out of my brain, without fully comprehending any of them. *"Given up for adoption." "Weren't ready to be parents." "Wanted to contact both of us when we became adults but knew that it wouldn't be fair given his 'line of business' and the fact that Daniel became a sheriff and I, a Catholic priest." "Knew that if he told us before his death it could make everything worse for him, but now that he's dead, there's no more reason not to let us figure it all out."* What the heck does all of this even mean? Figure what out?

Mr. Greenberg finishes with a flourish.

"You now inherit 25 million dollars each. Believing neither of you would approve, we were instructed, by the documents prepared in advance by your father, to divest all of his shares in each, well, 'unique' company he silently provided financial support for, including the business he ran directly out of this beautiful estate. You also have full control over his 'sex suit' project. It's yours to do with as you wish, although I should tell you he was in the final stages of Research and Development and has a full team of MIT graduates and other professionals in a variety of fields working on bringing it to fruition right here in New Mexico. If you bring the sex suit to final production, 25 million will be the equivalent of the value of a mere penny to the bank account of the richest man currently alive. Can you imagine a perfectly functioning sex suit? I can only humbly request you retain me as your counsel should you decide to proceed. There are also other parts of your father's life I can help you sort through when, and not 'if,' they arise in your future. Thomas Victor, your father, had a very, well, colorful past."

***

After signing a number of documents, Mr. Greenberg personally escorts the sheriff and I back to the sitting room, both of us in a state of pure numbness. The butler arrives with Detective Renae after summoning her from the Albuquerque fresh air.

"Ah, Detective Gambke. It's nice to see you again. Please let me know what you've decided when you're ready." Mr. Greenberg already knows her, a fact both the sheriff and I notice even with the immensely important news we've received.

Ignoring his outstretched hand, she turns to me and pleads.

"I've got to talk with you, Father, now." She's been crying, and the sheriff moves beside us. She looks at him then back at me, not wanting to speak in his presence. I'll explain to her later what has just transpired.

"It's all right, he can hear. What's wrong? Are you okay?" I place my right hand on her shoulder, trying to calm her.

She hesitates, looking back and forth between us again.

"Really, it's fine, Renae. What happened?"

She holds up a can of Sir Walter Raleigh tobacco. "I smelled it as soon as I walked in here." Her sobbing is immediate.

My mind can't immediately make the connection. It's on overload already.

Sensing my confusion, she thrusts a photo frame of Thomas Victor at my face, the biological father that Daniel and I never knew we had, and a wrenching cry emanates from deep within her. Flopping back onto a brown leather couch, we join her on either side. Trying to calm her as she gasps for air, she lets out emotions that apparently were still bottled up from nightmares of long ago. Between attempts to catch her breath, she wildly attempts to get us to understand.

"This is the guy that raped me, that kidnapped me! The guy I told you about! The friend of Cameron Gambke's!"

Mr. Greenberg hastily exits the room, and we are all left to mentally process what has just transpired.

Chapter 49

"Have you found Matt?" I ask.

"No."

Detective Renae meets me at the entrance to Burning Man, 2013, an annual event held in the Black Rock desert of Northern Nevada that I read all about in the local Reno paper this morning after catching some sleep in a Motel 6. I tried to drive all the way through from Albuquerque, but couldn't go any further once I reached the lights of the "Biggest Little City in the World."

She and, well I guess my brother, Daniel, have been here a few days. They flew directly to Reno right after the reading of the will in New Mexico. I'm thankful for the time I had to drive across Arizona, through Las Vegas, and up through the State of Nevada. It has given me the time to try and process this totally unexpected sea change in my life. The sheriff and I agreed to have our DNA tested as soon as we get back home to be absolutely certain. We also agreed that because our biological father was the one who completely wrecked her world, we would wait until the test results verified our fraternity to tell Detective Renae our own shocking news.

The revelations surrounding Thomas Victor, and how he has played a part in our lives, have thrown the three of us into a tailspin. We're understandably tense, so our collective desire to find Matt Gambke in "Black Rock City" may prove to be a welcome diversion. We collectively decided that no matter what, we need to see this trip through.

Seeing the bewildered look in my eyes, Detective Renae says to me: "Father, let me tell you well in advance. You are about to be amazed, awed, and in many respects, deeply offended by what you are about to see, all right?"

I nod my head and cover my eyes as a brief yet determined windstorm kicks dust from the playa directly into our faces. Maybe the timeless elements of nature don't want us here, either.

"I would like you to meet Ranger Dirk Donavon, our tour guide," she says.

"They call me Ranger Danger Dirk. Funny people out here, eh?"

Shaking the outstretched hand of the friendly 30-ish year old, I notice he's adorned in a uniformed khaki outfit. He waves to the gatekeepers as I drive my car through the entrance. I try to stay far enough away from his Jeep 4x4 to avoid being completely consumed by the dust being kicked up by his rear tires. My efforts prove fruitless.

I'm reminded of scenes from a favorite movie of mine, "The Road Warrior." I make a mental note that if anyone asks me about my first impression of Burning Man, I will suggest they watch it because I would find it hard to describe it in any other way that would do it justice albeit with one important twist – this is Mad Max on steroids.

Within a few hundred yards, Ranger Danger Dirk stops and points to where he would like me to park my vehicle, then waves for me to hop into his Jeep's backseat. I wonder if Detective Renae has told him I'm a Catholic priest. I'm wearing casual clothes, brown hiking boots I picked up at a shoe outlet along the way, my usual black pants, a long-sleeved white cotton shirt, and a beige Columbia desert hat. I wasn't sure what to wear, but within moments I realize that anything would have been acceptable.

"Hi. I'm Rosa. Rosa Marie Antoinette Herrera. But my friends call me Rosie." My riding partner is in her late teens or early 20's and dressed in the same outfit Ranger Dirk has, save the multiple streaks of pink starkly contrasting the rest of her brown hair.

"Hello, Ms. Sanchez. I'm Jonah."

We shake hands.

Peering at us from the rearview mirror, Ranger Dirk shares that Ms. Sanchez is 'interning' at this year's event.

"Do you live around here?" I ask Ms. Herrera, glancing out the dusty windows to the vast nothingness that surrounds us.

Her laugh is quick and joyful.

"That's funny!" she says, slapping my leg. "Only a small handful of people live around here, Jonah. Nope, I'm here from Wendover, Nevada. Not Wendover, Utah – Wendover, Nevada.

My family is still there. After high school I traveled around the State, hanging around old towns like Tonopah and Goldfield, and even Virginia City. I love the old haunted mining towns, the abandoned mines, all of it. That whole era intrigues me. But, I can't find a job. Do you know of any?"

She's direct and confident, yet not disrespectful. Plus, she doesn't seem to have an attitude. I like her already. She kind of reminds me of what may have been a younger Detective Renae, who is at present sitting in the front seat, staring at the impromptu circus that has formed around us.

"Well, uh, I'm not from around here." Nodding my head towards the detective, I add: "We're from North Carolina. Gardensville for me, specifically."

"Well, I've never been back there before. Sounds nice. Do they have any good jobs back there?" she continues.

"Well, I guess it depends on your skill set," I add.

"I am a quick learner and am very smart. If I ever go back there, can you hook me up?" She looks hopeful.

"Uh, sure, yeah. I'll do what I can." I have no idea how this young lady would have the means to travel across the United States, but if she arrives, I'll stay true to my word and at least try to help her.

Ms. Rosa Marie Antoinette Herrera smiles, and quiet momentarily fills the vehicle.

"Pretty amazing, huh?" Ranger Dirk laughs, his hand motioning to the spectacle outside the Jeep. "This City rose from the ground over a matter of weeks, a genuine phoenix rising from the dust and ashes of last years' event."

"I don't even know what to say, Ranger Donavon," I comment.

"First-timer?" he asks.

"Yes." I reply, my eyes battling the dust that has found a new home in unwelcomed places. It's almost impossible to capture or comprehend it all. You name it, I see it in front, beside and behind us, art, theme camps, full- or half-decorated bodies walking or riding a variety of moving vehicles, everything from bespangled bikes, golf carts, motorcycles, to solar-powered contraptions.

"How long have you been working here?" I ask.

"This is my fifth year. Want the three-minute spiel?" he says.

"Sure," hoping he'll roll up his driver's side window. The heat is intense, however, and I'm not sure what good it would do. There's powdery dust everywhere, and the A/C would just suck it inside and probably make matters worse.

He slowly drives down the makeshift road as he begins.

"Okay. This thing began on the beach in San Francisco in 1986. Just a small group. They got pushed out of there and ended up here. This area was all covered in water about 60,000 years ago. Before this group found it, it was primarily used for attempts to set land-speed records with rocket cars. In 1991, there were only about 250 people who attended. This year there are over 68,000 participants, including the small dedicated staff and volunteers, like me. Sold out three years in a row, and it just keeps getting bigger, way bigger. Last year, about 40 percent of the group were first-timers, like you. Most people think it's a bunch of freaks, but I've met people from all walks of life and, for the most part, they are all very cool. Doctors, business owners, moms, dads, kids, all races, and I would imagine all religions, although you wouldn't know it when they get into these city limits because all of what I described just evaporates, or meshes together, or is a hybrid of well, whatever."

"Thanks for the info," I say. "I'm just here for the day, but I appreciate it."

"It's perfectly all right, you don't have to participate, and everyone likes to watch." He smirks, and Detective Renae seems immediately embarrassed. At this point, it's highly likely she hasn't told him my profession.

"Wow!" he yells, slamming on the breaks as the sound and fiery impact of a flamethrower protruding from a converted Chevy Suburban gets our united attention.

"Gotta really watch what's happening out here," he laughs, waving to the revelers as they scoot by.

"Do a lot of people get hurt out here?" Detective Renae asks.

"Oh, you mean from stuff like that?" Nah. Well, not many. They're just having fun. Everyone has been well-versed on keeping it safe for themselves and everyone around them. There are rules out here like respecting everyone else, but every once in a while, someone does something stupid. Like last night. Some guy decided to race out on his scooter into the playa without his lights. Had so much fun with that, he decided to turn around and do it coming back. Hit a motor home and the impact killed him instantly, but no one else was hurt. So, things like that do happen, but for the most part, it's very safe. But at nighttime, you can barely see your hand in front of you if you wander off. People get lost who did some type of drug or drink combo they shouldn't have – or maybe just wanted to find absolute silence – and when they're reported missing, we have volunteers go find 'em. That doesn't happen a lot, but, with this many people, *something* is going to happen, so we have to be prepared for it.

"Even though this looks crazy, there's an incredible infrastructure. The organizing group works year round. There's like 25 project managers, who all have professional backgrounds in select areas, supported by up to 3,000 volunteers, who build this city before everyone gets here. Every year it becomes the fifth largest city in the State of Nevada. It's all laid out in this incredibly accurate grid, with street names and everything. We see Fed Ex deliveries all the time, and I've even seen Chinese food delivered all the way from Reno. Crazy!" His friendly banter enlivens my mood, and he reminds me of the kooky character in Mad Max who flew that helicopter contraption before crashing it. Although I'm increasingly offended by the surreal circus in front of me, I'm actually glad he's with us. I need a reason to smile.

"Do you know how many different volunteer groups exist to make this happen?" I ask, recalling how Sheriff Luder told me Matt might be one of them.

"Not exactly," he says, shaking his head. "Last count there were, like, 30. There are groups that deal with art installations, earth guardians, lamplighters, greeters, perimeter and exodus folks who watch for people sneaking in but also focus on traffic control when this thing breaks up. Those gatekeepers we passed have a big job, too. They have to make sure everyone has a ticket and no one is trying to sneak in. People can be and are pretty ingenious trying to slip in here without a ticket, for whatever the reason. Maybe they're cheap; maybe they just can't afford it. There are also a ton of EMS personnel, and even a special group of people that deal with Mental Health issues – especially if anyone has been sexually assaulted – so, really, like any city, if someone really needs something, for the most part, it's here."

"Are there a lot of sexual assaults out here during this event?" asks Detective Renae, her interest piqued. Ranger Danger shrugs his shoulders and answers.

"I don't know the numbers but, I mean, look at this environment. You have people frolicking around fully or partially nude, and common sense and experience tells me there's substance abuse going on, even though they know they're in big trouble if we catch 'em. The alcohol consumption alone makes a shaky environment even riskier. And then you throw it all in to a pot of just plain people wanting to have a good time and letting it all hang out, getting crazy and wild, and, well, like I said before, something's bound to happen. But, if it does, shit, what were they thinking coming out here and running around with no clothes on and putting themselves in this situation to begin with?"

He laughs again, but neither of us can find the humor in his last statement. He sees her frown, and catches my own concerned look in his rearview mirror.

"Hey, like I said, I don't really know how much it happens. But, I also don't want to give you the wrong impression. Yeah, sex happens out here, just like it does in regular cities everywhere. And I suppose there are some sexual assaults that take place, but I've seen people making love here and there all the time, and it sure doesn't look forced. But there's so much more to it. I mean, look around. People are here for a million different reasons, you know? I mean, maybe they are here just to find themselves, or just to forget the world behind them. I've heard people say they feel their life is so controlled by everyone and everything 'out there' they just want to come out here each year and do whatever they feel like, whenever they want, without judgment. No one is going to look at them as though they're not accepted or acceptable, dominate them, or say how bad they are for doing whatever they are doing."

His smile is immense; his joy clearly evident as he continues.

"You know how amazing it is to see these people from all around the world just reaching out to one another, offering their time just to help each other out, and giving things of their own when other people need it, offering to help them put their art structures up or tear them down, whatever? I mean, there's a lot of effort put in around the year by these participants to build and transport all the stuff for their theme camps – close to 1,000 of them and around 350 or so art sculptures this year – so they need help to put them up and break 'em down. And people do it, no questions asked. Sure, some are volunteers who have specifically said they will help with this job, but many are just participants who see someone else in need and just do it. I mean, if these people saw each other on the street in regular life, they wouldn't give each other the time of day, but they have a purpose here and it's simple, really – just to help, be loved, and to love others, you know?"

What Ranger Danger Dirk has just described strikes a chord in me. This search for happiness, a longing for peace, a sense of purpose that I've felt along with all the other pilgrims to the Marian apparition sites is what he seems to be describing. And I can see it on the faces of the people around us, too, as we continue to drive down the main street. They do seem happy, content, at peace. They are having fun, and lots of it. They're giving, and although their self-expression may seem eccentric at times, who am I to judge? Undoubtedly, I see many mocking religion, and the erotic nature of this place sets all of my alarms ringing, but I've also seen others who don't seem to be part of that scene. For them and maybe all, this is probably very cathartic, very transforming. My concern is that if they aren't in the fire, they are dangerously close to it.

"And you want to know how big this thing has gotten, I mean, outside of this area in Nevada?" he asks.

"Sure," I reply.

"It's gone global over the last few years. Spain, South Africa, Columbia, South Korea, Israel – I can't even name them all, there's like 30 different countries – that want to have their own Burning Man. So, who knows, I may have some international travel in my future to lend my expertise. Man, wouldn't that be great?!"

"Can I go with you?" Ms. Herrera blurts out, suddenly reengaged in the discussion.

"Well, let's just see how you do this year, okay?" he smiles.

Pulling the vehicle to a stop, he points.

"This is the epicenter, if you will. This years' theme is 'Cargo Cult,' and has something to do with how our earth is kind of oblivious to how we get the things we get, and always seem to wonder where all the other stuff will come from in the future that we can use. Maybe it comes from outer space, who knows? Aliens."

I shake my head, now better comprehending all the strange-looking designs and outfits around me.

"What's with the structure of a man on top of that spaceship, revolving around like the Seattle Space Needle?" Detective Renae asks.

"I guess 'the man' means something different to everyone. Maybe an old boss, current boss, old relationship, current relationship, old memories, current memories – who knows?"

Exiting the vehicle, we stand side by side. A senior citizens tour bus pulls up, its inhabitants slowly making their way to the structure. Ranger Danger chuckles.

"We gotta make sure we keep all the locals happy. In truth, we actually do appreciate how they support us each year."

Motioning towards the massive structure again, he encourages us to follow the endless stream of uniquely dressed, partially dressed or completely undressed participants, all merging with the senior citizens, the latter snapping digital pictures and having a grand time of it.

Detective Renae and I stare in the direction of the masses heading into the space ship, and my eyes catch two smiling characters dressed in altered black, white and red nun habits, with the words 'Satan Rocks and Rolls' emblazoned across the back, their faces painted green to match the alien theme, fake red eye contacts finishing off the ensemble. Ranger Danger continues, ensuring he covers the important high points of our "tour."

"Check it out. You gotta see the inside of this pavilion.

There's this 'Temple of the Navigator.' It's supposed to be an altar with six different prayer wheels, all in line with the theme of asking whomever provides our earth with all the goods, to help us again. You don't want to miss it because you won't be able to see it tomorrow."

"Why?" I ask.

"Because tonight we burn him." He turns to me.

"You burn him?" I try to process what I'm hearing.

"Duh. It's called 'Burning Man' for a reason." He laughs, and Ms. Herrera playfully smacks my shoulder.

I'm embarrassed since I didn't actually put it all together until just now. My head is spinning and I need some water and Kleenex, wondering how bad all this is for my sinuses and lungs.

"Yes, tonight this whole thing will be torched. And if it's like previous years, it will be wild, absolutely insane. You gotta hang around to see it. It's this massive bonfire that's accompanied by pyrotechnics, choreographed dancers with flames, and EMS personnel standing everywhere to protect the participants if it gets out of hand. Last year it was a crack up. Me and other guys are trying to work on crowd control, right? Crowd control, that's funny. The 'man' is lit up, and like 50,000 people go running toward it, like bugs to one of those bug zappers. And there's just a handful of us saying 'Don't. Stay back.' Shit, I could only hold my arms out for so long. They couldn't hear me through my fire suit, or if they did, they didn't care. We just moved out of harm's way and, in the end, no one got really hurt so it wasn't a big deal."

He's laughing as he heads back to the Jeep. Looking over his shoulder, he adds, "If I'm out here when you're done, I'll give you a ride back. You can grab some coffee or water at the café over there if you want."

Ms. Herrera puts out her hand and we shake. I wish her luck in the future.

"I'm gonna look you up someday," she says, smiling.

"If it be God's will." I return the smile as she jogs after Ranger Danger Dirk.

Following Detective Renae with my head down to protect my eyes from the sudden windstorm, I notice my black pants are completely covered in dust. I'm not one bit surprised that we haven't found Matt Gambke in this sea of costumed and decorated humanity. Even if he's here, he could be any one of them, dressed in heavy makeup and other-worldly costumes, with features that won't allow us to come close to identifying him.

I want to leave here as soon as I can. I miss the peace of the Nevada desert south of here, remembering the old towns of Goldfield and Tonopah that I just drove through less than 24 hours ago in my air-conditioned car, the same ones Ms. Herrera is apparently familiar with and very fond of.

***

"We've heard he's been here and may still be here," says the sheriff. We've caught up with him at the Ranger command post. Until we get the DNA test back home, I've now decided I'm not going call him my brother. That, in itself will take some getting used to, even if the DNA tests prove positive.

"He was probably a volunteer who somehow got a hold of a ticket and has just melded in. It's the proverbial 'needle in a haystack' dilemma," he continues, fixing his gaze on me, before adding: "I ran into our old friend Chaffgrind."

"What's he doing out here?" I ask.

The sheriff rolls his eyes and continues.

"Seems like his son, Alex, the 'famous' porn producer, is setting up shop and his dad is here to help out. He wanted to know if I was asking about permits, like I work for Burning Man or something. Seemed real nervous but relaxed when I told him I was just looking for someone. I showed him the picture of our suspect and Chaffgrind recalled him as a student in his class. Said he dropped out right before we sat in that night, right before the school break. Told me he saw him wearing a medical crew volunteer shirt earlier today. Looks like Matt touted himself as someone who has a medical background from his stint with the old folk's home."

I bristle, the disgust in both our eyes now matching in intensity.

"Hasn't seen him since, though. However, Matt told him he may come back tonight to make sure everything is going well, and to help out with the filming, if any was needed. We're also working with the guy that heads up the EMS function here. They're doing a search but have their hands full right now since this Burning Man thing is in full swing. In short, it's not their priority."

Nodding, I look inside the large domed tent, and note the film crew setting up, with an altar in the middle and "actors" dressed in Montezuma/alien-like outfits. The three of us will wait, since its dusk outside and they begin filming in 30 minutes according to Chaffgrind. The sheriff said he's all buddy-buddy with him and told him he and anyone who wants to join him can stand inside while they film.

We are on the outskirts of Black Rock City, and I can vaguely make out the temporary orange plastic fence that has been placed around the perimeter. Outside the fence, I see an official "Burning Man" vehicle slowly driving by, monitoring for deviants choosing to sneak in to the event rather than follow the rules. We sit quietly for a while, taking it all in.

"Can you believe the filth that's around here?" the sheriff asks us, our little group now sitting on open chairs just outside the tent. The majority of the city inhabitants appear to be making their way to the Temple of the Navigator, readying for the ultimate burn, the grand finale. Tribal drums began playing an hour ago over the loudspeakers, their crescendo slowly building, urging the throng forward for the definitive spectacle.

"I've seen all sorts of things here, and I still don't know if I will ever be able to explain it. Much of it is very creative and fun in many respects, but, yes, there're a great number of things I am concerned about," I reply.

"Explain it? I say we just bring some of our military out here and bomb the shit out of it." He stands, looking towards the temple while using his sheriff's hat to try in vain to whack the dust off his jeans.

"I hoped you would finally be of the mindset to help them, to show them another way," I say.

"I already tried that a few times today. It didn't work. They aren't interested," he offers.

"I hear ya. But would you actually resort to violence to force them to your position if you really could?" I realize it may take some time before he and I see eye to eye on a multitude of topics, no matter if we validate that we are, indeed, brothers.

"Yes, I want to rid the earth of them. If we did, September 11th, the Boston Marathon bombings, the Colorado movie theatre, the Connecticut elementary school, Columbine, heck, all of that wouldn't have happened. Ever."

He lowers his head, punching the toe of his cowboy boot into the playa. I refuse to let him continue with this errant thought pattern.

"Neither you nor I have any real idea what these people believe in nor do we know all the reasons they are here. But no matter what they believe, we both have already agreed that our world needs to change, remember? However, we can never forget that Jesus taught us that we must love others as we love ourselves. Long-term, meaningful change does not happen with violence. Although violence, even war, is sometimes necessary, it should never be our first option. Our first choice always must be to talk to people, work with people, love people, live our lives as a walking example – not to try and force them into our way of thinking."

Our attempt at communication is getting heated, again. Uncomfortable with the exchange, Detective Renae stands up and walks a few feet away.

"Sheriff, c'mon in, we're beginning in just a few minutes," Dr. Chaffgrind says. His painted smile disappears when he sees me with the sheriff.

"Professor," I nod, as I follow the sheriff and the detective inside. Entering the tent, we stand behind two beefy security officers. I ignore Chaffgrind and he chooses to do the same with me.

The plot that I can vaguely make out is that a Montezuma-alien tribal chief is trying to find the ultimate human female sacrifice for the alien god – apparently to, what? Appease the gods? Make these people/creatures more prosperous? The acting reminds me of a play I had to do in school with a few classmates. We won a first-place ribbon – in third grade. I'm wondering why anyone would even buy this crap to begin with. Oh, that's right, this is porn.

The scene in front of us quickly moves from the alien guards choosing the potential victims, to the victims individually 'servicing' the chief in their own erotic way, and if he disapproves, they are cast off to the side where the 'alien guards' can then have their way with them. Within 10 minutes, a massive orgy has ensued. Flesh on flesh – it's that simple – and this industry makes a mint. I shake my head.

"Do you know if Matt has any distinguishing body marks?" the sheriff asks Detective Renae, while intently staring at each actor. If he's somehow worked his way into the cast, spotting him won't be easy without a distinguishing mark since they are all now completely naked, save for their grotesque masks.

"None that I know of," she replies, shaking her head.

I don't need to see any more of this debauchery. Maybe I will be able to see Matt outside of the tent somewhere if he's not even part of this; maybe I will just sit and look up at the stars telling God how sorry I am for everything that has gone so astray with so many of His children and ask His forgiveness – for them; for all of us.

Turning towards the exit, a strange scream suddenly erupts from the chief causing me to pause – his version of what a Montezuma-alien would sound like, I guess. He's made his way to the front of the 'altar,' and from what I can gather, to the female that has serviced him the best. This is the one, the chosen 'sacrifice.' All orgy activity stops, the female actors move off camera, and the male alien guards line up one after the other – I count at least a dozen. Apparently, her ultimate sacrifice will be to service the Montezuma-alien chief and the leftovers will be taken by his military unit.

The naked chosen female, previously ordained, of course, by the director of the film and set apart with a headdress that is unrivaled by her peers, suddenly turns and intentionally looks straight towards us, her eyes fixated on the sheriff. His feet are riveted to the playa inside the tent, his stare locked with hers. He has seen those eyes before. She slowly turns, steps up out of the crowd and onto the altar, holding her position just long enough for us to plainly see the letters, "EBYT" tattooed across her lower back. I'm certain they will photo shop that out of the final video before going to market, that is, unless the sheriff gets to her first.

Within seconds, an incredibly loud yet, horrible, outer space-tribal genre of music begins, drowning out the sheriff's anguished scream. He lurches towards the altar, knocking Chaffgrind to the ground and attempting to push through really big Security Guard #1 and even bigger Security Guard #2. They subdue the sheriff quickly, escorting him outside. I follow, and glance back at a beaming Michele as she lies back on the altar, the Montezuma-alien chief taking her then, and the alien guards standing in line awaiting their turn.

Chapter 50

Detective Renae and I attempt in vain to follow the sheriff as he sprints towards the temple. He disappears quickly, absorbed by the thousands standing around the perimeter. We try our best to scan the crowd as choreographed dancers circle the structure, illuminated by the dancing flames of the torches. The beating drums grow louder as each minute passes. The crowd is in a steady yet growing frenzy; I trip over a few having sex on the fringes of the masses as I try to follow where I thought the sheriff went. Looking back, I realize that I've now also lost Detective Renae.

Within 45 minutes, the dancers finish with a flourish. All eyes turn to the center structure – the enormous 'man' standing on a massive make-shift alien saucer towers above the masses – as it is lit with a dozen torches. I recall what Ranger Danger Dirk said earlier about how crazy this is about to get. No one is moving towards it just yet, which is good because I only see a spattering of brave EMS volunteers in silver fire suits between them and certain death.

All around me is organized chaos. Singing, yelling, screaming, hugging, kissing, holding, crying. New Year's Eve on amphetamines. It appears the entire range of emotions are being felt by this monstrous group, each experiencing the phenomenon in a way truly unique to them. Peering towards the flaming structure, I give up hope that I might find either the sheriff or the detective until this all settles down. Making my way just two rows from the front of the crowd, I find myself in the middle of an impromptu mosh pit, revelers bumping and pushing me, jumping continuously full of unbridled exuberance.

At that moment, as though it couldn't get any more bizarre, it does. As the entire superstructure is enveloped in a raging blaze, I detect a figure emerging from its base. The wind has picked up, either from a storm moving in, or as a result of the spontaneous combustion erupting 40 yards in front of me. The dust and smoke are pummeling my senses. Sparks are flying everywhere. My eyes are burning. I rub them furiously to make sure they aren't playing tricks on me – causing me to see something that isn't there. But just like the certainty the sheriff vehemently expressed regarding his near-death experience when I first saw him in the hospital earlier in the year, what I now see unfolding before me is undeniably real, just 30 yards now and closing fast. Now 20, then 10. No one seems to notice, nor even look his way. Without a doubt in my mind, he's coming straightaway for me.

Moving effortlessly past the people standing shoulder to shoulder in front of me, he positions himself inches from my face, glaring into my eyes. Curly, ancient, ashen gray hair is protruding under his vintage top black hat. The giant 'Cargo Cult spaceman' and saucer – now fully enflamed – towers above and behind this being, his own frame eclipsing mine by at least a foot. The dark barren landscape, now completely aglow from the stupendous bonfire, allows me to see that he's wearing a matching black frock coat, neatly pressed black pants, white and black spectator spat boots, a black vest with a red cravat, and red gauntlet gloves. Unlike my black pants that may need to be thrown away after my excursion here to the Nevada desert, there is not a spot of dust nor any apparent burn marks on him, and his shoes literally shine from the light emanating from the raging inferno behind him. A glowing golden walking stick finishes up his Victorian-era trappings.

Either the noise around me has dinned, or the words now coming out of his mouth are at a much higher decibel. At any rate, it's in Latin. My seminary training comes back to me, if only in snippets, and I catch a few words and sentences: *"my targets," "you are fighting a losing battle,"* and *"my territory and hunting grounds,"* from his barely controlled, verbal tirade. Swiveling my head right and left as he speaks, I wonder how not even one person is looking our way, how no one at all is apparently catching this. It's just the two of us in a separate dimension. I now know who he is, though, and have a good idea why he has sought me out. He's always after Our Lord's shepherds, for if he can defeat us, the sheep will follow. It's been one of his methods of operating since the beginning.

Reaching into my pocket, I remove my Rosary beads, revealing in the palm of my hand Our Lord on an oversized crucifix. I'm also suddenly grateful for the brown scapular I wear daily around my neck, underneath my clothes. My world which was previously spinning calms immediately, my triumphant stare leveling his way.

"Never forget, He wins and has the faithful under His mantle of protection, and she will safeguard me and all her children. You lose," I say, God's grace holding me firm.

The 'Cargo Cult man' crashes on top of the spaceship behind this preternatural master of temptation and destruction, and the collective roar of all the pleasure-seekers brings me back to the moment. He doesn't flinch at the thunderous collapse.

A demented chortle spurts from his mouth, the deathly smell of his breath causing my face to immediately wince in disgust. The recollection of that awful stench emanating from the young girl at Lourdes just a few months ago threatens to overpower me once more.

"Oh, but I will always be waiting for and watching you, Fr. Jonah Lee Bereo, I promise you that."

No longer able to restrain themselves, the crowd sprints forward, almost knocking me to the ground. I'm forced to move with them lest I be crushed. The Prince of Sinners has vanished. As the celebrants race madly forward to the ever-beckoning radiation from the all-consuming conflagration, I make my way back to the direction of my car with Rosary beads still in hand, recalling the second and third of the 15 promises of those who pray the Rosary devoutly – that Mother Mary has promised her special protection and the greatest graces to all those who recite the Rosary, and that the Rosary shall be a powerful armor against Hell while destroying vice, decreasing sin, and defeating heresies.

Slowly making the sign of the cross, I recall what Pope Emeritus Benedict XVI once said about the devil and man – that on our own, we can't oppose Satan's power, but since Lucifer is not a second God, if we unite ourselves with Jesus, we can be certain of conquering him.

I thank God profusely for what just occurred and His

continued gifts and blessings, and ask for His continued help, guidance, and protection – for myself, family and friends; for every single person alive today and all those in the future. I pray especially for those who want nothing more than to believe that the Prince of Darkness doesn't exist, just so they can live an illusion – a consequence-free fantasy life. I thank Mother Mary, too, for her God-given protection, and ask that we all be given the grace and will to always remain worthy of His gifts.

Pausing to get my bearings, I notice I've moved at least 50 yards from the primal dance floor, staring into the endless blanket of stars above. I want to be in Heaven, right now. But knowing it's not God's will at this time, I recommit once more to never doing anything that might cost me eternity with Him.

Suddenly, an arm reaches out to grab mine, pulling me around. I can't see the face clearly due to the dark Nevada night, but I recognize the voice.

"They found him," Ranger Danger Dirk says firmly. The outlined frame next to him I assume to be Ms. Herrera.

"Found who?" I ask, wondering when this bad dream of a day will end.

"The guy you and Detective Gambke were looking for earlier today." He's slightly winded.

"Matt Gambke?!? They did? Where?" I ask, Ms. Herrera and I trying to keep up with him as he begins jogging in the direction of the crime scene.

"Right on the outside of the boundary line of our city, right past the orange plastic fence. Seems like whatever happened was done right after our patrol car made its second to last round of the night, so we figure about 30 minutes ago. On the trip back around, they caught him in their headlights. He's in pretty bad shape, I guess. Strung up."

"What do you mean 'strung up'?" I grab his arm to force him to stop. The noise of the crowd is getting louder since we are close to the center party zone, and I need to make sure I'm hearing him correctly. He turns, the outline of his face now clearer thanks to the raging fire that will burn for hours.

"Well, all I got over the radio was that some guy they

identified as your suspect has been tied up to some heavy, long wooden planks, formed like a cross. His balls are gone. We got there within two minutes of the call. I guess the dude began screaming like bloody murder after they pulled a sock from his mouth, and hadn't stopped by the time we came to find you guys. EMS was on their way. Pretty gruesome scene."

Ms. Sanchez abruptly leans over with her back to us, and I hear the vomit as it spews from her mouth onto the cracked playa desert. Clearly this isn't the adventure she was searching for.

Chapter 51

"This whole experience has been insane, a wild roller coaster ride, I tell ya."

I'm catching Fr. Jack up-to-date, and for the last 15 minutes have been describing what has transpired since our last conversation.

"That's an understatement, Jonah. Satan is very real, isn't he? Most people don't want to believe that at all; it's easier for them that way."

"I fully agree, Father."

We pause for a moment, and I offer more prayers of thanksgiving and continual assistance for God's protection.

I've already told him that Mrs. Susan Bellers admitted to embezzling $70,000 over a 13-year period from the collection proceeds. Apparently, she kept a separate set of books and would routinely walk out with the money in a brown paper bag. She'd told Fr. Bernard, when he actually had the courage to ask her one day, that, being environmentally conscientious, she was merely recycling her lunch bag. Sadly, she was able to get away with this for so long because she ran the show, and no other volunteers helping out in the office ever questioned her activities. She had full control and worked very hard to keep it that way.

She also intentionally never left an electronic paper trail by not transferring money from the parish account to her own. She simply used the easiest way because she saw no reason not to – the old-fashioned "cash in a bag and out the door" method. However, her luxurious lifestyle and purchases – none of which could be supported on her modest household income – were fully exposed by the diocesan investigator and auditors. Checks and balances? Unless Fr. Bernard stood up to her, they weren't going to ever be put in place. He never did, and they never were. That is, until the auditors showed up.

The spy camera her nephew, Dennis, had installed in my office the Saturday I walked in on them, ended up helping my cause immensely. Apparently, the morning after Michele Jerpun tried to seduce and then frame me, Bellers was so excited she came into the office early to grab the video – she had every intention of reporting me to the diocese even if Michele chose not to. She was fully convinced I actually did molest Michele and that the proof would be on the video. She didn't expect to see Fr. Bernard there that early, so she couldn't go into my office and remove the camera which was streaming video to her desktop. I'm still not sure what excuse she gave for planting the camera to begin with. At any rate, she also made the mistake of mentioning she had "proof" of the porn on my computer when she thought it would play to her favor, but it tipped off the investigators to visit Dennis' home with a search warrant where they found my laptop. Apparently, Bellers and her nephew had staged the break-in months ago in order to try and get computer evidence against me. That got her, and him, into even more hot water. After hearing my version and trying to tie it back to how Bellers could even know what she professed to have knowledge of, the auditor and the diocesan investigator found the spy cam – and the subsequent video traced to her computer owned by the diocese sitting right there on her desk. Her plan and scam were irrevocably foiled.

Not only did the story I had shared with Fr. Bernard check out with the exact date and websites I had visited, but the video footage showed exactly what had transpired with Michele Jerpun in my office. To boot, this same video feed provided the investigators with clear evidence of her embezzlement. It clearly showed that after she and a few committed volunteers performed their weekly count, she would place "her take" in the brown bag. In the end, she wasn't as smart as she thought she was, and her desire to ruin me boomeranged and landed her in prison. Her confidence and past success in this scam made her lazy and cocky. Part of her sentencing requires she pay full restitution. Although I have now increased my prayers for her true conversion, I must admit that I "high-fived" everyone I came into contact with that day.

"She put herself in that position, Jonah. That's why she's going to prison," Fr. Jack had commented, which I fully agreed with.

I said I felt sorry for Fr. Bernard, though, and Fr. Jack felt the same. His calling and his training were to be a shepherd to His people, not a full-time business manager. He just didn't have the skillset to run the administrative office, and was forced to place his full trust in his sister-in-law. He officially retired in October – just a month after she was arrested – embarrassed and headed home to the mid-west.

I am now the pastor of Our Lady of Perpetual Help Parish. The diocese is satisfied with the end result of their own inquiry; in other words, I've been fully and completely exonerated. Quite a few parishioners have still chosen to leave the parish – convinced of my guilt – but that's out of my hands. I've been relying on temporary help as I revamp the policies and procedures in the parish with the assistance of the auditors from the diocese.

"As for Matt Gambke, the night they found him at Burning Man, they determined his testicles had been removed with a clamp used for cattle, and a hastily prepared bandage had been applied to try and stem the bleeding. Whoever did this didn't want him to die right away, if at all, but they definitely wanted him to experience a great deal of pain. Had the desert patrol not found him when they did, he might have bled to death by morning. What I find of great interest is that right above his private parts, well, what was still left of them, were the tattooed initials 'B.H.R.,' which is exactly what was tattooed on his dad."

"What does that mean?" Fr. Jack had asked.

"I don't know, and no one will tell me. I asked both Daniel and Renae and they changed the subject rather quickly. They clearly know something I don't and are unwilling to tell me. They didn't seem surprised to see the initials, though.

"Plus, when I visited Matt in the hospital back here in North Carolina after his immediate extradition, I unintentionally interrupted Daniel and Renae talking in hushed tones. They stopped as soon as I walked up, but it seemed a little heated. All I heard was "he's been embedded in the group all along." They didn't offer any more information, and I didn't press. 'Official Law Enforcement business,' apparently.

"I did get out of Daniel that when EMS got Matt stabilized

and to the hospital in Reno, he wouldn't say who did this nor give any details about the rape of Gina. But later Renae told me he did turn in the other two guys who were part of the attack – buddies of his from high school who apparently routinely gang raped girls around the area and threatened them with their lives if they told. His deranged purpose in doing what he did to Gina was to try and impress Dr. Chaffgrind's porn-producing son with a video highlighting sex with a physically handicapped person. His buddies wore masks for the filming because it added to the 'surprise rape' screenplay. He didn't wear one because he knew from past experience that she wouldn't remember him or his accomplices anyway due to the drugs. He just never expected her to go into a coma. And you know what? He expressed absolutely no remorse about what happened to Gina. Either he's a great actor trying to hold in his feelings, or he's that numb to the pain he inflicts on others, especially his own family members.

"What got me was that Michele knew Gina was with him that night as he picked her up for the movies, but apparently he told her she had wandered off at the theatre when she said she had to go to the bathroom, and that's apparently when she was 'kidnapped.' I really don't know why she believed him because she doesn't seem to miss a thing, but he had this all planned out and his alibi stood. I don't know, this whole connection with Michele and Matt still seems strange to me."

"Jonah, from what you've just described, nothing would surprise me about Michele Jerpun, but I'm a little confused. If Matt Gambke wasn't talking, how was all this information discovered?"

"From the tape recorder," I say.

"The tape recorder?" he asks.

"Yes," I reply. "When he was castrated that night, he was forced to speak into a tape recorder that the investigators later found in his back pocket. They couldn't find any fingerprints on it, though.

"Of course, when the investigators played it for him, he denied it all. His defense attorney – who just happened to be the same attorney for Cameron Gambke along with Thomas Victor, Mr. Greenberg – claims the tape is inadmissible in court because he was under duress and fear at the time. He claims he only 'made up' this story because his attacker told him that if he didn't tell the truth, he would be castrated. He told the first story that came to mind, his attorney later said, but then was still castrated to be 'taught a lesson.'"

"A lesson about what?" he says.

"No one knows, and he isn't saying. At any rate, two major pieces of evidence are still against him. The Crime Lab analyzed the video from the neighbor, and it's definitely Matt and Gina. Further, and much more damning, is the actual video he gave to Chaffgrind's son at Burning Man. They turned it over to the police and Matt was so bold, so confident he had this all figured out, that he put his own name on it as the Director. At any rate, he's out of the hospital and the case is locked up in the courts."

"Confident or just stupid?" Fr. Jack has seen many personalities over the years, many who fit the mold of Matt Gambke.

"It's hard to say, Father, but I intend to get to know Matt further in the future. I've also overheard this may not have been his first attempt at producing porn. The more his young world is unraveling, the more he's looking like he's as seasoned a criminal as a man three times his age, and making porn was just when he was bored. How he has stayed off the law enforcement database up until now is well beyond me."

What I'm not going to tell Fr. Jack is that Daniel carries around a tape recorder, although I know that doesn't prove anything. We've talked for a while already, and I'm ready to tune in to the soccer channel.

"What about Michele Jerpun? Where's she at?" he asks.

"The last I saw of her was at Burning Man. They found her at the temple and brought her back to the scene of the crime. She was interviewed on the spot, and since she had an alibi – the filming of the porn flick – she was not detained. However, given the circumstances, she is still a suspect. Daniel and Renae were also interviewed, given their 'beef' against Matt, and I was interviewed, given what I now firmly believe he did to Mom. Nothing has been resolved, and the case is still an active investigation. Even so, she and Gina kind of dropped off the radar again, at least my radar, and I'm okay with that as it relates to Michele."

"Unbelievable. Do you ever regret having left Brooklyn?" he laughs in order to break the tension.

"Like I said, insane, huh?" I'm shaking my head, clicking through the channels absentmindedly.

"It certainly sounds like it. And how is Renae doing with all these discoveries?" he asks.

"This has all been very hard on her. Daniel and I, and my sister-in-law, Jean, all met with her once the DNA results came back. It was a difficult discussion, but it all needed to come out so the air could be cleared.

"If you can pray for her I would really appreciate it. It is truly heartbreaking what she has experienced and is still having to go through. First, having to deal with the death of her father, who although she couldn't stand him, was still her father. And then after all these years, to finally put a name to the face of the man who had raped and terrorized her, has created a tremendous mental burden, especially since we have become friends. And now having to deal with her brother, Matt, as the evidence has mounted against him, only exacerbates the pain she's experiencing. Fortunately, she's intensified the EMDR therapy with her aunt, and by all indications is making some solid progress. It will just take time.

"Renae told Daniel about the letter from Cameron. And Daniel even opened up and talked about his out-of-body experience, something I could see Jean hadn't heard about in detail. It was a tense and sad evening, yet cathartic all the same. One big upside is after Jean gave Renae a tight hug when she left, Daniel gave her a hug, too. A quick and weak one, but a friendly embrace nonetheless. *That* I was really happy to see.

"She's going to really try to tear apart the letter now, and we're going to help her because, at a minimum, this whole 'Cameron Gambke / Thomas Victor' connection is odd to say the least."

"And how is it going with your new-found big brother? I notice he's moved from 'the sheriff' to 'Daniel'," he says, that

417

chuckle that I miss the most immediately lightening the mood.

"Well, once the shock wore off, we seem to have settled in. I'm very encouraged he's praying the Rosary every day, along with the Divine Mercy Chaplet. He's also wearing a blessed miraculous medal, which makes me very happy.

"After Renae left that night, Jean wanted to hear more about the out-of-body experience. I get the sense she is making an effort to at least meet him halfway in their relationship. I tried to leave to give them privacy, but Daniel wanted me to stay since we're all family now, he said, and she didn't seem to mind. He replayed the message to her. He felt better knowing that the 'both of you' comment must refer to him and me. He feels bad that somehow our biological mom was trying to tell us to protect Thomas Victor and we didn't do anything about it. I think that's why he's going to really try to help Renae figure this all out, for his own sake, too. Who 'the others' are remains a mystery, but one that I intend to lend a hand in solving.

"We have our father's business to get our heads around, but so much has been happening for both of us we just haven't had the time to do so. We certainly don't feel compelled for his sake, because we at least agree that had we known Thomas Victor while he was alive, we wouldn't have liked him much at all. Daniel just wants to see the sex suit to fruition because he thinks that's what Mom was also telling him in the message. He has told me on a few occasions already that it must be what God wants, but I most definitely disagree. I can't imagine He ever intended this when He created man and woman. We have a long road ahead of us on this issue, no doubt."

A brief pause, and then I add, "We did agree on a new challenge, though."

"I see. And what's that?" he asks.

"He challenged me with coming to grips with my health worries and to also get the new church built. If nothing else, he's convinced that a larger building will allow more people to take advantage of the sacraments, and will be a place of solitude for many. He promised he would help me in any way he could, but he's not sure that's how he wants to spend his new-found fortune.

I'm not sure what to ultimately do with mine, either. I mean, I want to do something really positive with it, but I'm praying for God's guidance to show me. If it means a larger church, so be it, but maybe He wants the entire parish family to participate and not just me to foot the entire bill. At any rate, I challenged Daniel with overcoming his sex addiction and recommitting completely to his marriage with Jean. It's close to a new year, so we're jokingly making these our New Year's Resolutions."

"Very good. It's almost my lunchtime, Jonah, so tell me, what have you learned?"

Fr. Jack has always been predictable with this, forcing me to try and make sense of my world as seen through the eyes of God. I don't mind though. All I need to do is think of him and what he's meant to me in my life and I can't help but smile.

"I knew you were going to ask me that," I laugh.

"A bad habit of mine, eh?" he laughs in kind.

"No, not at all – it's helpful – to always try and guide me along," I reply. Pausing to consider my response, I summarize as best I can.

"Well, to your question. The other day I read that many people think St. Paul was obsessed with trying to eradicate and control all human sexuality, but that wasn't the case at all. Even back then, he was merely trying to point people in the right direction and away from the disordered lives they were living. He was telling the world then, and I keep telling Daniel now, that human sexuality is a gift from God, but only if we experience it according to His plan.

"Sex was always meant to be *part* of a beautiful life that could be lived and experienced as husband and wife. Unfortunately, sex has become the most important thing for far too many people in this world. Sex has become their beginning and their end; their goal, their means, their objective, their 'salvation.' It has become the *only* thing that keeps many excited in life, yet it's rife with pain and agony when misused – shades of the addict's cycle. The *disordered misuse* of sex has caused so much pain in this world.

"And in so doing, they all have become what they think about most of the time. Cameron, Matt, Michele, Daniel, Renae and even Jean."

"And you with your health?" he prods.

"Yes," I agree, "and me with my health. I'm a perfect example of how this truth plays out in real life, aren't I?"

"If I may offer, Jonah, let me leave you with this thought. Undoubtedly, sexual sin is very bad for a person's soul. But what is worse is when a person's mind and heart are closed to God, because only He can bring the peace, love, acceptance and caring that the world has always desired, if we remain open to it and continually ask for it."

"Very well said. And you're right," I say.

We sit in silence for a moment before I continue.

"That's why I need to talk my family and friends into joining me next year on our trip to Kibeho. There's so much more for all of us to learn, and at least money won't be an issue now."

"I agree. That won't be a wasted trip at all from what I understand has occurred over there. Oh, before I forget, what happened to the young lady with Down syndrome?"

"Gina? Well, again, I haven't seen her in a while, but apparently the last thing she said to Renae was really a question. She asked if Renae knew whether on the day sexual predators die, if they themselves know when they get out of bed that very morning that it's going to be their last day on earth. I guess Renae said she didn't know, but that Gina might want to ask me that question when we see each other again."

"A very perceptive young lady," he says, a yawn quickly following.

"I think she's smarter than anyone gives her credit for," I add.

It's time to bring our conversation to an end.

"I'll stay in touch and give you an update down the road, Fr. Jack."

"Can't wait, Jonah. Your life is much more exciting than mine these days." He laughs as he hangs up.

Powering down my laptop, I look out the window of the rectory. Daniel pulls up unannounced in his sheriff's car. Renae is riding shotgun, a serious look engulfing her face.

About the Author

A.I. Robeshin is a former executive, married, with children, based in the United States of America. An active life-long Catholic once equipped with only a fair grasp of the true teachings of the Church, Robeshin's materialist goal seeking was shattered when one child was gang raped – twice. This on the distant heels of a mother raped by a stepfather when she was just a child, and a mentally challenged sister who was sexually molested by two healthy and able bodied co-workers while in her late teens.

This book is the result of an absolute need by the author to get off the sidelines and onto the battlefield to address an ever increasing number of degrading and violent sexual sins. To reach out to the victims and give them hope. To wake up a largely naïve or indifferent society. To attempt to equip the world to turn the tables and effectively hunt the sexual predators who are preying daily on existing and new victims, female or male.

If you are interested in pursuing the topics listed herein, you may find these resources helpful. Please note that some of these web sites may not still be in operation at the time you are reading this book.

CATHOLICISM / APOLOGETICS / EVANGELISM

Be a Man! (Becoming the man God created you to be), by Fr. Larry Richards. Ignatius Press.

Beginning Apologetics Series. www.CatholicApologetics.com.

Beginning Apologetics (How to explain and defend the Catholic faith). (CD). Steve Wood and Jim Burnham. Family Life Center International. www.familylifecenter.net.

Between Heaven and Mirth (Why joy, humor and laughter are at the heart of the spiritual life), by James Martin, SJ. HarperOne.

Catechism of the Catholic Church – 2nd Edition. Libreria Editrice Vaticana.

Also, *Compendium of the Catholic Church.* United States Conference of Catholic Bishops.

Catholic Essentials: A Franciscan Living Room Retreat (DVD), by Fr. Angelus Shaughnessy, OFM. EWTN Global Catholic Network.

Catholic Sexual Morality (CD), by Father John A. Hardon, S.J., S.T.D. Eternal Life.

Changing Sides (How a pro-life presence changed the heart of a Planned Parenthood director) (DVD). Ignatius Press.

Church Fathers (From Clement of Rome to Augustine), by Pope Benedict XVI (Emeritus). Ignatius Press.

Cosmic Origins (The scientific evidence for creation), presented by Fr. Robert Spitzer, S.J., Ph.D. Ignatius Press.

Divine Providence (God's design in your life), by Francis Cardinal Arinze. Roman Catholic Books.

Double Standard (Abuse scandals and the attack on the Catholic Church), by David F. Pierre, Jr. www.themediareport.com.

Every Man, God's Man (Every man's guide to…..courageous faith and daily integrity), by Stephen Arterburn, Kenny Luck and

Mike Yorkey. Waterbrook Press.

From Wild Man to Wise Man (Reflections on male spirituality), by Richard Rohr (Franciscan priest). St. Anthony Messenger Press.

God: The Evidence (The reconciliation of faith and reason in a postsecular world), by Patrick Glynn. FORUM / Prima Publishing.

Good News, Bad News (Evangelization, conversion and the crisis of faith), by Fr. C. John McCloskey, III, and Russell Shaw. Ignatius Press.

Heaven (Classic talks by Mother Angelica). 3-part home video series. EWTN Global Catholic Network.

How the Catholic Church is the same and how it is different from other Christian Churches (CD), by Franklin J. Dailey, MD.

Jesus of Nazareth, by Pope Benedict XVI (Emeritus). Doubleday.

Jesus of Nazareth (Holy Week: From the entrance into Jerusalem to the Resurrection), by Pope Benedict XVI (Emeritus). Ignatius Press.

Men of Brave Heart (The virtue of courage in the priestly life), by Archbishop Jose' H. Gomez. Our Sunday Visitor.

Newsflash! (My surprising journey from secular anchor to media evangelist), by Teresa Tomeo. Bezalel Books.

Reasons to Believe (How to understand, explain, and defend the Catholic faith), by Scott Hahn. Doubleday.

Search and Rescue (How to bring your family and friends into – or back into – the Catholic Church), by Patrick Madrid. Sophia Institute Press.

The Catholic Faith Handbook for Youth. Saint Mary's Press.

The Complete Idiot's Guide to the Catholic Catechism, by Mary DeTurris Poust with Theological Advisor David I. Fulton, STD, JCD. Alpha Books.

The Complete Idiot's Guide to Understanding Catholicism, by Bob O'Gorman and Mary Faulkner. Alpha Books.

The Didache Series (Introduction to Catholicism; Understanding The Scriptures; The History of The Church; Our Moral Life in Christ). Midwest Theological Forum.

The Essential Catholic Survival Guide (Answers to tough questions about the faith), by the staff of Catholic Answers.

www.catholic.com.

The Life of Christ, by Guiseppe Ricciotti. Roman Catholic Books. (A few other very useful and informative editions of this work also exist).

The Fathers Know Best (Your essential guide to the teachings of the early church), by Jimmy Akin. Catholic Answers.

The Footprint of God series (The story of salvation from Abraham to Augustine), by Stephen Ray. Ignatius Press.

The Incorruptibles (A study of the incorruption of the bodies of various Catholic Saints and beati), by Joan Carroll Cruz. TAN Books and Publishers, Inc.

The Passion of the Christ (DVD). ICON Productions.

Also, *"Changed Lives, Miracles of The Passion"* ("Here's powerful poignant evidence of how God has used Mel Gibson's movie to change lives in remarkable ways" (Lee Strobel, author, The Case for Christ and The Case for a Creator)). (DVD). GoodTimes Entertainment.

The Light of the World (The Pope, the Church, and the Signs of the Times), by Pope Benedict XVI (Emeritus) with Peter Seewald. Ignatius Press.

The Ratzinger Report (An exclusive interview on the state of the Church), by Joseph Cardinal Ratzinger (Pope Emeritus Benedict XVI) with Vittorio Messori. Ignatius Press.

The Ten Commandments (with Father Benedict Groeschel CFR). EWTN Global Catholic Network.

The Navarre Bible (Old and New Testaments). Four Courts Press (Dublin) / Scepter Publishers (New York).

This is the Faith (A complete explanation of the Catholic faith) (CD and book), by Canon Francis Ripley. TAN Books and Publishers.

United States Catholic Catechism for Adults (CD). St. Anthony Messenger Press.

Welcome Home! (Stories of fallen-away Catholics who came back). Ignatius Press.

What Catholics Really Believe (52 answers to common misconceptions about the Catholic faith), by Karl Keating. Ignatius.

APPARITIONS, MYSTICS, MIRACLES

Blessed Jacinta Marto of Fatima, by Msgr. Joseph A. Cirrincione. TAN Books and Publishers.

God's Miracles (Inspirational stories of encounters with the divine), by Lesley Sussman. Adams Media Corporation.

God-Sent (A history of the accredited apparitions of Mary), by Roy Abraham Varghese. The Crossroad Publishing Company.

Lourdes (In Bernadette's footsteps), by Father Joseph Bordes (Rector Emeritus of the Lourdes Shrine). MSM.

Marian Apparitions of the 20th Century (A message of urgency) (VHS). Marian Communications, LTD.

Mary and the Apparitions of Guadalupe, Lourdes and Fatima. Catholic Classics by Regina Press.

Mystics & Miracles (True stories of lives touched by God), by Bert Ghezzi. Loyola Press.

Our Lady of Light (World-wide message of Fatima), translated and abridged from the French of Chanoine C. Barthas and Pere G. Da Fonseca, S.J. The Bruce Publishing Company.

The Apparitions of the Blessed Virgin Mary Today, by Fr. Rene' Laurentin. Veritas Publications.

The boy who came back from heaven (An accident. A miracle. And a supernatural encounter with angels and life beyond this world) (DVD). TYNDALE Entertainment.

The Call to Fatima (Graces and Mercy) (DVD). www.TheCallToFatima.com.

The Day Will Come (Answers to your questions about mystics, prophecies & miracles), by Michael H. Brown. Anthony Messenger Press.

The God of Miracles, by Michael H. Brown. Queenship Publishing.

The Miracles of Lourdes (EWTN Original Documentary) (DVD). EWTN Global Catholic Network.

The Wonder of Guadalupe (The origin and cult of the miraculous image of the Blessed Virgin in Mexico), by Francis Johnston. TAN Books and Publishers.

The Woman Clothed With the Sun (3-part DVD series). EWTN

Global Catholic Network.

The Wonders of Lourdes (150 miraculous stories of the power of prayer to celebrate the 150th anniversary of Our Lady's Apparitions). Magnificat. Publisher: Pierre-Marie Dumont.

The Youngest Prophet (The life of Jacinta Marto, Fatima visionary – Updated Edition), by Christopher Rengers, OFM Cap. Alba House.

To Heaven and Back (A doctor's extraordinary account of her death, Heaven, angels, and life again – a true story), by Mary C. Neal, MD. Waterbrook Press.

Understanding Miracles (How to know if they are from God, the Devil, or the imagination), by Zsolt Aradi. Sophia Institute Press.

Unsolved Mysteries (4-disc DVD set). FIRST LOOK Home Entertainment.

Visions of Heaven, Hell and Purgatory, by Bob & Penny Lord. Journeys of Faith.

Where Miracles Happen (True stories of heavenly encounters), by Joan Wester Anderson. Ballantine Books.

Where Wonders Prevail (True accounts that bear witness to the existence of Heaven), by Joan Wester Anderson. Ballantine Books.

www.miraclehunter.com

SEXUAL PREDATORS / CRIME

An Affair of the Mind (One woman's courageous battle to salvage her family from the devastation of pornography), by Laurie Hall. Focus on the Family Publishing.

At the Altar of Sexual Idolatry, by Steve Gallagher. Pure Life Ministries.

Breaking Free: 12 Steps to Sexual Purity for Me, by Stephen Wood. www.familylifecenter.net.

Common Threads: Stories of Life After Trauma (DVD), by Amber Ward. Shadow Lane / Productions.

Crime, Shame and Reintegration, by John Braithwaite. Cambridge University Press.

Criminology (Theories, Patterns, and Typologies – Sixth Edition), by Larry J. Siegel. West / Wadsworth Publishing

Company.

Dirty Fighting, by Andy Puzyr. Desert Publications.

Fraternity Gang Rape (Sex, brotherhood, and privilege on campus – 2nd Edition), by Peggy Reeves Sanday. New York University Press.

Halting the Sexual Predators Among Us, by Duane L. Dobbert. Praeger Publishers.

How to Protect Yourself from Crime, Reader's Digest (The most comprehensive guide to safeguarding yourself, your family, your home, and your business – 4th Edition), by Ira A. Lipman. The Reader's Digest Association, Inc.

I Never Called It Rape (The Ms. Report on recognizing, fighting and surviving date and acquaintance rape), by Robin Warshaw. HarperPerennial.

Inside the Mind of Sexual Offenders (Predatory rapists, pedophiles, and criminal profiles), by Dennis J. Stevens, Ph.D. Authors Choice Press.

Let's All Fight Drug Abuse. L.A.W. Publications.

Lying: Moral Choice in Public and Private Life, by Sisella Bok. Pantheon Books.

Obsession (The FBI's legendary profiler probes the psyches of killers, rapists, and stalkers and their victims and tells how to fight back), by John Douglas and Mark Olshaker. Simon and Schuster.

Our Sexuality (Eleventh Edition), by Robert Crooks and Karla Baur. Wadsworth Cengage Learning.

Personal & Home Defense Magazine. www.tactical-life.com.

Physical Abusers and Sexual Offenders (Forensic and Clinical Strategies), by Scott Allen Johnson. Taylor & Francis.

Pornified (How pornography is transforming our lives, our relationships, and our families), by Pamela Paul. Times Books.

Pornography: The Secret History of Civilization (From the walls of Pompeii to the Internet; 2,000 years of sex). (DVD). KOCH Vision.

Predators (Pedophiles, rapists, & other sex offenders) (Who they are, how they operate, and how we can protect ourselves and our children), by Anna C. Salter, Ph.D. Basic Books.

Sadistic versus Non-Sadistic Sex Offenders (How they think,

what they do) (DVD), by Anna C. Salter, Ph.D.
www.specializedtraining.com.

Screaming Through the Silence (Memories, truths and a hope towards understanding), by Mary Ann Ricciardi. AuthorHouse.

Self Defense Women's Seminar (DVD). Stoney-Wolf Productions.

Sex and Violence (Issues in representation and experience). Routledge.

Sex Crimes (Patterns and Behavior – 3rd Edition), by Stephen T. Holmes and Ronald M. Holmes. Sage Publications.

Sexual Predators in Public Places (DVD). www.education2000i.com.

The Evil that Men Do (FBI profiler Roy Hazelwood's journey into the minds of sexual predators), by Stephen G. Michaud with Roy Hazelwood. St. Martin's Press.

The Gift of Fear (Book and CD), by Gavin De Becker.

The History of Sex. MPH Entertainment, Inc. for the History Channel.

The Invisible War (DVD). New Video Group.

The Violence of Men (New techniques for working with abusive families: A therapy of social action), by Cloe' Madanes with James P. Keim and Dinah Smelser. Jossey-Bass Publishers.

Truth, Lies, and Sex Offenders (How they think, what they do) (DVD), by Anna C. Salter, Ph.D. www.specializedtraining.com.

Why Does He Do That? (Inside the minds of angry and controlling men), by Lundy Bancroft. Berkley Books.

www.freetacticaltips.com

MISCELLANEOUS

50 Voices of Disbelief (Why we are atheists). Wiley-Blackwell.

Abnormal Psychology (An integrative approach – Fifth Edition), by David H. Barlow and V. Mark Durand. Wadsworth Cengage Learning.

Burning Man. HardWired.

Burning Man: Beyond Black Rock (DVD). Gone Off Deep Productions.

Degenerate Moderns (Modernity as rationalized sexual

428

misbehavior), by E. Michael Jones. Ignatius Press.

Expelled (No Intelligence Allowed) (DVD), by Ben Stein. Vivendi Entertainment.

Midwest Center for Anxiety. www.stresscenter.com.

Quiet Desperation: The Truth About Successful Men, by Jan Halper, Ph.D. Warner Books.

Red Wolves (And then there were (almost) none), by Meish Goldish. Bearport Publishing. www.bearportpublishing.com.

Speechless: Silencing the Christians, by Rev. Donald E. Wildmon. Richard Vigilante Books.

The Truth about Cheating (Why men stray and what you can do to prevent it), by M. Gary Neuman. John Wiley & Sons, Inc.

The Wolf Almanac (A celebration of wolves and their world), by Robert H. Busch. The Lyons Press.

Your Life, Your Choices – Right or Wrong. L.A.W. Publications.